the

INCANDESCENT

the

INCANDESCENT

A School Story

EMILY TESH

TOR

Tor Publishing Group | New York

THE INCANDESCENT

Copyright © 2025 by Emily Tesh

Excerpt from "Tarkington, Thou Shouldst Be Living at This Hour" copyright © 1947 by Ogden Nash, renewed. Reprinted by permission of Curtis Brown, Ltd.

Designed by Jen Edwards
Map by Virginia Allyn

A Tor Book
Published by Tom Doherty Associates / Tor Publishing Group
120 Broadway
New York, NY 10271

www.torpublishinggroup.com

Tor® is a registered trademark of Macmillan Publishing Group, LLC.

The Library of Congress Cataloging-in-Publication
Data is available upon request.

ISBN 978-1-250-83501-7 (hardcover)
ISBN 978-1-250-83502-4 (ebook)

Our books may be purchased in bulk for promotional, educational, or business use. Please contact your local bookseller or the Macmillan Corporate and Premium Sales Department at 1-800-221-7945, extension 5442, or by email at MacmillanSpecialMarkets@macmillan.com.

First Edition: 2025

Printed in the United States of America

0   9   8   7   6   5   4   3   2   1

For A. K. Larkwood

O adolescence, adolescence,

I wince before thine incandescence!

Thy constitution young and hearty

Is too much for this aged party.

—OGDEN NASH

AUTUMN I

chapter one

RISK ASSESSMENT

DOCTOR WALDEN LOOKED GLUMLY AT THE form she had to fill in. At the top it said RISK ASSESSMENT. She'd designed the form herself, in a burst of optimism. They would have fewer accidents if people just stopped to think. It was an unfortunate truth that in the Venn diagram of 'qualified to teach magic' and 'still alive,' the overlap consisted almost entirely of people who had always been much too sensible to accidentally get eaten by a demon. Walden's colleagues—in particular, those who were her responsibility, the loosely grouped Faculty of Magic here at Chetwood School—possessed, as a body, an admirable and well-judged lack of imagination. In the three years since she took the post as Director of Magic, she had had someone in her office once a term to weep on her shoulder and say *but why would anyone ever—*

Some of these people had been teaching for *years*, and yet they still managed to be surprised by how bloody stupid the average teenager could be, given a group of friends to impress and a

fifteen-second video about major invocation that they found on the
internet somewhere.

Walden's innovations in her role as Director of Magic, so
far: aggressive, highly specialised content filters on the school
network—a project which had given her comrades in arms among
the IT staff, and perpetual enemies among the students. Arcane
safety refreshers every term for every year group, which bored the
pants off the older ones but had in fact improved the incident statis-
tics Walden tracked. And, for the teaching staff, the risk assessment
form. It was supposed to lead you gently, bullet point by bullet
point, through every enormously dangerous and dim thing your
students might decide to do. There was a column for planning what
you were going to *do* when the worst inevitably happened. There
was a helpful checklist on the back. There was a colourful box
at the bottom with a quick banishment cantrip, a basic shielding
charm, and the extension number for the infirmary.

Everyone hated it. Even Walden hated it. The last thing you
wanted to do at ten o'clock at night when you were teaching first
thing tomorrow was fill in the bloody risk assessment.

Unfortunately, being senior management meant you had to
stick to your own procedures or live with the knowledge that you
were an unspeakable hypocrite. Walden preferred the former. Besides, she had her Upper Sixth first thing for a lab practical, and
if you were going to skip a risk assessment, the lesson where you
intended to have four seventeen-year-olds summon a medium-
sized demon for the first time was not a good choice for it. The
old-fashioned wooden wall clock—inherited from the long line of
former Headmasters who had previously lived in this Victorian
suite of rooms—ticked over to ten past ten. If Walden had another
coffee now, she'd get no sleep at all.

FIRE, she wrote next to the first bullet point, and in the risk mitigation column, FIRE DRILL PROCESSES; EXTINGUISHERS (2) + TRAINED STAFF MEMBER; QUENCHING CANTRIP. She considered for a moment and then wrote out the cantrip as well, in the neat academic notation that was second nature to her: words in black ink, gestural inflections drawn in sharply and accurately with one of the red biros she always had lying on her desk. If you were doing something, you ought to do it properly. Walden believed this deeply, which was probably the reason she kept looking up from her desk at 10 P.M. and realising she'd worked another fourteen-hour day. It wasn't that she didn't believe in work-life balance. It was just that her career was her life.

She kept working down the list of bullet points, imagining disasters in order of likelihood. The block capitals were also automatic; a precaution, so that someone else could easily refer to the form if Walden herself was unavailable because she'd been eaten by a demon. There was a digital version of the risk assessment, but the thought of wrestling with the printer at this time of night was dire. INJURY (MUNDANE); INJURY (ENCHANTED); SUMMONING ARRAY MISFIRE; LESSER WARD FAILURE. Walden thought about the precise makeup of the sixth form class she was teaching in the morning and added MAGICIAN ERROR (OVERCONFIDENCE) AND MAGICIAN ERROR (UNDERCONFIDENCE). These forms always went fast once you actually started. The electric desk lamp with its old-fashioned fringed green lampshade gave off a warm light, and the wood-panelled walls shone with the rich glow of a century of care and polish. Out of the corner of her eye, Walden spotted a pile of marking she hadn't done yet and elected to ignore it. Finish this form, go to bed, coffee and double Invocation in the morning.

Just as she had this thought, there was a knock on the door.

Walden gave the door a baleful look. If it was an emergency—at a boarding school you expected the occasional late-night emergency—her colleagues all knew to come straight in. Only one person would have the temerity to come to Walden's office at this time and *knock*.

She sighed, pushed the risk assessment form to one side, and arranged her face into an expression of inquiring courtesy. "Come in!"

And—of course—it was Laura Kenning. "Good evening, Ms Walden," she said.

Every other bloody adult on the school site would have said *Sorry to bother you, Saffy*. But Kenning had chosen her rules of engagement and Walden would stick to them. "Good evening, Marshal Kenning," she said. "It's *Doctor* Walden, if you don't mind."

"Apologies, Doctor," said Kenning blandly, which Walden, a connoisseur of passive-aggression after a career spent with teenagers, interpreted as *You can take your DThau and shove it up your arse*.

Kenning, like Walden herself, was young for her post, certainly younger than Walden; perhaps thirty-two or thirty-three. She looked irritatingly bright-eyed and bushy-tailed. It was possible she was on a night patrol and only just starting her shift. Her short fair hair was neatly combed, her silver-chased armguards polished to a mirror shine and strapped precisely in place over the white sleeves of her uniform shirt. Her black leather boots shone almost as bright, and her shortsword hung neatly at her hip. Walden glanced at it with displeasure. It rubbed her the wrong way, seeing the Marshals wander around the school fully armed. There was no need for it, and it sent the wrong message. This place was *safe*. Walden worked extremely hard to make it safe and keep it safe. No one was going to get eaten by demons here, so Laura Kenning had no need to swagger around the place looking like she was about to go on the hunt.

Marshals were demon hunters and demon killers. The

enchanted shortswords were an ancient, traditional part of their official kit. Other traditional accoutrements had been discarded in the last two hundred years. Religious symbols were now felt to be an emotional rather than practical support against demons. Full suits of rune-engraved plate armour were both difficult to make and not noticeably more effective than just making the runes smaller and putting them all on the armguards. But Marshals had other resources besides the swords. Walden had written a paper during her MThau on the unique sets of physically defined spells that they employed in combat. No member of the Order of Marshals would ever call themselves a 'magician'—that word belonged to the academic tradition—but they were certainly, in the inelegant phrasing of modern generalist accounts of magical practice, magic-users.

So Laura Kenning and her squad had plenty of tools at their disposal for managing the minor demons that cropped up every day in the natural course of putting six hundred teenagers in one place and letting them learn magic. The thing that set an enchanted sword apart was not that it hurt demons, but that it could also, very easily, hurt people. That felt wrong to Walden. Her students should not feel themselves perpetually on edge around Laura Kenning's squadron of paranoid paramilitary brutes.

Walden would never put it quite like that out loud. The Marshals were of course 'a valued traditional element of the rich fabric of Chetwood life, here above all to ensure the safety of our students and staff.' Walden visualised the relevant page of the school prospectus—with a large photograph of Kenning on it; the woman photographed well—and gave the Chief Marshal a bland and professional smile. "What can I do for you, Laura?"

"I'd like to discuss Nicola Conway," said Kenning.

Nikki Conway: seventeen years old, originally from South London, the most talented teenage magician that Walden had come across in nearly twenty years, and for more than a decade now a ward of the school. There was absolutely nothing to discuss, or at least nothing that the Marshals hadn't made clear already in their repeated, annual formal protests, which they had been making ever since Nikki started studying magic in Year Seven—like *every single child in the school*—years before Kenning even took this job. On top of that, Kenning seemed to take Walden's polite stonewalling about the whole thing personally. Over the last three years, they had had this conversation so many times that Walden could probably have done it in her sleep. It had been bad enough during Nikki's GCSEs, and even worse since she had started her Invocation A-level.

The Marshals' problem with Nikki was not based on her grades (outstanding) or her character (remarkably level-headed, for a teenager). It was simply that when she was seven years old, Nikki had been responsible for the demonic incursion that had killed her mother, her father, and her younger brother. Marshals did not believe in extenuating circumstances. They were not interested in second chances.

And this was the real core of why Walden found herself having a conversation like this one with Kenning every couple of weeks. Both of them—Walden as Director of Magic, Kenning as Chief Marshal—were responsible for the magical security of the school. Walden, at deputy head level, technically outranked Kenning within the school hierarchy. But the school's squadron of Marshals reported not to her—which they *should*, in Walden's opinion—but to Chetwood's Board of Governors on the one hand, and the Knightly Council of the Reverend Order of Marshals (District of Buckinghamshire) on the other.

In an ideal world they would have been working harmoniously together to share expertise on magical security issues. The problem was that they disagreed profoundly about nearly every issue.

Sometimes they disagreed that there even *was* an issue. Kenning clearly felt she outranked Walden on any issue with potential demonic involvement. As far as Walden could tell, Kenning's position was that demons were so dangerous that no one should ever risk doing any magic at all. Which was certainly *a* view, and she was entitled to hold it; but then why on earth take a job at a school which taught magic?

Walden was winning the Nikki Conway debate, and intended to continue doing so. Kenning was not going to get any benefit from her 10 p.m. ambush.

"As you are no doubt aware, I'm concerned, Dr Walden," said Kenning. "Perhaps you're not aware that the best predictor of a serious incursion is the magician's history? If it happened once, it's infinitely more likely to happen again. And we both know Nicola wouldn't even be here if it hadn't happened once."

"I'm familiar with the research, yes. The study you're talking about—"

"—doesn't control for age, you're going to say. But caution is never a bad idea. I know Nicola is your star pupil." (Walden barely resisted grinding her teeth.) "I just think your relationship with her, as her teacher—especially given her family situation—is getting in the way here."

"Are you questioning my judgement, Marshal?"

Kenning said, "That's my job."

A pause. A chill in the room was not a demon—though Walden was almost tempted, just to even things up a bit—but the shared knowledge of an unspoken threat: Kenning could try to go over Walden's head, to the District Commissioner of the Marshals, or else to the school governors.

It wouldn't work. Walden would win those arguments too. But it would be extremely annoying to have to attend more meetings.

"I've become aware that you're teaching a practical tomorrow morning," Kenning said. "Which I should really have known already. May I repeat my request for clear schemes of work, with *dates,* at the start of term?"

"We do our best, Marshal," said Walden, "but teachers' plans seldom resist first contact with the enemy."

Kenning didn't even smile. "Nicola must be excluded from that lesson."

"Request denied," said Walden, as if it had been a request. "I would much rather Nikki learn advanced invocation where I can see her than try it herself unsupervised."

"You admit that she might try it unsupervised?"

"Show me a young person with her brains and talent who wouldn't," said Walden. "Marshal, I understand your concern. As you say, it's your job. My job, among other things, is to consider the needs of our students. I don't deny that you're an expert on demons; will you grant that I am an expert on teenagers?" And *on demons, more than you,* she could have said. She had multiple university degrees in academic magic. Kenning had the eighteen-week Marshal training course, probably over a decade ago now, and whatever she'd picked up along the way in terms of practical experience since then. There was no comparison. But Kenning already knew all of that—*Ms Walden,* indeed—and Walden didn't need to antagonise her any more than she already was.

Instead she tried—not for the first time—being straightforward and reasonable. "Nicola Conway is going to deal with demons in her life. She is far too talented to avoid it. She is already considerably more thoughtful, and more careful, than most magicians her age—precisely because of the history that worries you so much. In my professional judgement, she and her classmates are ready for this practical. Delaying it would only create more risk of a demonic incursion. And if one begins, I would rather it happened in front of me, in a lab I warded myself, rather than in someone's bedroom at two in the morning."

"I'll be observing," said Kenning.

"We'd be delighted to have you," Walden lied.

They stared at each other a moment longer. Walden became aware that she was wearing a white towelling dressing gown over a ratty set of pyjamas she'd owned since university. If Kenning was going to make a habit of dropping in impeccably uniformed and unannounced at this time of night, then Walden would have to start spending her evenings in the outfits she thought of as her professional armour—sharply cut blazers, A-line skirts, a brooch from the jewellery box she'd inherited from her grandmother.

"I apologise for disturbing you so late," said Kenning abruptly.

You could have led *with that,* Walden thought. "Not at all," she said. "I'm always willing to listen to my colleagues' concerns. I'll see you in the morning, Marshal."

"Did you know that clock is possessed?" Kenning said, gesturing to the wall clock. "I can sort it out for you."

"That's quite all right," said Walden. "It's not doing any harm."

"It's a *demon.*"

"Only a very small one," Walden said soothingly. "Good night, Marshal."

After Kenning was gone, Walden sat back in her chair and sighed. The risk assessment form glared accusingly up from her desk. The wall clock, in an unusual burst of activity, gave out thirteen very fast chimes and then manifested a cuckoo which emerged with glowing red eyes, opened its beak, and screamed.

"Yes, yes, I don't like her either," Walden said, and picked up her pen for the next bullet point. DEMONIC INCURSION, she wrote. In the risk mitigation column, she put: ME.

chapter two

UPPER SIXTH INVOCATION

"PHOTOCOPIER'S ON STRIKE," SAID THE Head of History to Walden when she walked into the staffroom.

"Thanks, Marie," said Walden. She would have guessed anyway, just from the harassed expressions of several hovering teachers clutching textbooks and printed worksheets. Chetwood had been founded as a school of pure magic, turning out fully trained magicians who were masters of all the arcane disciplines—invocation, evocation, instantiation, and the long-since discredited fourth school, divination—and, as a bonus, could usually add, subtract, and write their own names. But all that was back in the fourteenth century, some six hundred years before the advent of the National Curriculum and OFSTED's private-sector shadow, the Independent Schools Inspectorate. These days Chetwood School was a specialist foundation, like a technical or musical college, with a full complement of academic teaching staff alongside the magicians. Walden, who was an alumna, remembered an uneasy rivalry between the magical teachers and the academic side back in her own school days. The current Head had stamped on it hard. Good teachers knew that in a school there was only really room for two sides: Us, and Them.

The photocopier was a hulking grey beast looming in the corner of the staffroom. On the noticeboard behind it was pinned a laminated A4 sign: DO NOT EXORCISE. Walden navigated her way through the hovering crowd with polite good-mornings to her colleagues and opened the maintenance panel. "What's the matter with you?"

Two fiery purple eyes peered up at Walden from the dark, unknowable depths of the multipurpose tray. *Strike!* squeaked the demon possessing the photocopier.

It was only a minor imp, of the first order. Walden knew it quite well at this point. Demons were attracted to complexity and to personhood. Laypeople assumed that this meant every magician was on the brink of getting possessed all the time, but really demons entering the mundane plane moved into complex and person-shaped spaces, like hermit crabs moving into shells. That *could* mean a human being, but it took a very strong demon to do it by force. If you were unlucky enough to meet a magician with a demon looking out from behind their eyes, you could usually assume they'd invited it in.

More common was a demon possessing an animal—it could happen randomly, if an opportunistic demon found a weakness in the fabric of reality and a living creature about the right size on the other side, and it was also the source of the old cliché about magicians summoning familiar spirits into black cats. Of course, that sort of thing was frowned on these days as being rather unfair to the cat. Technology, complex and intricate, was always a risk; hence Walden's clock—hard to find a magician's clock that *hadn't* been possessed at some point—and the school's draconian, much-protested mobile phone policy. Impossible to detach several hundred teenagers from their phones altogether—and their parents would have been appalled if the school had tried—but, actually, a middle schooler didn't need a little demon box in their pocket at all times. No, they didn't. No, turn it off. Yes, it *does* have to go in the dormitory safe overnight. The commonest incident reports that came across Walden's desk were repetitive to the point of grim comedy: twelve-year-old with a secret second phone hidden under their mattress, awake at one in the morning scrolling through a social media app they were not legally old enough to sign up for, and shocked, shocked, when the imp possessing their phone started trying to eat them.

So modern technology was one risk. But actually, if anyone had ever looked at something and called it 'you'—assigning it a self, whether it deserved one or not—then a space had been made, and in that space something could live. Provided, of course, that there was enough magic around for the demon to make the crossing from its own plane to this one.

Since Chetwood was lousy with six and a half centuries' worth of adolescent wild magic, and the staffroom photocopier was called variations on 'you bloody bastard thing' by dozens of people every day, there was no point trying to keep it clear. You just ended up re-exorcising it once a week. Even the Marshals had given up. Its current inhabitant was a known quantity, and there was a large bowl of salt next to the fire extinguisher in the staffroom, in case of emergencies.

"Who told you what a strike is?" Walden asked the photocopier.

"Probably my fault," said Marie. "We're doing labour movements with Year Nine."

"Not to worry," Walden said. "Besides, arguably, it does work here." No consent on the school's part, no employment contract, but if they preferred this fairly benign imp to the other potential in-habitants of the photocopier—and Walden *did*—then it was worth trying to keep it happy. Making agreements with demons was the heart of her academic discipline, and keeping the school's wild magic problems under control was one of her core responsibilities as Director of Magic. She would have liked to have her coffee first. "All right," she said to the photocopier, "what are you striking for? Better working conditions?"

The demon said, *Blood!*

"All our staff are entitled to sick leave, pension contributions, support from the employee assistance program—"

Blood! shrieked the photocopier. *No representation without exsanguination!*

There were some chuckles from the crowd of teachers. "No blood," said Walden firmly. A meal of human bodily fluids was the fastest possible way to turn a minor demonic possession into a major demonic problem. "Would you accept a digestive biscuit?"

The fiery flecks of the purple eyes in the depths of the multi-purpose tray flickered. The imp said, with an air of deep cunning, *Chocolate.*

"Very well," said Walden. She fetched a chocolate digestive from the staffroom kitchen and carefully fed it into the photo-copier's maintenance hatch. The demon ate it in two sulphurous snaps. Then the machine let out several loud beeps. "Now what?"

Staples! demanded the demon.

Walden fetched a box and tipped it in. Another gulping sound, and a strong smell of rotten eggs: then the photocopier began to spit out perfectly stapled packs of worksheets about—Walden read sideways—the Luddites.

"Thanks, Saffy," said Marie. "Should I just give it a biscuit next time?"

"A small demon is still a demon. Better not," said Walden, which was much more diplomatic than saying *I ran an entire training session on handling low-level demon issues last INSET day, come on.* The main advice she'd given her non-magician colleagues on how to handle low-level demon issues was 'don't.' Chetwood had constant imp problems, and yes, they were annoying; yes, it was tempting just to deal with it yourself. But it was dangerously easy for a non-specialist to accidentally agree to a more serious pact than they'd meant. "Call me down, or any of the magic faculty, or else"—she sighed mentally, but it was what they were for—"one of the Marshals."

The episode had taken up the time she'd meant to use to have her leisurely morning coffee. Walden filled a travel flask with coal-black caffeinated sludge from the coffee machine instead, and hurried across the quad to the arcane labs.

Outside Lab Three, uncharacteristically early and flicking brazenly through his phone as if he'd never heard of a personal electronics policy, was one of her Upper Sixth. He'd arranged himself, his school rucksack, a rainbow collection of lever arch folders, and a hefty bag of sports kit all in an array on the floor, in such a way as to present a tripping hazard to unwary passersby. "Will," said Walden. "Legs."

"Sorry, miss," said Will, and drew his long legs in black jeans—*not* the smart trousers mandated by the sixth form dress code—up into a tightly acute triangle, which improved the situation only slightly.

"*Will.*"

Will looked up from his phone and bestowed upon Walden his most winning smile. "Sorry, Doc," he said.

"William Daubery, clear this corridor right now or face my wrath," said Walden. "I ought to dress code you and PEP you."

School rules inevitably turned into verbs. *To dress code*: to send a child back to their dormitory to change. *To PEP*: to confiscate a misused mobile phone. The personal electronics policy was relaxed a little for sixth formers, but Will, who was more than halfway through A-levels in Invocation, Evocation, and Further Evocation, ought to know better than to play with a tasty little electronic device right outside the arcane labs. Yes, the risk was low, because Walden ran a tight ship. But part of keeping the arcane labs magically secure was knowing that 'low' and 'nonexistent' were very different beasts.

"Whoops," said Will, but he obediently got up and hefted his possessions over to the wall, and the phone—a large and expensive-looking model, he would no doubt be very annoyed if it *did* get possessed and had to be destroyed—went into the front pocket of his rucksack. "Haven't you had your coffee yet, Doc?"

"No, I haven't," said Walden sternly. "And so I'm in a very bad mood. Don't test me."

Will faked a shudder. "I'll warn the others."

"See that you do," Walden said. "And turn your phone *off* in the arcane corridor, and don't spread your things all over the floor again. Someone will trip and break a leg. Remember, I have eyes in the back of my head."

"Yes, miss. Doc!"

Walden unlocked Lab Three and let herself in. There was just time before the bell to finish her lesson prep and gulp down about half the black-sludge coffee. She plucked the risk assessment out of her pile of papers and slapped it down front and centre on the big desk at the front of the room.

The lab was otherwise almost empty. The science labs, on the other side of the building, were fully equipped with sinks and Bunsen burners and fume cupboards and all the other apparatus of a twenty-first-century scientific education. Modernity had taken magic in the other direction. The arcane labs were stripped down as far as possible; the less there was in here, the less possibility that someone would accidentally start you-ing something and invite in an unwelcome demon. The room was painted white floor to ceiling, and had no desks except the teacher's and no chairs at all. There was a whiteboard on the wall behind the desk; the pens were kept in a jar of salt, because Walden knew from bitter experience how easy it was to accidentally say *Where are you?* to a missing board pen.

When she taught magical theory, she booked one of the seminar rooms upstairs, so her class wouldn't have to work on the floor. But for practical work, the arcane lab was a necessity.

Very stark in black and yellow against the white safety paint were the incursion wards: north, south, east, west, one over the door, one over the fire exit, one for each of the windows. They were repainted every half term. Walden checked them for errors, fading, or alerts, as she did before every lesson. Then, slowly and with great care, she introduced a minor location error into the ward above the fire exit, changing its area of effect from 'this laboratory' to 'this place.' It took her almost to the bell, with two minutes to spare. She swallowed another bitter gulp of coffee.

She shuffled through her papers for Upper Sixth's homework— four problem sheets on arcane attribution, handed in last week and marked yesterday evening. The work was about what she'd expected: Nikki outstanding, Will slapdash, Aneeta careful, Mathias skipping questions that worried him. Walden put them to one side. She paused to straighten her shoulders and arrange her face, putting aside her late night and Laura Kenning and the photocopier demon, putting on—like the armour of blazer and skirt and brooch—the total good-humoured calm of Dr Walden, teacher.

The bell went.

"Come in!" Dr Walden called.

And in they came, shambling, sauntering, seventeen years old: Upper Sixth Invocation.

Walden did not do much frontline teaching anymore. Director of Magic was a deputy-head-level role, and the further you climbed the ladder of a career in education, the less you got to actually teach. Her work calendar was full of meetings, conferences, presentations, project deadlines. There was blocked-out time for boundary patrols and spot checks, and apparently free time which always filled up immediately with crisis management: constant variations on the stern talking-to for the middle schooler with the secret phone under the mattress, along with the diplomatic but firm talking-to for the loving parent who had purchased the phone.

On top of that, there were the hours upon hours she spent maintaining Chetwood's magical infrastructure. Children were such easy targets for opportunistic demons that even ordinary schools needed a couple of solid incursion wards on site, just in case. One of the things Walden had brought in as Director was the sixth form volunteering club, who went around the local primary schools repainting what were usually faded, half-arsed protections against demons. Magical specialists were expensive, and waiting for the county council to get around to hiring someone was a mug's game. But at least in a normal school, the worst you were likely to encounter on the demon front was a determined imp, encouraged by a talented but inexperienced child who'd watched too many unhelpful videos on the internet.

Chetwood, with its long magical history, and six-hundred-odd half-trained adolescent magicians living on site, was a different kind of problem. Ordinary schools did not have a dedicated team of Marshals stationed on site. Ordinary schools did not need incursion wards in every building. But Walden's biggest problem was not the mobile phone incidents, the difficulties of politicking with Marshal

Kenning, or keeping the incursion wards up to date. All of those paled next to her most vital responsibility: managing the intricate system of nineteenth-century wards, which had been the height of cutting-edge sorcerous-industrial invention around 1855. They depended on an enormously complex set of old-fashioned thaumic engines, built into and impossible to move from a large room adjoining the Headmaster's suite in Brewers Hall. The mechanisms were more than a hundred and fifty years old, comically clunky, inherently vulnerable to demonic possession, and a nightmare to maintain. They were also so absolutely integral to the way the rest of the school's magical defences worked that if they failed, there was a good chance that Chetwood School would just collapse out of mundane reality altogether and disappear into the demonic plane, taking six hundred children with it.

No pressure, the Headmaster had remarked to Walden wryly when he hired her. David Bern had been selected by the school governors to attempt to save Chetwood's faltering academic reputation, and he was doing a good job on that front, but his background was geography, not sorcery. That was why he lived in a rather nice five-bedroom house in Chetwood village, while Walden lived in the old Head's suite, sleeping in the room next to the thaumic engines.

She'd had to get out of bed in the middle of the night to fix them three times in the three years she had worked here. It didn't sound like much, unless you understood what was at stake. The whole system ought to have been shut down and rebuilt from scratch to modern standards, but to do that would take about five years, and those would be five expensive years in which no fees came in. Chetwood School would not survive. Instead, like most schools, the institution went on from year to year by doing what had always more or less worked, or at least seemed to work, or at any rate kept things going.

So Walden's days were filled, and she barely got to teach. Which was sad, because she loved to teach. She did, at least, do the Year Seven arcane safety course, on the teaching carousel with Relationships Ed, debating, Mindfulness in Schools, and beginners' yoga. It gave her three weeks with each class, just enough time to learn all their names. Her sixth formers—Years Twelve and Thirteen—were the only sets she saw all the way through; four times a week, for two hours at a time, for two years.

It was unusual for a deputy head to take on an A-level examination set, but invocation, Walden's subject specialism, was hard to hire for. Modern academic magic was divided into three disciplines. Evocation was what most people thought about when they imagined someone doing magic: magicians using their own physical strength, speaking words and making gestures, to cast spells with immediate results. Instantiation was a more recent academic term for what had once been called alchemy, the branch of magic that used the physical fabric of the world to create long-lasting magical effects, like the warding produced by the thaumic engines.

Invocation was the discipline of the demon summoners.

Anyone from the Evocation or Instantiation Departments could teach the basics, just as Walden could have taught Year Eight Magic without any difficulty. Magical fundamentals were the same across all the arcane disciplines. But a magical A-level was a demanding academic course, and needed a confident teacher. Chetwood continued to advertise, and Walden regularly sent out feelers through her old academic supervisors and colleagues, hoping for a talented postgraduate. In the meantime, she would rather sacrifice her sleep and Sundays to work than have sixth formers taught demonic invocation by someone whose skills were not up to scratch.

It was October now of her fourth term with this set, and she felt she knew them rather better than she knew her own family, most of whom she hadn't spoken to since last Christmas.

Take them in order:

William Daubery first, because he was the sort of young man who tended to put himself first. He was a scion of one of the bona fide old English magical families, the sort that barely existed these days, with an ancestor who'd stormcalled for Elizabeth I and sunk half the Spanish Armada, at least according to Will. In Walden's experience, all that 'old magic' meant was that children arrived at school with a collection of bad habits to unlearn, and Will was no exception. His magic was effective but careless, and he rolled his eyes every time a teacher gave him the safety lecture. Blue-eyed, curly-haired, always smiling, always pushing at the edges of the dress code—those black jeans! Irritating boy—Will was set fair to become one of those lucky young men who sailed cheerfully through life on a comfortable tide of bullshit. If he had been an adult colleague, Walden would have found him very tiresome. Since he was a schoolboy, and since they had worked out together the limits of Walden's tolerance for bullshit (low) by this time last year, she was able to be amused by him instead.

Nicola Conway—brilliant Nikki—was Black British, wore her hair in an elbow-length cascade of braids, and carried herself with an air of quiet confidence that meant she succeeded in looking rather cool, even in the sixth form dress code of plain shirt, smart trousers or skirt, and jacket. She was hanging on to her South London accent by a thread after a decade of boarding school: sometimes posh Home Counties vowels came out of her mouth by accident, which seemed to disgust her. Her tragic history was not something she shared. Walden was fairly sure that even Aneeta, who was among Nikki's closest friends, had no idea beyond the bare facts of 'parents dead, ward of the school.' Nikki's magic was brilliant. In lessons she worked with an intensity which sometimes unnerved her classmates, making Will joke nervously about geeks, making Aneeta worry she wasn't trying hard enough. Though she was closest to Aneeta, she always sat next to Mathias.

Mathias Wick was a tongue-tied and perpetually anxious white boy with terrible acne, who on the face of things could not have been more different to cool, confident Nikki; but like her, he was a ward of the school. He'd been removed from his family home by the state and placed at Chetwood when he was thirteen. As Walden understood it, it was a shame that the state had not got there sooner. Mathias's parents had joined one of the handful of obscure religious sects—Walden thought, but would never say, *cults*—that still conflated 'demon,' the magical concept, with 'devil,' the theological one. They had felt that Mathias's natural inclination for magic was proof of inherent evil, and had been correspondingly cruel.

Walden did not know many of the details beyond that. Mathias did not discuss it in lessons, and since it was not directly an academic or magical issue, it was not her business. The school's traditional role as one of the few safe places to foster a powerful underage magician was, at present, firmly separated from the school as educational institution. School House, where Nikki and Mathias and their handful of younger foster siblings lived, was the domain of Ebele Nwosu, the pastoral deputy head, known in accordance with tradition as Matron. She was a woman whom Walden respected deeply for her endless patience, her academic expertise—before taking the deputy head role, she had been Head of Psychology—and her genius for pastoral work, which was one of the hardest parts of teaching. Her husband, Reverend Ezekiel, was the school chaplain as well as being the only other magician teacher with the invocation skills to handle an A-level set. He taught the current Year Twelve.

Nikki had adopted Mathias when he arrived at Chetwood, and

still seemed to look on him with a kind of mother-hen protective-ness. The powerful foster-sibling bond of School House, and the loneliness that lay behind it, clearly meant something to both of them. As far as Walden could tell, they had little else in common beyond a fierce talent for magic—both of them born with the rare, wild magical ability that would manifest even totally untrained, the talent that Chetwood's scholarship and bursary funds were dedi-cated to supporting in one of the few parts of the school's carefully PR-massaged mission statement that Walden was totally uncynical about. Mathias found theory challenging, but on a good day he was the strongest magician of the four. Unfortunately, his good days were rare.

Last but by no means least was Aneeta Shah, a chubby Indian girl who wore glasses with round frames. Aneeta, alone of the group, was taking a magical course in sixth form as an interesting sideline to her education, rather than the main event. It was a char-acteristic, very quiet, very intellectual boast that she had chosen the most difficult and least practical arcane discipline to study as an 'extra' on top of her A-levels in Maths, Chemistry, and Biology. The A-level Invocation class was tiny compared to Evocation and Instantiation. Most people just found it too difficult. Of course, anyone could learn magic, if they tried, but it was bloody hard work if you did not have the knack, and quite hard work even if you did. Aneeta was not afraid of hard work. Walden saw some-thing of herself in how the young woman approached magical theory, as a complex and fascinating puzzle undertaken for its own sake. Her practicals brought her predicted grade down from the precious, coveted A* to an A. Since she was comfortably expecting A*s in all her other subjects, it was unlikely to hinder her university applications.

As for the other three: Nikki would get the A*. Will was probably capable, but that depended on whether his competitiveness with Nikki overcame his natural laziness early enough for him to do some actual work. Mathias would scrape a B if he was lucky—and that only because in such a small group, with three overachievers as his classmates, Walden felt able to dedicate a fair amount of lesson time to what was effectively private tutoring. A-levels, like the thaumic engines grinding away in the room next to Walden's suite, were something that more or less worked, had always been there, and would be very difficult and complicated to rebuild from scratch. But every time Walden had a student like Mathias, it was impossible not to be appalled by the unfairness of public exams: two years of work by a determined, complicated, talented young person, reduced to a single brutal letter grade.

Walden gave them back their homework. Will immediately tried to negotiate his mark upwards. "Check your work next time," Walden advised. Aneeta and Nikki swapped problem sheets to look at each other's answers to the tricky question at the end, which neither of them had quite solved, though both had got close. "*Oh,*" said Nikki after a moment. "It's a substitution." Walden nodded approval.

Mathias folded his crumpled worksheet in half and shoved it deep into a pocket.

"All right, Upper Six," said Walden, "remind me what we're doing today."

"Shouldn't you know, Doc?" said Will. "Don't they pay you for this?"

Walden took a seat on the teacher's desk—the four sixth formers were in their usual semicircle on the floor—and said crisply, "Thank you for volunteering, Will, take us through it, please."

Will pantomimed stab-to-the-heart betrayal, but he did it. "Major summoning, fourth level. Uh, contain, invoke, reify, query, dismiss."

"Good," said Walden. "Off you go, then."

They all stared at her.

"What?"

"Aren't you going to tell us what to do?" said Mathias.

"I've spent a year and a bit telling you what to do," said Walden. "I hope you were paying attention. Come on." She picked up her mark book. They all looked at it with distrust. "I'll be taking notes," said Walden. "Oh, and Marshal Kenning should be joining us at some point. Don't mind her, just carry on as usual."

The sixth formers exchanged looks and mutters. It was all very well to say 'Don't mind her.' They were seventeen, not stupid. They knew what Marshals were for.

"All right," said Nikki, getting to her feet. "Let's do it."

"Are we allowed to work together?" said Aneeta.

Walden crossed her legs and propped her mark book on her lap. She flipped to a blank page and held the pen poised.

"She'd say if we weren't," pointed out Will.

Who's she, the cat's mother? Walden thought. Wearing her teacher outfits always made her own mental voice start to sound a bit like her grandmother. She took a note. Since she had nothing important to record yet, she wrote down what time it was.

Aneeta read it upside down. "We're being timed!"

"I didn't say that," Walden said. "You have the whole double."

"So . . . summoning circle, right? Salt, chalk," said Will. "Let's go." He fetched supplies from the cupboard in the corner of the classroom, along with a metre ruler. "Big and central." He got on his knees and started work on the pentagram.

"Shouldn't we check the perimeter wards first?" said Aneeta.

"It's a school lab, they're fine," Will said.

Walden said nothing.

Nikki said, "Aneeta's right. Safety check first. Oi." She scuffed her black school shoe across the chalk lines Will had drawn.

"Seriously?" said Will.

"North, south, east, west, windows, door, fire exit," said Nikki. "Matty, you take this half of the room, I'll do that half."

The split ended up being one-third to two-thirds, because Nikki was a lot faster at spellreading. But Mathias was responsible for the fire exit which Walden had altered. She took care not to watch him any more than the others. Mathias was exquisitely sensitive to the attention of authority figures. He would notice, and panic.

"Done? Can we actually get on with this now?" said Will.

"This doesn't look right," Mathias mumbled.

"It's a school lab, it's fine."

"It doesn't."

"What's wrong with it?"

"I dunno," Mathias said. As usual, his instinct for magic was outstripping his grasp on theory. Reading the logic of someone else's spell was not always easy, but they'd spent a long time on incursion wards last summer. Walden bit her tongue. Normally, she would have encouraged Mathias to at least *try* before he gave up; but the point of this exercise was to let the class figure things out by themselves.

Aneeta came and peered up at the ward next to Mathias. After a moment she gave a little screech. "Nikki!"

"What?" Nikki had moved on to ostentatiously checking on the fire extinguishers.

"Again, guys, school lab, school ward—" said Will.

"Oh shit," said Nikki, staring at the streaks of black and yellow paint.

Will paused.

"Language," said Aneeta, with a glance in Walden's direction.

"Actually," said Walden serenely, "'Oh shit' is the correct reaction to finding an error in an incursion ward."

Will finally joined the other three, clustered around the fire exit. He frowned. "Is it—"

"It's the location," said Nikki. "It's too vague."

"'This place,'" Will read, translating the loops and swirls of arcane notation on the wall.

"Could mean anything," said Nikki. "This room, this building, this school, this whole country— Nice one, Matty."

"Yeah, good shout," Will said, and gave Mathias a hard slap on the shoulder. After three terms, Mathias seemed able to accept this as a gesture of friendship. At the start of sixth form, Walden was fairly sure he'd been terrified of Will.

"Was it a test?" said Aneeta, and then, watching Walden's face, immediately decided: "It was a test."

Walden inclined her head. "*Always* start with the safety check," she said. "Every time. Don't count on me, don't count on the school wards. Don't count on anything. Mistakes happen. Check, then check again. What will you do now?"

"Fix it?" said Aneeta.

"Fix it," said Nikki.

Nikki roughed out a correction to the incursion ward on the back of her homework. Spellwriting was a fiddly business of symbols and shorthands. Technically it was a form of instantiation, though only the handful of students in the Instantiation A-level set—Nikki among them—would do much original spellwriting in school. But you could not do invocation safely without learning how to adjust within the boundaries of someone else's prewritten spell. The entire discipline depended on summoning arrays and their accompanying layers of wards. At the secondary level, that meant memorising a selection of the vast bank of designs which already existed.

Walden could create an accurate adjustment to an incursion ward without planning it out first, because she had years of experience, but she was pleased that the sixth formers didn't risk a freehand change. They crowded around Nikki, peering. "Looks good," was Will's verdict. "Let me get the paint."

When Walden had changed the ward, she had done it by the force of her magical intention alone. That skill too was the result of long experience. Paint was easier. Will painted up the correction and then went back to the large salt-and-chalk summoning array he was drawing on the floor. The others, by unspoken agreement, let him get on with it, while the three of them wrote out and then argued about the steps for a fourth-order summoning. Will's unshakeable self-belief was his best asset. He was the fastest in the group—and the second most accurate—at arcane notation, because he never fell into the trap of hesitant sketching. Mathias and Aneeta both did that constantly, with tentative, wobbly spellwork as the result.

"Yeah, good," said Nikki to the finished pentagram. "Go over the upper meridian again, maybe. What do you guys think?"

Walden made a note in the column she'd labelled TEAMWORK.

"If you're both happy," said Aneeta.

"Matty?"

Mathias shrugged.

"Seriously, mate, you spotted that bad ward," said Will. "Hit me, I can take it."

"It's really good," said Mathias.

"Okay," Nikki said. "Then we're ready. Positions, guys. Dr Walden, can we have the dagger?"

At this point Walden intervened to check their work, because there were limits to self-directed learning, and 'actually summoning a demon' was one of them. While she was making minor corrections to the sixth formers' summoning array, Laura Kenning came in and took up a position in the corner of the lab, arms folded, silent. "Good morning, Marshal," said Walden in a friendly way, because it was important to model professionalism and good manners in front of the children.

Kenning said, "Morning." The sword on her hip caught the light from the window, a bright glint of silver. Her cropped blonde hair was a golden halo. She looked like she'd escaped from the school chapel's stained glass, a butch take on an avenging angel.

The sixth formers gave her uneasy looks.

"All right!" said Walden, snatching back their attention. "Good work, everyone."

"I have a question," said Nikki. "What would we summon a fourth-order demon for? I mean, in the real world."

Ah, the utilitarian question. All teachers got this sometimes, and the real answer—*Education is more than a skills checklist for a job application*—seldom satisfied most teenagers. Walden could have said: *Not everything worthwhile in life is useful.* She truly believed that. She could also have said: *We are using this esoteric academic skill in the real world* right now, *and its purpose is to turn you into a person who is undaunted by complex, high-stakes, multistage brainwork.* But that wouldn't have been fair to the spirit of Nikki's question, so she went for a less abstract answer.

"Nothing, I hope," she said. "There is absolutely no piece of magic you can do by summoning a demon this size which you could not also do in some other, much safer way." This was untrue, she realised as she spoke. Having Kenning in the room was putting her on edge. Never enjoyable to be observed teaching, and particularly unpleasant to be observed by a hostile person carrying a sharp object. "I beg your pardon, I misspoke. What I meant to say is: there is no piece of magic you *should* do which can only be done with the assistance of a demon. If you remember our magical ethics topic from last year."

"There's military stuff," said Will. "My uncle does it."

And absolutely should not have mentioned it to you, Walden thought, but she said, "Yes. There is, as you say, military stuff."

Aneeta said, "Did you ever, like—do it?"

"I was approached by the Pentagon when I lived in the United States," said Walden. "I told them no."

She would not normally have shared this titbit with the group. She was immediately annoyed with herself, because she knew she'd said it to impress Kenning. Why did she need to impress Kenning? Kenning was just a rather difficult colleague. But Walden couldn't resist glancing over, trying to gauge the effect of the boast: *I am considerably more knowledgeable about demons than you, and I have the alarming job offer to prove it.*

Kenning appeared to be looking out of the lab window. She probably wasn't even listening.

But the sixth formers were. *"Wow,"* said Will.

It was too late to unsay it. Walden resigned herself. "Were they scary?" said Mathias, clearly envisioning some sort of gun-toting, sunglasses-wearing hit squad.

"Not at all. When Americans are trying to recruit you, they are extremely nice to you." Walden remembered the recruiters—a man and a woman, both in conservatively cut suits—offering plums one after another: funding, unlimited; never worry about research grants again; lab space, state of the art; opportunities for promotion; no need to relocate, there's a California campus; fieldwork, of *course* not, unless that's a direction you'd like for your career; and then the final twist of whipped cream on the military-thaumaturgic trifle: *Considering your relationship with Dr Chan*—how pleased they'd been with their munificence, and their frightfully modern and relaxed attitude to lesbianism—*eventually, we're sure you'll be thinking about citizenship.*

Walden had said she would think about the offer. And then she had booked a flight back to the UK. Her relationship with Rosalind Chan had been dying already; doomed, really, since the day Roz said to her, *Honestly, Saffy, I think babysitting is beneath you. You're too good to waste on high schoolers—and what's a schoolteacher anyway but a failed academic?*

Back at home, the Ministry of Defence had never approached Walden, though she'd been half expecting it. Presumably the MOD had a plentiful supply of people like Will's uncle. Or perhaps they'd just found out that she'd said no to the Americans, and felt they couldn't top that offer on a civil service budget.

"All right, that's enough of that," she said, before the class could dive any further down this particular personal history rabbit hole. "Let's summon a demon, everyone."

They took up positions around the five-pointed array—pentagrams were a classic for a reason, one of the safest and simplest of all the summoning forms. Walden joined them, placing herself at the northern point of the pentagram so that she would be able to anchor the students if necessary. "I'll demonstrate good form for you again, and then we'll go one at a time," she said. "Everyone ready?"

Nods, mumbles; a clear "Sure!" from Nikki. In the corner of the room, Kenning shifted position subtly, though her arms stayed folded.

"On my count. Three—two—one—"

Walden nicked the tip of her left index finger and let a drop of blood fall towards the pentagram. The first layer of protections written into the summoning array went into action as it hit the ground, and the blood drop fizzled out of existence. Just the scent of it, the promise of human power and human vulnerability that it represented, would be enough to tempt a demon closer. Walden felt the inhabitants of the demonic plane notice what was happening and turn their attention to the classroom.

And then she summoned a demon of the fourth order.

She hardly needed the pooled power of the four students to support the invocation. She pulled some magic down from them through the array anyway, so they would know what it felt like, but fourth-order summoning was well within her capabilities. Demonic size in theory kept going forever in exponential progression, but in practice no one had ever found one bigger than the twelfth order. Only a handful of magicians in the world had ever summoned anything above the ninth.

Walden didn't mention it often—after all, it was hardly relevant to a schoolteacher's career—but she was, in fact, one of that handful.

She had to send her power diving through the demonic plane like a hook to scoop up a demon small enough for this pentagram. She felt the others scattering away from her in fear. In the real world Walden was a short thirty-eight-year-old white woman with mouse-brown hair in a neat bob. On the demonic plane she was a swaggering giant.

YOU, she said to her captured demon. *COME.*

The air over the pentagram boiled and split, glowing with the dull purplish light of a controlled demonic incursion. It was considerably more exciting-looking in the ultraviolet spectrum. The demon manifested, and as Walden moved power through the summoning array it began to shape itself not to the contours of possession but in a form of its own choosing. Reification, this was called. Not hugely attractive, it had to be said: the demon was about four feet high and consisted of an inkblot collection of wobbling black shapes, some of which might have been limbs. Halfway up there was a mouth, which opened to show serrated rows of needle teeth.

Query. Walden asked, "What is your name?"

The mouth let out a furious shriek, and the demon said, *Vazirikal! Vazirikal!*

Demon names were attached to them by humans and usually made useful handles to control them. "Thank you," Walden said. With a hard downward slash of a hand gesture, she dismissed it. The inkblot shapes disintegrated. The purplish glow of incursion faded. The arcane lab was quiet. Walden's students wore solemn expressions. Walden resisted the urge to glance over her shoulder at Kenning again.

"All right! And that's how it's done," she said. "And now you know its name, which should make things a little easier. Will, you first." She passed him the dagger. "Off you go."

One by one, the sixth formers summoned a demon.

Walden had picked Will to go first because she judged him least likely to get nervous. He rushed it—she had to sharply remind him to slow down as he chanted the words of invocation—but he got Vazirikal back, managed to compel it down to a convincing reification although the teeth were less distinct, and asked it what was for lunch in the school canteen that day. *Chips!* howled the demon.

"Nice," said Will, and dismissed it, fairly neatly. Then he glanced across the pentagram at Nikki. "Beat that, Conway."

Nikki rolled her eyes.

"Very well done, Will," said Walden, in a no-nonsense tone. "Aneeta, your turn."

Aneeta wore an expression of grim concentration as she ran through the invocation. She could not get Vazirikal's form pinned down to more than a vague conglomeration of shadows, but Walden was pleased with her control otherwise. For her query, she rattled off an equation Walden did not recognise. The demon spat an answer, and Aneeta dismissed it with a little gasp of effort.

"Good work. Though I'm afraid I have no idea if that was correct," Walden said.

"I'll check it," said Aneeta. "It's from my Chemistry home-work."

Walden gave an assessing glance to the two remaining. Mathias was wearing a familiar strained expression: *Please don't pick me!* Walden had mercy on him. "Nikki," she said.

Nikki did the summoning perfectly: steady pace, tight control, an elegant and precise reification. She asked Vazirikal what she ought to give Matron for her birthday. The demon said, *Knit!*

Nikki dismissed the demon and said, "I'll make her a scarf." Walden caught her smug glance at Will and hid a smile. A little competition could go a long way in a classroom setting. "Excel-lent work, Nikki," she said. "I couldn't have done it better myself. Mathias, your turn. Stay calm, take it slowly."

Mathias looked a little sick. But he needed this practical, and Walden did not want to humiliate him in front of his peers by not even letting him try. She thought he could do it. She was sure he could do it.

He put too much power into the invocation. Mathias never quite *believed* how strong he was. Walden felt the blowback hit her through the pentagram, and watched the rest of the class wince. Will said, "Oof, Matty."

Walden saw Mathias's focus slip.

The roar of power in Mathias's invocation did not have the cold and dangerous edge of Walden's long experience. In the demonic plane her magic said, *Watch out, here comes a predator.*

Mathias's said, *I'm big and slow, come eat me.*

Enormous interest suddenly surrounded their pentagram and its little scissor-slice incursion. Vazirikal got eaten even as Mathias was groping for it. Walden said calmly, "I'm taking control of the summoning. Mathias, on three."

Mathias didn't seem to hear her. He was still trying to summon Vazirikal; except that what was left of Vazirikal had been incorporated into a seventh-order archdemon. It would burst the boundaries of their fourth-order array without difficulty if it managed to get a foothold, and he was blindly offering it one. *"Mathias,"* said Walden sharply, and then she didn't bother with the count or being gentle. She shoved all four children out of the magical working and took sole control as she threw her own power between the assembly of demons and her students. There were gasps and shouts as the four sixth formers flew backwards and either sat down hard or thumped into the white walls of the arcane lab.

In the demonic plane, most of the descending scavengers scattered. The archdemon, not yet reified, was imperceptible by sight, but Walden could feel the spiked weight of magical distortion it gave off. It gave her the equivalent of a considering look, trying to decide whether a delicious meal of teenage magician was worth the risk of taking her on. Walden returned her best cold schoolmistress stare: *Do you really think it's a good idea to try me, kid?* The demon couldn't actually see her expression any more than she could see it, but part of being a magician was knowing the relationship between your solid, mundane human body and the magic it performed. If you wanted your presence in the demonic plane to be frightening, it helped to be a good actor. This performance of inarguable authority was more or less the skillset you needed to manage a roomful of teenagers anyway, so Walden got plenty of practice.

The archdemon seemed convinced. It wavered.

Then it reared back in alarm.

Walden was startled until she realised that Kenning had jumped into the pentagram, shortsword drawn. This was reification in reverse, the mundane world brought into the demonic plane. The magical weapon manifested as a glowing blade of white light. Kenning herself was also projecting into the demonic plane, much harder than Walden, the avenging angel manifest as a stalwart figure of muscle and defensive magic. *Oh,* thought Walden, *she's actually quite good.* She had assumed—well, *talented* demon hunters tended not to end up as school security.

She also thought, as a minor corollary: *Oh, she's gorgeous.*

An awkward thing to notice about a difficult colleague in the middle of facing down an archdemon. But the archdemon had already decided they were too much trouble and was slouching away. Kenning spoke a rapid four-syllable banishment—Marshal spells were so *fast*—to give it a good kick in the behind as it went. Walden waited for her to pull out of the pentagram so that she could begin the dismissal sequence and close the incursion.

The archdemon disintegrated.

Kenning said, "What did you—"

"Laura, *get out of there,*" snapped Walden.

But it was too late.

chapter three

OLD FAITHFUL

THEIR NEW VISITOR WAS HARD FOR WALDEN'S magical senses to perceive clearly, in the way that an ocean is hard to comprehend by standing on the seashore. Walden felt the great catspaw of its intentions land across the summoning array—which was, after all, only a fourth-order pentagram drawn by students—and start to force it further open. "No, you don't," she said, and by a solid effort of will managed to manifest a secondary pentagram, drawn in lines of pure force, around their original array. She had lost track of where the sixth formers were. She prayed they had the sense to stay quiet and out of the way. "Laura!"

Kenning was right underneath their new visitor. What was she doing?

Oh, Walden realised a second later. She was trapped.

Kenning was tangled in a great mass of demonic magic, more like the wild growth of a jungle than the elegant, ordered lines of magical intention that Walden taught to her students. She was hacking hard at it, her sword and little slices of combat spells doing the work of a machete, but the demon's power was gigantic and the tangling spells were regrowing as fast as she could cut them down. All the while, at the edge of her thoughts, Walden could hear soft, cruel whispers.

She closed her mind to them, invoking layers of personal defence and warding, as the demon poked and probed for insecurities, doubts, and desires. This was not a dim little imp to be satisfied by chocolate digestives. It was not even a mere archdemon, a creature of force and hunger. This worrying at Walden's mind was subtle, complex, and vicious—the work of a gigantic, malevolent intelligence.

Kenning had stopped fighting. She stood still in the morass of coiling magic that was boiling out of the pentagram. It had started to reify into pale, writhing shapes, like a heap of coiling maggots. Walden swore. "Laura!" she shouted. "Marshal Kenning! For the love of God, don't listen to it!"

Thankfully Kenning heard her. This was, after all, what she was trained for. She brought up her sword. Walden threw the full force of her own magic behind the Marshal as Kenning sliced through the white maggot-shapes—they withered into nothingness—and then slammed home a deep stab with the sword and a triple-strength banishment at the same time. For a moment the two of them worked in perfect harmony. *YOU HAVE NO PLACE HERE,* they roared at the demon. *BEGONE.*

And still it was not enough. The demon bent under the force of their attack, but its monstrous will clung firmly to the original penta-gram. It wanted the mundane world. *Oh,* how it wanted. It wanted Chetwood, specifically: six and a half centuries of wild magic, plus a smorgasbord of half-trained teenage magicians and their untested strength. What demon could resist such a feast? And once it had consumed them all, what human power could contain it? It would swallow up Chetwood village, the meadows and ponds and little woodlands. From there it would spread its dark wings over the Home Counties. It would lift up its monstrous, writhing head, staring greedily southwards, scenting the air, tasting magic and complexity and systems and millions upon millions of selves. Then at last it would begin its slow oozing advance down the Great North Road, through the commuter towns one by one, vacuuming up the Green Belt, rolling over the traffic jams on the M25 without glancing down as the little cars buckled under the force of its passage and burst into flame, bent on the magnificent feast of London.

You'd get the full force of the RAF on you before you got close, thought Walden: but 'nuclear strike on Hertfordshire' was only a slightly less terrible an outcome than 'capital city consumed by a higher demon.'

Minor possessions were common, but minor *incursions*—true manifestations of demons in the mundane world, reified, uncontrolled, wild—those were rare. Major incursions were very rare, and archdemonic incursions almost unheard of. This thing was bigger than an archdemon. Officially, those topped out at the ninth order. Tenth- and eleventh-order demons, theorised in the nineteenth century but not confirmed by experiment until the twentieth, were the higher demons—the principalities. *The big boys,* Walden's thesis advisor had called them.

There was only one higher-demonic incursion in recorded history. It had followed an attempt at a twelfth-order summoning in the USSR in 1968. No one had tried a twelfth-order summoning since. Not officially, anyway.

BEGONE, BEGONE, BEGONE, chanted the combined force of Walden and Kenning, while the higher demon worried at the pentagram's edges like a cat that had seen something small and tasty scuttling into the cracks of a crumbling brick wall.

I belong here, Saffy, its voice whispered in Walden's thoughts, clear and coherent and terribly familiar. She had worked at Chetwood for three years and not seen a flicker of this thing; but it had been here all along, and it knew who she was. *I still belong. You know me. You know I do.*

And then it was dislodged. Something shook it loose from the summoning array and suddenly the full force of Walden and Kenning together was enough to send it whirling away into the void. Walden's chest heaved as she panted. There was sweat dripping down the back of her neck. She was almost surprised to see the white walls of the arcane lab come back into focus. The black and yellow paint of the incursion wards had all turned scarlet. Kenning, still standing in the remnants of the now inert pentagram, collapsed into a crouch and gasped for breath. "How did you do that?" she demanded.

"That wasn't me," Walden said. She turned to the teacher's desk.

Nikki was standing there, wide-eyed with fright. Aneeta, Will and Mathias were clustered behind her. Nikki held in her shaking hand the risk assessment form that Walden put down on the desk at the start of every lesson.

There was a colourful box at the bottom of the page with a quick banishment cantrip. It was, intentionally, the sort of spell that it was easy to cast in a hurry in an emergency. Walden had felt it slide under the demon's grip on the summoning array and pry it loose.

"Quick thinking, Nikki," she said. She felt a certain measure of smugness. Laura Kenning and her narrow Marshal assessment could not have been more wrong about Nicola Conway. "Well done. Have a house point."

In justice, after a narrow miss like that, Walden would have had a sit-down and a nice cup of tea. Unfortunately, there was still half an hour of the double left. She drank the last of her cold coffee instead, and regretted it immediately. "All right, let's review," she said. "I'm sure you've already guessed that your homework is to write up a report on today's practical. What have we learned?"

A painful silence. Kenning had taken up her stance in the corner again. She looked tired.

"Was that him?" said Will. "Old Faithful?"

Of course; Will had a long family connection to Chetwood, he would have heard of the school's largest and most alarming demonic pest if anyone had. "*It* was a very large demon, yes," said Walden. "Precise identification would be difficult without summoning it. Should we summon it?"

"*No,*" said Aneeta immediately.

Good. "Why not?"

"Um, because it would kill us?"

"Correct," Walden said.

"Did anyone else, like—hear it?" said Aneeta. "It said—"

She stopped.

"Remember our higher demons topic. These creatures are predators. The more intelligent ones will absolutely try to play on your emotions in order to create a weakness. I promise you, nothing it said was worth listening to," said Walden. "We had the bad luck to run into something rather bigger than we were expecting. That can happen. What did we do right? What should we have done better?"

"I froze," said Mathias, miserable.

"Yes," said Walden gently. "You did. That can also happen. Let's see what we can learn from it, so it's less likely to happen again."

It took a while to get the group talking, and it was a good ten minutes before Mathias said much more than monosyllables, but by the time the bell went for morning break, they all seemed to have recovered from the incident. "All right, do me a practical report. Use the structure in your notes, and it's due next week. Yes, as in Monday next week," Walden said, fully expecting to have the reports all in by Wednesday-ish. "Will, could you stay behind a moment, please."

Always difficult to tell off a Year Thirteen, and particularly difficult to tell off someone like Will, who as well as being unshakeably self-confident was more than a foot taller than Walden. Scolding was much easier when you could loom a little, but short of magical cheating, Walden could not physically intimidate someone who was six foot three. She knew how to make her tone of voice make up the difference, though. "Do you know why I want to speak to you?" she asked Will when the others were gone, in tones that any intelligent child would instantly parse as 'alarmingly neutral.'

Will shrugged, which was a fairly good start, because it meant he *did* know and preferred not to admit it. "It was Matty's fault, though."

"We're not talking about Mathias just now, Will," said Walden, and then waited. Silence was a powerful tool when you were dealing with a teenager who knew they were in the wrong.

"Okay, okay, okay," said Will. "I only said *oof.* I didn't know it would distract him."

"What's the arcane safety standard for secondary casters in a major invocation?" Walden asked.

"Silence," Will admitted.

"So you do know," said Walden. "Good. I was concerned that I hadn't taught you anything. And I am disappointed, Will. You put yourself and your classmates at serious risk through pure carelessness. By now you should be a much better magician than that."

"But—"

Walden raised her eyebrows.

"It was all fine in the end, though, wasn't it? It's not a huge deal."

Kenning spoke up. Walden had forgotten she was still there. In a flat voice she said, "That was at least a ninth-order archdemon. If it had succeeded in forcing an incursion, it would have eaten you all alive, followed by the rest of the school. The main reason it *didn't* succeed is that you are lucky enough to be taught by one of the most skilled invokers in the country. If someone under my command made a mistake that stupid, I would have him kicked out of the Order."

Will's mouth worked. He said, "Oh."

That was a little harder than Walden had meant to hammer him, but it seemed to have worked. "Think about that," she advised. "I think you owe Mathias an apology. Do I need to call you both into my office, or can I trust you to speak to him yourself?"

Will said, "I'll do it."

Walden made a mental note to follow that up later. Will was almost never actively malicious, but he could be slippery, and he tended to conveniently forget anything that he would find difficult or embarrassing to deal with. "And I will look forward to reading your practical report next week," she said. "It goes without saying that I expect a clear analysis of *exactly* what went wrong today. Now, off you go."

When Will was gone, looking chastened, she said, "Well. Thank you for your help this morning, Laura. Shall we go and get a cup of tea?"

"I need to write up this incident," said Kenning. She still looked annoyed. "So do you, don't you? That boy should be punished. Detention, at least."

If Walden thought that a lunchtime detention would have

the slightest effect on Will, she would have given him one. But he was the sort of boy who laughed off official punishments, or even boasted about them, and then forgot they had ever happened. Shame, on the other hand, would stick with him. "I assure you," she said, "having to apologise to someone, and then write a report explaining that he got something wrong, will be much harder on him. If you'll leave the discipline to me, please."

"What was an archdemon that size doing here?" Kenning said. "That thing was at least ninth order. It was intelligent! Why didn't I know about it?"

"Tenth order," said Walden, stifling a sigh. "Or possibly eleventh. And I'm sure you did know about it. The previous Chief Marshal must have mentioned Old Faithful."

"Old Faithf—yes, as a joke to frighten the newbie!"

"Not a joke, I assure you," Walden said. "Old Faithful has been hanging around Chetwood School since the seventeenth century at least. It's fairly quiet but it makes an occasional push."

"It's been here for *three hundred years*? Why has no one killed it?"

"It's been tried," said Walden. "Haven't you seen the memorial in the chapel? The Headmaster who died in 1926. I think that was the last serious attempt. After that they tried moving the school site, but Old Faithful just followed, and the new campus was less magically secure—so back we came. Since then, efforts have focused more on keeping it out, and preventing wild magic bleeding through between the planes, so it doesn't get too much to eat."

"How often does it get through?" Kenning demanded.

You should already know this, Walden thought. *Surely it's your job to know this.* But she also felt guilty. The former Chief Marshal had been a tired man in his sixties plodding towards retirement. Shouldn't Walden have checked that he'd actually trained his replacement properly on Chetwood's security position? Wasn't it her responsibility too?

If she'd known Kenning was actually good . . .

It was probably Walden's job to know.

"Its attempts are very rare, and its successes are rarer," she told Kenning. "A lot of magicians have worked hard to defend Chetwood, over the centuries. And a lot of Marshals, of course. The last serious incident was in 2003."

Kenning frowned. "I've seen that memorial," she said. "By the cricket pitches. A boy died."

"Yes. The school's most recent student death. And, of course, we would all prefer to keep it that way. If you like, Marshal, we could set up a meeting with the archivist and I'll talk you through everything Chetwood has on our unwelcome demonic squatter. The earlier records are rather piecemeal, but if the information is useful for you . . ."

"Yes," said Kenning. "As soon as possible. I want everything on the 2003 incident, to start with." Of course she did. Walden already regretted offering the archives session; but it was a personal regret, not a professional one. Professionally it was exactly the right call. Kenning added, "Before your time, I suppose."

It took Walden a moment and then she laughed. "Thank you very much. I was *seventeen* in 2003."

Kenning looked embarrassed. "I didn't mean—"

"It's quite all right," Walden said. "When you spend your days with teenagers, you age fast. Spiritually, if not physically, I really am an ancient crone. Sometimes they explain the internet to me."

"We had *internet* in 2003."

Walden snorted. "Try telling them that."

chapter four

SITE MANAGEMENT

ALDEN GOT HER CUP OF TEA. THE TEN minutes she spent collapsed into an armchair in the staffroom having a not very interesting conversation about weekend plans with a German teacher were blissful. *Not much. You? Oh, haha, not much*—both of them fully understanding the real purpose of the ritual, which was to spend ten minutes being a human person with a name, perhaps some hobbies, and a rich inner life, not Dr This, Frau That.

Of course no one ever really had weekend plans in term time—apart from the chatty group of newly qualified teachers in the corner of the staffroom, who buzzed with the enviable energy of youth. To Walden's eyes they looked barely older than the sixth formers. Their ringleader, blonde-ponytailed and enthusiastic, was Lilly Tibbett, who was the NQT—a newly qualified teacher—in the Evocation Department this year. Walden, as Director of Magic with oversight of all the magical departments, had sat on that hiring committee. Lilly was a talented young magician with a CV full of scholarships and prizes; almost no actual experience, but you expected that at twenty-three. She had the makings of a good teacher, which was to say she knew her stuff and she was good with people. At twenty-three, the good-with-people was mostly raw charisma, rather than skill, but charisma was a valuable place to start. Her students already called her, lovingly, *Tibbs*.

"Duty calls," said Frau Cole, as the bell went. "My bad Year Tens, so pray for me."

"Good luck," said Walden. "I ought to be in a meeting."

She had a meeting, and another meeting, and a phone call with a parent, and another meeting, and lunch with colleagues where—naturally—everyone only talked about work; and the Admissions briefing after lunch, and her direct report meeting with the Head of Instantiation, and a one-hour arcane safety single lesson with 7C. Last on her docket was the weekly two-hour state of play with the site manager. Todd Cartwright was a wiry man in his sixties whose bald, domed head rose gently through a shoulder-length shock of grey hair. He had been at the school for forty years, longer than any other member of staff, a Chetwood institution. His current title recognised what he actually did, and had in fact been doing for years, but before that he'd been called caretaker, handyman, security guard, van driver, and most importantly—and the reason Walden had fought tooth and nail to keep him reporting to her, rather than reorganised into Operations in the most recent shakeup—Keymaster.

The ancient title was as old as the school. The Keymaster was the keeper of the school's Great Key. It locked the outer doors to the chapel, which were traditionally kept open, and the gigantic oaken Chetwood Gate, which was usually shut—with the postern gate open instead—to discourage country ramblers and tourists. Some people saw the beautiful rolling grounds of a boarding school, charmingly filled with young people doing traditional outdoor boarding school activities, and just could not comprehend 'private property,' or indeed 'you cannot wander around a school in term time taking photographs of the children.' Yes, Chetwood was absurd, ancient, privileged, beautiful—but to the children who lived here, their school was not an aesthetic. It was just life. They had a right to get on with life without being goggled at.

Todd now had a team of friendly security people in high-vis jackets who gently explained this to unwelcome visitors. He seldom had to bundle people off the site himself. He still wore the Great Key on a chain around his neck every day. Keymaster was not just an honorary position. Walden had once had to explain this at length to a governors' meeting. The Victorian thaumic engines in the great room adjacent to her suite looked very impressive and did a lot of work. But Chetwood had been here much longer than they had. The school's ancient boundaries and gateways were part of a much older and subtler set of protections against magical danger, and the Key secured them. *Shouldn't it be given to a trained magician, then?* she'd been asked. *Or perhaps the Chief Marshal?*

On paper, perhaps; but Todd had what he called a 'knack' and what Walden thought was probably a spectacular untrained talent for magic. She'd tried to suggest adult lessons, more than once, and the old man always just laughed. In any case, his nose for the fluctuations of magic around the school grounds was second to none. Several times now, he'd been the first person to alert Walden to a minor magical security issue before it could grow to a major one. In the 2003 incursion, more than twenty years ago, he'd been first on the scene, before any of the trained magicians on staff, before the Marshals.

Laura Kenning would probably want to know that, and talk to him about it. Walden put it out of her mind. She'd offered to sort out that session in the school archives. It could wait until then.

Todd was in a glum mood today. He'd been in the boiler sheds all afternoon. "Two years," he said. "Two years of life left in those if we're lucky. And the insulation's gone to pot. Last time anyone looked at it was in the seventies, far as I can tell. Ten to one we'll have to get an asbestos crew in."

"I'm sorry, Todd," said Walden.

"Sorry, sorry. It's not in the budget, they said. Took it to the Bursar, do you know what he told me? 'Maybe next year, Todd.' Maybe next year! Well, when those boilers go, we'll be lucky if it's a whimper and not a bang. Even if we're not cleaning up an explosion, I tell you, you'll still have ice forming up on the inside of your classroom windows all through January. You're going to need those old fireplaces in your suite, Dr Walden." Todd was meticulously hierarchical—Walden suspected him of finding it funny—and refused point-blank to call her Saffy. "Meanwhile the Bursary lot are sitting in their swish offices in the new building counting pennies. The kids'll be freezing their fingers and toes off over in Scrubs. You can tell 'em it's a history lesson. Not in the budget! What do they think the budget's for?"

Walden had some sympathy for the Bursar's plight, because she'd been in the meetings and seen the spreadsheets. Chetwood was rich, of course, with its ancient foundation and its hefty school fees. But it was also poor, because the whole institution was just enormously expensive to run. A boarding school was an education crossed with a hotel, and in the twenty-first century, the parents who paid eye-watering sums to send their offspring here expected the education to be first-rate and the hotel at least three stars. Day-to-day running costs, on top of staff payroll, ate up an astonishing amount of those eye-watering sums. And the ancient and gorgeous school site might photograph beautifully, but almost nothing in it was fit for purpose. The oldest parts of the school—the chapel, its adjoining colonnade making up the west side of the quad, and the Old Refectory at the other end—were Grade II listed antiquities, part of the original fourteenth-century foundation. Their cold, stony grandeur went hand in hand with the eye-watering cost of the heating bills. The other three sides of the quad were a Georgian replacement for a previous collection of sixteenth-century buildings. The classrooms were cavernous high-ceilinged affairs adorned with classical-ish plasterwork of dubious quality, all exactly the wrong size for twenty-eight desks and a smartboard. Hugging the back of the chapel was School House, also a victim of nineteenth-century enthusiasm for replacing things. In the school archives there were some sketches of the original School House, which had been a rather pleasant traditional farmhouse dating probably from Tudor times, with a substantial kitchen garden. Now it was a red-brick attempt at Gothic fantasia, featuring a small tower which was notable for being out-of-period for every possible period the Victorian architect could have had in mind.

The school had acquired other boarding houses in haphazard fashion over the centuries, naming them after benefactors or patron saints: Kings, St Edmund's, St Jude's, Lady Margaret, Brewers, and New House—so called because it only dated from 1904. The house buildings, mostly erected before the advent of modern plumbing and on the assumption that every student would be male, had become ever more inconvenient and impractical. In the 1960s a forward-thinking Headmaster had sold them all off except Brewers and New House and used the profits to buy the school a secondary campus, an expanse of former farmland on the other side of the main road into Chetwood village. There he erected a new boarding house, heavy on the concrete, to house the whole student body. He named it, grandly, Universal House.

The students called it Wormwood Scrubs.

This had been abbreviated to just Scrubs by Walden's own time at the school, and Scrubs it remained to this day. Walden felt very fond of it despite how ugly it was. After all, she had lived there for most of her adolescence. She knew that the Bursar also felt very fond of it, because it was one of the few school buildings that didn't require an expensive specialist in historical construction techniques every time something needed repairs.

With the exception of the seven young sorcerers being fostered in School House—where they had their own bedrooms—all the college's boarding students lived in single-sex accommodation in Scrubs during term time. The younger ones slept in dormitories of eight, graduating to smaller groups of four further up the school and double rooms by sixth form. There was also a substantial minority of day pupils, who lived in the village and in the surrounding countryside. The names of the old boarding houses had been retained as organisational and pastoral units; every student, day or boarding, was assigned to one. The younger ones took house sports and the annual house point competition very seriously, though most of them lost interest, or at least felt they were too cool to admit they cared, by Year Ten or so.

Walden's meeting with Todd ended just after half past four. He'd had nothing of substance to report except that morning's excitement in the arcane labs, which of course Walden knew about already. "Key picked it up," he said—Todd always attributed his remarkable awareness of Chetwood's magical fluctuations to the Key, though as far as Walden could tell it had no earthly way to detect anything of the kind—"but I knew you were teaching in there, and I'd already seen Marshal Kenning heading over."

Walden otherwise got on with Todd very well, but she wished he didn't have quite so much respect for the Marshals.

"Old Faithful rolling over in his sleep?" Todd said.

"Something like that," said Walden.

The old man gave her a thoughtful look. "Something, all right," he agreed. "Bit like the boilers, if you ask me. Better to sort it out before it goes bang."

By the time Walden got out of her meeting, the school day had officially ended. There were still plenty of people about. She paused for a moment in the colonnade on the west side of the quad. She had barely had a chance to look out the window, let alone step outside, since she had started her working day at half past six that morning.

It was a glorious October afternoon. The light had that peculiar autumnal clarity that made the quad look like an antique print of itself: greens, reds, blacks, a blue and golden sky. The shadow of the chapel's angular roof cut a neat diagonal across the lawn. A chattering line of students in scarlet uniform blazers snaked out of the door to the tuck shop in the Old Refectory and round the edges of the perfectly mowed green. Half a dozen Year Sevens were playing a game with light spells, evoking beginners' firework illusions in pink and orange and shouting excitedly as they weaved in and out of the columns of the colonnade. Some Year Elevens walked past in a tight, conspiratorial cluster, giggling about something on a phone. Under the tightly pruned oak tree at the far side of the quad, a pair of sixth formers had claimed a favoured spot—the quad's only bench—where they were sharing a packet of crisps. The staffroom's outer door was open on their left, and Walden could see a group of teachers sagging into armchairs and drinking tea. At the doors of the chapel stood Reverend Ezekiel, a tall middle-aged Black man in dark gown and clerical collar. He caught sight of Walden and waved.

Walden waved back. She felt a glow of warmth for the whole scene: the buzzing, noisy, complicated, exhausting, surprising, entertaining, endlessly delightful life of a healthy school. She was well on the way to another sixteen-hour work day, she could feel it—she had marking and lesson planning still to do, there was a faculty meeting to chair tomorrow morning before registration, she needed to set up that session with Kenning and the archivist, spend an hour tuning the thaumic engines, and in fact write her own incident report on Old Faithful's attempt this morning—but it didn't trouble her. Walden loved her job. Chetwood was hers and she belonged here, in this place where she did good and meaningful and interesting work every day of her life. What had she spent the last two decades working for, if not this?

She thought of Old Faithful's shadow bearing down on the arcane lab that morning. Todd was right: if the great demon was stirring, precautions needed to be taken as soon as possible. So Walden would take them. She was expert and unafraid. *Come on, then,* she thought, watching the children toss dancing lights from hand to hand, the sixth formers flirting, the teachers gossiping, two small birds darting in and out of the branches of the great oak tree. Something bright and sizzling curled in the back of her thoughts, and she folded her arms, making sure to catch the sleeves of her blazer over her wrists. *Come on,* she thought at the monster in her school's shadow. *Come and have a go if you think you're hard enough.*

Walden was at the shiny, glass-fronted faculty meeting room in the new Bursary building bright and early next morning, early enough that she bumped into Dinah from Catering dropping off the croissants and tea urn. The meeting was due to start at 8 A.M., which gave her half an hour before the official start of the school day to run through an agenda with thirteen items on it. Everyone was going to be yawning and bleary and thinking about their lesson for Period One, and anyone on house duty would already have done Revs—as the first wake-up register of the day was traditionally known—before sending their teenage charges off to breakfast.

She sat at her laptop and gave her colleagues friendly smiles and greetings as they stumbled in and flung themselves gratefully at the tea and croissants. "Morning, Victoria—good morning, Simon—hi, Lilly—good morning—"

"How's it going, Saffy?" said Ezekiel, taking the red plastic chair to her right.

"Busy, busy, but I can't complain," said Walden. "Did you get a croissant?"

"Can't stand the school pastries," said Ezekiel. He was wearing his clerical collar, but he'd left off the gown. Tuesday morning, so no chapel service today. He pulled out a notebook and fountain pen ready for the meeting—Ezekiel resented his laptop and used it as little as possible—and said, "Are you still coming by for that observation later?"

Walden had in fact completely forgotten that they'd planned a lesson observation, but she clicked subtly to her calendar and there it was: *Period Two, obs Ezekiel Y11 GCSE Invocation.* "Of course," she said, "I'm looking forward to it."

"Should be a good one," said Ezekiel. "They're a nice set, and I'm carrying on with the ethics topic."

Magical ethics at GCSE level was one short-answer question and a box-ticking exercise—*Should you summon demons to help you commit crimes, yes or no* well, that was an oversimplification. Not much of one. Walden hid her disappointment—she'd been hoping to see

Ezekiel teach something interesting—and glanced up at the clock. Three minutes past eight. "Good morning, everyone!" she said. "Shall we get started?"

You did not expect a full faculty meeting to be a lively exchange of views. There were too many people and too much to cover. Seven Evocation teachers, four Instantiation, and two—Walden and Ezekiel—to make up the Invocation Department. Walden ran through her agenda as quickly as she could. Magical security reminders: leading, today, with the fact that Old Faithful had stirred on campus again. "Please stay aware and make sure your lab wards and risk assessments are up to date," she said. "I'll be meeting the Chief Marshal for a further assessment later this week. While I'm on the subject, can I remind you all that the Marshals would *really* appreciate knowing in advance when there's an elevated chance of demons. If you find yourself teaching an advanced practical that isn't already noted on the scheme of work for that date, do please drop an email to the Marshal duty address. It makes staffing easier and it means they can get there faster in a crisis."

Unconvinced expressions around the table—well, academic magicians tended to be dubious about the utility of Marshals. Walden was no exception. But Kenning had been undeniably very good—fast, decisive, effective—during that summoning-gone-wrong yesterday. Very good, and gorgeous.

Oh hush, Walden thought at herself. But she felt positively saintly for passing on Kenning's tiresome complaint about schemes of work. No one could accuse *her* of being a problem colleague.

She rattled through the rest of the meeting, reminding Chetwood's magical faculty about the upcoming exam board consultations, useful conferences, this year's professional development cycle, the importance of interdisciplinary lesson observations *including* with our colleagues in academic subjects, and how to report a weakness in the school wards. She handed off to Victoria for a check-in; she was the Head of Instantiation and doubled up as subject lead for the middle school Magic curriculum. Walden had very little to do with the middle school beyond her arcane safety carousel, since no one started formal Invocation until the GCSE course began in Year Ten. Were Years Seven to Nine learning anything? Apparently yes, they were; and Year Nine were coming up to GCSE choices after half term. Early mutterings looked good for the magical departments. Walden made a note to herself to check the date of the Options Fair, which was when either she or Ezekiel would have to sell GCSE Invocation to their department's potential students for next year. It was a few years since she had taught a GCSE set, but once she lost her current Year Thirteen it might be a nice change of pace to go back to a younger year group.

Then Simon, the Head of Evocation, introduced Lilly Tibbett's NQT project: a fun new magical sports approach to Year Eight Evocation, with outdoor lessons. Everyone made interested and supportive noises and Walden made another note: refocus the school's outdoor demon defences next time she tuned up the thaumic engines. *Any* loose magic attracted demonic attention, and she couldn't think of anything more likely to produce uncontrolled bursts of magical energy than a gang of middle schoolers doing competitive spellcasting. Then she nodded to Ezekiel, not as Head of Invocation—with only two of them officially in the department, they didn't need to waste meeting time, they could just email each other—but as senior house staff.

"Just a short one from me," Ezekiel said. "A reminder to check the register codes for sorcerers in your lessons. We have seven living in School House at the moment, one at the local primary and the other six Chetwood pupils, and there are a few others in all year groups except the current Year Ten. Remember to use your judgement when you respond to misuse of magic around the school, with these students in particular. Be aware that the youngest ones, especially, often aren't doing it on purpose. That doesn't mean *be lenient*—they need to learn!—but do be kind. And I'll be running my session on childhood sorcery, what it means, and how it develops at the twilight INSET before half term; if you haven't heard me talk about it before, this might be a good time."

'Sorcerer' was the current term for the people who had once been called 'rogues' or 'erratics': people who would find themselves doing magic without ever having been taught any, who attracted demons before they knew what demons were. They were much, much rarer than laymen thought. In Walden's opinion, most of the children noted as potential sorcerers on the school's register were probably just reasonably talented to start with and then came from families where they saw other people casting spells. People like Nikki and Mathias—strong, wild magical talents, capable of summoning demons by accident before they ever finished primary school—were rare enough that the dozen or so currently studying at Chetwood, half of them fostered at School House and nearly all of them on scholarships or bursaries, probably made up most of England's current population of sorcerers under eighteen.

Ezekiel's update was the last serious point on the agenda. Walden asked for Any Other Business—there was none, of course, and most people's expressions just said *Let me out of here I need to finish my marking*—and then said, "Thank you very much, everyone, we'd better stop there," a precise two minutes before the bell. "I'll email the minutes round later. That was our last faculty meeting this half term—it'll be back to departments in this slot for the next few weeks. And remember—do your risk assessments, check your wards!"

There were still a few chewy, unconvincing school croissants left, so she snagged an extra before heading back to her office across the road in Brewers. Her schedule for the day was rattling through her thoughts. She didn't see Upper Sixth on a Tuesday, but she did have an arcane safety lesson with 10T before lunch. Write up and circulate those minutes, spend Period One doing emails and an incident report about Old Faithful's little feint yesterday, and then observe Ezekiel's Year Eleven. Break, lesson planning, Year Ten early lunch. And then she'd blocked out the afternoon, weeks ago, for a long session working on the thaumic engines. Everything planned and prepared. Everything under control. Nothing could go wrong.

Ezekiel, like most teaching staff at Chetwood, had a classroom that was *his*. It was one of the things Walden missed most from frontline teaching. Lab Three was her regular lab, but you could hardly personalise an arcane laboratory. Ezekiel's teaching room felt like his own, with his fountain pens and notebooks on the desk, his laptop jammed into a corner, and a framed photograph balanced precariously on the stationery cupboard: Ezekiel and Ebele outside the chapel with the school choir last Christmas. He was a form tutor in the Lower Sixth, and his tutees had decorated their form noticeboard with a circus theme, featuring their own school-photo headshots stuck onto the bodies of cartoon clowns: all very good-humoured and really only lightly disturbing. They'd stuck a photo of Ezekiel in the middle as ringmaster.

The other noticeboards around the room were looking smart too: middle school posters about philosophy and religious studies, Year Ten Invocation work featuring colourful annotated diagrams of first-order summoning arrays. Walden, arriving before the bell for Period Two, went and peered at that display and discovered it was a few years old. One of the diagrams had Aneeta's name on it. She wouldn't point it out. Technically, displays of student work were supposed to be refreshed every academic year, but it was one of the things that always fell by the wayside. Who had the time?

Year Eleven Invocation turned up in dribs and drabs once the bell went, plumping rucksacks on desks and gossiping with each other in little knots. A few of them greeted Walden politely, which was unusually good manners with an adult they did not know well, and boded well for this year group as sixth formers next year. Chetwood's general standards of behaviour hadn't been affected as badly as some schools by the pandemic a few years ago—when you locked down a boarding school, it just went on being a boarding school—but most of the day pupils had been pulled out for the duration, and of course a lot of the younger children now coming up through the middle school had been primary schoolers at the time. There was a feeling among the staff that general maturity levels had slipped, a sign of children who'd missed out on key bits of socialisation.

Walden opened up the observation form on her laptop and made a note: good behaviour even before their teacher arrived. A nice set, as Ezekiel had said.

Lesson observations could be very dull. What was wanted at the end was a beautiful A4 page of admiring notes that Walden and Ezekiel could both put in their prof dev folders ahead of the next pay review cycle. After all, there were very few surprises involved in good teaching. Different people had different styles, but the fundamentals were consistent across age groups, across disciplines, across all different kinds of schools: *Know your students*, and *Know your subject*. All you could really get from an observation was a handful of ideas for things to incorporate into your own practice: activities, structures, turns of phrase.

Ezekiel arrived, unhurried, two minutes after the bell. He

walked into his classroom and was instantly the centre of it. Year Eleven went silent, rapidly pulling out notebooks and tucking away rucksacks under desks, not needing to be told. Walden did a quick headcount: there were twenty of them, a medium-large set for a GCSE in a magical subject. Ezekiel waited in amicable silence until all of them were prepared and watching him, and then said, "Good morning, Year Eleven. Back to the grindstone; we're carrying on with our magical ethics discussion. Dr Walden is joining us today," with a nod in her direction, "as I'm sure you've noticed. Let's get started."

Walden began her A4 page of admiring notes: *Clear routines & established behaviour expectations. Immediate sense of purpose.*

She'd seen Ezekiel teach before, and always enjoyed it. His style was stricter on the surface than Walden's—Will Daubery would never have risked attempting his brand of schoolboy bullshit on Reverend Ezekiel—but that strict structure gave him room for a relaxed, conversational approach. Year Eleven obviously liked and trusted him. He opened with a quick-fire question-and-answer session, recapping their last lesson: *When and how can you use magic on another human being?* Hands went up every time he asked a question, but Ezekiel ignored the volunteers and called out names: "Anastasia, what do you think? The principle of consent, good, we discussed it last time. Connie, do you agree with Anastasia? Why? Yes, excellent. Zachariah—" A pause; Ezekiel raised his eyebrows and glanced at the bin in the corner. The luckless Zachariah obediently got up, walked over to it, and spat out his chewing gum. "You're not off the hook yet," Ezekiel said, when the boy got back to his seat. "Better make it good. Anastasia and Connie made good points. How would you disagree with them?"

"Uh, I wouldn't?" said Zachariah, attempting a charming smile.

"Try," said Ezekiel, good-humoured and patently uncharmed.

"Pause, think about it. Everyone else, I want you to think about it as well. Make notes if you need to. I'll be picking someone else to speak once Zack's had his turn."

Walden was busily adding to her observation notes: *Use of names, strong questioning technique, praise and encouragement, behaviour management, THINKING TIME, contribution is strongly expected / not a punishment, no one gets to hide.* All normal parts of a good classroom discussion, and she did all of it herself, but doing it with twenty fifteen-year-olds of mixed magical and academic ability was a lot more impressive than doing it with four talented Year Thirteens. Ezekiel clearly knew his students extremely well—picking out a confident speaker to start the discussion, getting a quiet one to expand on an established point, identifying minor misbehaviour and immediately correcting and refocusing. Zack took his thinking time and then said, "What about if someone's unconscious and you're trying to help them?"

"Go on," said Ezekiel. "Why would that change anything?"

"Well—"

The discussion kept going for rather longer than Walden would have allowed if she'd been teaching this topic. The class covered the basic exemptions to the principle of magical consent and from there dove deeper: What about medicine? Does a doctor need your consent to save your life? If a person is unconscious, can you assume they probably *would* consent to being helped? What if you don't speak the same language? What if someone has a developmental disability and doesn't understand what you're asking? What about age, does that matter? Can a child consent to having a spell cast on them? Can *you*?

A forest of hands shot up. By this point in the discussion Ezekiel was barely speaking at all, only glancing around and calling out names, occasionally injecting another question as the class wrestled the last one to a standstill. Walden was starting to pick out names and personalities: Anastasia, a tall blonde girl with a slight unplaceable accent, was loud and opinionated; Alec, a rather overweight boy with long, lank hair, contributed less often but almost everything he did say was very clever indeed; another boy, Ibrahim, loved to argue but seldom thought his point through before he started talking; quiet Connie needed coaxing and encouragement but clearly *wanted* to join in; Zachariah thought he was funny and was sometimes right—and so on, and so on. Some of these children would become next year's A-level Invocation set. Walden was already hoping for Alec.

"Very good," said Ezekiel at last, cutting the conversation off. Walden glanced up at the clock and saw that it had been nearly twenty minutes. *Much* longer than she would have spent on the magical ethics topic at GCSE, when really the whole thing could be boiled down to the five bullet points listed in the syllabus. You could just hand them out on a worksheet. But Ezekiel went to the board and wrote *CAN YOU USE MAGIC ON A PERSON?* Then he drew five blank bullet points underneath, and said, "I want you to boil down the discussion we just had to what *you* think are our five most important points. You can work with the person next to you, and you have eight minutes."

Walden got up to peer over shoulders as Year Eleven worked. The atmosphere in the classroom was focused, the conversations nearly all on topic, and Year Eleven were busily deducing the syllabus for themselves, with an air of satisfaction. She went quietly to Ezekiel's side at the board and murmured, "*Very* nice. Socratic, even."

"I try," said Ezekiel.

"Stretch and challenge?"

"Wait for it."

Walden waited, watching the students scribble their bullet

points. As the eight minutes wore on, some of them—mostly the girls—got out highlighters and gel pens and started decorating their notes. Zachariah had finished early and was looking out the window. On her way back to her laptop in the corner, Walden casually read his notebook upside down and saw that although his handwriting was terrible, he had in fact written down four of the five key points he needed. Walden would not usually have trusted such a large group to do this much thinking for themselves. *High expectations*, she added to her observation notes when she sat down again. *Open discussion—above GCSE level.* She *should* teach a GCSE set again. It would be good for her, and it would be fun.

"Yes, Alec?" said Ezekiel.

Alec put his hand down. "Sir," he said, "how are we defining 'person'?"

"*Good* question," said Ezekiel. "Expand it."

"Well—what about animals?"

"Is an animal a person?" Ezekiel asked.

"An animal *could* be a person," said Alec. "Like a dolphin, or a gorilla. If an animal is as intelligent as a person—"

"Oh, wait, what about *aliens*?" said another boy. "Could you do magic to an alien?"

"Obviously an alien would be a person!"

"Would it, though?"

"But even if an animal isn't a person," someone said over this, "you still can't just—"

"What if it's a bug? What if it's a *worm*?"

"You mean like if an alien was a worm—"

"Sir," said Alec over all of this, "I was just wondering—"

"Let me ask all of you a question," Ezekiel said, and waited until the room was quiet, focused on him. Then he asked, "Is a demon a person?"

Walden looked up from her keyboard.

"That's what I was wondering," Alec said. "Is it?"

And there was silence in the classroom. No one knew the answer. Walden would have been extremely surprised if they did know. The exact nature of demonic sapience was one of the most contested questions in modern invocation. But Ezekiel let the silence stretch—letting them think about it.

"Demons are so stupid, though," one girl said.

"Is a stupid person not a person?" asked Ezekiel.

"Because," said Alec—no hand up, this time, and Walden thought he was too absorbed in the question to remember classroom manners—oh, he was going to be a *good* A-level student—"everything we do in Invocation is about doing magic to demons." *With demons*, Walden thought, but it was a fine distinction. Alec's point was fair. "And if it's wrong to do magic to people without their consent, and demons are people, then—"

"But it's got to be all right," objected a small girl sitting near the front, "or *you* wouldn't be doing it, sir."

"Ah yes," said Ezekiel, and tapped his clerical collar. "I called up God and had a quick chat about the issue, and he told me it was fine." He smiled at the class. "Is that what you wanted me to say?"

Laughter, embarrassment. "Um—"

"Well, this is a question that the GCSE syllabus doesn't bother asking, but I think it's a good and important question," Ezekiel said. "I could give you a potted summary of my thoughts on the matter, but as it happens, we have someone in the room with us who did a doctorate on this sort of thing. Dr Walden, take the hot seat, help us out. Is a demon a person?"

Walden had been expecting it. She didn't stand up—this wasn't her lesson, she wasn't the teacher—but she leaned forward in her chair, opening up her body language, as the Year Elevens craned their necks to look at her. "It's a fascinating question," she said, which was filler while she rapidly thought through how to pitch what she knew into a useful mini-lecture for a class at this level. "The answer, helpfully, is both *yes* and *no*. Demonic personhood is a contested topic, because it ties into the very nature of what demons are, and *that* is a contested topic as well. Let me ask you all: Is a demon a human being?"

Headshakes, negative murmurs: that was an easy one. "Is a demon *like* a human being?" Less certainty this time, but a general *no*. "I agree," Walden said. "A demon is not very much like a human being at all. So is a demon an animal, or like an animal?" Even more uncertainty. Ezekiel was watching her thoughtfully. Walden answered her own question: "*No*, on the whole, is the truest answer; but there are elements of *yes* as well. Demons are constantly experiencing one of the key pressures of the animal kingdom. In the demonic plane, they are all predators and all prey. Managing an invocation safely becomes much easier and safer when you keep those pressures in mind. Like most opportunistic predators, demons are unlikely to pick fights they are not certain to win. A trained modern magician is too much of a risk for all but the strongest demons, and they can tell; they have a raw sense for magical power and control that goes well beyond the senses we all develop in our magical practice. So to keep yourself safe, you only need to make it clear that the risk calculation of attacking you doesn't work out in the demon's favour. Most of the time, they accept that. After all, we have something they want. Our world is a kind of escape for them, a restful alternative to the merciless pressures of their own plane. It's been argued that a first-order imp that moves itself into a nice safe home possessing a washing machine or a TV remote is engaging in a kind of self-domestication, like cats."

Year Eleven looked thoughtful. A hand went up to ask a

question. But Walden glanced at the clock: no, she couldn't take up too much of Ezekiel's lesson on tangents. She gestured *hands down*—a flattened palm in the direction of the curious student—and asked them all the critical question: "Is a demon *alive*?"

"Yes," said the young man Alec, decisively.

But one of the others—a sturdy girl with glasses, Walden hadn't caught her name—said, "No?" When Walden nodded at her to go on, she said, "Well . . . MRS GREN, right? *Movement, respiration, sensitivity, growth, reproduction, excretion, nutrition—*" GCSE Biology in action; some of the others were nodding thoughtfully. "Demons do *some* of those, sometimes," said the girl, "but they don't do all of them—do they? Do demons respire? Do they breathe?"

"Only when possessing something that breathes," Walden said. "And they don't reproduce—at all, as far as anyone can tell. Rather, they seem to spontaneously generate in areas of high magical activity. So our answer is in fact both *yes* and *no*: demons are and are not alive, because they are life forms—we are fairly sure of that—but they are not *biological* life forms. In the demonic plane they generally lack physical substance altogether. Demons are *magical* life forms. They come from magic, and they are made from magic, and they eat magic."

"Nutrition," someone said.

"Just so—but not, as far as we've observed, excretion. Magic goes in, it doesn't come out. Now, obviously the demonic plane, which demons inhabit, is magical in nature. That doesn't mean that demons are totally disconnected from physical reality. Magic is real, it is measurable, it has meaningful physical effects. But their experience of that reality is by definition nothing like ours. They are *not like us*. They are much more unlike us than a dolphin or a gorilla. In fact, the most useful imaginative comparison probably *is* an alien. The key thing you all need to remember is that demons are not social. There is no such thing as demonic family or demonic friends. Because they don't reproduce, they don't conduct even the very basic social negotiations that most sexually reproducing animals need in order to produce offspring. Researchers spent centuries trying to learn the language of demons before concluding—fairly recently—that there really isn't one. Which means that any demon that manages to communicate with us in English is actually doing something terrifyingly intelligent: it's deducing human speech from first principles, without any help, without any of the underlying brain structures that let us learn language as babies. The first-order imp which seems so very stupid to us is probably, really, orders of magnitude cleverer than any of us could ever be. It's simply that all that cleverness is being used up on something we have a biological cheat code to handle." Year Eleven were truly interested now; some of them had fully turned around in their chairs to watch her speak. "Demons are not social; they don't form groups; arguably, 'demon' is barely even a useful category. Every individual demon is a species unto itself, and the only thing they all seem to have in common are the predator-prey relationship which they apply without exception to every single other living thing they encounter: demon, human, animal. Some of them share hunting strategies— you might have heard of skinner demons, a subtype of archdemon which turns its prey inside out—but that seems to be a copycat behaviour, not a meaningful relationship. All of which brings us to the personhood question. Is a demon a person? Do we need to treat it as we must, morally, treat other people? If being very stupid doesn't make someone not-a-person, does it follow that being very intelligent makes someone *more* a person?"

"If a person is trying to turn you inside out, you don't have to be nice to them," said the opinionated Anastasia.

"Inarguably correct. And—arcane safety—what will all demons do if you let them?"

"Eat your brain," chorused the class.

"Good. What I would say, though I'm by no means an expert, is that morality, the right and wrong of how human beings treat each other, is social. Therefore it is very difficult to apply the rules of morality to a totally asocial, totally amoral life form."

"If it's difficult," said Ezekiel, "does that mean we shouldn't try?"

Walden gave him a raised eyebrow: *What, even I get the Socratic treatment?* His grin was a there-and-gone-again flash in his dark face. "I think that's an individual decision," she said austerely. "But do bear in mind the essential principle of all invocation is the demonic contract, which works in exactly the same way as a human contract. 'I give you this, and in return, you give me that; this we agree, and we promise to abide by the agreement.' All the spells, arrays, and wardings you are learning are elaborate extensions of that principle. What we offer to demons, as magicians, are slices of physical reality, something which has enormous value to them. And what they offer us is *power*—which, of course, we must use responsibly. It all operates on that same principle of consent. 'Here's what I want, and here's what I'm willing to give you for it.' The demon is a willing participant."

"Though bear in mind," said Ezekiel, "that there is almost always a power imbalance, one way or the other. Which makes 'willing' a tricky word."

chapter five

THE ARCHIVES

W ALDEN MANAGED TO GET THE LESSON observation properly typed up and emailed over to Ezekiel during her lunch break. She made a note to find a meeting time with him to talk it over in person—she was interested in his opinions of those students, and which ones he thought would go on to A-level. And she needed to float taking Year Ten next year, which meant asking *him* to take Year Twelve, she couldn't do both with a management workload; and that would leave him with two A-level sets, which was a big ask. Add it to the list. There was always more to do.

After lunch, in the high room next door to her flat, surrounded by heavy glass panels set into walnut-and-brass facades, Walden tuned up the thaumic engines. She didn't deal with the physical, mechanical side—that probably *should* have been handed off to an Instantiation teacher, but in practice none of them was as good at it as Todd Cartwright, who'd been adjusting misaligned gears and replacing damaged pneumatic tubes for the better part of forty years. Walden's business was the invisible magical web of defences that the engines powered. She worked with salt and red chalk, drawing intricate miniaturised warding arrays on the wide parquet floor with the humming engines surrounding her—miniaturised because they were a mere fifteen feet across, rather than the several acres they needed to be to cover the whole school site. Every time she finished one, she flipped half a dozen brass switches. The engine's hum deepened, and the latest refreshed ward flashed gold and then vanished as it got picked up and projected outwards.

Today, Walden spent longer than usual on the ward against higher demons. *I belong here. You know I do*, something whispered— not a true demonic whisper, just a memory sharpened by worry. It was rare for Old Faithful to stir. The old monster had been feeding on the ambient wild magic of Chetwood for centuries, and that was usually enough to keep it satisfied. It was very bad luck for a magical working as small as a sixth form lesson to attract its attention. If only Mathias wasn't so strong!

Walden kept a close eye on Mathias in their lessons that week, but he seemed fine: shaken, but fine. Will was making a show of being friendlier and more considerate towards him than usual. Aneeta was quiet in lessons—well, she was a quiet person. Nikki, meanwhile, seemed to be enjoying the fourth-order summoning topic. She wrote notes frantically fast in their theory lesson on Thursday, and peppered Walden with questions. She really was a delight to teach. Walden had to be careful not to let herself get drawn into the weeds: several times she found herself saying *That's a bit too advanced for what we're doing here, Nikki, but if you want to read up on it* . . . By the end of the week she'd dug out her undergrad copy of *Nielle's Arrays*, very dog-eared—Walden had once referred to it several times a day, though nowadays she had most of it by heart— and very useful. Nikki accepted it with an air of determination. "Thank you, Dr Walden," she said.

"Nerd," said Will across the classroom. Nikki only glanced at him, uninterested, and then started flicking through the book. Will looked disappointed not to get more of a reaction.

That was Friday afternoon. On Saturday morning, with gloom in her heart, Walden climbed the spiral staircase opposite the staffroom to reach the funny little loft above the library that housed the school archives. She had promised Laura Kenning a meeting, and a meeting they would have.

The archives were lit only by a small skylight with a slatted blind. The chilly light of the October morning came through in pale stripes. Walden was late, apparently, although not according to her watch; Kenning was already there, and the archivist— Philomela Jones, an older woman in a soft grey dress, occasionally and unwillingly also the assistant school librarian—was talking to her. Or *at* her, rather. Philomela was always a bit more intense than people expected.

"Now, this is a copy of the royal grant of suspension," she was saying, "barring Marshals from the site—this is the Tudor period, academic magic occupies a bit of a legal grey area at the time, and the Marshals are sometimes little more than acquisitive thugs—oh, not *you*, Marshal Kenning, I'm speaking historically. The grant is signed by Henry VII—the original still has his seal but it's not here, it's in the Tower of London. The impetus probably came from his mother, Margaret Beaufort. She was a patron of the school, of lots of educational institutions in fact, hence Lady Margaret House which we still have, and the portrait, a small-scale eighteenth-century copy of the famous Wewyck portrait from about 1510, which is hanging in the staff dining room now—it's not a very *good* copy, of course, they sexed her up a bit by eighteenth-century standards, but that's to be expected. Now, *this*—"

Walden leaned against the doorframe, folded her arms, and

tried not to smile meanly. Kenning kept opening and closing her mouth, trying to find an opening. It was basically impossible to get Philomela on topic politely. You just had to interrupt the steady stream of history. "Good morning," Walden said at last, just as Philomela began "Of course once we beheaded King Charles," sounding as if she personally had sharpened the axe. "I'm afraid we need to focus it a bit for Chief Marshal Kenning. Shall we start with the Dorking Record?"

"Oh—yes—Headmasters!" said Philomela. "Let me just . . ."

William Dorking, Headmaster from 1660 to 1682, had kept a meticulous diary, consisting almost entirely of daily summaries of his meals and bowel movements, and a list of women's names. "Prostitutes," said Philomela, "is the usual explanation, although I think some of these poor girls were most likely just locals in domestic service. But . . . here we are, volume fourteen."

Volume fourteen of the Dorking Record contained the earliest evidence of Old Faithful on the school site. "'On this day the great demon returned & consumed two wizards entire,'" Philomela read aloud with relish. Walden couldn't actually manage Dorking's handwriting, but she'd seen a transcript before and that sounded about right. "'Wizard' rather than 'magician,' because we're before the nineteenth-century academic movement. Interesting that it's 'returned,' isn't it?"

"Does that mean it's been here even longer than that?" asked Kenning.

"Almost certainly!" said Philomela. "Now, let me see what else I can find for you."

Filing cabinets, straining cardboard boxes, old wooden travellers' chests. Walden and Kenning stood close together in the one clear patch of floor in the middle of the archive as Philomela darted around them. The slatted blind on the skylight gave

Kenning's short fair hair a zebra stripe of light and shadow. She looked uncomfortable. "Letters from schoolboys," said Philomela, "bills for repairs; here's the deed of gift from the Worshipful Company of Brewers, which of course is how the school could afford to build the thaumic engines—and Brewers Hall to put them in, naturally. There's still a Brewers scholarship every year. Now once you get to the twentieth century things get a little interesting—*this* is a letter to *The Times* from 1913 that mentions a 'greater demonic power' in the context of Chetwood School—you can see the contemporary politics behind it, because of course we're building up to the First World War and everyone has started thinking about demons as weapons . . ."

"What about incursions?" demanded Kenning.

"If I may," said Walden, and pointed. Philomela gave her hands an assessing glance—they were clean, of course—and then handed her the stiff folded card. Walden showed it to Kenning. "The order of service for a funeral," she said. "Rodney Merringham. The Headmaster who died in 1926."

"We actually don't know very much about him!" said Philomela. "He was an alumnus, of course—there have only been a handful of non-alumnus Headmasters, our current Mr Bern among them. And like practically all Englishmen of his generation, he was a survivor of the trenches. Most of his contemporaries from school were already dead—you've seen the memorial board in the chapel, haven't you?" She took the funeral order of service gently from Walden's hands. "He was quite young, only forty-something. And people were rethinking it all in the twenties—arcane safety, as they say now—after everything that had happened during the war. I'm sure it must have influenced his decision to try to destroy Old Faithful. Of course he failed. Technically this was for a memorial service, not a funeral. There was no body found, you see. That's a common thread in Old Faithful's incursions. Here's the next one."

In 1926 there was a major incursion. Three minor ones followed: 1929, 1935, 1938, and then Old Faithful slowed down after a retooling and expansion of the thaumic engines. In 1961, another major incursion, with two deaths, following an attempt to move Chetwood's school site across the county. It had turned out that abandoning a centuries-old set of protections was not a good idea. Old Faithful had seized the opportunity, the school had moved back to its original site after the disaster, and the Headmaster had resigned in disgrace. In 1962, a minor incursion, aftershocks. In 1978, another minor. Then a long period of quiet. "By this point," said Philomela, "the school's defences have the problem more or less under control. Provided everyone is sensible, of course. Sometimes, people aren't."

And that brought them to 2003. The photographs were all in colour now, the records printed, not typed. Philomela said, "Here he is," and took out a school photo, the traditional rows of children in smart jackets, names listed underneath. She pointed to the top corner. "Charles Green. This is a house photograph—he was in St Jude's. Of course, he was also a School House boy. One of Chetwood's traditional functions, as a school, is the education of young sorcerers."

Walden looked at the photograph and said nothing.

Kenning peered at it. "Bad hair," she said.

"Well, he was a teenager, you know," said Philomela, but she laughed a little. "I'm afraid this one is a very typical story of schoolboy hubris. Green attempted to summon Old Faithful on purpose—heaven knows why. I believe he even talked some classmates into helping him. His was the only death, which was honestly very lucky, considering. Awful for him, of course."

"Kids can be stupid," said Kenning.

"They can, can't they?"

Walden said nothing, and said nothing. She possibly *should* have said something. But it wasn't Kenning's business, or Philomela's, not really. The purpose of this meeting was to give Chetwood's Chief Marshal a clearer picture of the scale of what was lurking in the school's magical shadow. It wasn't to wake up old ghosts.

"Well, that's completely fucking terrifying," said Kenning as they walked through the colonnade and then cut across the quad for the staffroom door. It was ten o'clock and there was simply no way to avoid having a polite cup of tea with her, short of inventing a meeting or an urgent phone call. "There shouldn't be a school here. You realise that, don't you? There's a demon the size of an elephant here, so there shouldn't be a school."

"Biomass is a tricky measure," said Walden, "but I think a more accurate comparison would be *whale*, not *elephant*. One of the larger species of whale."

Kenning gave her an exasperated look. "Not my point, Dr Walden."

"You know," said Walden, "most of my colleagues do call me Saffy. So where, exactly, were you thinking of sending the students?"

"What?"

"Chetwood School is closed on the recommendation of the Marshals," Walden said. "We have just over six hundred pupils and all of them know *some* magic. Where are they going to go?"

"A normal school," said Kenning. "With normal people in it. It'd be good for most of them."

Walden inclined her head. "Good luck persuading their parents."

"Fine. A *different* boarding school. One without, again, the giant demon."

"And where do you think the giant demon will go," said Walden, "when it's not getting anything to eat?"

Kenning stopped walking. They had just reached the oak tree on the far side of the quad. The grounds team came most days and swept up the leaves and acorns that it dropped at this time of year, but they didn't work on Saturdays. The gnarled ground and the wooden bench underneath the tree were heaped with curling dry leaves, and a low breeze stirred them, making faint rustling sounds. Kenning said, "So are you actually saying that it's fine to keep feeding an occasional kid to the big demon, if that keeps it happy enough to leave the rest of them alone?"

Walden just looked at her. She looked until Kenning glanced away, embarrassed. "No," she said at last. "I don't appreciate that accusation, Marshal Kenning, and I am very sure you don't actually believe it."

Kenning tucked her hands in her pockets. "It's just crazy," she said. "That thing is here and no one has done anything about it. It's crazy."

"I think the problem with this conversation is that you have cause and effect reversed," Walden said. They kept walking; the tense moment was over. And Walden *did* need to work with this woman, and she *was* good, and it was not unreasonable to be upset about the presence of a giant demon on the school site. Walden also found it upsetting. "You're acting as if the demon was here first and some complete idiot decided to build a school on top of it. But it's the other way round. The school was here first; the demon is here because of the school. If the school was somewhere else, or if the *students* were somewhere else, that's where the demon would go too. That's exactly what happened when they tried to move the school site in the sixties. Powerful demons *become* powerful by going where the power is and digging in. Old Faithful became what it is by moving into Chetwood's shadow in the demonic plane and staying there."

"I don't have to like it."

"I don't think anyone *likes* Old Faithful, no. But the work we do keeps our students safe from it."

"No big incursions in twenty years," said Kenning. "And thirty years before that."

"A couple of blips in a five-decade record of excellent arcane security," said Walden, and then hated herself for it. "'Blips' is not the word. Even a minor incident is a terrible disaster when a higher demon is involved. But Chetwood exists to protect its students as well as to educate them. That's true of any school, but it's doubly true here. I think we do it well, on the whole. Tea?" The relaxation end of the staffroom—well away from the possessed photocopier—was all sagging, comfortable armchairs and institutional mud-brown carpet. There was a fresh pot of tea already brewed in the little attached kitchen.

"The work we do," muttered Kenning, and then nodded *yes* to tea. "Listen, Dr Walden—" a pause, and then Kenning corrected herself, abruptly, "Saffy. I think we need a reset."

"A reset?" Walden passed Kenning a mug of tea. Kenning started shovelling sugar cubes into it.

"I mean—" Did the woman always stop and start this much when she was talking? "Look. You're not my boss. I know you don't like that, but it's true. Marshal work, my team's work, it's not the same as the kind of magic you do. You don't *understand* the work we do." Walden raised her eyebrows—she could have said *Actually I wrote a rather well-received paper on*—but Kenning was barrelling on. "You've been a magician probably all your life, and you've never been a demon hunter. You've never seen the amount of damage these fuckers can do to a normal person's life. But I get that you're good at this and you care. Well, I'm good and I care too. We ought to be working together. We can disagree like grown-ups, probably."

"Would you say that we haven't been grown-up until now?" asked Walden.

Kenning gave her a Look. "'It's only a very small demon,'" she said.

Walden remembered saying it, but she didn't remember sounding quite so condescending. "'Good evening, Ms Walden'?" she answered.

Kenning snorted. "Sorry. Your face—well. Yes, all right, childish. You agree we've been childish?"

"It's the school environment," Walden said. "It brings out everyone's inner teenager."

Kenning laughed faintly, and drank some tea. Walden noticed, again, that she was gorgeous. This was out of character for her. She needed more of a non-school social life, probably, which was something she would add to her to-do list as soon as she had the time. "A reset, then," she said. "We can share expertise more productively. I couldn't agree more."

Share expertise productively, Kenning mouthed, and then took another mouthful of over-sugared tea in apparent despair.

Walden decided to ignore this as leftover childishness. "Shall we start by setting up a standing meeting? I have a slot on Sunday afternoons."

"You work on Sundays?"

"Well—" Technically, officially, Walden did not. But what else was she going to do with her time? "Friday morning, then."

"No mornings this term. I'm leading the night shift," said Kenning. "Have you got an evening?"

"Thursday," said Walden, though it was going to eat into her lesson prep time. "We can meet on Thursday evenings. I'll look forward to it."

It was Saturday, so she had a single with the Upper Sixth before lunch. Keeping hundreds of children busy at the weekend was one of the great challenges of boarding school life. Saturday morning, Saturday afternoon sports teams and academic societies, Sunday morning chapel—optional, but if you weren't attending you were expected to be either in the library or on the sports fields—and Sunday afternoon for clubs and excursions, usually to the village but occasionally a larger and more exhausting trip to a zoo or a theatre or a theme park. All of those needed to be supervised, which meant staff didn't get a full weekend off either. Usually you got either Saturday or Sunday. If you put in for cover early enough and could arrange swaps with enough colleagues, occasionally you managed both.

It wore on people. It even wore on Walden. She always tried to plan her easiest teaching for the week in the Saturday morning single slot.

This week, for example, she had them all doing practice questions for the A-level exam, timed and in silence. This had the double benefit of being extremely good for them—of the four, only Aneeta could be relied on to practise exam technique on her own initiative—while being fairly restful for Walden. She put the Thursday evening meeting with Kenning in her calendar. She replied to some emails. She looked up and said, "Yes, Nikki?"

"It's about the book you gave me," Nikki said.

Walden raised her eyebrows. "Does that mean you've finished the work I asked you to do?"

"Well, I just—"

"Timed and in silence, Nikki," Walden said. "Thank you."

She glanced around at the other three. All of them had their heads down over their work. Mathias's worksheet had developed some doodled star-shapes in the corner, which meant he'd got stuck somewhere and hadn't wanted to ask for help. Walden went over and began to speak quietly to him. She was aware, with a teacher's sixth sense, that Nikki had gone back to work, with a wronged and mutinous air. Well, she might be one of Chetwood's best, but she was still a teenager, with a teenager's tendency towards overreaction. She would get over it.

chapter six

ANEETA

W ALDEN SPENT SATURDAY EVENING SLOG-
ging through her marking and carefully scheduling
several emails to send at 8 A.M. on Monday. Ten
o'clock found her still dressed—not in ratty pyjamas tonight, thank
you Marshal Kenning—and still at her desk, poking at the draft
of Monday's school assembly. Assemblies were a bit of a dark art;
no tougher crowd than six hundred adolescents who had heard
three of these a week for years—Monday, Wednesday, Friday—
and would rather be asleep. Walden's assembly-writing was further
hindered by her distaste for the tried-and-true genre of 'personal
anecdote with an awkwardly forced moral.' Halfway through writing she remembered with a groan that she'd also agreed to take
next week's non-denom assembly. Non-denom was the optional
alternative assembly for the students who didn't want to attend
Wednesday morning chapel, which was most of them. More than
a third of Chetwood's pupils were Jewish, Muslim, Hindu, or Jain.
Most of the rest were carol-service-only, which Walden couldn't
fault, since it had also been her approach to chapel when she was

a student here. She attended most Sundays now, because the music was nice and Ezekiel was an excellent speaker, but she would not have described herself as religious.

The knock on the door was a surprise, but also a bit of a relief. Walden felt that she'd reached a détente with Laura Kenning today. Perhaps this encounter would be the next stage of their reset. *And* she wasn't wearing pyjamas this time. "Come in!" she called.

It wasn't Kenning.

Aneeta was in slippers, tracksuit bottoms, and a puffy pink outdoor coat. She must have walked across the road from Scrubs like that. Walden was shocked. She could not think of another time when a student had dared to disturb her after hours in her suite, which was tucked out of the way in Brewers and right next door to the extremely off-limits thaumic engines. She was not a house-mistress or a form tutor—she was senior enough not to be really part of the pastoral structure at all—and while she always tried, on principle, to be kind and pay attention, she knew very well that she was not one of the *approachable* teachers. Walden *had* people skills, because you needed them to do the job well, but they were learned and practised. Warmth did not come naturally to her. Children with problems usually took those problems to someone else. Even after hours, there were always staff on duty in the boarding house: a night porter, Marshals on patrol, and several younger teachers who lived in the flats on the ground floor and could be woken up in emergencies.

Aneeta's expression was a dreadful mixture of misery and embarrassment. She hovered in the doorway, cringing as if she expected to be shouted at. "Sorry" was the first thing she said.

"Aneeta?" said Walden. She bypassed *This is not appropriate*; it wasn't, but Aneeta clearly knew that, and had come looking for her anyway. "What's wrong?"

"I promised not to tell."

Walden stood up, really concerned, when she heard Aneeta's voice wobble. Aneeta was, to her certain knowledge, both clever and sensible. She would not be here out of an ordinary fit of teenage hysterics. They told you in teacher training to listen to your instincts, and Walden's were yelling at her right now. Something was badly wrong. "Come here, have a seat—have a tissue—what's the matter?"

"It's Nikki," said Aneeta, and burst into tears, right there in the doorway.

"Aneeta!"

Walden went and took her by the shoulders of her puffy pink jacket, and steered her gently into a chair. Aneeta was crying too hard to speak. She took off her steamed-up glasses. *Tissue*, thought Walden, and gave her one. *Glass of water*—there was a jug on the desk, spare glasses on the side. A sensible, even-keeled seventeen-year-old in floods of tears, breaking a promise to a friend and coming to find a senior authority figure about it—there were a number of possibilities for what this could be, none of them good, some very bad indeed. Walden summoned up the calm and patience and authority of her teaching persona. Warmth was hard for her, but she could do reliable, she could do nonjudgemental, she could do trustworthy and confident and, most importantly of all, *safe*.

Make no assumptions, ask no leading questions. It took Aneeta a moment to be calm enough to talk. Walden let her wipe her eyes and drink from the glass of water and gather her dignity. No one that age wanted to cry hysterically in front of a teacher. "Can you tell me about it?" she asked, when Aneeta looked ready to talk.

"The demon," said Aneeta. "The one from last week, the big one, the one that talked. Nikki, she—she—" A gulp. "—she said she knew it."

It took every inch of Walden's professionalism not to turn white as she immediately saw the shape of the problem. Aneeta was still talking. "—and it talked to me too, it said . . . but I thought, 'That's not true, that's just something I'm scared about, so it's up to something,' and then I thought, 'Aren't demons too stupid to lie,' so I looked it up and it would have to be a big—like a really big—but Nikki—"

"Did Nikki tell you what the demon said to her?" said Walden, very, very calmly.

"It's the one that . . . the one . . ." Aneeta swallowed. "She said, it's the one that killed her mum and dad. That's what it told her. She told me today."

"I see," said Walden. She understood now why Aneeta had bypassed housemasters and tutors and come straight to the school's Director of Magic. Doubts, desires, insecurities: Who had more of those than a teenager? Their unwelcome visitor hadn't been able to get a grip on Walden's own mind during that summoning gone wrong, but she had not stamped hard enough on Aneeta's question about its whispers. In a class with Mathias in it, it was easy to forget that all of them were vulnerable. She needed to set up a one-to-one meeting with Nikki in the morning—probably she needed to telephone School House tonight, in fact; Ebele would still be up—best to check in on Mathias too—even Will—

"And she said I mustn't tell," said Aneeta, "and she wouldn't talk to me anymore, but," and she pulled from the pocket of her puffy pink coat a dog-eared, ancient paperback, now decorated with dozens of pink Post-it notes.

Nielle's Arrays. Walden's undergrad copy. She reached out and Aneeta passed it to her with rapid gratitude, as if she was handing off a large spider. Walden opened at the first pink Post-it. Chapter eleven, triple arrays, meant for summoning archdemons. Nikki's familiar looping handwriting on the Post-it said, *CHECK how big is big enough???*

"She left it on the table at lunch," Aneeta said. "I don't think she knows I've got it. But I looked at her notes and . . . she *wouldn't,* but what if . . ."

What if. Nikki had been asking aggressive, high-level theory questions all week. She had tried repeatedly to go off topic in lessons and pick Walden's brain on advanced summoning. She had been acting *differently,* in a way that Walden had not perceived as worrying because it was consistent with what she already expected from her best student. She hadn't said *Why are you asking, Nikki?* She'd given her a book of advanced summoning arrays.

Walden closed *Nielle's Arrays* carefully. She couldn't let Aneeta see how frightened she was.

"I've been thinking about it all day," Aneeta said. "Maybe I'm just being silly, but—I went to bed and I was lying in bed thinking and then I read the book some more and I looked at her notes and—I know Nikki's loads better than me, but I'm not *bad* at invocation. I think I know what she's— And then I texted her. And she didn't text back."

Walden knew she hadn't fully controlled her expression this time. She said, "Thank you, Aneeta." *You should have come to find me hours ago,* but there was no use telling her that now, when she was already here and already in tears. Walden picked up the office phone and dialled the extension for School House.

No answer.

She tried again. She felt herself willing Ebele or Ezekiel to pick up. This time the phone didn't ring.

Walden put the handset down. Aneeta was staring at her, still crumpled and wet-eyed though she'd cleaned her glasses and put them back on. Walden forced herself to step back into her teacher persona. Dr Walden was calm. Dr Walden was certain. Dr Walden always knew what to do.

Her first responsibility was the child in front of her. She could not send Aneeta back across the road to Scrubs now. Safest to assume the worst-case scenario. Nikki was no match for Old Faithful. If a wild incursion started on the school grounds, a student wandering around by themselves would be a juicy snack for anything that came through. She could not leave Aneeta alone in her office, with its filing cabinets of confidential student information. The rest of the Victorian suite was Walden's private refuge. Living in a boarding school could send you mad if you did not carve out a space to be a real adult human being. No student—and very few colleagues—had ever been permitted to cross the holy threshold between Walden's office and her sitting room.

"I'm going to nip over to School House and check everything is all right," she said. "I'd like you to stay here, please, Aneeta. Not in the office—through here."

It could not have taken more than a few moments to ensconce Aneeta on Walden's elderly sofa and grant her permission to watch TV and to help herself to anything she liked in the kitchen. Walden's personal laptop was on the side, already signed into her work email; she sent a quick email to the Scrubs night-duty address, letting them know where their missing sixth former was—perhaps another thirty seconds of work. It all felt like hours too long.

Walden left Aneeta there sitting on the sofa and clinging to her phone. She kept thinking about the dial tone when she'd tried to call School House. Back in her office, something occurred to her. She turned to the possessed wall clock. "Hey, you."

The clock's resident demon—a second-order imp—manifested its eldritch cuckoo obediently. Walden breathed a sigh of relief. If something big had crossed over from the demonic plane to the mundane world, its presence would create a thaumic vacuum, hoovering up the wild magic that sustained lesser possessions like this one.

And then her relief shattered as the imp evaporated.

"Fuck," said Dr Walden, and started running.

Her senses were thrown open as she pelted down the stairs and weaved through the corridors—out of Brewers Hall and in through the back of New House, round the shortcut by Modern Foreign Languages and past the locked doors of the arcane labs, out the other side to the colonnade of the main school building. She felt the imp in the staffroom photocopier go, and the haunted radiator in a third-floor Maths classroom, and the peculiar being that made its home in the chapel organ and could sometimes be heard singing windily to itself on moonless nights. One by one they were swallowed up, the canaries in Walden's personal coal mine. The incursion wards that were all over the school—painted over doors and printed out on posters and carved into the fourteenth-century masonry of the Old Refectory—groaned and began to glow under the strain. A fire alarm started ringing. Walden met a Marshal—not Kenning, one of her squad—standing around uselessly in the colonnade. "Bar the road!" she snarled at him, and kept running.

The tarmac expanse of the main road was a natural barrier, but not much of one. If the incursion jumped across it, there were four hundred children asleep in Scrubs.

Walden stumbled to a halt outside School House. She had already had no doubt. But the sight of the red-brick building swathed in shifting curtains of purplish light confirmed it. An incursion ward was incorporated into the design of the stained glass above the front door. It glowed white, but it was holding.

Gathered in a huddle on the grass outside: Ebele Nwosu, in a dressing gown and bonnet, and four children. Walden slowed as she reached them, counting. There were seven children currently fostered in School House: she could see four. A Year Eight, two Year Nines, a Year Eleven. Ebele grabbed Walden's arm. "He went back in," she said.

"Get further back," said Walden.

"Saffy—"

The door of School House burst off its hinges. The incursion was worse inside, much worse, but the ward over the door hung on; raw magic boiled against the opening and did not get through. Out of the shadows came Ezekiel, right fist closed as he maintained a precisely spherical magician's shield of pale, silvery light. Over his left shoulder he had the fifth of School House's seven young sorcerers: a six-year-old boy.

Ebele flew to them. Ezekiel embraced her and handed her the little boy in the same movement. Then he turned to Walden.

"I couldn't get near the tower," he said. "Nicola and Mathias both have bedrooms up there."

Walden looked up at the building. Other people were gathering. The fire alarm had woken everyone up. The tower was a black blotch against the night sky, shrouded in a dull glow of deadly violet. Walden exchanged a look with Ezekiel and saw in his eyes the same grim calculation she was making.

Two fully trained magicians on the spot. One of them a married man, father of three and foster father of seven. The other was Walden, who was single and unattached and hadn't spoken to most of her family since last Christmas.

She had a momentary vision of her own memorial plaque in the chapel, a shiny brass record underneath the unfortunate Headmaster from 1926. DOCTOR S. WALDEN, 1986–2025, ALUMNA & DIRECTOR OF MAGIC, REQUIESCAT IN PACE.

She was the most senior person present. This was her school, and Nikki and Mathias were her students.

"Get someone to call the Headmaster if they haven't already," she said. "And don't let it cross the road."

Ezekiel nodded gravely.

"Are you planning to go *in* there?"

When had Kenning shown up? Walden had no idea. "That's correct, Marshal," she said.

"Are you *out of your mind*?"

"We can discuss it later," said Walden, an automatic sentence out of her teacher phrasebook, and then she had to stifle a laugh. "If you'll excuse me."

She was not expecting Kenning to grab her by the shoulder. The Marshal had a strong grip. "Absolutely not," she said. "Demonic incursions are a Marshal matter, Dr Walden. The Marshals will deal with it."

Walden shook her off. "Then where are they?"

Kenning said nothing.

"Chetwood School employs six Marshals full time in case of magical emergency," Walden said. "Two of them are supposed to be on patrol at all times. Where *are* they, Chief Marshal Kenning? Where's your squad? The last one I saw was dithering until I gave him an excuse to run in the opposite direction." Kenning still didn't answer. Walden lost patience entirely. "Let's face it, Laura. If a person is any good at demon hunting, then they don't apply for the job where the most difficult thing they have to do on a daily basis is *intimidate children*. You say this is a Marshal matter? The Marshals aren't here. I am."

"We should still wait for support," Kenning said. "You can't send someone into a wild demonic incursion solo. It's madness. It's suicide."

"Wait how long? If it takes much longer for help to get here, there'll be nothing to do but force an incursion collapse from the outside. Now kindly stop wasting my time."

Kenning opened her mouth to say something else, but she was interrupted. Out of the worried little crowd clustered on the lawn emerged someone who should definitely not have been there. He'd thrown on a hoodie with the school crest on it, and he was holding his phone.

Will.

Walden had a sudden mental flash of Aneeta, still tearful and frightened, alone in an unfamiliar place with no way to know what was going on, clinging to her phone. Texting a friend for support. *I keep making mistakes.*

"You're going to collapse the incursion?" Will demanded. His expression was wild. "If you collapse it with Nikki and Matty in there they'll *die*."

"Will"—*what the hell are you doing here*—"get back," Walden said.

Will ignored her. "What the fuck are you doing!" he yelled at Kenning. "What's the *point* of you people if you don't even do your job and fight demons?"

This was more or less what Walden had just been saying, but that didn't mean she was happy to hear a student shouting it at the school's Chief Marshal. "William!" she snapped.

Will rounded on her. "You can't just leave Nikki to die!" he said, and then his expression settled into determined lines. Walden saw what he was going to do the instant before he did it. She grabbed hold of him.

A spell, she thought afterwards. *I should have used a spell.* But when you saw them every day, when you were treated to a front-row seat for all their tantrums and absurdities and interpersonal melodrama, you *knew* they were children. And so it was possible to forget that a person who was seventeen was also very nearly an adult. It was possible to forget that they could, and would, make decisions without you. It was possible to forget that they were *bigger than you.*

The contest of strength—a short thirty-eight-year-old woman who hadn't darkened the door of a gym in months, versus a tall seventeen-year-old boy who went rowing four mornings a week—went predictably. Will shoved Walden away. She fell on her backside into the grass. He dashed up the steps and through the violet magical maw that was the front door of School House.

"Will!" Walden shouted uselessly after him. Kenning helped her to her feet.

"Right," said Walden. "Now there's three of them in there. I hope you're done arguing. Give me two hours. If I don't come out, collapse the incursion." She unpinned the owl brooch she was wearing from her blazer and slipped it into her skirt pocket. The blazer would restrict her arms too much if she had to cast a spell in a hurry, so she left it in a pile on the grass. She didn't look back.

Kenning caught up with her on the steps. "What," said Walden, exasperated.

"A demonic incursion is still a Marshal matter," said Kenning. Her shortsword gleamed in her hand. Violet light danced, reflected, from the line of silver runes that ran down the blade. "You can't go in solo. I'm coming with you."

chapter seven

THREE-STEP PLAN

EVERY TEACHER WALDEN KNEW HAD OCCASION- ally resorted to the three-step lesson plan, which was to say, the lesson you planned in the three steps it took you to walk into the classroom. It was just a fact of the job: there was never enough time to do everything right. She'd comforted her share of overwhelmed perfectionist trainees, up all night working on six full lesson plans for the next day. She'd *been* that person, well into her NQT year. But it was unsustainable. You had to forgive yourself for imperfection. You had to teach the lessons, let them go, do better next time if you could. Ultimately, *some* lessons got the full minute-by-minute detailed plan that you learned in teacher training. Some, with experience, you pulled out of your pocket based on a half-remembered activity you'd cooked up years ago. Some you begged colleagues to lend you their PowerPoints for. And some you just had to make up on the spot.

Walden had never walked into a critical incursion before. She didn't have a plan. No one could. No risk assessment would help her now.

Three steps took her through the ruined front door of School House.

She felt raw demonic magic descend around her, greasy and claustrophobic. The air smelled of sulphur and gunpowder smoke. When she glanced back, the doorframe was still there, but the world beyond was gone. There was nothing but a louring darkness. Getting out of here again was not going to be straightforward.

"Stay behind me," said Kenning. "You do realise we're basically *in* the demonic plane here?"

Walden *obviously* knew that. She caught herself before she snapped about it. Kenning wasn't tense because of her; this wasn't the moment to restart what they'd both agreed were really just childish squabbles.

Kenning was ignoring her anyway. Her focus was on setting up the cast for a magical shield: not a pale sphere like Reverend Ezekiel's, but a shifting and layered shimmer in the air which hooked into one of the runes on Kenning's left bracer for support, so it would self-sustain for a few moments if she was distracted. It was very neat work, especially since Kenning took an extra moment or two to get it precisely balanced, with an attention to detail that Walden didn't usually expect from a non-academic magical practitioner. She had written about Marshal magic during her MThau, but the Marshals she'd interviewed had been suspicious and unwilling to give away their secrets. Academic invocation specialists like Walden were, traditionally, their enemies. She'd never seen the spell Kenning was using before.

"What beautiful shielding," she said.

Kenning glanced at her. She seemed to think she was being patronised. "I'm not a trained magician. We use what works for us."

"I was being sincere," said Walden. "I do know academic magic isn't the only way to do things." During their brief shared life as postdocs at Stanford, Roz Chan had taught an undergraduate course on non-elite and non-Western magical traditions, shared with a junior professor from the Anthropology Department. It was interesting stuff, and the lecture hall had always been packed to the gills even though Roz had been objectively—Walden could think it without unkindness now—a pretty bad teacher.

The Marshal shield really was lovely. She said, "How do the layers"—and seeing Kenning's closed expression—"never mind."

They were advancing as she spoke, along School House's front hall. Walden probably shouldn't have been talking, but few things were as ghostly and unnerving as dead silence in a school building. Through the swirls of shadow and the dull purple gleam of loose magic, she glimpsed coat hooks, a jumble of black school shoes in various sizes, family photographs of Ebele and Ezekiel with their children and foster children in assorted combinations, and a child's bicycle. No demons here. No sign of Will.

He hadn't got far. They found him in the kitchen.

Also in the kitchen was a seventh-order archdemon. In this place, as the demonic plane and mundane world overlapped and blurred together, it had assumed a physical form without difficulty: a ghastly collection of sucking toothless mouths and fleshy tentacles. Will was unconscious, his head under the kitchen table. Walden rather thought he'd run straight in without any defences up and hit the wall of malevolence the archdemon was throwing off. It was giving her a headache even through Kenning's shield.

"Leave the hostile to me," Kenning said.

Walden was not an expert on magical combat per se, so she was perfectly happy to do so. She cast her own shield, since Kenning presumably needed all her focus for the fight—she used the traditional one she knew, which manifested as an upturned bowl of white light—and went to her knees next to Will. Blood in his curly chestnut hair meant a head wound. Not the demon's work—it would have taken his head off completely. He'd hit the table on his way down, and the kitchen floor was stone flags.

He was still breathing. He was still alive. The main reason he was still alive was that the archdemon was big enough—just—to be contemplating a possession, and not quite big enough to have forced it already. Anything smaller would have started eating Will by now. Anything bigger would already be settling down to a comfortable new home inside him.

"You have a charmed life, William Daubery," Walden told the unconscious boy softly. "You have no idea how lucky you just were."

Magical healing beyond the most basic first aid required a medical degree before they even let you try. Walden certainly did not want to go poking around in a potential concussion. She looked up, intending to offer Kenning support.

And then she took a moment to watch in frank admiration.

Kenning was *very* good.

It wasn't that she was strong, although she was. Indeed, she was throwing around quite a lot more raw power than Walden would have been in her position. Her spellwork did not have the stripped-back precision of an academically trained magician; it shimmered at the edges, and drew lines of thaumic aftershock through the raw magical ambience of the demonic plane. In any case, simple magical power did not impress Walden. Any demon had it, and any talented schoolchild. She herself had been strong to start with—not a true sorcerer, but strong—and she had spent decades since then becoming expert. Very few people these days could call on more magical power than her.

It was the way Kenning *used* what she had.

She cast wordlessly, or in brief staccato syllables, relying above all on gesture: hands, feet, the motion of her body. It was the motion that arrested Walden's attention, the smooth flow from one stance to another; the way the magical sword, blazing with white light, functioned as an extension of the Marshal's right arm; how she wrapped the ambient power of the demonic plane around herself and turned it into traps and tripwires for the archdemon's groping tentacles. Kenning's face was set in calm, concentrating lines as she battled the monstrosity. This was hard work for her, but in the way that a marathon was hard work for a serious runner. Walden could tell she wasn't needed at all.

She did gasp when the archdemon disarmed Kenning. The sword clattered on the stone flags of the kitchen floor, its light blinking out. But Kenning didn't panic, didn't flinch; the white blaze reappeared in bunches gathered around her fists and feet. Walden watched her force the archdemon back with blow upon blow: fast kicks, jabs with her fists, even her elbow. It was losing its grip on reified physicality, the tentacles evaporating one by one, leaving a quivering pink core. Kenning lunged forward and tackled it flat, letting out a shout—*ha!*—that was mostly a sharp explosion of breath.

The archdemon writhed and struggled under her, but Kenning was now striking repeatedly at that quivering core, magic shining around her fist. Before long it collapsed into fine pink mist, which evaporated.

Kenning picked up her sword, got to her feet, and caught her breath. Walden caught hers too. *Good grief,* she heard herself think.

"You, er . . . know karate?" she said.

"MMA," said Kenning. She wiped sweat off her forehead. "How is he?"

"He'll live," said Walden. "If we get him out of here fast enough."

"Couldn't have been one of your small students, could it?"

Kenning said, eyeing Will's prone form. "I can get him into a fireman's lift if we drag him out from under the table."

"No need," said Walden, and levitated him.

It was a bit showy—like all magic that involved really serious disagreements with physics—but she had the very good excuse that a child's life was at stake. In any case, she doubted Kenning was going to be much impressed by a mere temporary abeyance of gravity after a demon-killing performance like that. Walden was already regretting what she'd said, about talented Marshals not ending up working for Chetwood; though a part of her was also thinking, *Why on Earth is someone like you working for Chetwood?*

Kenning recast her multilayered shield and they took Will back down the corridor to the front door. Walden frowned at the darkness beyond it. "Well, that won't do," she said. "If you could just stand back for a moment?"

Kenning did.

Walden would normally have summoned a mid-level demon for assistance with punching a controlled planar portal. What was the point of being an invocation specialist otherwise? But summoning anything in the middle of a critical incursion was decidedly unsafe. She opened the portal herself, with a sharp gesture and a grunt of effort, and felt the minor earthquake under her feet as the view past the doorway shimmered and resolved into the late-night lawn at the front of School House. She was pleased to glimpse that someone—most likely Ezekiel—had had the sense to set up a perimeter. "If you take him through," she said. "Thank you very much."

"You first," said Kenning. "In case any nasties try to follow us out. I'll cover you."

"I'm not coming," Walden said. "There are two more of them still in here, Marshal. I'm going for the tower."

Kenning looked grave. In the tones of a medical professional delivering an unhappy diagnosis, she said, "Dr Walden, it's already been too long. You must know there's no chance."

Walden inclined her head. "As I said before. Give me two hours. Then collapse the incursion."

"You're throwing your life away," said Kenning. "I know we've had our disagreements, but this isn't the time for an argument. Listen to me. Please."

She meant it. Walden was touched. It didn't change anything about what she had to do. It was her fault Nikki and Mathias were trapped in here; her fault, because she hadn't seen it coming; her fault, because Old Faithful had first got its claws into Nikki during her lesson; her fault, for another reason too.

I still belong. You know me. You know I do.

"Thank you for your help, Laura," she said. "I must apologise for what I said earlier. You are very good at your job. And it's been a privilege."

And then, since Kenning didn't seem inclined to move, she cast a modified wind spell to give her a little shove out of the door, and sent Will floating through alongside her. She had just enough time to let the levitation down gently before the strain of holding the portal open grew to be too much. Walden felt the sting of magical backlash when it snapped shut, as if something had just tried to close needle-sharp teeth on her fingertips.

Then she was alone in School House, alone in a critical demonic incursion. She could no longer make out the lines of the front hall—the coat hooks, the family pictures, the bicycle—through the fog of wild magic. The doorframe behind her stood alone in an expanse of shadow that was punctuated only by a boreal shimmer of shifting purple light.

No sign of Old Faithful yet. That was not a hopeful thought.

Walden knew it was here; and if it was not paying attention to her, then it was paying attention to something else.

Nikki and Mathias were in the tower. They were still alive. Walden chose to believe this because the alternative was unbearable.

She turned away from the door and headed in.

chapter eight

INCURSION

INVOCATION WAS WALDEN'S MAGICAL SPECIALTY and her life's great passion. She was an expert in creating tiny and tightly contained demonic incursions, overlaps between the mundane and demonic planes, in order to conduct her carefully managed trade: pieces of mundane existence, which could be as small as the vibrations in the air she breathed, in exchange for a demon's effortless facility with magic, the stuff that was as natural and intrinsic to their existence as water to fish. Incursions were by nature unstable and temporary. A single incursion ought to be just big enough to allow one demon of predictable size to travel from one plane to the other for a very short period of time, without gaining any foothold in material existence beyond a temporary reification. But 'ought' was doing a lot of work in that sentence; 'ought' was about expert practice and effective risk management. The truth was that there were ways to make bigger incursions, and to have them last longer. These were mostly very expensive in raw materials, beyond the reach of any individual magician who was not personally a billionaire—and also, of course, insanely dangerous and highly regulated. But Walden had seen one such mega-incursion, created under controlled conditions in a lab in the Arizona desert, which had been going for nearly forty years.

This incursion—a *critical* incursion, with a demon in control—was shaping up to be bigger than the one in Arizona. But then, Old Faithful was bigger than anything anyone had ever dared summon for mere research purposes. The archdemon that had been going for Will must have been a secondary scavenger. Walden saw a few others about the same size as she made her way through School House, as well as plenty of smaller imps feeding on the household electronics and delighting in the unexpected treat. There was nothing larger. Anything big enough to present a challenge to Old Faithful was also smart enough not to pick a fight with it.

In a peculiar backwards way, Old Faithful was an asset to Chetwood. They had far fewer serious demon problems than a school full of underage magicians should, because the one higher demon they did have was so huge and so terrifying that it had scared off all the competition. And, in turn, Old Faithful was so big that the everyday half-trained magic of schoolchildren was barely enough to tempt it. It lay quiescent, uninterested, lazy: a great white shark swimming among the little fish, unwilling to waste effort on anything less than a plump and juicy seal.

Unfortunately, a pair of talented sixth formers fit the demonic definition of 'juicy seal' almost perfectly.

Walden, under the barrier of her glowing white shield, tried to move quickly. The physical geography of School House, which she knew well, was of limited help. She made it back to the kitchen, but could not find the staircase which she knew ought to be there. She only had two hours. "Think, Saffy," she muttered aloud when she felt herself starting to panic.

Silence. And in that silence, another sound: a series of treble yelps and whimpers, and a regular *swish* and *crack*.

It took a moment for Walden to understand that she was hearing the sound of a child being beaten with a cane. Horrific. But she went towards the noise, because it was what she had. She found herself walking through a wall which, come to think of it, must have been put up when the kitchen was last remodelled, and into a room that no longer existed: a wood-panelled teacher's office out of a history book, rather like Walden's own. Next to the desk, the phantom figure of some sadistic Victorian schoolmaster was caning a boy whose age Walden could only place as 'too young for secondary school'—perhaps eight or nine. Chetwood had been offering a complete education for young magicians since the fourteenth century. At one point, it had accepted pupils as young as five.

She murmured a variation on the standard banishment and sent it towards the apparition with a sharp gesture. The schoolmaster disintegrated. Hard to guess what it had been. An imp latching onto a memory of strong emotion was more likely than a true ghost.

The little boy pulled up his flannel shorts. His legs were pale and knobby-kneed. He had not been affected by the banishment. "Hello," Walden said, before remembering that no one had greeted people that way before the invention of the telephone. "I mean—good evening."

No reply. The child started walking away from her.

"Wait!" Walden said, and took a few steps after it.

They seemed to have been steps in time. The boy grew into adulthood before her eyes. His hair was turning grey by the time Walden recognised him from the oil portrait hanging in the school hall. He was the doomed Headmaster from 1926. "Mr Merringham?" she tried. "Rodney Merringham?"

"They sent a witch?" said Merringham. "I beg your pardon; a lady magician." The correction was one that would have mattered a great deal in the 1920s, Walden seemed to remember. The contemporary definition of 'witch' varied depending on who you asked: possibilities included the straightforwardly sexist 'female magical criminal,' the fairly disrespectful 'non-academic practitioner'—by that definition, Kenning was a witch, though Walden would never have used the word that way—and of course the defiant 'academic magician with strong feminist views.' Roz had called herself a witch for a while. Walden herself had never really got on with the term.

Merringham was peering anxiously at Walden through gold-rimmed spectacles. He wore a black academic gown over a threadbare suit. His voice had had a blurred and distant quality, like listening to a poor-quality recording from long ago. "I need to get up to the tower," Walden said, watching him carefully. This one, she thought, *was* a ghost. Merringham had been dead for a century. But some part of him lingered, imprinted in the magic of the demonic plane where he'd died.

"We can't have it threatening our boys," Merringham said.

"Indeed not. The tower, Mr Merringham?"

"Death, the Fool, the Ten of Swords, the Tower. A poor prospect, very poor. But we can't have it threatening our boys."

Divination, once held to be the fourth arcane discipline—invocation, evocation, instantiation, divination—was totally discredited; a dead science, like its kinsman astrology. Even a century ago it had been on its last legs. "Please, Mr Merringham," Walden said, "do you know the way up?"

Something in her tone made him frown. "Women," he said, "are too emotional to truly master magic. It is essentially a manly pursuit—like cricket."

Absolutely no point having an outdated argument with a confused ghost. "I'm sure you're right, Mr Merringham," said Walden. "There's a boy trapped in the tower. How do we get up there?"

That got the ghost's attention. "Can't have it threatening our boys," he said again. Ghosts were not Walden's area at all, but she rather thought he was stuck on that idea, skipping and repeating like the ancient recording he resembled. "This way, young lady."

You died in your forties. You've got ten years on me, if that, Walden thought. But she took her grandmother's owl brooch out of her skirt pocket. She jammed it pin-first into the wall, with some force, and looped a spell around it to make sure it stayed firm. When she let it go, the enamelled owl was shining with pale golden light: a beacon, to mark the way back.

Walden followed the ghost.

This was definitely not the present-day School House. The staircases groaned and sagged underfoot in a way that spoke to terrible rottings and splinterings in the dark below the floorboards. Todd Cartwright would have been appalled. And although it was hard to see detail through the greasy fog of the demonic plane, the rooms here seemed much smaller and darker than the light and airy house that Ebele ran now. Walden at one point caught a glimpse of a wall-fitted gas sconce. Occasional figures moved through the fog; imps latched onto echoes of emotion, perhaps, like the schoolmaster she'd dismissed. Boys, mostly. Chetwood had been a single-sex establishment until 1963.

The sobbing was hardest to bear. It rose and fell, and the timbre varied, though it tended towards the treble. Boarding schools nowadays prided themselves on being homes away from home for your darling offspring, all life and fun and well-resourced pastoral support teams. In the nineteenth century, 'pastoral' meant poems about sheep. Walden followed Merringham's ghostly figure through spartan dormitories with glitters of frost on the insides of clouded windowpanes. The stifled whimpers of unhappy children echoed in her ears. She reflected in passing on how much history had been made by men presumably suffering from the aftereffects of traumatic childhood neglect.

A welcome stretch of relief came when Merringham's ghost led her across a silent space which seemed to be the long-lost kitchen garden from School House's pre-Victorian incarnation. A bit peculiar, since by that point they'd climbed several flights of stairs, but Walden caught a trace of lavender scent and saw a knee-level motion in the fog which might have been the suggestion of a chicken. *I ought to be taking notes,* she thought. Critical incursions were poorly understood, mainly because they were very dangerous and everyone tried to make sure they never happened. Attempts to simulate a crisis like this took place in areas where no one lived, or wanted to live. But School House's long history was casting its shadow over the demonic plane here.

Eventually, a doorway became visible through the fog from a distance. Painted on it in lines of white light was the intricate shape of an incursion ward. Not an old one either. Walden knew what modern spellwork looked like. She only became more certain as Merringham led her closer. She'd marked enough of Nikki's homework to recognise her handwriting.

"I can go no further," Merringham said when they reached the door. Walden was startled again by his blurred and distant voice, by his accent with the clipped consonants of long-ago BBC announcers. "I rather think I must have failed. Did I fail?"

Walden looked at the ghost, academic gown and bad suit, gold-rimmed spectacles and greying hair. The plaque in the school chapel and the painting in the hall were all that remained in the world of this man. He had left so slight a mark on history that she doubted he even had a Wikipedia page. His brow was furrowed, his mouth anxious and sad.

And what more will remain of me, she thought, *when this is all over?*

A photo, rather than an oil painting. The visiting photographer had been in a hurry at the end of a long day slogging through all Year Seven. The image on Walden's staff ID wasn't even a nice picture.

One thing you learned, as a teacher: it was very seldom helpful, or kind, to lie to a person about themselves. They usually knew you were lying. It never made them feel better.

"I'm afraid you did fail, Mr Merringham," she said.

"I had the most rotten teachers, as a boy," said Merringham. "I wanted to be a good teacher, that's all."

"You were," Walden said, feeling it was true, though she could not know. She had never seen him in a classroom.

"It seemed like the least I could do," said the ghost. "We can't have it threatening our boys."

The incursion ward shone brightly on the door, reversed. It was painted on the other side. Its light made it hard to read the childish plaque that said, in pink bubble letters, NICOLA'S ROOM.

"I'll take it from here, Mr Merringham," Walden said. "Thank you for your help."

The ghost faded away. The outline of its body became part of the shapes and shadows of the landing. Walden stood at the top of the stairs in the present-day School House's tower. She had not been back here in twenty years. Opposite the door with Nikki's name and the incursion ward, another door hung open, revealing through a thin layer of magical fog the detritus of teenage boy—scattered hoodies, forgotten plates, a gaming console. No sign of Mathias himself.

Walden found herself praying—*oh God oh God please*—as she tried the door of Nikki's room. No atheists in foxholes.

The door would not open.

It was not the incursion ward preventing Walden from entering. A badly drawn or overgeneralised ward might accidentally exclude humans as well as demons, but this one was written with Nikki's characteristic precision and verve. The identity clause directing it against any unwelcome demon was perfect to the last dot and curve. There was nothing to find fault with at all, in fact, except that there was not enough power in it to present a serious barrier to anything larger than an eighth-order archdemon. Even that was a *lot* of power for a sixth former. Mathias was in there too. He had to be. Nikki could not have put that much force into a ward alone.

So something else was barring Walden's way.

She frowned at the door. It took her a few seconds to spot the subtle, smoky shapes of demonic spellwork. Demons very seldom actually *cast* spells, in the same way that birds seldom needed aeroplanes. The logic and formality of spellcasting were an intellectual step too far for most of them anyway. But Old Faithful was no ordinary demon. The spell barring Walden's way forward was a subtle and powerful piece of magic. Again she felt the researcher that she no longer was clamouring for her attention: *If only you had time to take notes!*

She glared at the demonic barrier. It was a spell and therefore it would be possible to analyse it and unravel it. The smoky shapes tried to shift away from her gaze. "No, you don't," Walden said, pinning it in place with a glare. The spell had a location clause, she saw, but no weaknesses there—though it defined School House in confusingly roundabout terms, including a timeframe element that ran backwards as well as forwards, which had startling implications. And the identity clause—

Ah.

Those who do not belong, said the demon's spell. *Those who have no right to enter.* Unforgivably vague, if a human had written it, but Old Faithful had more than enough power to hold its concept of not-belonging firm without sacrificing overall spell stability.

Nevertheless, it was an opening.

"I am the Director of Magic at Chetwood School," said Walden. "I am a senior member of school staff, undertaking safeguarding duties in accordance with my professional obligations as outlined in my employment contract. There is nowhere on the school grounds where I have no right to go, *particularly* if I believe a child is in danger. And your incursion seems very dangerous, my friend."

She put her hand out and caught her fingers in the spell as she spoke. It twisted away from her, trying to escape—oh, this was not a passive defence; Old Faithful had certainly noticed her, and it was paying attention now. But the principles of invocation relied above all on the inviolability of a bargain; to a demon, the wording of Walden's employment contract carried as much magical force as any summoning array. Walden closed her fingers on the greasy, smoky heart of the barrier spell. *Dr S. Walden, D.Thau, M.Ed, Director of Magic, alumna.* Chetwood School knew who she was. She had every right to be here.

The barrier fell apart. The door of Nikki's bedroom swung open.

Walden could see nothing through it. The fog of demonic magic was thick as the soup from the school canteen. But she heard a low cry of alarm in the distance. Opening the door had disrupted Nikki's incursion ward, and its white light was fading. Walden stepped over the threshold, slammed the door shut behind her, and sent a firm blast of power into the ward to shore it up. It was much too late to actually prevent this incursion, but every ward still functioning would help to slow its growth. As the spell's glow grew brighter, the fog around Walden receded a little, revealing that Nikki's bedroom floor was an absolute tip—shoes, clothes, a ragged-looking stuffed rabbit perched on top of a beanbag, a slipping pile of lever arch files all bursting at the seams, two stray hockey sticks. "Nikki!" Walden called sharply, before she tried to pick her way across. "Mathias!"

There was an answer. Walden recognised Nikki's voice. It sounded frightened, and very far away.

"Stay where you are!" Walden called back. "I'm coming for you."

She threw some more power into her upturned pale bowl of a shield, and then for good measure added another layer to it, remembering how neatly Kenning's shield had reinforced itself. Then she set out across the floor.

Old Faithful, or else the peculiar geography of the demonic plane, was playing tricks. There was much more floor than was logically possible at the top of a tower, and all of it was covered with mess. Nikki couldn't possibly *own* this much stuff, and Ebele would never have let her leave all her possessions lying around like this. Out of the corner of her eye, Walden caught sight of a battered blue guitar, decorated with stickers and propped on its amp. The skin on the back of her neck crawled. Neither Nikki nor Mathias was musical.

She began to be afraid that the absurd obstacle course would go on forever. She did not spot the summoning pentagram until she was almost on top of it.

It was a big one, a triple array straight out of *Nielle's Arrays,* and very competently done; Walden would have graded an undergraduate highly on a piece of work like this, provided they hadn't then used it to try to summon something about five times bigger than it was designed to hold. The first and second circles had broken down completely. There was so little left of the outermost pentagram that

Walden had already stepped over it before she realised it was there. The second circle still had some traces of power remaining, but most of it was sputtering sadly, useless and undirected.

Nikki and Mathias were trapped in the innermost circle.

The third pentagram, at their feet, had transformed from a drawing in salt and chalk to a sucking black void. Walden saw Nikki step towards it, two little shuffling steps, and then back away with one big step; then forwards, two more little shuffles, and back: dragging herself away. If she stepped into that darkness, she would be possessed at once. The demon was pulling her in. Mathias, on the other side of that black maw, was on his hands and knees, shuddering.

Small mercies, Walden thought. *It started with the tougher nut to crack.*

There was no time to plan or to hesitate. Walden went briskly forward under her shield. She put a teacherly hand on Nikki's shoulder and shoved her sideways. Nikki stumbled and fell, shrieking in terror as Old Faithful's tug dragged her forwards at the same time.

"I think not," said Walden, and stepped into the black hole that was the central pentagram.

There was a howl of irritation somewhere in the violet fog of the demonic plane, and the void roiled under her feet. Walden felt Old Faithful trying to tug her down. She held her right hand high and her left hand spread out—the oldest, simplest gesture of sorcerous command—and spoke in syllable after precise, focused syllable. The spells rolled confidently off her tongue, defining, compelling, demanding. A thousand years of the European magical tradition, six centuries of Chetwood School, and more than twenty years of study and practice had created Dr Walden. Old Faithful was a lot bigger than she was, but it had never had to *work*.

Her hands were trembling and her blouse and vest were stuck

to her back with sweat by the end. The void still licked at her shoes. "BEGONE," she finished. "Or else."

The black maw closed over. The central pentagram ceased to be a howling hole into endless darkness and became Nikki's scuffed bedroom floor.

Walden, with a gasp of relief, let go of the threads of spellwork she was holding. Only her pale shield remained, and around it a spiderweb of perception and awareness, in case the demon tried to sneak back up on them. Nikki was still on the floor. Her head was in her arms, and her shoulders were heaving as she sobbed. Walden cast a worried glance at Mathias, who hadn't moved. He was curled on his hands and knees, almost a foetal position. Walden did not dare check on him herself. Old Faithful, faced with a slightly more challenging opponent, had withdrawn—but she was not arrogant enough to think she had actually beaten it. It would be around here somewhere, watching for an opening or a distraction.

Walden's focus had to be her defences. She did not have enough magical reserves left to do all that again. She could not afford to slip.

"Nikki," she said, carefully modulating her tone into kind-but-firm, the voice you used when you *needed* them to listen. "This isn't the time to go to pieces. I know you're a sensible girl. I need you to stop crying and stand up. Now."

Two more awful, gasping wails. Then, with a visible effort, Nikki lifted her head. Her dark brown eyes were still full of tears, her curling lashes stuck together with dampness. She looked younger than seventeen. Her voice was on the verge of breaking into a wail again as she said, "Dr Walden, I'm *so sorry*."

"Don't worry about it now, Nikki," Walden said. Kind but firm. "I need you to get up for me, and find out what's the matter with

Mathias. I'll be right here with the shield. Come on. Up you get. You can do it."

Nikki crawled over to Mathias. She looked exhausted. It had to be after midnight by now, and she had spent most of the last hour trapped at the heart of a critical incursion with Old Faithful on top of her. But Walden's concern had to be a distant, floating thing, next to the immediacy of maintaining their defences. They were nowhere near safe. One mistake on Walden's part would most likely doom all three of them.

"Matty? Matty?" she heard Nikki say, and then, "I think he's having a panic attack."

Can't blame him, Walden thought, but oh, that was an unwelcome complication. "Nikki, I need you to get him up and walking," she said. She could hear the tension leaking through her professional calm. Nikki was far too bright not to know how much trouble they were all in. Her glance up at Walden was frightened, and then determined.

Walden focused fiercely on her shielding and scouting spells, and tried not to listen while Nikki talked softly to Mathias. A twitch at the edges of her perception; Old Faithful was testing how attentive she was. Walden narrowed her eyes and turned to face that way. Another twitch, now directly behind her. She turned again. She still hadn't actually seen the demon. It was too big. Now it tugged at Walden's spiderweb in two places at once. She had a feeling it was laughing at her.

"Dr Walden, I think we're ready," Nikki said. She'd got Mathias standing, and had a protective arm around him. Mathias was alarmingly pale, the scattering of his acne a livid constellation of red on his forehead and chin. He was still breathing too fast. But Nikki at least looked better, if still very tired. Walden had hoped that having someone else to look after would calm her down. It was the main reason *she* was calm, after all.

"All right," Walden said. She made direct, intentional eye contact, first with Nikki and then with Mathias. "We're all going to walk together. Stay calm and stay with me. Don't try to hurry. Don't attempt any magic yourselves. I've got you shielded and I will keep you safe. Do you understand?"

Nikki nodded. After a moment, Mathias did too.

"Good," said Walden. "Let's go."

How long ago had Walden left her enamelled owl brooch jammed into the wall of School House's kitchen? The twist of magic looped through it was a shining beacon to her now. The distorted space of the demonic plane was under Old Faithful's control and did its best to confuse her, throwing up classrooms that no longer existed and dormitories that had long since been emptied. The great demon was pulling in spaces from the rest of the school now: a section of Brewers Hall, a space punctuated with columns from the colonnade, the shining glassy conference room walls from the new Bursary building, even a double room from Scrubs. Walden bit her lip when she noticed but said nothing. She did not want to frighten the children.

She'd left Laura Kenning outside School House, and she remembered that glimpse of a perimeter. Walden had colleagues who knew what they were doing. If the incursion started spreading quickly, then collapsing it was the only option. An incursion collapse would be experienced by everything inside it as an explosive detonation. Death would be fast, if Walden dropped her shield; or slow, eaten alive by hundreds of demons, if she tried to save herself. How far away now was her two-hour deadline? If the three of them could not find their way out in time—

No use worrying. It would be more dangerous if they tried to run.

Walden did notice, as they moved, that the lesser demons she'd spotted on her way up to the tower had all disappeared. Had they fled, or had they been consumed? Neither possibility was comforting.

She stifled a sigh of relief when they reached the disappeared Victorian office where she'd met Merringham's ghost. No sign of him now, but the thread of magic tied to her brooch led straight through the wall. Not far now. Nikki and Mathias were both very quiet, but they had started to look less scared. Walden touched the wall and it shimmered. "Walk straight through," she said. "Imagine it's not there, and it won't be."

They walked through the wall. It disintegrated, revealing School House's airy present-day kitchen on the other side. Walden put her arm out abruptly. Mathias walked into it. She did not glance over at him. She did not dare look away.

Her owl brooch was no longer jammed into anything. The thread of Walden's magic looped through it jiggled and twisted as the figure sitting on the table tossed it from hand to hand. Left, then right. Left, then right. He set it on one end on the kitchen table and gave it a spin. The enamelled owl clattered away and fell onto the stone flags.

The figure looked up at them and grinned. He had slightly wonky canine teeth. His jeans were threadbare. Demonic power hung around him in a malevolent cloud.

"Hey, Saffy, you made it," said Old Faithful, in the voice of a boy who had been dead for twenty years. "I was starting to get worried."

chapter nine

CHARLIE

W ALDEN LOOKED AT THE BOY IN THE
threadbare jeans and said nothing.

"You got good! Like, really good! Congrats on the
doctorate. Fancy."

She took a breath, and raised one hand, and spoke the opening syllables of the strongest banishment she knew. Her hand was shaking. She tried to force it steady.

"Oh, come on," said Old Faithful, unbothered, smiling. "Don't waste your time. You can get out from here. I won't pick a fight. But you're not getting both of them past me. You know it, I know it. Which one are you leaving behind?"

"Neither," said Walden.

"Why not?" said the demon. "You left *me* behind."

"Dr Walden?" said Nikki.

"Don't listen to anything it says," said Walden.

"Yeah, you've done enough, Niks, haven't you," said Old Faithful. It put on a sonorous tone. "*I had your mother and father, girl, I licked your brother's little bones clean, and if you desire vengeance then you know what you must do*— Ha, can't believe you fell for that! You must be pretty thick, huh? Or maybe you've just got a shit teacher."

"Don't listen," said Walden.

"And you had to drag poor Matty into it," Old Faithful said. "Matty thinks he has to please people or they'll start hating him, just because his mum and dad did. Pretty sad, mate. And you took advantage, Nicola, so what does that make you? A bitch, right? Maybe it should be you who gets left behind."

Walden said, in her most quelling voice, "That's enough nonsense, thank you."

"*Oooooo,*" said the demon. "Yes, miss." It laughed. The laugh was easy and carefree, a schoolboy's laugh.

"I know what you want," Walden said.

"Yeah, I think I've been pretty clear," said Old Faithful. "Lunch." It slipped off the table and picked up Walden's enamelled owl brooch. "I remember this. Wasn't it your gran's? Want it back?"

"I know what you want," Walden said again. "And I know your power. If you really intended to consume my students, you could have done it an hour ago."

The demon glanced up. In its eyes she saw a sharp, interested hunger. "Yeah?" it said. "But I didn't, did I, Saffy? They're only kids. Maybe I'm just nice. Maybe there's something left in here that isn't all demon. Did you think of that?"

Yes, Walden had thought of that. She had thought of it at once, and known it for pitiable wishful thinking. The demon smirked at her expression.

"Let's make a deal," Walden said. Deals with demons were her business. "First, you let both of them go."

"Oh, I do, do I?" said Old Faithful. "What about my lunch?"

"You kept them alive this long," Walden said. "They were never what you wanted. A pair of half-trained teenagers is barely even a light snack, for you."

"Yeah?" said Old Faithful. Its voice had dropped to an eager whisper. "You know me so well, Saffy, huh? What's my big plan, then?"

"The most powerful magician to step into your hunting grounds this century," Walden said. "Me."

She heard Mathias gasp. Old Faithful faked an unimpressed look, but she had its full attention, that was clear. "Sounds pretty noble!" it said. "The whole self-sacrifice! Making up for last time? Remember last time?"

Doubts, desires, insecurities: Walden shoved them away. *Saffy, Saffy,* the demon kept saying, but she was Dr Walden. She wore her adulthood like armour. "I have no intention of sacrificing anything," she said. "Let me make my terms clear. We both know that I could easily force my way past you right now, taking one and possibly both of my pupils with me. I would then be out of your reach. My offer is this: if you let both of them go now, guaranteeing their safety by solemn oath, then I will stay here and fight you. If you win, you win. Lunch, as you say. If I win"—she paused—"I *will* kill you."

Old Faithful licked its lips. Walden heard Nikki whisper, *"How is it like—a person?"* She held the dead boy's gaze.

2003: the death of Charlie Green. A typical story of schoolboy hubris, Philomela had said, as if Charlie had been just any boy, an interchangeable boy, the Platonic ideal of adolescent foolishness—a concept, not a person. There was a photograph of him gathering dust in the school archives, a memorial plaque outside Scrubs, and a tree planted near the site of the old cricket pavilion that after twenty years no longer looked new.

Walden—Saffy—had been seventeen years old. The Marshals

had dragged her away screaming, before they collapsed the incursion.

Charlie must have shielded himself through the detonation. He'd still been alive. He'd still been alive, the last time she saw him, before he was left behind for Old Faithful, alone.

The body—the corpse—that Old Faithful was wearing had not aged a day, of course. He probably even had his guitar calluses still. Walden remembered finding him fantastically fit. Impossible to see it now. Nothing had changed: he was still tall, blond, with the chin-length shaggy haircut that every teenage boy with pretensions to counterculture had worn in the noughties, but these were not the things that struck her now. Instead she could only see how his skinny height had not yet filled out in the shoulders and torso, how the last traces of childhood chubbiness lingered around his soft cheeks, how badly he'd shaved the erratic blond fluff on his chin and upper lip. *You were so young,* Walden thought. She could have wept. *Oh, Charlie, you were so, so young.*

"Did you miss me, Saffy?" Old Faithful said sweetly.

Walden had spent a considerable portion of the twenty years since Charlie was consumed by this monster becoming one of the world's foremost experts on higher demons. She was not fooled. "No need for games, thank you. Just your answer. Now," she said. "Do we have a deal or not?"

"But if I let them go," the demon said, "what's to stop you leaving too? I felt you punch that portal earlier." It grinned at her— Charlie's earnest, sideways grin, with Charlie's wonky canines. It reached into the pocket of its jeans and pulled out a familiar penknife. "Give me a guarantee."

Walden fumbled the catch, and had to stoop and pick up the penknife without taking her eyes off Old Faithful. She knew what it was asking for. Blood pacts with demons were an ancient practice—a largely *obsolete* practice, because the risk so reliably out-weighed the reward. If you gave a demon a piece of your physical self, you were giving it an opening that would last as long as you lived. The profound stupidity of what Walden was about to do weighed on her. But she could not see another way to force it to let both Nikki and Mathias go.

Be realistic: if she won this fight, Old Faithful would be destroyed, and the blood pact would not matter. And if, as was infinitely more likely, she lost . . . well, then nothing would matter.

She rolled up her sleeve. It was something she would never normally do in front of students, but it was hardly worth worrying about now. Old Faithful raised its eyebrows at the stark colours of Walden's tattoos. The lowest band of black-and-scarlet spellwriting circled her forearm a little way above her wrist. Walden wore long sleeves all year round to cover the designs, partly because the parents who sent their offspring to boarding school tended to be a conservative bunch, and partly because she had no interest in discussing them with children. She did not discuss them now.

"I give my solemn oath," she said, "that if you let these two children, Nicola Conway and Mathias Wick, go freely and unmolested from your domain, and never again attempt to harm or distress them in any way, then I will remain here to face you in combat, the outcome to be freely determined between us. And I seal this oath," she nicked her wrist and held it out, "with my own blood."

Old Faithful came towards her. Its footsteps were light on the stone flags of the kitchen. It was wearing battered old Converse trainers, and one of its shoelaces was undone. Walden tried not to notice. She stared the demon down, and did not flinch when it grasped her hand, swiped chilly fingers across the cut at her wrist, and then stuck those fingers in its mouth. "Mmm," it said, pulling them out again with a pop. "Deal. Off you go, kiddos. Door's unlocked." It stepped theatrically to one side. The kitchen door behind it swung open, revealing the front hall of School House and the doorframe at the far end. The view through the doorway was dark, but not the roiling dark of the demonic plane. It was nighttime out there, back in the world, the real world, where Walden would almost certainly never set foot again.

She was terrified. But she could not sound terrified. "Go on," she said.

"Dr Walden—" said Nikki. Mathias gave her a big-eyed look. Neither of them moved.

"Don't worry, I'll be right along," Walden lied ruthlessly, and when that didn't seem to work, "You'll only be in my way."

Old Faithful chuckled.

"Go," Walden said, putting all the authority she could muster into her voice. "Tell Marshal Kenning—"

But of course there was no need to tell Laura anything. She was good at her job. Walden's plan for this fight was to spin it out as long as she could and pray her two hours ran out before Old Faithful managed to possess her. Incursion collapse would seal them both in here, and then it wouldn't matter in the least who won. Walden had a pretty clear idea of the odds. Hopefully Nikki and Mathias coming out of the incursion with the story of what Walden had agreed to would prompt Laura to act sooner.

With a certain amount of chivvying, the sixth formers finally set off down the corridor. Walden watched them go with her heart in her mouth. If she'd made a mistake—if Old Faithful went back on the deal *now*—

"Don't worry," said the demon, who was standing unexpectedly at her elbow. Walden could not suppress a sudden, awful startle. "I don't need them anymore. It's you I want."

Walden backed away from it. Her wrist still hurt where she'd nicked it. She started unbuttoning her blouse. "Oh, wow," said Old Faithful. "This is sudden, Saffy. Can't we make out first?" Again Charlie's engaging grin. "I didn't want to die a virgin. It just happened."

Walden finished with her blouse and shrugged it aside. Underneath, because it was October, she was wearing a sensible vest. The demon's eyes moved over the tattoos on her arms; bands of spellwork on both, creeping florals woven around them on the left, the exuberant reds and oranges splashed across Walden's right bicep. "Those are new," it said.

"Not really," said Walden.

"Sure we can't kiss? For old times' sake?"

"I am thirty-eight years old," Walden said flatly. "I have no interest in being pawed by a monster wearing the corpse of a child."

"You really are no fun at all," said Old Faithful.

"I'm a teacher, Charlie," Walden said. "I'm the opposite of fun."

The demon smiled at her. Walden heard her own slip a moment late: *Charlie.* This wasn't Charlie, had never been Charlie.

"When I'm you," Old Faithful said, "I'm going to walk out there and they won't know."

Walden said nothing.

"I'm not some pathetic little imp who hides in a photocopier and eats biscuits. I can *think.* I can *lie*," the demon said. "And I'll know everything you know, because I'll have your brain. It'll be my brain. Your doctorate will be my doctorate. Your office will be my office. And I'll call the naughty children into my office, and I'll have a little snack." Charlie's crooked grin got broader. "Just a little snack. A little here, a little there. I won't get caught. I'll get stronger and stronger. And there's nothing you can do."

Old Faithful had agreed to fight. It hadn't agreed to fight fair.

This was no different than what it had done to Nikki when it pretended to be the demon that killed her family. It was looking for weaknesses, because Walden frightened and distracted would be a lot easier to take down. But she was frightened, she was distracted. Her body, her expertise, and her career as tools for this ruthless predator: it was an awful picture.

"Ready?" said Old Faithful.

"Yes," Walden said.

It pounced.

Not physically. Charlie's body stayed where it was, grinning. But Walden went to one knee under the force of a solid wave of magic that roared across the airy kitchen towards her. It went through her shield like tissue paper. She recast it, frantically fast, and felt only the aftereffect of whatever that attack had been, like the prickling of a thousand tiny knives. Very nasty.

Magical combat was simply not Walden's area of expertise. It was what Marshals did, with their shining swords and their rune-marked vambraces, or else it was a personal enthusiasm pursued by academic specialists in evocation. Walden's style of doing magic was almost exactly opposite. Invocation, in its purest form, was meticulous and elegant and beautiful and *slow*. It was worked out at a desk beforehand, or memorised as a series of complex, overlapping annotated diagrams. It was satisfying, challenging, intellectual, and totally unhelpful when a giant demon was trying to stab you with thousands of sorcerous knives.

She had already tired herself out shutting down Nikki's pentagram and getting the two sixth formers out of that trap. She regretted, now, levitating Will earlier; she should have let Laura carry him. She had not reached this far into her own reserves in years. A schoolteacher—even a schoolteacher teaching A-level Invocation—just did not need to use this much power this fast. No point trying to get fancy. Walden struggled upright from her half-kneeling crouch and spoke a banishment, one she'd written herself, years ago now. The syllables echoed off her tongue and took on shuddering form in the air of the demonic plane, each a solid little ball of magical force.

Old Faithful took them all to the face and shoulders and then shook itself hard. Walden had seen Charlie react that way to getting caught coatless in February sleet: *Ooh, ow, feck,* and then shaking himself like a dog when they got indoors, breaking into laughter. There was no laughter now, but no caution either. That banishment really hadn't bothered the demon at all. Walden revised her estimate of its size upwards: she'd assumed tenth order, but this was eleventh, definitely, and maybe tending towards the twelfth. She *knew* that spell would have a destabilising effect on a tenth-order demon. She'd developed it for exactly that purpose.

Old Faithful sent another overwhelming wave of knife-sharp magic towards Walden. She managed to break the worst of it on a counterspell like a flood barrier before it hit her, but the hem of her smart John Lewis skirt turned abruptly into unravelling rags, and when Walden conjured her pale shield back into existence, she could not get it wider than the three feet around her. It kept trying to shrink further down. At this rate she was not going to last out the rest of her two hours.

Walden bit her lip and called down power through the bands of spellwriting tattooed among the flowers on her left arm.

Years since she'd used this. It hurt worse than she remembered. The spellwork illuminated with ruddy golden light and did what it was designed to do, siphoning ambient power from the environment around them, turning it into something Walden could use. This was the demonic plane: there was a *lot* of ambient power. Walden let out a gasp of pain and then shoved all of it into her shield, just as Old

Faithful frowned and sent out another hammering wave of malevolence in her direction. This time it shattered against Walden's shield, washed away undirected, and then got picked up by the power-siphons tattooed on Walden's left arm and chanelled back to her.

It was agony. Walden had to shut the tattooed spellwriting down again even as she gratefully poured more magic into her defences. She could feel the lines of pain on her arm still, and smell the faintest hint of roasting meat.

So. She couldn't risk too much of *that*.

"Cool," said Old Faithful. "Look at you, eating magic like you're one of us. Can't wait to try those."

It was an ancient horror, not a teenage boy, but it certainly tried to wind you up like a teenager would. Charlie's memories were in there. But Walden was used to children needling her for reactions, and she refused to give this thing the satisfaction. She cast another banishment, a drifting, elegant, sideways creation that wasn't hers. It belonged to her ex-girlfriend Dr Roz Chan, who had also worked on higher demons. For years now Walden hadn't spoken to her beyond the occasional polite Facebook exchange, but she had fallen in love with Roz's beautiful magic once.

The spell managed to tangle Old Faithful up a little—*Yes, Roz*, thought Walden—and gave her an opening for a binding, which she took. Charlie's face twisted in irritation as she narrowed down the demon's field of play. It could still hit her, but it wouldn't be able to cast any more of those overwhelming waves of destruction without leaving itself wide open to a counter. "Think you're pretty clever, don't you?" said the demon.

"I *am* pretty clever, thank you, yes," Walden said.

"Well, I'm *bored*," said Old Faithful. "Let's get this over with."

It charged her.

Walden wasn't expecting it at all. She had been thinking of this as a *magical* duel. But that wasn't the deal, was it? She went down flat on her back with Charlie's weight on top of her, skinning her elbow on the stone flags of the kitchen floor. He had been lanky, not fit, but that made very little difference given how much bigger than her he was. Walden yelled and writhed and did her best to knee him in the groin; her knee connected, but the demon only snarled. Spittle fell from its lips onto her face. It wrestled Walden flat, pinned both her wrists with one hand, and with the other brandished the penknife she'd used for the blood pact. Walden could somehow only see the hand, the nails untrimmed and grown too long, the knob of bone at the base of his thumb, the bumps of his knuckles, a perfectly normal teenage boy's hand. She thought, *Oh God, oh God, oh God.*

Old Faithful dragged the knife down her left arm, a long shallow cut that sliced through every band of tattooed spellwork. It *hurt.* Walden shrieked. The demon stared down at her out of Charlie's grey-green eyes. "These are different," it said, touching the edge of the knife to the uppermost band on her right arm, just above the curling pattern of scarlet splashed there. "What do they do?"

Walden panted for breath. There were tears of pain and despair at the corners of her eyes. She swallowed hard. "Above your level," she said. "Come back when you've got a degree."

"I'm having *your* degree," Old Faithful said, and it grabbed a handful of Walden's short brown hair and twisted hard. "You lose, little witch. *You should never have left me here.*"

Walden couldn't hold it back any longer. The sob that broke out of her felt like it had been building for years. Charlie's eyes, Charlie's hands, Charlie's smile, Charlie's memories somewhere behind that demonic snarl. She'd mourned him twenty years ago. He wasn't any less dead because a monster was puppeting him now. But she wept and said, "Charlie," and "I'm sorry," and "I'm *sorry.*"

She saw the demon's look of growing triumph. *I was supposed to last longer,* she thought. But maybe all her adult life had been leading her back here, to die the death she'd narrowly escaped as a schoolgirl. Maybe you never really stopped being that stupid, stupid child. Maybe this was what you deserved for getting away.

As she had this thought, a blast of white light, sizzling with power, lifted Old Faithful bodily off her and threw it across the kitchen. It slammed into the wall by the fridge and fell in a ragdoll heap.

Walden thought, *What?*

"GET UP," bellowed Laura Kenning, framed in the kitchen doorway, "AND GET OUT OF MY WAY!"

chapter ten

—————

PHOENIX

W ALDEN HAD NEVER BEFORE APPRECIATED the motive force of a really good shout. She prided herself on being soft-spoken in the classroom. But the Chief Marshal's roar triggered some hindbrain instinct that obeyed without thinking. Walden got up and dived for the cover of the kitchen table.

Laura let loose another blast of percussive magical force that drove Charlie's body to its knees as it struggled to stand up. Then another. She was advancing with sword in hand, eyes narrowed. The blasts kept coming, each one dizzyingly bright and accompanied by a thundercrack of displaced air. Walden saw after a second what she was doing. Old Faithful might be possessing a human body, but it was not human, and all Laura's spells were designed to hammer it right where a human's physical senses would confuse it most: balance, vision, sound. It seemed to be *working*.

Oh, she was so, so good.

And she reached the kitchen table and scowled at Walden and said, "What are you doing? Run!" Old Faithful was up again now and casting; that thousand-knives blast, but Laura's shield absorbed it without difficulty, the top layer flaking away and the next one coming smoothly up to take its place.

Walden said, "What are *you* doing? Laura, get out of here!"

Laura spared an instant to favour her with a speechless glare. She turned back towards Old Faithful and hurled another bombshell blast of combat magic towards it. Then she pivoted back again, grabbed a handful of Walden's sensible October vest, and kissed her hard and fast on the mouth.

Walden spluttered. "Laura!"

"Busy," snapped the Marshal, returning her focus to the demon. Charlie's body was firmly back on its feet, face twisted in fury, demonic magic bubbling dangerously around him. "Doesn't matter. Go."

"I can't," Walden said. "I made a blood pact with it. If I don't kill it here it can follow me anywhere—Laura, it's no use, there's nothing to be done—for God's sake get out there and collapse the incursion— *Did you just kiss me?*"

"You have to kill it?"

"It's eleventh order!"

"Fine," Laura said. "Then we kill it." But Walden heard the grimness in her voice. She already knew that Laura's next words would be—*or die trying.*

Then they had to stop talking, because Old Faithful was on them.

It had been holding back before. It had been playing with Walden like a cat playing with a mouse. Too big to be intimidated by her raw power, it had assessed her as an actual threat and concluded—correctly—that she wasn't one. But the Marshal *was* a threat, and the demon was not playing now. For a confused three minutes or so, all Walden could do was frantically pour the last of her magical reserves into her shield, expanding it to cover both of them, and pray it was helping. Laura's marathon-runner focus was not calm and easy now. But she did something—a dismissal, though not one Walden recognised at all—and Old Faithful backed off, retreating to the other side of the kitchen and watching them narrowly. Behind it, on the fridge, Ebele had stuck up some of her six-year-old foster son's artwork with magnets shaped like colourful fish.

Walden had exactly one trick left. She'd thought she wouldn't get a chance to use it. She probably *still* didn't have a chance. The problem with academic magic was that doing it properly took such a bloody long time.

But Laura didn't look like she was willing to walk away. So unless they were both doomed to die here, Walden had to make the attempt.

"Can you keep its attention off me for three minutes?" she said.

Laura could have asked why. She didn't.

She said, "I can try."

Old Faithful recovered its bearings and descended on them in a storm of demonic magic once more. Walden forced herself not to pay attention. She retreated further into a corner of the kitchen and turned away from the spectacle of Laura under the lash of its dreadfully powerful magic, turned away from Charlie's puppeted body and its expression of inhuman, murderous glee.

The tattoos on Walden's right arm were not spell-siphons. The bands of spellwriting had been done for her by the same San Francisco artist who'd handled the spellwork and florals of her other sleeve: a handsome trans man with a short beard and a flirtatious smile, whom Walden might have taken up on his offer of a coffee date, if she'd been single at the time. But the image underneath the bands of spellwork, spectacularly red and gold, taking up all of

Walden's upper arm and spreading down towards her wrist, had come later. It was not ink.

Walden worked slowly. The more complex an invocation was, the more important it was not to rush it. She tried not to notice the battle going on in the same room, tried not to see the splatter of blood across the kitchen table when one of Old Faithful's knife-waves hit, tried not to hear Laura's cry of pain. Each band of spellwriting had taken months of laborious development before she finalised the designs. They illuminated one after another. They did not burn as the siphons had; they were not affected by the strong magical currents of the demonic plane. They were, intentionally, as self-contained as it was possible for a work of magic to be. They depended on Walden and on Walden alone.

Only a handful of magicians in the world had ever summoned a demon above the ninth order.

Walden was one of that handful.

She had not chosen the form her fellow traveller took. She had been expecting it to be horrible; reified demons were usually horrible. But the image trapped under her tattoos was rather lovely, really: a coiling, long-winged firebird, feathered with rich red and golden plumes, a sharp raptor's head with a wickedly hooked beak, two scaly feet spread wide, each adorned with a violently orange spur.

This demon was of the tenth order. It had not had a name when Walden first summoned it. So she called it Phoenix: because she'd met it in that high-security lab in the Arizona desert, and because it was glorious. It had been totally quiescent ever since Walden finished her dissertation defence. But as she went oh so slowly through the layers of spells that bound the demon to her skin, it woke.

She felt it first; the rich and sensual warmth of a suddenly enormous pool of magic at her disposal, like being presented unexpectedly with a marvellous hot bath. Only then did she see it move. The feathers under her epidermis ruffled. A scaled foot flexed open and closed. The firebird opened its eyes.

Out of pure curiosity, Walden had done this in front of a mirror once. So she knew that by now her hair and fingernails had taken on a flame-bright tone, and her eyes were a solid glowing gold.

Look at you, Old Faithful had said, *eating magic like you're one of us.*

You have no idea, Walden thought.

And as demonic power spread its wings inside her, she turned back to the struggle that was Chetwood's Chief Marshal losing and losing badly to Old Faithful. As she watched, Laura's sword sliced deep into the demon's upper arm. It did not react at all. Pain was not something it chose to feel.

When Walden spoke, she spoke softly. She had always prided herself on being able to control a classroom without raising her voice. "May I have your attention now, thank you," she said. 'Thank you,' not 'please': a trick she'd picked up from her first teaching mentor. Don't ask them politely to cooperate. Assume they already have, and thank them for it. Be courteous, be kind, let them feel good about it; but leave no openings. Your authority is not optional. It had made sense, and come naturally, to a magician who had been studying formal demonic invocation since she was fourteen.

And it worked. Charlie's body looked up sharply.

Walden let the Phoenix take over.

This was not, now, a fight between a higher demon and two outmatched humans. It was a fight between two higher demons. One of them was older and stronger, but it had trapped itself in the body and brain of a schoolboy who had never even finished his A-levels. The Phoenix was much younger but only a little smaller, and it had a tremendously unfair advantage. It had Walden, and

Walden's expertise, and Walden's self-discipline, and Walden's years of experience in outwitting schoolchildren.

Walden was the fellow traveller now. She watched her own hands casting spell upon spell with some wonder. She recognised all the pieces that went into the Phoenix's use of magic, but not the way they were being used. The higher demon regarded Walden's knowledge of the limits of spellwork as a collection of flimsy little birdcages, meaningless at the best of times, utterly laughable in the demonic plane. It knotted together disparate strands of invocation and evocation and instantiation into effortless, fluid expressions of will and power. Microsummoning, thought Walden, recognising that some of its spells were being powered by imps who appeared and disappeared in mere heartbeats, far faster than any human could have worked through an invocation. Molecular instantiation, as the Phoenix discovered with satisfaction the lithium batteries of an abandoned toy car on the kitchen counter and blazed through them in seconds, leaving dust in its wake and a great wash of power in its hands. Classical evocation—Did Walden have any idea how much power she was carrying around in her great sack of water and meat, the hidden potential of her blood and bones, the coiled kinesis lying in wait in her muscles?

Watch out, I'm not—!

The Phoenix, outraged, was discovering the displeasure of a pulled muscle. It did not speak—not in words—but Walden felt its disapproval at the waste of such a fine natural advantage. It was the first time a demon had ever told her she ought to be stretching daily.

Quiescent, but not numb; bound, but not imprisoned; the Phoenix had dwelt in Walden's flesh for years, and neither of them had wasted the time. It had *her* understanding of magic. It was sophisticated, technically fluent, and as up to date as any magician could be who was not actively part of a research institution. And along with that expertise, it had its own nature, which was to be magic, and come from magic, and eat magic. The siphons on Walden's left arm were burning again, though bearably now. The Phoenix could handle the raw power of the demonic plane much better than she could. It was having, in fact, a perfectly wonderful time. Like Walden, it enjoyed success.

Old Faithful was outmatched.

Walden saw the moment when it realised. It braced itself to flee. *"No,"* she said, and the Phoenix, with its hunter's intelligence, its predatory instinct for the kill, agreed with her.

They caught it the same way Laura had tried to, with a flurry of physical spells that targeted the exploitable weaknesses of a human body. What about the strengths—the power of blood and bone— *What blood,* said the Phoenix, *when the fool killed its host years ago?* Blind, dizzy, deafened, Charlie's lanky figure stumbled over its own feet and then collapsed and did not get up again.

The Phoenix was delighted. It was a demon. It had won a fight. Now it wanted to feed. It wanted to *grow*: to gorge itself on Old Faithful's centuries of power and become bigger, stronger, cleverer, deadlier than Old Faithful had ever been.

Walden's spell-tattoos had been designed with very precise tolerances. The Phoenix nearly doubling in size would overwhelm them. She would be possessed at once—if she did not simply burn alive, releasing a new monster into Chetwood's magical environment in the process. "No," she said firmly, and activated the leashing element written into every strand of the spell. Her body, her power, her authority. She left no openings.

Not fair! howled the demonic firebird as its cage slammed closed, and perhaps it wasn't. But Walden had seen its mental picture of taking chunks out of Charlie's helpless body with Walden's nails and teeth, and her stomach was already turning at the thought. No, thank you. The red and golden feathers splashed across her arm went still. Walden went to her knees beside the body and turned it over.

She did nothing else for a moment or two. Just looked at him.

A shadow fell over her. Walden had somehow forgotten all about Laura Kenning.

"We could try an exorcism," Laura said. "Drag it out of him, cut it into pieces, banish the remains. It's been done. Not on anything this big, but it's been done."

God, how that would feel. To walk into this incursion looking for three lost children, and come out with four. But the Phoenix's scorn for Old Faithful had been well founded. Walden shook her head. She reached for the cut in Charlie's checkered shirt where Laura's sword had gone into his arm, and held it open. The injury underneath was deeper than she'd thought. Down past the layers of blackened, bloodless flesh, Walden could see bone.

"It's all that's holding his body together," she said. "Exorcism wouldn't change anything now. It would just make it harder to kill."

Laura had her sword in hand. "Then let me."

Walden looked down at the face of the boy in her arms. He was so young.

Look at us now, Charlie, she thought. *Look at me.*

Look at me, with my hair dyed back to brown, long sleeves over my tattoos, cosplaying my own grandmother most of the time; look at me, nearly forty, not speaking their language, not getting their jokes—oh, you would laugh. But you should have been here too. You should have travelled like you wanted to, you should have visited me in California, you should have kept making music. Maybe it would have worked out, maybe not. Maybe by now you'd be married with children, losing your hair and putting on weight and playing guitar at the weekends and you'd have learned what I've learned, that there's joy in finding good work to do and doing it, there's joy in looking back along the path you walked and knowing you wouldn't change it. Oh, we wouldn't have believed it, and you never got the chance to find out, but Charlie, Charlie, it feels so good to grow up.

She saw his fingers twitch. Old Faithful was trying to regain control. It was down, but not defeated. Not yet.

Charlie's body was cold. She stroked his shaggy hair. She looked up at Laura.

"Go on," she said.

Laura brought her sword down squarely through Charlie's chest. There was a blaze of glittering silver in the strike, and each rune along the length of the bright sword illuminated. The whole body convulsed as if struck by lightning.

Old Faithful died.

Walden gritted her teeth through the thaumic reverberations as its death poured past her, a wave of suddenly undirected wild magic washing away in all directions. Charlie was withering in her arms, becoming a shrunken mummified husk, still dressed in old jeans and band T-shirt and chequered shirt. When Laura withdrew the sword from his chest, still shining bright and totally clean, nothing changed. It was over. More than twenty years later, it was all over.

Walden carefully closed the dead boy's eyes and laid him down on the stone kitchen floor. She folded his hands over his chest.

"It's done," she said.

Well. There was no point sitting around feeling sad. Walden stood up, stretched with a wince—the Phoenix had used her body hard in that fight, everything ached—and tried to gather some professional detachment. "The incursion should shut itself down, now, I think," she said, "without that monster holding it open. It's much too big to self-sustain. Shall we?"

Silence.

"Laura?" Walden said.

She turned towards the Chief Marshal and found herself staring down the length of a silver shortsword. The tip was at her breast.

"Ah."

"You're possessed," said Laura.

She'd seen Walden wake the Phoenix, of course. And she was a Marshal.

Walden met her eyes steadily. "Other way round, actually," she said. "I possess."

"I'm supposed to believe that?"

"I still have my doctoral thesis somewhere if you'd like to read it."

"Dr Walden," said Laura unhappily.

"I really don't know what I can do to prove it to you," Walden said. "If I am possessed, then I have been for years, and it hasn't caused any problems yet. But, if you'll forgive my pulling rank on this one—I *am* an expert on demons. More than you. And I feel quite confident that the Phoenix is under my control, and harmless."

"You think you're the first magician to say that about a demon?"

"Well, no, of course not," Walden admitted. "The difference is, I'm right."

"I have a duty," said Laura. "I swore an oath of service. I can't let a higher demon walk around loose in the mundane world."

"It's not loose, it's extremely carefully caged," Walden said. "But I do see your point." God, she was tired. How on earth to get Laura to leave her alone about this?

Then a sudden inspiration. "Would you care to swear an oath about it?"

Laura stared at her. "A what?"

"An oath," said Walden. "A geas, you know, that sort of thing. I understand, Marshal Kenning. The Phoenix is potentially quite dangerous, yes. But I can give you the power to sort it out in a pinch, if you really don't feel you can trust me."

The shortsword finally wavered, before Laura's wrist stiffened and she brought it back to its threatening position at Walden's breast. Walden thought, for a moment, about the kind of courage it took to watch something take down an eleventh-order demon, and then decide it was your duty to fight it.

She took the tip of the silver sword between thumb and forefinger. "I give my solemn vow," she said, "that the demon named *Phoenix* presents no threat to anyone or anything in the mundane world; that all my skill and all my power are at work in maintaining this state of affairs; and that if I fail, I submit myself at once to the judgement of the Order of Marshals and especially to the Chief Marshal Laura Kenning. By this oath I lay my fate in her hands. If the Phoenix wakes, she shall know of it, and she shall be granted all power to act." Magic curled around Walden's fingers and the sword as she spoke. She was being intentionally vague with the wording—too vague, if she'd been dealing with a demon. But Laura was human and Walden was not afraid of her. The whole thing was just a formality really. The Phoenix had been living quietly on Walden's arm for so long that most of the time even Walden forgot it was there. But for Laura's peace of mind, she finished, "And I seal this oath with my own blood."

She turned her fingers over and nicked them on the sword's sharp edge. Then she offered them to Laura.

Laura let the sword fall and took her hand in an abrupt motion. She brought Walden's bloody fingers to her face, hesitated, and then kissed them awkwardly. Then she let go at once. Walden breathed out, feeling the pact take hold. She'd never made any kind of binding magical contract with a human being before. The underlying principle was the same as in any invocation, but the sensation was very peculiar. Laura's magical essence was so much smaller and stranger and more complicated than the glowing presence of a demon.

"That's that. And now please let's go," she said. She carefully didn't glance down at Charlie's shrivelled corpse by her feet. Now was not a good time to burst into tears. "I don't think I can bear to be here another moment."

The purplish shimmer of wild magic grew thinner and brighter, reinforced by the remnants of Old Faithful, as they walked together towards the broken front door of School House. The fog of the incursion was starting to lift. Laura tripped over the child's bicycle in the hallway and swore.

In the absence of the great lurking threat, smaller demons were already creeping back. *More will come,* said some part of Walden that was forever a professional. *We are going to have a problem soon.* But then she forgot again, because a pair of apparitions, imps latched onto memories of emotion, were kissing by the coat hooks. She held up a hand, *Wait.*

Laura said, "But it's *dead.*"

"That's not Old Faithful," said Walden.

Charlie as she'd known him, bright eyes and crooked smile, grinning down at his girlfriend, who was a desperately tiny waif with violently bleach-blonde hair. "Oh," Laura said behind her. Walden remembered that dye job, done herself in a Scrubs bathroom while a friend kept watch for patrolling teachers. She watched her teenage self—had she really looked that young?—go up on tiptoe to say something in Charlie's ear. She couldn't remember what she'd said, but whatever it was, it made him laugh. Teenage Saffy was laughing too. Then the two of them went on, hand in hand down the hallway, past Walden and Laura as if they were not there and further into the depths of School House: a pair of giggling children who had never met a consequence that mattered.

It was amazing how stupid teenagers could be, Walden thought, with enormous, grieving fondness. She knew she wouldn't change them for the world.

chapter eleven

REFLECTION AND TARGET-SETTING

W ALDEN STEPPED THROUGH THE DOORWAY feeling tremendously relieved; the incursion was shrinking behind them, and would collapse itself before long. But outside School House there was a depressing scene of chaos. No one seemed to be in charge. The two people with direct responsibility for leading magical security at Chetwood had both been *inside*.

She had a whole ten seconds to take in the scene of useless milling about around the edges of School House's lawn. There were far too many people, including an ambulance crew and an additional squadron of Marshals who seemed to be arguing with Laura's second-in-command. Ebele and the younger children were gone, but Ezekiel was still there, his power sunk into the magical perimeter, his face a mask of effort and exhaustion. Several younger magician teachers were holding the perimeter too; they must have been woken up from their comfortable beds in the Scrubs flats. Lilly Tibbett was wearing purple plaid pyjamas and enormous fluffy slippers. Then Walden's attention was arrested by the sight of Nikki, Mathias and Will, sitting in a glum little circle on the grass with foil first-aid blankets over them—good grief, why had no one got them out of here? At least Will seemed to be conscious—

And then she spotted the lurking figure on the edge of things whom she recognised, with a sinking heart, as a self-appointed journalist from the *Chetwood Village Inquirer.* Oh God, no.

Silence fell when the crowd finally noticed Walden and Laura on the steps of School House. Walden took an assembly every other week and was used to an awkward hush and a lot of eyes on her, but just now she did not feel strong enough for it, not at all. She closed her eyes for a moment.

Her school, her students, her responsibility.

"Everything is under control," she announced, pitching her voice to carry through the night and the crowd. "The demon is dead and the incursion is closing."

There was a further moment of silence which was, Walden re-alised, everyone looking at the Marshal standing next to her for confirmation. Laura said gruffly, and not quite loudly enough, "Dr Walden is correct."

Walden looked over the heads of the crowd and met Ezekiel's eyes. He looked not at her, but at the house behind her—which was, after all, his home. After a moment he nodded gravely, and then she saw him release the power in the perimeter and sag with exhaustion. The other magician teachers followed his lead, and slowly the protective magical shimmer dissipated. Walden breathed out.

She would have liked to go and speak to him—to thank him, to tell him what had happened, to have a moment to express how completely dreadful all that had been to someone who actually understood—but it was impossible, because the entire bloody crowd was descending on the steps of School House at once.

It took ten minutes before someone appeared with enough of an aura of power to manage the mob. The power was not magical. It was something much more effective than that. It was the power of inarguable, hierarchical, institutional command. As the crowd fell back politely, Walden looked with enormous gratitude into the face of the Headmaster. As always, David Bern had an air of profoundly reassuring middle-aged solidity. He was in his heart the quintessential Geography teacher, unshakeable as the foundations of the earth, and despite being woken up in the middle of the night to the news that his school was under attack by a higher demon, he'd had the presence of mind to put on a tie. He looked warm and professional and more than capable of dealing briskly with the journalist. The last thing any school wanted, ever, was attention from the media.

"You're dead on your feet, Saffy," David said firmly. "Get to bed. I'll handle this lot."

"Thank you," Walden said. "Mr Bern will answer all the rest of your questions, everyone. Good night."

Then she slipped away through the crowd. She looked for Ezekiel, but he was already gone; to his wife and to bed, hopefully. Instead Walden rescued her blazer from its crumpled heap in the grass and put it on, feeling a bit of relief when she was no longer bare-armed in the October cold with her very unteacherly tattoos on display. But she still could not leave. There were three more problems to manage, and David had given her a firm instruction with a simple glance and nod. Walden buttoned the blazer with relief and, thus armoured in good tailoring—never mind the ragged mess that Old Faithful had made of her skirt—she marched over to the gaggle of Marshals.

They were still arguing about something, now with Laura in the middle. Two yawning young men with trainee stripes on their sleeves were standing guard over the pathetic tableau of Nikki,

Mathias, and Will. Mathias was fidgeting compulsively with the edge of the foil blanket over his lap. Will seemed to have given Nikki his school hoodie.

"—not possible!" said a Marshal Walden didn't recognise, spitting it at Laura. His rank insignia suggested he was a district commander. Wonderful.

"Would you kindly explain," she said, in her coldest and most schoolmistress-ish voice, "why you have chosen to keep these children sitting on the ground in the cold in mid-October?"

She saw the tone hit. The district commander flinched. It did occasionally happen that you triggered someone's long-suppressed memories of getting told off at school, and Walden wasn't above taking advantage. She raised her eyebrows at him, giving off her best impression of *detention imminent*. "Uh—is it Miss Walden?" said the Marshal.

"Doctor," said Laura.

"Dr Walden . . . we have to keep them all under formal observation," the Marshal said. Rallying a bit, he added, "You as well. In case—"

"I see," said Walden, even more coldly. "Is there any particular reason this observation has to take place *here*?"

The district commander admitted, in a mumble, that there was not, and suggested vaguely that the district barracks in Milton Keynes . . .

Walden shut that down firmly. "Since you and your squad aren't DBS checked—in fact, I've seen no formal identification at all—I certainly can't let you remove these children from school grounds. Fortunately, Laura here is Chetwood's Chief Marshal. Perhaps you'd be good enough to take charge of the observation requirements, Laura? I'm sure the commander has a great deal to be getting on with."

"Of course," said Laura, expressionless. Walden thought she caught a flicker of appreciation in her eyes.

Walden went over to the huddle of teenagers. They all stared up at her. They looked extremely pathetic. She adjusted her expression from *very scary deputy head* to *just Dr Walden, you know her.* Somewhere to do a formal observation—somewhere magically secure, self-contained, and separate from the rest of the school, but with enough beds for all the exhausted children to get a decent night's sleep—

There was only really one place in Chetwood's grounds that qualified.

Walden wasn't free of responsibility yet. When was she ever? "Come on, you lot," she said. "Up you get. Sleepover in the Director of Magic's flat."

Aneeta was awake, still curled on the couch with her phone. She looked miserable and exhausted. When she heard them come in, she leapt up. "Nikki!" she shrieked, and flung herself at her friend.

Walden graciously pretended that she had very urgent non-teenager things to do while Aneeta hugged first Nikki, then Mathias, then Will, then Nikki again, and the four of them all talked at once about their ordeal. Laura followed her lead and helped Walden retrieve clean towels and bedsheets for the guest rooms. "How are they still this loud?" she muttered.

"'O adolescence, adolescence, I wince before thine incandescence!'" Walden quoted, and at Laura's blank look, said, "It's a poem. I think about it a lot."

The flat was sized for a small family, and Walden by herself rattled around in it a bit. Getting the two spare bedrooms ready took long enough that by the time she returned to the living room, the sixth formers seemed to have calmed down a bit. They were all still talking at once. "—can't believe you were that *stupid*," Nikki was saying to Will.

"I thought you were going to die, Conway!" Will protested. "And I haven't even asked you to Leavers yet so like—"

Nikki's mouth dropped open. "You're asking me to Leavers?"

In the pause that followed, Aneeta said in a loud, entertained whisper, "Oh my God *it's happening*."

Mathias sniggered. Will had turned violently pink.

Walden swallowed a laugh. Teenagers. You knew them so well and yet in some ways, of course, you didn't know them at all. She'd parsed Will's dash into the incursion as idiocy, not adolescent knight-errantry—but, after all, the two were not mutually exclusive. She knew very well how easy it was to be seventeen, in love, *and* an idiot. *Oh Charlie*, she thought. *Oh sweetheart. You were so young.*

"Ahem," she said, and all four of them looked up. "It's well past your bedtime, children." You couldn't call Year Nine 'children' without offending them, but by the time they hit Upper Sixth they always found it funny again. Walden couldn't resist adding, though it was a little cruel, "Sort out your interpersonal issues in the morning."

Various mortified looks as all four of them realised belatedly how loudly they'd been talking. Walden smiled to herself. What was the good of being the grown-up if you didn't get to embarrass them a little? She sent them off to the guest rooms. She fetched them glasses of water, and old T-shirts for the girls to sleep in; the boys were going to have to make do in their day clothes, because Walden had nothing that would fit. She left Nikki and Aneeta cuddling up together in the double bed in the smaller guest room, and Will and Mathias doing rock-paper-scissors for who got the bed and who got the futon in the bigger one. She went back into the kitchen.

Laura was there.

"I'd offer you a gin and tonic," Walden said, "but we're in loco parentis. I don't think I'll be able to sleep for a while yet, so if you'd like my room—"

"I'm doing a formal observation, thank you," said Laura. "No. I'm going to sit up and observe how few demons there are in here and it's going to make me feel a lot better. I was on a night shift anyway, I slept all afternoon, don't worry about me. You should go to bed."

Walden shook her head. "What I really want is a coffee," she said. "What I'm going to have is a cup of tea. Would you like one?"

They had tea. Walden had a vast collection of mugs, because students kept giving them to her. She put the kettle on and fetched down one that said WORLD'S BEST TEACHER and another decorated with a cartoon of a cat.

"Do you want to talk about it?" Laura said abruptly. She was, Walden was coming to realise, actually rather an awkward person.

She poured boiling water over the teabags. "There's not much to say."

"I forgot you were an old girl," said Laura. "The 2003 incursion—"

"Yes, I was there. I was in sixth form," said Walden. "I admit that I should probably have mentioned it earlier. I do find it quite hard to talk about. How many sugars?"

"Two," said Laura.

Walden had to hunt in the cupboard for sugar. Laura had definitely taken more than two when they had tea in the staffroom, so she got the whole bag and let her sort it out herself. Her own preferred brew was teacher tea: teabag mashed against the side of the travel cup for two minutes in the staffroom kitchen, splash of milk, rush off to your next lesson. She passed Laura the WORLD'S BEST TEACHER mug, sat down opposite her at the kitchen table, and took a sip from the cartoon cat mug. The tea was still much too hot. She already felt better.

Laura was still looking awkward. Walden felt she had to say a bit more. "Yes, all right, I was there. We were seventeen years old," she explained, "and very talented. Worse, we knew we were very talented. Charlie was a School House boy, a sorcerer—you know what that means, of course you do, you've worked here long enough. I didn't actually know very much about his background, I realise now. I'm sure he didn't want to tell me. But you don't end up as a ward of Chetwood School without a ferocious talent for magic. He was good. So was I. When I look back, I still don't know if it was his idea or mine. There's no excuse. We weren't tricked into it like poor Nikki was tonight. We just wanted to see if we were good enough to summon and control an absolutely enormous demon. And, of course, we weren't." She drank some more tea. "It was May half term, right before our A-levels. Charlie had an Oxford offer—an EE offer, if you can believe that; he must have really impressed the interviewer. So did I, but my offer was three As. Which I knew I would make. We felt like lords of the world, magician-kings to be, masters of the arcane disciplines . . . you know. Children. Old enough to know better, but we didn't, yet."

Laura had set her tea down and was watching her gravely. Come to think of it, it was a long time since Walden had told anyone this story.

"The school was mostly empty," she went on, "though there are always a few still here over the holidays. My parents were in Barbados. Charlie . . . well, as I said, he was a School House boy. We had just enough sense not to try it in a dormitory. We snuck out to the old cricket pavilion. Hence the *new* cricket pavilion, because in the course of trying to fight our way out, we demolished it. We failed, of course. Really, we should both have died, but the school

Marshals took the very risky decision to send a team in after us. Looking back, it was very brave of them. At the time . . ." She shook her head. "It was already too late for Charlie. They dragged me away. I heard him screaming. And then they collapsed the incursion."

"No wonder you don't like Marshals," said Laura.

Walden rolled her eyes. "Give me some credit for being an adult, Laura, it was twenty years ago. I don't like Marshals *in school* because, frankly, I don't think intimidation is the best way to persuade children to think about the consequences of their actions. It certainly didn't work on us. Does that answer your questions?"

Laura said, "So he was your . . ."

"Boyfriend," said Walden. "We were going to attend Leavers as a couple, actually, which in sixth former seriousness terms is only a few steps down from getting engaged. God knows what would have become of us at Oxford. Probably broken up by the end of Michaelmas term of first year."

Laura said, "Oh," and then, after a moment, "I thought you were . . ."

"Bi," Walden said. Despite her best efforts, she felt her mouth twitch with amusement.

"Right," said Laura, looking embarrassed.

"My turn for a question," Walden said. "Why are you working for Chetwood? I mean, not to put too fine a point on it, you're obviously *extremely* good, and it's—"

"—a career dead end," Laura said. She wrapped both hands around the WORLD'S BEST TEACHER mug. "I know. Everyone told me. Nicola Conway."

"What?"

"Nicola Conway is why," Laura said. "Or, well, not exactly. She doesn't remember me. But the Conway case—I was there.

Twenty-two years old, still a junior, barely knew what I was doing—but I was there. Whole family dead in a surprise incursion. Absolutely bloody awful."

"I see," said Walden, who didn't.

"The thing is that it was our fault," said Laura. "The Marshals. Oh, not officially, of *course* not officially, but there's a screening program in primary schools and we should have picked up the Conway kids and had tabs on them long before it got to that point. It was both of them, you know. Nicola and her brother. I went through the records afterwards. I was strongly encouraged not to, but I did." She made a face. "And we had Nicola on the record as one to keep an eye on—she must have been what, Year Two? And tested top of the range every year. Her brother had only just started Reception, but given Nicola's scores, we should have been keeping an eye on him as well. But they were both out sick with a stomach bug the week the Marshals visited their primary school that year, and no one followed up. The Marshals should have done it, but they left it to the teachers to organise, and the teachers were too busy to bother. Inner London state primary, you know."

Walden knew. Teaching was a hard job, but the version of it she did—reasonably well-paid, comfortable, straightforward, with the vast majority of students from overwhelmingly well-off backgrounds and speaking fluent English—all this was a breeze compared to the challenges many schools faced. She could see very easily how Nikki and her brother had fallen through the cracks. But at what cost?

Laura's expression was dark. "At the end of the day, it wasn't anyone else's job. It was on *us* to do that follow-up. Such a stupid basic lazy fuck-up. If someone had followed up, it would have saved three lives. If one person had gotten a good look at just how powerful those kids were getting and how fast—all it needed was an incursion ward with an alert on it somewhere in the family home, and the Marshals would have been there in time. But no one followed up. No one cared. No one takes the outreach and prevention side of the job seriously. It's just 'school security.' An easy place to put people out to pasture when they're too old to fight demons and not ready to retire." She sighed. "My squad aren't bad demon hunters, you know. They're not. Some of them were damn good demon hunters, five years ago, ten years ago. But when you're over sixty and you know your reaction times aren't what they were, you can't draw your pension yet and you'd like to live long enough to spend some time with your grandkids . . ."

"I understand," Walden said.

"Anyway. That's why I got into this, and it's why I'm still doing it. Though it was the shock of my life when I got to Chetwood and—you know, I had this picture in my head for years, this little seven-year-old scrap who just lost her whole family. Every time I wondered if I was really wasting my time, I'd remember. It kept me going. And then suddenly I'm here and she's five foot nine and doing her GCSEs."

Walden took a sip of tea to hide the fact that she suddenly didn't know what her face was doing. The sudden and forceful respect she felt seemed hard to express. Instead, she said, "They do that. Grow. The passage of time, you know. It shouldn't be allowed."

"It really shouldn't," said Laura.

Walden smiled at her. The warmth of respect was still in her thoughts, and Laura's repeated protests about Nikki's magical studies were taking on a new tone in her memories: not obstructive, but protective. Still *wrong*, of course. "Thank you for telling me," she said. "I am grateful. If you hadn't been there tonight, I would be dead or possessed by now."

"Still not sure about your pet tattoo monster," Laura said.

"If something goes wrong with my leashing spells," said Walden, "you will now, thanks to that oath, be the first to know. I don't think it's very likely. It's been there for nearly fifteen years, you know." Laura did not seem appeased. Walden changed the subject. "Do let me know if there's anything I can do to support your career. We work together, and I do have some," a hand gesture, "some professional capital, I suppose, to work with. I am very happy to, I don't know, write forceful memos to district commanders and so on. You're obviously completely right about prevention and outreach."

"I know I am," said Laura. But she looked pleased.

"You've lost out on quite a lot by sticking to it," Walden said. Opportunities, promotion, status, respect—you got none of those when you chose the career dead end. "I admire you for it. It's a sacrifice."

Laura snorted. "Look who's talking, Miss—sorry, *Doctor*—I-could-have-worked-for-the-Pentagon."

Walden laughed. "I'm pretty sure my ex-girlfriend took that job. Sometimes I think about how much money she must be making by now and want to cry. Not that I do too badly, of course. But even senior management in the private sector doesn't pay like US military R&D." She took another sip of her tea. "On the flip side, at least I can say with confidence that I am not responsible for any war crimes. Or even any things that technically aren't war crimes because no one has tried them yet."

"So we can agree," said Laura wryly, "that there are reasons why a highly qualified person might choose the job where she'll be underestimated and undervalued forever."

"Hah. Yes. Cheers to that."

They clinked their mugs together. Then they sat in silence for a while, drinking tea. Walden finished hers and stood to put the kettle on again. She still felt far too edgy to sleep. She kept thinking of more things to do. *The thaumic engines will need recalibrating . . . need to do a full boundary patrol . . . reset all the incursion wards . . . write up a safeguarding concern for Nikki—no, two, one for Mathias as well . . . got to meet with his TAC, is he even seeing a counsellor at the moment . . . sanctions . . . emergency assembly in the morning before the student rumours get out of hand . . . report for the governors . . . there'll be an investigation, someone's going to get the blame, I might—let's not think about that.*

Something reassuring to go out to parents . . . have to meet with David first thing . . . double Invocation tomorrow after lunch . . . why did we leave Charlie's body in there, can I go back for it . . . and did I ever mark that problem sheet?

"I owe you an apology," Laura said, while Walden was staring blankly at the kettle and writing an impossible to-do list in her head.

"What?"

When Walden turned around with the milk carton in hand, Laura was looking wretched. "I was—that was—terribly unprofessional of me," she said. "Earlier. I apologise."

"What?" said Walden again and then while Laura went red remembered all at once: that *kiss*. "Laura—"

"Look," said Laura, shoulders squared like she'd spotted another demon to fight, "would you like to get drinks at the Red Lion with me sometime?"

Walden said, "I don't think that's a very good idea."

Laura deflated. "Right. Of course. Sorry."

"That's the only pub in the village," Walden said. "Which means it's the *student* pub. So unless you want our first date observed with interest by half of Year Thirteen—plus a couple of Year Tens hiding in the corner and praying we don't notice them—"

"Oh," said Laura. She started to smile.

"Counterproposal," Walden said. "Next time I have a free day—which I'm afraid won't be till half term, but it's only a couple of weeks off now—we can catch the train into London and I'll take you to a little place I know near Camden Town. And then, I don't know, we can see a film or something. It's been years since I went on a date but I think I remember the steps."

"Sounds nice," said Laura. "I'll look forward to it."

"Me too," Walden said. And with that, exhaustion fell onto her like a weight of stone. She looked at the mug of tea in her hands and could think of nothing worse than trying to stay awake long enough to drink it. "I think I should go to bed," she said. "Are you sure you're all right to sit up?"

"Sitting up for an observation is part of my job," said Laura patiently, "which I am good at. And I was on a night shift, and I'm completely fine. I'll write my report if you can lend me a laptop or something."

"Of course."

"One more thing, though—"

Walden paused.

Laura grinned at her. "I've always wanted to know. Did your parents really name you 'Saffron Walden'? Like the train station?"

Walden, taken completely by surprise, started laughing. "I've never been able to decide if that would have been better or worse. No, no. I'm afraid it's 'Sapphire.'"

"Oh my God."

"I know." It was a beautiful, romantic, totally un-English sort of name. It belonged to someone about as different as could be imagined from the person Dr Walden chose to be. She'd always found it embarrassing.

Laura rallied admirably. "That's pretty, though," she said. "Like your—"

She stopped, probably because she'd noticed herself being unforgivably cheesy. *Eyes,* Walden finished mentally for her, and laughed. "I haven't heard that one in a while," she said. "There's a reason I go by Saffy. I do prefer it."

The truth was that she was barely even Saffy, most days. Dr Walden was the self she had made, the home she possessed, a person with knowledge and experience and power and status and a place to belong. *Saffy* was a compromise, because people liked you to have a human side. And of course she did have a human side. Who didn't?

She felt very human just then, smiling at a good-looking woman in her kitchen at two in the morning. For a moment—just a moment—she was not really, not at all, thinking about her job.

"Good night, Saffy," Laura said. "I'll see you in the morning. And I'll look forward to half term."

"Likewise," said Walden. "Good night, Chief Marshal Kenning."

"Oh, for—"

"Laura," said Walden, and she felt very human indeed, and quite brave, when she boldly dropped a kiss on the Marshal's cheek, before she left her sitting in the kitchen and went to bed.

OCTOBER HALF TERM

chapter twelve

REPUTATIONAL DAMAGE

"DR WALDEN, THANK YOU FOR WAITING," said the Chair of Governors. "We've agreed a compromise."

Walden's gaze flicked round the meeting room—panelled walls, oil paintings, uncomfortable blue plastic folding chairs around an ancient long refectory table—trying to assess what 'compromise' meant. Two intensely busy weeks had passed since Old Faithful had made its move, broken through in a critical incursion, and died at Walden's hands. The governors were mostly male, though there were a few women among them. They were all well-dressed, and almost all white. David, as Headmaster, sat at the Chair's left hand. His expression gave nothing away. This meeting was the final stage of the governors' formal investigation into the disaster.

"Chetwood is one of the leading schools of magic in this country—I daresay, in the world. You were appointed Director of Magic as part of that mission. Now, our whole school community must take this demonic incursion very seriously."

It was quite something to be accused of 'unseriousness' about demonic incursion by a person who had probably had to look up eleventh-order demons on Wikipedia two weeks ago when he got the phone call. Sometimes Walden regretted being a grown-up. It meant you could not say what you actually thought. But she kept smiling. She had no leverage here. It was quite likely that she was about to unceremoniously lose her job. She had been deep in crisis management for the last two weeks. She knew how many angry and frightened phone calls from parents there had been. She knew that next year's eleven-plus entrance applications were down. The bloody local journalist had not been able to resist the drama: a critical incursion, an eleventh-order demon, right here in our sleepy Buckinghamshire village—just think of what could have happened to the children! And think of what could still happen to our *house prices*!

And then, nightmarishly, the BBC had picked it up, and now the whole thing was in the school's search results. For a private school, which needed parents willing to pay school fees in order to survive, reputational damage was an extremely serious problem. Old Faithful was no one's fault. But once you got to Walden's level, things that were no one's fault were still your responsibility.

"We considered your points very carefully," the Chair said. "You made some forceful arguments—as did David, of course." Walden and David had met before this meeting to go over every single headline they needed to hit. It was always a relief to have a good Head in your corner. "I want to say, on behalf of the board, that we are all impressed by your dedication to your students."

What had become very clear, in the course of the investigation, was that the governors expected someone to take the fall for what had happened. It had been indicated—not very subtly—that since recruiting a qualified Director of Magic halfway through the academic year was going to be very difficult and expensive, they were happy for the blame to be put on a pair of reckless young people from troubled backgrounds. Someone had said that, 'troubled.'

Walden had not been in the meetings twenty years ago. Perhaps someone had said the same sort of thing about Charlie.

So she and David fired back: our duty of care. Our *mission*. Our school's long and noble history as a safe haven for young sorcerers with nowhere else to turn. Our institution's charitable status, said David solemnly, and got some nervous looks: 'charitable status' was a tax issue. And then Walden had looked around the room and reminded herself that most of the governors were people who sincerely believed in the importance of Chetwood School and the mixture of magical and academic education it provided. Plenty of them were alumni. Not a few had children at the school. They were frightened. It was a shutting-the-stable-door kind of fear. They wanted to act, at once, in a way that would make them feel like they had done the right thing.

Let me tell you about Nicola and Mathias, she'd said.

The sob stories had worked on some of them. The magic words 'Oxford candidate'—Nikki had put in her application at the start of October, and Walden thought her chances were good—had worked on others. And then they'd invited Laura Kenning to come in and give her final account of the incident, along with her analysis as Chief Marshal.

Walden had been expecting it to be a disaster. Laura was such an abrupt and awkward person. She didn't have the years of practice addressing a group that any teacher got as a matter of course. Besides, there *had* been several mistakes in how they'd handled Old Faithful's incursion. Walden lay awake at night thinking about them. If she had just paid more attention to Nikki in the days following that summoning gone wrong. If she hadn't let herself be worried about Mathias, and distracted by the need to scold Will, and then caught up in the countless meetings and observations and phone calls and emails that were also her job. If she'd taken more time answering Aneeta's question about Old Faithful's whispers that day. If she hadn't given Nikki the *book*.

There were several mistakes in the handling of this incident, Laura had begun, in an abrupt and awkward way.

Then she'd thrown herself on her sword.

Walden had felt fairly awful listening to it. Laura had clearly done her own share of lying awake. What was the good of a Chief Marshal on a school site, if not to protect children from demons? *Insufficient threat analysis,* Laura said. *A historical culture of carelessness regarding the eleventh-order demon known as 'Old Faithful'—like sitting on a volcano and assuming it would never erupt, just because it hadn't for a while. Lack of personnel. Lack of preparedness among those personnel who were on duty. Lack of leadership by the Chief Marshal. Patrol schedules too heavily focused on the student dorms and known hot spots, requiring school staff with little training or experience to cover gaps on an ad hoc basis. Frankly,* she'd paused, and looked grim, and finally said, *a lot of people should have died.*

And then, while everyone still looked solemn about that, she'd gone on: *The only reason this incident was just a frightening mistake, and not a horrific tragedy, is Dr Walden.*

Walden hadn't been expecting it. She did not quite know what to do with her face for the next part. You could not sit there and smile blandly while a person called you a hero; it was too awkward. Laura gave a stripped, professional account of their trip into the incursion to recover Will, Nikki, and Mathias. Somehow, she managed to make it sound like Walden had been tremendously efficient and highly competent the whole time, instead of full of adrenaline and making it up as she went along.

"At the very least, the three children in the incursion should have died, or worse," said Laura in the end. "I wouldn't even have tried to save them. And if I had tried, I would probably have failed. I don't know how to explain to you all just how dangerous an eleventh-order demon is. A volcano probably is the best thing to imagine, or any kind of natural disaster—that's what a higher demon is, a natural disaster. It's not just a question of being brave or doing the right thing. To take on something like that, you need skills that most people simply don't have. The Order of Marshals keeps track of the magicians in this country who do have those skills, and it doesn't take much effort, because I could count them on my fingers.

"I want you all to be clear about what I'm telling you. Chetwood just lost an apex predator that's been lurking in the school's magical shadow for hundreds of years. That doesn't mean the school is safe. It means it's open season until a new higher demon moves in to claim that hunting ground—and there *will* be a new one. No demon can resist the sheer quantity of wild magic that a large group of teenage magicians is always going to generate as a matter of course. You need to substantially step up the magical security operation on the school campus. You need to increase the number of Marshals, and the new squadron should include at least two pairs of active-duty demon hunters. And it would be absolute madness to get rid of the only member of staff you've got who is capable of handling the problem personally if all else fails."

Laura had scared them. Her blunt, abrupt, awkward speech—her obvious *sincerity*—had worked. The Chair of Governors didn't actually say so, but as he laid out his compromise, it became clear that something had shifted in the whole room's perception of Walden. They had thought of her as—well, as the person she was: academic turned educator turned school management. Which was to say, not *real* management—even people who sat on boards of governors were often a little unconsciously woolly about the fact that the people running a school were effectively the C-suite of a medium-sized business enterprise—but essentially the same kind of person they all were: an educated middle-class professional, doing a normal, everyday kind of job.

But Laura was a Marshal. Marshals were not normal and everyday. The Order of Marshals was even older than Chetwood, another mediaeval survival dressed up in a twenty-first-century org chart. It had endured down the centuries since its inception by changing, and changing, and changing. There were Knights Mareschal in Robin Hood stories, or projected backwards in time into legends about King Arthur. They had hunted demons first as mendicant monastics, then as organised thugs. They had been enforcers for the Church in the days when demonic exorcism was the job of the village priest and God help him if he wasn't up to it. They had been a crusading knightly order in the Middle Ages, and witch-hunters in the Protestant Reformation. They had dwindled in the Enlightenment, when gentleman-wizardry was on the rise, and grown again with the Industrial Revolution, as demons discovered the joys of technology. Marshals had fought in the First World War, the first and last modern conflict where both sides had openly summoned demons onto the battlefield, pouring monsters into machine-gun emplacements and early tanks and the very first aeroplanes. There was a long strip of no-man's-land, near the site of the Battle of the Somme, where even now the boundaries between the mundane world and the demonic plane were thin, and it was a very bad idea to switch on your mobile phone.

Marshals—including the first Marshals-Distaff, female recruits— had stood with silver swords drawn on the rooftops of London during the frightening stage of the Blitz when everyone had been convinced the Nazis would crack demonic bombings any day.

There'd been quite a good BBC miniseries about it a few years ago.

These days, of course, the Order of Marshals was essentially a specialist branch of the police, funded by council tax, plagued with all the usual problems of a modern UK police force: understaffing, bureaucratic complexity, organisational inertia. But Laura Kenning was a Chief Marshal. Though hardly anyone actually paid attention to the Order's traditional internal ranks, Walden guessed she could probably tack something like KMC—Knight Mareschal Capus— onto her name, if she wanted to. She was slightly too young to get KMCD, for 'Distaff.' The Order had taken an amazingly long time to admit that having a separate set of ranks for female Marshals made no sense, but they'd caved at last in about 2006.

When a tough and beautiful person wearing rune-inscribed armguards and a silver sword stood in front of you, very visibly the inheritor of nearly a millennium of demon-hunting hero-tales, it was quite hard to shove her back into the place where some part of the Chair of Governors clearly *wanted* to shove someone with no university degree and an Essex accent. Laura too clearly knew what she was talking about. She looked like a hero, even while she insisted that she had been the key point of failure. If she said Walden was an astoundingly capable magician and the person Chetwood needed, it was hard to disbelieve her.

"The students in question must, of course, face appropriate consequences for a very serious error of judgement," the Chair said, "but I would not dream of interfering with the school's processes, David, when it comes to what those consequences should be. The safety of the school community is paramount, naturally. The governors are sure you will consider the best interest of all the children under your care."

Walden murmured agreement, as did David in the Headmaster's

seat. The Chair was quite right, after all. A little patronising, but quite right. And what he was really saying was that they had *won*, won what they had been fighting for all through the investigation process: another chance for Nikki and Mathias. Walden had not been expelled from Chetwood for bringing Old Faithful down on top of herself as a teenager—and she probably should have been, because she had done it on purpose, and someone had died. But then, teenage Saffy's parents had been alumni and donors. Charlie had taken the blame: conveniently dead, with no one to speak for him, another young person from a troubled background.

And so Walden was not immediately losing her job. She was, despite everything, a little surprised by that.

"Chief Marshal Kenning," said the Chair, "we have considered your assessment as well. As the Marshal on the spot—and as a key stakeholder in the school's magical security arrangements—we felt we had to take you very seriously. We have also spoken to the Marshals' District Commander for Buckinghamshire about this matter."

Ah, thought Walden, before he said it. She caught David's eye and saw that he already knew. She felt awful. It was Laura who was losing her job. In front of a roomful of people, no less. That was a nasty way to do it. But you did not become a fantastically successful hedge fund manager—which was what the Chair was, when he was not generously donating his time to the school—without an edge of ruthlessness in you. *Someone* had to take the fall for what had happened, and Laura, with her blunt and honest review of her own mistakes, had volunteered. With the Chief Marshal gone, the school could put out a statement: *immediate reorganisation and improvement of our magical security operations*—it wouldn't repair all the damage done by the BBC News article, but it would be a start. Walden also had an edge of ruthlessness in her. She could feel awful for Laura and at the same time appreciate that it was the neatest solution possible to Chetwood's problem. It was one of only two solutions, in fact, that avoided the practical consequences of Old Faithful's incursion coming down like a hammer on the vulnerable children in the middle of the disaster. From the governors' point of view, either Walden or Laura had to go. They must have been discussing it before they invited her in. David had hired Walden himself, and liked her; that would have tipped the balance.

Laura took it on the chin. Walden saw that she'd been expecting it. Perhaps the District Commander for Buckinghamshire had warned her. She got out some dignified platitudes: *it's been a privilege* and *grateful for the opportunity*. Then the Chair dismissed her, and she left fast.

"All right, moving on. Dr Walden, please take a seat," said the Chair. "Obviously, our next concern is the future development of Chetwood's magical security operation. We have talked extensively with the Order, but we felt there were concerns about their suggested approach."

Walden took the offered seat. She was no longer on trial. "I have my disagreements with the Order's theoretical approach," she said, "but they are generally fairly good at what they do. What kind of concerns?"

The governors exchanged looks. "To put it bluntly," said a woman sitting near the end of the long refectory table, "they're quite old-fashioned. Their idea of a plan is just to throw more warm bodies at the problem. Nothing but respect for the organisation, of course, but having a bunch of Marshals hanging around the school doesn't seem to have actually achieved much in a crisis. As David has pointed out, it was your skills, as a fully trained academic magician, that made the difference. So we were hoping to achieve something a little more *agile*—"

—*and a little less expensive?* Walden thought. But she was now at the bottom of this room's hierarchy, and so she did not say it. Besides, she'd been in the Ops meetings, she knew enough about Chetwood's finances. The governors were right. Laura's suggestion—doubling the Marshal squadron that the school paid for, bringing in the crack frontliners of the Order, the active-duty demon hunters—Knights Mareschal Venitant—would be wildly expensive, and unsustainable. Especially if eleven-plus entry was down.

"We have decided to bring in a magical security consultant," said the Chair. "Say hello, Mark."

Walden's hackles immediately rose. 'Consultant,' what did that mean? Magical security was *her* job. It looked like they'd planned a replacement for her, not for Laura. David gave her a warning glance. It was clear he'd used plenty of his own capital with the governors, fighting to save her career. She'd said so many times to him that Chief Marshal Kenning was obstructive and unhelpful. That had probably fed into his decision to back the governors getting rid of the Marshal now. Office politics—don't think about it! Who was *Mark?*

The man at the far end of the table gave a charming, faintly embarrassed smile and a little wave. He had been introduced at the start of the meeting as a representative of the school's 'wider community,' a phrase so vague it could mean absolutely anything. His expression now seemed to say: *Sorry about that, bit of light skulduggery!* He was a white man with conservatively cut curly hair, a slight tan of the just-got-back-from-Provence variety, and the faintly ageless look of a person who had always been good-looking and was now committed to maintaining it. Walden guessed he was in his forties, but equally he could have been mid-thirties and outdoorsy, or mid-fifties with some light plastic surgery. He was wearing a very good suit, with a shirt open at the collar. No tie, no wedding ring.

Walden had an unaccountable sense of familiarity. Her field was not huge. Had she met him before?

"Mr Mark Daubery, Dr Sapphire Walden," said the Chair. "Mark is an expert on magical security in general and demonic issues in particular. He's worked for the highest levels of the government, and we are very fortunate to be able to call on his expertise at Chetwood. He's going to do a full review of the school's magical position. He's also going to take over Chief Marshal Kenning's role as active security lead, until the end of this academic year. So you'll be working closely together."

Daubery. Well, that explained it. And it also gave Walden a better guess at his age: he had to be an alumnus, but she had no memory of ever meeting him, so he was at least half a decade older than she was. She gave Will's uncle, a magician who did 'military stuff,' a friendly and professional smile. There was no way to avoid having him imposed on her, that was obvious. And there was no need to assume the worst. But she did not like that she had never met him before. She did not like that he was a consultant, outside the school hierarchy; it was clear that she was not supposed to be able to tell him what to do, nor even to go over his head to David.

On top of that, knowing perfectly well that it might be unfair, she was immediately suspicious of the charming smile and good suit. Will as a schoolboy you could tell off for his nonsense was bearable, and even quite funny. Will as an adult colleague presented a range of unpleasant possibilities, including but not limited to 'incompetent bullshitter' and 'absolute bastard.' No sensible woman over the age of twenty-five felt anything but dubious in the face of a smiling posh chap with good cheekbones.

Mark Daubery's smile was easy, but his eyes were cool and assessing. "The famous Dr Walden!" he said. "William talked about you right through Christmas dinner last year. It's a pleasure."

chapter thirteen

RED LION

THE MARSHAL BARRACKS WAS A SMALL HOUSE on the edge of the school site: two storeys, four bedrooms spread over both floors, a communal kitchen and living room, shared bathroom, peeling magnolia paint. *This could use some smartening up,* Walden thought as she let herself in that evening.

Keeping the school site pleasant and attractive was a roll-the-boulder-up-the-hill task. The grounds and maintenance team that Todd commanded obviously had to prioritise the areas that the students used. No matter how many tidy-up initiatives or environmental awareness days or stern school assemblies you arranged, it was impossible to prevent a large group of teenagers from being, essentially, a mindless hurricane of destruction. They stood on desks and plastic chairs and broke them; they were ungentle with the blinds and broke those; they leaned the wrong way against some ancient piece of plasterwork and broke that too. They made paper aeroplanes and used wind spells to fly them everywhere, and then never got around to collecting them up again. They lost pencil cases and schoolbooks and PE kits. They ate crisps and forgot to put the packets in the bin, they ate apples and chucked cores into bushes. They unbent paper clips and tried to scratch their names into the ancient wood and stone of the school chapel, joining a tradition of bored adolescent vandalism that stretched back six hundred years. Walden's own initials, interlocked with Charlie's, were etched secretly somewhere under a pew in there.

The site needed constant development as well. The school buildings were mostly not fit for purpose. Everything was either in need of restoration or in need of a complete rethink. There was always scaffolding somewhere. At the moment it fenced Scrubs, which in the 1960s had been a gloriously modern testament to the power of concrete, and now, more than half a century later, was a depressing lesson about the long-term viability of concrete. Scrubs was not even the biggest problem. Looming five years in the future was the dreadful spectre of the chapel roof. You could not just leave a beautiful, much-loved, constantly used example of fourteenth-century religious architecture to collapse in on itself—especially not when it was listed! But there were only a dozen people in the country with the skills to work on that roof, and they all got booked up years in advance and cost an absolute fortune. The Bursary was already working on building up a fund for it, but sooner or later it was going to come down to another alumni donation drive.

Understandable, then, that the Marshal barracks had fallen off the school development radar. But Laura was in her thirties, and most of her squad were older. Not all of them lived here, of course. A couple had families—there was one who lived in the village, and one who commuted from the nearest town. Still, Walden found it dissatisfying, knowing how very nice her own school-provided lodgings were, to see that Chetwood's magical security team were living in accommodation that looked like a second-rate undergraduate rental. It could not have helped with that 'historical culture of carelessness'

Laura had talked about either. If you did not feel like your job took you seriously, why would you ever take your job seriously?

At the very least, all of this needed repainting. And not in magnolia either, even if it was cheap.

Laura had a ground-floor room with a plaque on the door: CHIEF MARSHAL. Walden knocked. "Come in!" she heard.

The room was already half stripped. Laura was packing her life at Chetwood into two big suitcases. She wore a black tank top and faded old jeans. Her silver sword was hung on a bracket on the wall, with her armguards next to it. "Good evening," Walden said. "Sorry to interrupt."

Laura said, "Was that meant to be 'Good evening, Marshal Kenning, I'm here for an informal valedictory interview,' or 'Hi, Laura, I don't have normal conversations very often'?"

Walden snorted. "The second one."

"Hi, Saffy," said Laura. "Come in. Do you want a glass of water or anything?"

"We *are* going to do the valedictory interview," Walden said. "You gave the outlines of your assessment today, but I want—"

"A full review. I'll email. I wrote it all down earlier this week. And the consultant guy already spoke to me." Laura paused, as if she had something else to say about Mark Daubery, but she did not say it. Walden could guess.

There was a moment or two of rather awkward silence.

"Are you all right?" Walden asked.

"I was expecting it," said Laura, which wasn't an answer.

"You did your best," Walden said. "You did absolutely everything you could. You certainly saved my life, when you came back into the incursion for me. I don't want you to go away thinking you failed here."

"Saffy," said Laura, "I'm not in the mood."

"I apologise," Walden said. "I'm afraid I don't have normal conversations very often."

Laura turned and looked right at her for the first time since Walden had entered the room. "This is depressing," she said. "I promise I don't want a shoulder to cry on. I'm not really a crier. But look, it's half term. The kids aren't around to see us, and I could really use a beer. Pub?"

"Honestly, it was you or me," Laura said later. "We both know it."

She was into her second pint, while Walden was nursing a rather expensive gin cocktail. They were splitting a bowl of pork crackling as they relaxed in a booth in the corner of the Red Lion. They weren't the only customers, but it was close: the Lion had traditional trappings, but it was really a quiet country gastropub now, the sort of place that served pork crackling in locally sourced artisanal crockery. It had been a long time since this slightly wonky building was the actual social heart of Chetwood village.

"No regulars," Laura said. "I don't trust a pub with no regulars."

"Much too expensive to have regulars," said Walden. "But they do better in term time—laying in cases and cases of Bacardi Breezers for Year Thirteen on Saturdays. We do ask them to be strict about checking IDs and cutting people off."

"They would be anyway," Laura said. "Nothing but a mob of tipsy eighteen-year-olds, alongside the people who can afford houses around here—what a crowd!"

"It was you or me," said Walden, "but I'm still sorry it was you."

Laura's shoulders in her green puffer jacket sagged a little. She sighed. She took another mouthful of her lager. "Had to be me," she said. "Chetwood needs you more. You've got an absolute helljob coming up, I hope you realise. Of course you realise. Old

Faithful was scaring off everything else that might want to snack on a teenage magician. There's a lot of everything else out there and it's all going to come for you at once." She laughed, rather grimly. "Worst-case scenario, you haven't seen the last of me. The DC's over the moon. I was throwing myself away on school security, you know. Everyone told me."

"You're—"

"Back to fieldwork. It's what I'm really good at. It always was."

"What is your rank in the Order, exactly?"

"KMVC," said Laura. "That's right, four whole letters— Knight Mareschal Venitant Capus. They might take the C off me for a bit, as a slap on the wrist. Makes us look bad when there's an incursion right under our noses."

"You couldn't have prevented what Old Faithful did," Walden said.

"You think you could?"

Walden said nothing.

"No, you couldn't," Laura said. "It was coming. If not Nikki Conway, it would have been someone else. That demon was after *you*. It was huge and hungry and smart enough to keep quiet when a Marshal might be looking. I had no fucking idea what we were dealing with until the week before it hit. I should have known. It was my job to know. But that means it was planning an incursion all along. It was waiting for the right chance. You think it wouldn't have found a vulnerability somewhere? Six hundred kids, you think none of them would ever have listened to it?"

"I don't think I should be crying on *your* shoulder," Walden said.

"You're right, you're right. I admit that you're right."

They were quiet for a little while. The gin cocktail, although appallingly pricey, was actually rather good.

"So," said Laura at last. "About that date."

"Er," said Walden.

Laura caught her eye. "We really don't have to be awkward about this, you know."

"I just . . ."

I was punch-drunk on survival and exhaustion, and you had both kissed me and saved my life, and the children were safe when I really didn't think they would be, Laura, I really didn't, and—well—

Laura said, "It was two in the morning and we were out of our minds with relief. I'm about to be reassigned to a London chapter house. We could give it a go long distance, if you want."

"Well," Walden said.

"That's what I thought," said Laura. She gave Walden an awkward smile, and it seemed to be sincere. "Honestly, Saffy, you don't have to explain it to me. I'm a career girl too."

"I just don't know when I'd have *time*," said Walden. "And . . . I'm thirty-eight. There comes a point, when you're single and unattached and closing in on forty, that you do stop to ask yourself: 'Well, am I going to?' And for some people—certainly, for me—the answer is 'Actually, I like my life the way it is.' I know who I am. I'm rather good at being who I am. I won't say I don't miss sex occasionally, or never think that it would be nice to wake up with someone. But I also think it's rather nice to have my space to myself, and never have to worry about anyone's time but my own. Long distance would mean carving out—"

"—hours of the day, all your free time, all those train journeys," Laura said, "and phone calls or Zoom calls or *emails*—"

"God forbid, not more emails!"

Laura laughed. "Just one more thing to plan."

"I'm not saying it couldn't be worth it," Walden said. "Of

course these things often turn out to be worth it in the long run, for lots of people. Just . . . not me. Though I truly would have liked that date, I think."

"So would I," Laura said. "Let's say this one counts. I'll even walk you home."

"We live in the same place."

"No, we don't," said Laura. "You live in a cushy Victorian suite. I live in a magnolia box with a shared bathroom."

"There has to be some money in the estates budget to do up the Marshal barracks," Walden said. "It matters."

"I agree," said Laura. "It's one of the recommendations in my report."

Walden finished her gin cocktail and did not order another. The Red Lion had a low front door and a wonky step. "Can't they fix that?" Laura said, as they emerged slightly uncomfortably into the darkened pub car park.

"Original feature," said Walden. "Historical charm, you know."

"I always feel charmed when I fall down the stairs."

"It's very authentic," said Walden. "People have been doing it for centuries."

Laura snorted. "That's just Chetwood all over, isn't it?" she said as they struck out for the country lane that led back from the village towards the school gates. "Like living in a theme park. Acres of countryside—weird little chapel—teachers in fancy dress for assembly—tennis courts, rowing lake, a school *golf course* for crissakes—and when you visit, once a term, you can take your kids out to lunch in a pub with shitty beer where they charge you extra to hit your head on the doorframe."

"You won't miss it?" Walden said. She felt obscurely hurt. Yes,

Chetwood was, honestly, a bit silly. She thought of the school's silliness, its traditions and its poses and its absurd antique formalities, as the same species of fun and games as the annual house point competition. Laura sounded so annoyed.

"Oh—I don't know," Laura said. It was a full-moon night, and the moonlight slid across her fair hair and made fantastical spiked shadows out of the hedgerows that lined the lane. "It's very pretty. Have you ever taught in a real school?"

"Chetwood is a real school."

"You know what I mean."

"Real enough to the pupils," said Walden sharply. "Real enough to Nikki Conway, for example. If you mean, have I taught in a state comprehensive: no. There aren't many jobs for people like me in the state system."

"Because learning magic is only for people who can afford the school fees," said Laura.

"Take it up with the Department for Education," Walden said. "The only government work I was ever offered, I turned down. And Chetwood is genuinely very committed to its scholarship programme for young sorcerers, you know. I *do* think it makes a difference. Oh— why are we squabbling about this? It's not a perfect system. I agree. I'm only a schoolteacher. I like my job. I can't fix the world."

Laura gave her a glance and a one-shouldered shrug. "Okay."

"Okay?"

"Would you send your children here?"

"I've never wanted children. All right, the hypothetical. Yes, I suppose I would. It's a good school. The magical education it offers is one of the best in the country. Yes, I think I would."

"Could you afford it?"

Walden considered. "Presumably, if I have children, then I also have a partner. So . . . with the staff discount . . . yes. Probably."

"Mmm," Laura said.

"Wonderful date chat, thank you," Walden said.

Laura laughed. "Sorry. You keep it bottled up, I suppose. I've been here four years. Nice place to work, pay's good, colleagues all right—one absolute bitch who thinks she's my boss, you know, but nowhere's perfect—"

Now Walden was laughing.

"—but I don't know, you walk in somewhere like this and you think, 'Fucking hell, this exists? This is real? All these kids, do they think it's *normal*, living in a picture postcard?' Little bit of bitterness, maybe. 'Why didn't I have this?' And the answer is I didn't have the sense to be born to parents with more money than God. Not your fault."

"Not more money than *God*," said Walden.

"School fees are there in black-and-white on the website. Fifty grand a year, not counting, what, uniform, sports kit, events, extras, the annual *ski trip*—"

"Yes, yes," said Walden, "but the Church is one of the largest landowners in the country. I promise you, God has a lot more money than Chetwood." Trying to be delicate about it, she asked, "So is that why you joined the Marshals? To learn magic?"

Laura laughed. "I joined the Marshals because I was eighteen, it pays all right, and I thought it might impress girls. Then I turned out to be good at it. I wasn't tragically longing for boarding school the whole time, promise. Once I'm over the sting, most of me will be glad to get out of here."

"You really won't miss anything about it?" Walden was embarrassed as soon as she'd spoken. What was she doing? Was there anything more pathetic than fishing for compliments?

Luckily, Laura didn't even seem to notice. "I will and I won't," she said. "How the other half live. Nice kids, as well. In justice you'd want them all to be absolute wankers, but they're mostly just kids."

"A few wankers, perhaps," said Walden demurely, not letting herself feel disappointment. Really, what had she expected? *I'll miss you, Saffy?* They didn't have that kind of . . . well. They were colleagues, with an acknowledged little mutual something that wasn't going to go anywhere. That was all.

"The future Mark Dauberys of the world. Good luck with that," Laura said, as they turned through the postern gate below the magnificent stone edifice of the Chetwood Gate, past Todd's neat little house that guarded the road, up along the avenue of lime trees that marked the road through the rolling expanses of sports fields towards the heart of the school. "I'll take the demons any day."

They parted where the path for the Marshal barracks turned off—a sad little pebbled path, with no signpost. There was a brief, terrible moment where they were looking at each other and neither of them seemed to know what to do about it. The soft wash of the moonlight scolded them both for their embarrassing inability to manage anything approximating romance. Finally Laura made an awkward little gesture and leaned in, while Walden changed her mind at the last moment about going in for another cheek kiss, so that both of them tipped forward and then pulled back, bobbing hopelessly in place. Laura snorted. "This was fun," she said. "Thanks for the beer. I'd better finish packing."

"Good night," said Walden. The failed kiss lingered in the air between them: dreadful. She turned away. She did not watch Laura disappear down the pebble path. She put her hands in the pockets of her sensible coat and went home and slept in her warm, comfortable, sensible bed, and did not dwell on it.

AUTUMN II

chapter fourteen

NOVEMBER

HALF TERM WAS GONE. THE STUDENTS WERE back. Chetwood sprang to life again, empty halls filled with chatter, empty classrooms with clutter, empty dormitories with interpersonal drama. The people Walden envied least in all the school were the Heads of Year. *She took my mascara—That's my mascara!—Well I heard he said to her that she said something mean about me because so-and-so told her that I—*

And the real problems, of course, mixed up with the ordinary chaos of humans living with other humans. Pastoral work was listening, patiently, so patiently, for the signal through the noise: the bullying hidden under of layers of *He's a loner, though, isn't he,* the academic struggle underlying *I didn't let her copy me, Miss, she just took a photo when I wasn't looking*—listening, thinking, and above all watching for the truest danger sign among teenagers: the sudden change. Who has gone quiet when they used to be loud, or loud and disruptive when they used to be quiet? Who has lost weight rapidly, who has given up doing their homework, who has developed mysterious bruises and then abruptly quit the swimming squad? The underlying causes—growth spurt, new friend group with bad study habits, clumsiness and coincidence; or eating disorder, depression, peer-on-peer abuse?

It happened at Chetwood, as it happened everywhere. Parents could spend a fortune trying to future-proof their children, but no one could make them entirely safe from the present.

It was November, the start of Autumn II, the worst half term of the academic year. Eight long uninterrupted weeks until the Christmas break, waking in the dark, going to bed in the dark, spending the brief hours of sunlight trapped in offices and meeting rooms and classrooms. Now came the dreary slog through the worst parts of the curriculum. Children learned incrementally; skills took time to develop; you *had* to put the hardest stuff as late as possible in a two-year course while still leaving yourself time to revise and consolidate before the public examinations in summer. What it always came down to was a block of hell with your exam sets in late November. Over and over in the staffroom you could hear teachers saying to each other, "If we can just get through it all by mocks!" Mock examinations, in January, were worse than the actual GCSEs and A-levels, because the students had a fraction of the time to revise almost the same amount of material. Year Eleven looked frazzled, and Year Thirteen grim, as the dark times bore down on them.

Upper Sixth Invocation had to master the fourth-order practical before the mocks whether they liked it or not, as well as covering triple arrays and advanced exorcism. It was a wan, unenthusiastic group who greeted Walden in the seminar room for their first theory lesson of the half term. Mathias had his head down, meticulously drawing more ballpoint geometric patterns on the dotted inside cover of his lever arch folder. Aneeta kept fidgeting with her glasses. Nikki was not taking notes and not asking questions. She sat by the window and looked out at the grey morning as if she was hoping the classroom would disintegrate into the clouds. Will turned up late enough that Walden gave him a demerit, laughed too loudly at the atmosphere, and attempted a few jibes of banter which, unusually for him, were misjudged badly enough to cross the line from 'schoolboy nonsense' to 'actively nasty.' Just as Walden began—"Highly inappropriate, Will, I am not impressed, and that's another demerit"—Nikki turned away from the window and said explosively, "Could you maybe just not be such a *shit* all the time?"

"Wow, okay, aggressive much," began Will, and Nikki abruptly stood up, grabbed her schoolbag, and then—oh, Walden's heart went out to her—managed a tight and miserable little, "Sorry, Dr Walden, I'm just—sorry," before she gave up and fled the classroom.

"I'll go," said Aneeta at once, getting up to follow her, leaving all her things on the desk.

Walden immediately and automatically did the necessary mental calculations. Objectively, both Nikki and Aneeta could afford to miss a short section of a lesson—they were conscientious, ambitious young women, and Walden had already given out the booklet she'd written for the class on triple arrays. Both of them could probably teach themselves the theory from there. In fact, Nikki had already taught herself the theory, hadn't she? It had been a triple array, competent but simply not strong enough, that had stood at the heart of Old Faithful's incursion. So Nikki taking a moment out of the room was not an *academic* problem.

And with teenagers, as well, there was the question of dignity. No one wanted to have an emotional breakdown in front of an authority figure and a classroom of their peers. A comforting hug from a friend in the girls' toilets, and a chance to fix her makeup and gather her pride before returning to the lesson, might be exactly what Nikki needed.

Or it might not.

Walden swept briskly into the next segment of the lesson she'd planned, a formal introduction to the theoretical underpinnings of the triple array, with one eye on the clock. Five minutes. Seven. She'd meant to do some group Q-and-A to check their fundamentals before moving on to notation. Will kept glancing at the door. Ten minutes. Walden rapidly reorganised the lesson plan in her head. "All right, Will, Mathias, let's have you two on the same table. I want you to collaborate and work through this problem sheet"—after a few years teaching you were always ready with spares of everything—"revising double arrays, before we carry on with the triples."

"I think we did this one last year," said Will, looking at the first question.

"You did. I still have your marks in my mark book. Let's see if you've improved. I'm just going to check if everything's quite all right."

Provided you knew where they were, and you'd told them what they were supposed to be doing, it was acceptable in a pinch to leave sixth formers to get on with some work by themselves. If it had been a Year Seven who'd disappeared from Walden's lesson, she'd have had to email the school office to go hunting—because if you left a classroom of Year Sevens unsupervised, you had only yourself to blame when they invented a fun game of Jumping On The Desk to Touch the Ceiling, No I Don't Know Why It Broke or the ever-popular Throwing Our Shoes Out the Window, No I Don't Know Where They Landed.

Corridor empty. The nearest girls' toilets were round the corner in the Humanities block. Walden was giving herself five minutes to find Nikki and Aneeta, and if she couldn't do it in that time, she was alerting the office to do a sweep.

It took two minutes. Nikki and Aneeta were not in the girls' toilets, but Walden followed a hunch and knocked on the closed door of the disabled toilet next to it, and they were in there, curled up on the floor in the corner together like two sad kittens in smart skirts and blazers. Nikki had her head in her arms. "It's okay," Aneeta was saying, "it's going to be okay, all right? Shh, shh, you're okay."

She was such a kind, thoughtful, good-hearted young person, and she was obviously doing her very best to support her friend. But to Walden's experienced eye this looked like it was above a fellow teenager's pay grade. *Eye level,* she thought, and crouched next to them. "Nikki?"

"She's all right, Dr Walden, she just needs a moment," said Aneeta protectively.

"Nikki, can you talk to me?"

A moment went past. Nikki shook her head without lifting it from the cradle of her arms. Then she said, muffled, "Dr Walden, I'm really sorry, can I—can I go to the nurse?"

"I'll look after her," said Aneeta at once.

Problems, priorities: an A-level lesson on a key topic still in progress, Will and Mathias alone in the seminar room, Aneeta trying to take on too much responsibility, Nikki an emotional wreck on the floor of the disabled toilet. Walden was not formally on the pastoral team. She didn't even have a registration group—when would she have time? The chain of command for Nikki's current state went form tutor, head of sixth form, pastoral deputy head—which was Ebele. But every child was every adult's responsibility. "I'm going to walk you down to the nurse, Nikki," Walden said, "and then I'm going to put my head round the door of the pastoral office and let

Matron know what's going on, all right? Aneeta, if you go back to the lesson, the others will explain the revision sheet we're doing."

Early in her career, Walden had still been sensitive to awkwardness. Interactions between adults and children were so often *so* awkward. They lived in the same world as you—exactly the same world, the same corridors and classrooms, the same bells ringing out the hours of the timetable—and yet in a world that was nothing like yours at all. The difference between a schoolchild and a schoolteacher, one of Walden's mentors had once remarked, is that a teacher who finds herself miserable at school can leave.

Fourteen years, that was the length of a modern English education: Reception to Year Thirteen. Fourteen years of corridors, classrooms, bells. Fourteen years of rules and restrictions and uniform requirements. Fourteen years of being told what to do. It was not surprising that children sometimes behaved badly at school. It was not surprising that they refused to do the work, or had emotional outbursts; that they made nasty jokes, or looked at you now and then with a silent, resentful sneer. You had a great deal of power, and they had almost none. You had many choices, and they had very few. The truth was that school—especially boarding school— could be a bit like the old joke about marriage: *fine, for people who like living in institutions.*

Walden's teaching persona, her mask, was a necessary shield. It created a wall of distance between herself and the young people she taught and listened to and genuinely cared for. It let her glide untouched past jokes and sneers, and stand serene above the outbursts and the awkward moments. But eventually the mortar in the wall began to crumble. You could not maintain the same kind of distance with sixth form that you held on to with the middle school. They came back after their GCSEs out of the red uniform jumpers, wearing the smart clothes which they had chosen themselves, and you reframed them in your mind: adults, almost. Normal people. Think of yourself at sixteen, seventeen, eighteen—were you really so different now?

But oh, it was awkward. When you lost the mask, you lost the scripts that belonged to it. Walking down the corridor beside Nikki—Nikki still looking crumpled and tearstained—Walden was terribly aware, and terribly sorry, that she could think of absolutely nothing worthwhile to say.

School corridors during lesson time never lost their uncomfortably liminal quality. Passing the closed doors of busy classrooms, Walden glimpsed colleagues at work, children with their hands up or with their heads down over exercise books; but out here, just their two sets of footsteps in the hush, and the wall displays in need of touching up, and the persistent smell of floor cleaner.

The infirmary was on the ground floor of New House, opposite the sixth form common room. The front half of the room was a cross between a doctor's waiting room and an admin office. Curtains blocked off the beds in the back half. The school nurse was behind the desk packing a medical kit with spare inhalers—Walden couldn't remember which trip exactly was going out this week. She looked up when Walden and Nikki came in, gave Walden the polite greeting that her status in the school hierarchy demanded, and immediately took over looking after Nikki—sitting her down, getting her a glass of water, asking friendly, inane questions just to get her talking. She was an expert, of course, on how to deal kindly and helpfully with a child who was having a bad day. Walden felt a little sting of professional envy for the skill that she did not have. "I'm just going to pop in and see Matron—I'll let her know Nikki's here."

"Dr Walden," said Nikki, suddenly and a little too loudly. Walden paused in the doorway.

Nikki took a deep breath—gathering courage. She lifted her chin. "Dr Walden," she said, "I think I should drop."

Walden stared at her.

"Invocation, I mean," Nikki said. "I think I shouldn't—I shouldn't do the A-level actually. I'm sorry—it's not that you're not a good teacher—you're really good," as if she thought Walden might take this *personally*, as if the problem with one of Chetwood's brightest dropping one of her three A-level subjects in November of Year Thirteen was that her teacher's feelings would be hurt. "I just think—I thought really—I think I shouldn't do magic anymore. So. I thought I should tell you."

Stall, thought Walden instantly. "Nikki, I disagree with you," she said—best to start clear and firm—"but I think we should have a proper conversation about this at a better time. The process for dropping subjects"—is that you *don't*, not this late in the game— "is a whole system, and I am not the person who makes the final decision." That would be the Head and the decision was going to be 'no.' "We'll discuss it at the right time. Let me just get Matron for you before I have to rush back to the classroom."

Ebele's New House office was one of the most pleasant spaces in the school. It was in origin another intimidating wood-panelled box, but Ebele had been fierce with redecoration: antique oil paintings swapped out for student artwork, soft cushioned chairs in white around a modern coffee table, the obligatory computer desk and filing cabinets hidden in the back corner and kept impeccably clear. A pastoral deputy head was not a therapist or a doctor, not a detective or a judge, but the job involved elements of all of those. This was the room where the worst problems came, and the worst conversations took place. The phone next to the desk was where Ebele made the calls to parents, to the county council, in the worst case to the police: *I believe this child to be in immediate danger.*

Luckily, Ebele was not in a meeting. Walden could see her sitting at her desk, wearing a sunny yellow dress and chunky woollen cardigan—a performance of good cheer and matronly kindness as surely as Walden's blazer and brooch and A-line skirt were a performance of traditional status and expertise. Just because you were performing, it didn't mean it wasn't true. Walden knocked and went in. "I've just dropped off Nikki at the nurse," she said.

Ebele's smile of welcome gave way at once to concern. "How bad is it?"

"She's going to pieces," Walden said frankly. "Walked out of our first lesson, and she just asked me if she can drop the A-level. She can't."

"Oh, *Nikki*," said Ebele, with deep sympathy. "All right, I'll go and check on her. We did a lot of talking over half term, that girl and I. Not enough, perhaps."

"We're not going to let her throw her future away over this."

"Of course not," Ebele said, and Walden realised with a start that *she* was on the receiving end of the soothing pastoral voice right now. She must look shaken, or worried, or— How embarrassing. But Ebele smiled at her comfortingly. "Don't worry, Saffy. She's been through a lot. And she's a proud girl, very serious, very thoughtful, she doesn't like to make mistakes. It's perfectly normal to have some wobbles."

chapter fifteen

VAPE

WALDEN TAUGHT THE REST OF THE LESSON, ignoring the atmosphere that lingered over the other three students. She went back to the infirmary at break time, but Nikki was no longer there. The door of Ebele's office was shut. Perhaps they were still talking; or perhaps Ebele was already caught up in the next crisis. There was always another crisis.

There was always another lesson; there was always another meeting; there was always another bell ringing, and this was one of the great comforts of school. Hour to hour the majestic machinery of the timetable moved hundreds of people around the corridors and offices and classrooms. You never had time to stop and worry. You did the job to the best of your ability, which meant you did what you could and moved on. When the problem of Nikki Conway came back in front of Walden, Walden would focus on it again. Until then, she had work to do.

Five o'clock, well after sunset at this time of year: now the end of Prep, and the double bell for after-school period, when the boarding pupils were shepherded to what the timetable called Enhancement Activities and the students called, obscurely, Trimmers. The day pupils who were not signed up to clubs streamed out of the school's front gates and into the shiny cars—BMWs, Land Rovers, Teslas—of waiting parents, or waiting au pairs. Headlights blazed through the gloom. The twenty minutes it took to clear them all off the school site were some of the most tightly orchestrated of the day.

Walden, as senior staff, was on sweep duty through the sports hall's basement locker rooms. Nothing the maintenance team could do would ever change the fact that this cramped underground maze of narrow wire lockers was where every teenager in the school dumped their sweat-soaked sports kit after Games. It smelled atrocious. She discovered a pair of malingering boarders, two fourteen-year-old girls, in the back corner of one of the girls' locker rooms. She gave them a mild look. They stuttered with unconvincing innocence and fled.

Walden glanced up at the vape detector on the low basement ceiling and frowned. There were chalk marks around it. She was tired enough that she did not bother with either word or gesture. She just folded her arms and glared.

The being that emerged from the detector as a little wisp of cherry-flavoured smoke was so minuscule it barely counted as a demon at all. It was just a puff of power and intention, given life force by the system it inhabited, and bribed to keep the alarm from going off with offerings of flavoured smoke. Honestly, quite clever work by whoever had done it. It was amazing how creative teenagers could be when they'd thought of something that you really did not want them to do.

"Get gone, you," Walden said, and the imp's fragile grip on the material plane disintegrated. As the red smoke dissipated she looked around and spotted in the corner, jammed between two wire lockers, a plastic classroom chair. Someone must have dragged it down here to stand on, reach the ceiling, and draw their little summoning array.

Walden had a board pen in her skirt pocket. She could follow health and safety regulations and fetch a stepladder and a second person to watch her standing on it, or she could just get the job done.

She was tired. It was November. She dragged the chair over and stood on it. She still had to go on tiptoe to reach the detector. Eight clean, firm strokes of the board pen—it was a green one, why did she have that, she didn't even like the green ones—and the vape detector was warded. The outline of the ward shimmered, green and gold-flecked, and then settled. It would hold for a few weeks, until Walden had time to come down here and paint up something more emphatic.

"Very nice," said a voice behind her, and Walden startled and fell off the chair.

'Fell' was not the word; she stumbled, the flimsy chair went one way and she went another. The heel of one of her neat black court shoes got caught in the back of the chair. It came off her foot, and Walden went sideways. She had just enough time to think in horror, *If this ends up as a broken ankle—*

There was a gust of wind—leaf-scented, outdoorsy, a welcome relief from the foul fug of the basement—and Walden, rescued just in time by someone else's spell, landed untidily and embarrassingly, princess-style, in Mark Daubery's arms.

He grinned down at her. "You know, Sapphire," he said, "we can't keep meeting like this."

"I *beg* your pardon," said Walden.

Instant change of tack: Mark's grin went from boyishly charming to collegially good-humoured, a change as subtle as it was obviously intentional. He set her politely back on her feet and then went to one knee on the basement floor in his good suit to rescue her shoe from the corner it had fallen into. "Sorry, sorry about that, completely my fault," he said, "like the Americans say—*my bad!* Annie in the office said I'd probably find you down here at this time of day. She also said I should just put a meeting in your calendar, but I thought I'd try my luck. Everything all right?"

Walden slipped her shoe back on and straightened her blazer. "Fine, thank you," she said crisply. "Did you need me for something?"

Like it or not, she had to work with this man. The princess catch and the cheesy line were outrageous behaviour, but it wasn't a crime to be flirtatious, or outrageous; given how he looked and sounded, both of those probably worked for him as often as not. Easiest to think of him as a forty-something variant on his nephew Will: basically unmalicious, basically selfish, basically manageable. To have one's career overseen by a smiling *consultant* was perhaps not that dissimilar to finding a demon in a vape detector. Yes, it was irritating. But Walden could handle it.

"Let's walk and talk," said Mark. "Or have you got a club to run now? Year Eight rugby? Year Ten knit and natter?" Two different feints, joke-shaped but not joking: *Not a team player, are you,* he was saying, *not the motherly type either; what are you?*

"Year Thirteen Oxbridge interview prep, usually," said Walden, "but in the magical faculty we rotate it among the Heads of Department. So I have half an hour, if you'd like to meet." She smiled at him. *I'm extremely good, you wanker,* was the answer, and he returned her smile with genuine enjoyment, understanding perfectly.

Mark admired her office. "You can feel the history, can't you?" He admired her big, old-fashioned, green-leather-topped desk. He peered at the antique wall clock. "I'm surprised it's not possessed," he said. "These old magicians' clocks usually are, you know."

"It was," said Walden.

"Ah," Mark said. "Thaumic vacuum when the big one made its move?"

Oh, so he did know something. Walden supposed you could not get away with acting as a magical consultant to the government if you were a complete fake. "Thaumic vacuum, extremely rapid," she said. "Straight through two layers of defences. The major incursion wards held on in this half of the building, but the demon just went under them."

"You must have been spitting nails."

"Excuse me?"

"Well, I would be," Mark said. "I don't know, I always like these little old possessions. Imp in a clock, imp in a rotary telephone. Ghost singing Vera Lynn out of an ancient radio. We had a lot of them in the house when I was growing up. Maybe you're the zero-tolerance type, but I never saw any harm in them. Sad, losing them all at once."

"That one manifested as a demon cuckoo," Walden said. "A lot of chiming and shrieking when it got annoyed. I confess I was quite fond of it."

Mark laughed. "Not that zero-tolerance, I take it. I think we can get on, then, don't you?"

"Do you chime and shriek?"

"Only on special occasions."

Walden, annoyed, saw that he'd somehow steered the conversation round to being flirtatious again. Had she not stamped on it obviously enough the first time? He took a seat in the chair in front of the desk that Laura Kenning had always ignored, and leaned forward. The smile, the open body language, the casual confidence—Walden hadn't the slightest doubt it was all intention-ally aimed at lowering her guard, but she could still feel it working. If Laura had been this good at making herself charming, Walden might have understood her sooner. "Is there anything in particular you wanted to cover in the next half hour?" she said. "I have quite a lot to do."

"Well, let's cut to it, then," said Mark. "Dave and the governors are expecting a nice tidy report from me. I'll be having chats with as many teachers as I can—maybe some of the sixth form, too, what do you think?"

"That depends on what you're trying to achieve."

"A holistic picture of the school's readiness to handle a major incursion, likely points of failure, and an elegant, inexpensive set of evidence-based solutions—you know the guff." Walden tried not to be too obviously disgusted. Mark's grin said he knew, but what could you do, you had to talk the talk. "Come on, you're the boss on this stuff. Who do I actually need to talk to?"

"The Marshals," said Walden. "And Todd Cartwright."

"Todd the caretaker? He's still around?" Mark laughed incred-ulously. "He was here when I was a kid!"

"The Keymaster. He knows the site extremely well, and I find his perspective valuable. And, yes, teaching staff and students. I recommend speaking to a cross-section, not just the sixth form. You'll find that the GCSE years and the middle school are every bit as involved in the issue. This is a magical school."

"Was it a kid who summoned an imp into that smoke alarm you were warding?"

"Of course. I don't know who yet," said Walden. The truth was she was unlikely to find out, unless someone developed a strong enough guilty conscience or a stupid enough urge to boast. "But most likely a Year Nine or Ten."

"Sixth form all too goody-two-shoes to vape in the locker rooms?"

"Sixth form have off-site sign-out privileges," said Walden drily, "and so they go and vape in the woods on the other side of the rugby pitches."

"Tut, tut. Kids these days. We just did cigs and White Lightning."

Walden remembered, suddenly and with extraordinary clarity, the taste of the cheap cider Charlie had got hold of one half term—using his last exeat card to catch the train to Luton, flashing his unconvincing fake ID at a corner-shop clerk who almost certainly hadn't cared in the least, sneaking the big blue plastic bottles back to school and hiding them in a hollow tree stump in, yes, the glade in the bluebell woods on the far side of the school sports fields. White Lightning! It tasted like bad apple juice and adolescent stupidity. The vividness of the taste-memory was a shock. "They don't sell it anymore, you know," she said, to chase the thought away.

"What, White Lightning? Really?"

"Discontinued in 2009. Because of," she allowed herself a thin smile, "the strong association with underage drinking."

"And just like that, I'm an old man!" said Mark. "I can hear my joints creaking already. Well, listen. I'm not just here to write a report for the governors. Though I'll do that, and you can think of it as me making your life easier, because it'll get them off your back. But I'm not planning to spend all my time sitting around taking up office space. Do you do a regular planar patrol here?"

A planar patrol involved creating a temporary portal to the demonic plane and sweeping the area clear of medium-sized demons. It was a lot of power expended for, in Walden's experience, not very much useful effect. But when Mark said it she saw, irritated, that now Old Faithful was gone—and who-knows-what would be starting to move into its abandoned territory—it was probably a good idea. With any luck, it would prevent nasty surprises entirely. "Not regular, no," she said, "but I agree that it would be worthwhile to add it to our system, for the time being." Part of her was already groaning. Planar patrols could not be dumped off on junior Evocation teachers. Adding it to the system meant adding it to Walden's own overloaded plate.

"Not much of a delegator, are you?" said Mark. "I just told you I'm not here to sit on my backside. Look, is it that you don't trust me?"

A beat. "Well, I didn't hire you," said Walden.

Mark laughed. "Need to see me in action? All right. Are you free Sunday afternoon?"

chapter sixteen

THE LAKE

I T DRIZZLED ALL DAY SUNDAY, IN FITS AND STARTS. The rain had the November quality of coming at you in sideways gusts, so that no umbrella could possibly keep you completely dry. Walden passed through the student lunch hall in the Old Refectory on the way to the staff dining room and saw the abandoned heaps of soggy coats and winter hats. Teenagers huddled together for warmth over their ham-and-cheese lunch paninis. Todd was lying on his side in the corner bleeding an ancient, uncooperative radiator. Like Walden, he seldom really stopped working.

Staff lunch was also paninis: ham and cheese, just cheese if you were vegetarian, no vegan option on a Sunday. Walden picked at the salad on the side, which was six sad unseasonable leaves and half a tasteless tomato. She did have a kitchen in her flat. She really ought to cook for herself sometimes. But cooking for one was depressing, and the school meals—one of the better staff perks, this—were free.

Todd joined her at the table halfway through the meal, still in his work overalls. He ate two paninis and a large bowl of tragic salad with every sign of enjoyment, which cheered Walden up, and he complained again about the state of the boilers. Walden inquired after his great-nieces and -nephews. Todd had never married, but everyone knew he kept meticulous track of his sister's grandchildren. The oldest was in Year Five, and his parents were starting to think about secondary school. "And the Marshals had a look in at their school, and funny old thing, the lad's got a bit of the fizz," said Todd, doing an obscure hand gesture which Walden understood from context to mean 'a knack for magic.' There were degrees of innate magical ability. Sorcery, the wild uncontrollable talent which *had* to be trained or else—that was extremely rare. More common—but still not actually common—was ordinary talent: the fizz, the knack, the baseline potential which made doing magic feel easy and natural. Some children were natural athletes, and some children were natural magicians.

That one of Todd's relatives should share his prodigious untrained talent did not surprise Walden in the least. These things often ran in families. But magic was not taught in state schools—too abstract, too impractical, too old-fashioned, and too bloody expensive. So unless Todd's great-nephew turned out to be a full sorcerer after all—unlikely, if he'd reached Year Five without a manifestation—there was not going to be any state funding for his magical education. Without a place at Chetwood, or one of the handful of other private schools like it, his talent was unlikely to go anywhere.

Todd knew it as well as she did. "So I told Jennie, well, why not put him in for here, then? And she said, no, no, we couldn't afford it even if they took him, and I said I don't know about that, I've got a little bit saved up, and you never know, there's bursaries and so on . . ."

He gave Walden a worried look, as if she might tell him off for his presumption. "Why not?" said Walden encouragingly. "That's what the bursary funds are for."

She found herself thinking, as the conversation went on, of Laura Kenning's wry look in the moonlight: *Why didn't I have this?* It was the same reason that Todd had not had this, an obvious, powerful, intractable knot of money and power and history, changing too slowly for most. "Have you thought any more about adult magical studies?" she said, which Todd seemed to hear as an abrupt change of subject, although in Walden's head it was not. "The Open University offers a short course—I believe it's all online these days—"

"Now, Dr Walden, show some sense," said Todd, with lugubrious good humour. "Some of us have work to do."

After lunch, she met Mark at Reception, the secure modern box that had been flung up to ruin the façade of the main school building in the nineties. The front desk was unmanned, and the glass-paned front doors were locked. Mark's Audi pulled up, doing a rather showy turn around the wide gravel circle at the front of the school. He parked in a reserved space, jogged up to the doors, and waved at Walden through them. He'd swapped the good suit for jeans and a chunky jumper, with expensive trainers, all underneath a battered old Barbour that he almost certainly never wore in London. Walden wore the same clothes on Sunday as she did on work days, though in deference to the weather she'd put on a raincoat and wellies. She buzzed him in, and noticed as she did so that there was a little frisson of *something* inhabiting the electronic keypad that kept the door locked.

Walden frowned at it. That was the second new imp she'd

encountered in three days. Yes, you expected minor possessions at Chetwood, but not this many, and not this quickly.

"Another one?" said Mark, peering over her shoulder as she murmured a banishment over the keypad. "Oh, it's only an imp. What's the harm?"

"I thought you were a security expert," said Walden. "You don't see a problem with stray demons in the security system?"

Mark laughed it off. "Fair, fair. Well, shall we? Where do you want to start?"

"Boundary sweep and work our way in, of course," said Walden. She flipped the hood of her raincoat up. "Umbrellas are in the stand over there, if you didn't bring your own."

She'd had a little bet with herself, but she lost it. Mark did not pull out an old-fashioned black umbrella with a carved bird's-head handle from the boot of his Audi. Instead he quite happily took one of the large, cheap red umbrellas branded in white with Chetwood's latest logo. School branding was one of those things that objectively mattered—those school fees paid our salaries, those parents had *expectations*—while being completely dire to think about. The current logo was a vague shield shape and a large letter *C*, vaguely reminiscent of banks and law firms and—most importantly—other expensive boarding schools. Mark twirled the umbrella over his head, unfazed by the rain. "Show me a lamppost, I'll do you a little dance."

"No lampposts, I'm afraid. We're starting by the rugby pitches," said Walden.

"Lovely weather for it," Mark said. "This brings back memories! They used to make us play in all weathers. You'd be shivering half to death in your Games kit till the mud coating warmed you up."

"I remember," Walden said. "Hockey was more or less the

same. We have a girls' rugby team now, of course." That was an innovation of the last ten years, amazingly enough. For long decades before that the gender divisions of school sport had been as observed as dutifully as the call-and-response prayers at Evensong. Boys' winter: rugby, of course, and certainly not football. Girls' winter: netball—a sport apparently designed on the principle that basketball would be more ladylike if it was less fun—and hockey. Boys' summer: cricket. Girls' summer: tennis. The whole thing had always been comically sexist, but it had taken a concerted student protest—boys turning up to netball lessons in borrowed Games skirts, girls tramping down to the rugby pitches—before change had come at last.

"You're never telling me they've dumped hockey," Mark said.

"Of course not," said Walden. "Chetwood actually wins at hockey."

"Did you play?"

"I developed," said Walden, "as early as possible, a strong interest in netball. If you weren't A-team material, and you managed to get one of the good positions—wing defence, say—you could spend most of a Games lesson standing still and gossiping with whoever was wing attack on the other side."

The rugby pitches were a generous sweep of land lying at the foot of a gentle rise. The little hillside beyond was crowned with ancient English woodland, which in April was filled with bluebells and on a day like today was probably not filled with vaping sixth formers. There had to be enough pitches for the First through Fourth XV to play home fixtures simultaneously—Chetwood would not have been able to host games otherwise—so the fields looked simply enormous as you came up to them. The grey mist of the rowing lake beyond was mildly picturesque in a Gothic sort of way. The combination of hilly rise and lake meant that these splendid school facilities, which got photographed in summer for the prospectus as a glorious expanse of green, were in fact a gigantic marsh. Canada geese browsed here most of the year. Only meticulous attention from the grounds team stopped the pitches from becoming approximately three acres of mud every autumn.

"Where are we putting the portal?"

"On the boundary, naturally," said Walden, and set off across the grass. Her wellies went *squelch squelch* in the saturated mud underneath the green. What you wanted for a planar portal, wherever possible, was a sense of liminality: a border-place, an edge-place, somewhere where it made sense to say you were crossing from one world to another. An actual doorway was ideal—the division between mundane world and demonic plane, during Old Faithful's incursion, had been marked by the front door of School House. Mark, bedraggled despite the red umbrella, looked hopefully towards the padlocked door of the boating shed. His trainers were muddy and his jeans were not doing particularly well in the driving sideways rain. "Did you ever row?" he said. "Cox, maybe?"

"No," said Walden, thinking uncharitably *And of course he's a boatie.*

"Shame. You'd probably have liked coxing. You strike me as the type."

"You mean short and bossy?"

Mark faked contrition. "I'd say *commanding.*"

Ignoring the promise of shelter in the boating shed, she struck out for the jetty. It was cordoned off, with a NO SWIMMING sign—the open-water swimming club would probably start running again in spring—but she just stepped over the low fence. Mark said, "Ah, of course," behind her as their footsteps sounded among the patter of raindrops on old wood.

"Technically," Walden said, "Chetwood School does not own

the lake." There was even a village rowing club, with its own rather smaller shed on the far side of the grey water. "This is as far as we can go. Welcome to the boundary."

School and not-school, private and public, and most importantly land and water; *The places we belong,* Walden might have said to a class, *and the places we do not.* Magic followed logical, consistent, learnable internal rules—until it did not; until you ran into the woolly edges where everything depended on the perceptions of the magician. It annoyed some students immensely. Walden had always found it delightful: beyond all the rules and systems so carefully worked out by so many scholars over so many centuries, at the boundaries of knowledge, a space full of beautiful mystery.

Mark came and stood next to her on the jetty. To Walden's surprise, he furled the umbrella. The rain poured down on him, rapidly soaking his hair and face and beading on the shoulders of his Barbour, but he did not seem to mind. "Smell that," he said. "Clean air, clean water. Does you good."

"It's certainly fresh," Walden said.

A grin, less calculated and the more charming for it. "Bracing," said Mark, "that's the word. All right! I brought salt and chalk, but they'd be sluiced away in seconds. Be honest—do you do this to all your new hires?"

"What on earth do you mean?" said Walden, as if she didn't know.

"Better be a *serious* magician," said Mark, "if you want to impress Chetwood's Dr Walden. Yes, ma'am, right away, ma'am! Just give me a second." He joined his hands together and stretched them above his head. "You'll let me off if I don't get it perfect first time?" he said.

"Well, I—"

Mark punched a portal.

It was pure evocation, no demonic assistance involved. Walden was certain, right away, that he was in fact a specialist evoker, or had been at some point. He had the smoothness and precision of an academic magician, balanced with the confident physical self-awareness of a sportsman. The very best evokers tended to straddle the borderline between youthful athleticism and middle-aged expertise. Mark was probably just over that line. No matter how good you were, you could not sustain the same amount of magical power out of the strength of your own body forever. Mark Daubery, it seemed, had followed a common path—evocation in youth, turning to invocation as he looked down the barrel of his forties.

Evocation teachers teach PE, instantiation teachers teach design and technology, and invocation teachers teach contract law, ran a common faculty joke, *and all of us think all the others are stupid and bad at magic.*

Mark's portal was a good one. It hung shimmering in the air at the end of the old jetty, taking the form of an arched doorway with a purplish curtain of raw magic hung across it. Rain fizzed and evaporated off its glowing edges. Mark glanced at her, *Well?* and Walden had no criticism ready.

And really, wasn't it better if he was actually good? Wasn't that exactly the mistake Walden had made with Laura Kenning—assuming she was less than competent, and then letting that assumption poison their whole relationship, so that they'd barely had a chance to actually know each other before Laura was gone?

You're being increasingly unprofessional about this, Walden told herself. It was one of the harshest pieces of self-criticism she could think of. *This man is trying very hard to set up some kind of worthwhile working relationship. He has gone out of his way to acknowledge your seniority and your expertise, when the position the governors gave him meant he could simply overrule them both. Meanwhile, you are intentionally making the experience of working together as difficult and unpleasant as possible. Laura would have lost her temper by now, and you would deserve it.*

And another, softer voice, somewhere in her heart: *Admit it, Saffy, you mostly resent him because he's not Laura.*

"Very nice," she made herself say, and winced: it had come out as if she was bestowing praise on a student, which of course sounded patronising in any other context. And she did not know Mark well enough to follow up with *I'm afraid I don't have normal conversations very often.* His brows quirked in amusement, which was a better reaction than being offended. "Shall we?"

"Ladies first," said Mark.

"How old-fashioned."

"Self-interest. If something is waiting for us, you get eaten first."

"Ah. I'm glad to know where you stand."

"Safely behind you, Dr Walden."

Walden shook her head and smiled. Basically an overgrown schoolboy, she reminded herself. Basically harmless. "Very well," she said, and readied a neat gestural banishment charm—a variation on the basic one on the back of her risk assessment—before she stepped off the end of the jetty, through the portal and into the demonic plane.

On the other side: nothing.

A vast pastel nothingness, blurred and softly grey. There was no lake. The demonic plane was hostile to the physical fabric of the real world, and water could only exist here when it was safely contained and cohered within a system of selfhood—an animal, a human being. The nothingness rippled around Walden's wellies. There were no demons waiting for her. She had not really expected them. There was nothing permanent, reliable, or persistent about a large body of water, not on the level that most demons could comprehend. There was nothing there to pin a sense of self to, unless you counted individual fish. A higher demon the size of the Phoenix might be able to develop a concept of 'lake' as a whole, and so tie its territory to a whole feature of the landscape. But why would a demon that strong waste itself on such a thin hunting ground, when the school was right next door?

"It's always spooky doing this," Mark said. "No one home? Good stuff. Let's check the shed."

He trudged over formless grey towards the land-water boundary, the school boundary. Walden watched without comment as he tried to step back onto what was, in the mundane world, school grounds. The external wards flared briefly golden. Mark sprang away, swearing loudly.

"I think you forgot your staff lanyard," Walden said. "You *were* given a staff lanyard to wear on site—weren't you?"

"Bloody buggering— What?"

"I picked up a guest pass from reception, just in case." She had it in her raincoat pocket. She fished it out and tossed it over. Mark caught it handily, turned it over to see the holographic outlines of detailed spellwork on the back, and said ruefully, "Daubery fails the test."

"No, the portal was very good," Walden said.

He was still examining the pass. The spellwork was Walden's own, an original design. "This can't be doing much to keep out demons."

"There's more to school security than managing the demon problem. What you just bumped into is actually aimed at unscrupulous human beings."

"Do you get those often?"

"As with demonic incursion," Walden said, "the way to assess risk to children is to decide not how often a bad thing happens, but how serious the consequences would be if it *did* happen."

"So you're talking, what, stalking, kidnapping——"

"Honestly, when an unwelcome adult tries breaking into the school grounds, the goal is usually simple theft," said Walden. "I sometimes think the ICT suite might as well have a target painted on it. But the things you mention are among the worst-case scenarios, yes."

Mark put the guest lanyard on. "Right. Boundary walk, then?"

"Let's get going." Walden crossed the external wards——feeling the welcoming shiver of her own spellwork passing over her, assessing her for belonging, and tidily identifying her as staff——and paused to take in the transformation. From formless foggy pastel, the ground underfoot went abruptly and violently green. The greenery was not grass but the idea of grass, the memory of it, the decades and decades of mowing and rolling and raining and trampling and browsing geese and shouting children. It looked like the brushwork of some abstract painter, which made it quite unnerving to stand on. Mark whistled. "Hear that?"

The shouting: young male voices, mostly, as Walden would have expected. Blurred running figures moving in the green distance. The demonic plane here was shaped by the school. It was not quite as clearly defined as the incursion in School House; but then, School House had been the site of a student boarding house for most of the last five hundred years. "I wonder when rugby was invented," she said.

"In 1845," said Mark. "At Rugby. Rugby School, that is."

"Less than two centuries, then," Walden said. "But I suppose we have been playing a *lot* since then."

"If the history makes a difference, I'm surprised we're not hearing anything off the water," said Mark. "Rowing's an old sport. The Ancient Greeks did it."

"But the lake is on the other side of the school boundary. And water does not mix well with demons."

Mark nodded, conceding the point. "Your report on the big incursion—you saw an echo of yourself in there, you said."

"Yes?" said Walden suspiciously. "What about it?"

"Wonder if I'm out on that field somewhere," said Mark. "Seventeen forever and covered in mud."

Walden tried to imagine it, and found it surprisingly difficult. Mark's overgrown schoolboy attitude didn't make him an *actual* schoolboy. There was far too much sophistication and intentionality about the way he deployed the charming smile. *Not an innocent person,* she thought. *But then, who is?*

chapter seventeen

THE HUNT

BY THIS POINT WALDEN HAD ADMITTED TO HER-self that a planar patrol was a genuinely good idea. And Mark was here and he did seem competent—overconfident, occasionally, perhaps, but competent. So if the patrol needed doing regularly, he might as well be the one doing it.

They walked the school boundaries, following the lines of hedgerows and ancient walls, and then spiralled in, sweeping through the site. It was impossible not to comment on what they saw. Everything on the original school grounds, on this side of the road, was dense and solid with the buildup of centuries of magic. From the outside, the school chapel was practically identical in the demonic plane to its mundane incarnation.

When they ducked through its great oak doors they were lashed with colour. The nave was thick with dream or memory or ghost of two hundred years of sunlight poured through dizzying stained glass. It went slipping and sliding across the flagstones in a brilliant kaleidoscope. Those dazzling windows had been smashed to fragments in the reign of Henry VIII, and light like this had not been seen here in the mundane world since.

Four demons in the chapel: one largeish imp that flew screeching overhead in the form of an eagle and then perched suspiciously in the arched ceiling and glared at them. Two fifth-order demons on either side of the sombre board of the war memorial with the long list of slaughtered alumni, posing in the shapes of gargoyles. In the vestry they found one archdemon, eighth order, roughly human in shape, faceless, gowned in something scarlet that oozed. That one was reasonably challenging to banish. Mark did the busywork of keeping it distracted while Walden drew an array to anchor her spell. It was harder to focus than it should have been. She was right-handed, and her right arm itched, from the wrist to the shoulder, the whole time the archdemon was there. Under her skin, something with coiling feathers was flexing and shifting, trying to come awake. To hunt.

Your assistance is not required, Walden thought firmly.

She nearly dropped her chalk when the Phoenix answered. They had been together for more than a decade and it had never spoken to her. Its voice in her head was a raptor's cry, the slash of talons. *Let me loose, let me strike,* it meant. *My prey is here; I am strong and fierce and hungry; let me fly!*

"All right there?" called Mark from where he was wrestling the archdemon. "Don't let me rush you—it's only a skinner!"

"You're fine," answered Walden, shaking off the hunter's song in her thoughts, gripping her chalk more firmly and returning to the detailed outlines of her array on the chapel wall. The stone here was as ancient and almost as solid as its mundane original. "I'll be right with you."

"Hopefully before it turns me inside out!" Mark called, but he was barely out of breath, and after patrolling with him for most of an hour, Walden did not actually think he was in trouble. He was no Laura Kenning—his spells did not have the speed or brusqueness of Marshal combat magic—but he was fine.

Banishment achieved; the skinner demon gathered its oozing scarlet cloak about it and tried to dash away. To Walden's surprise, Mark killed it with another evocation spell: an explosive lob of percussive force, expanding inside the demon's being into edged shards that sliced its selfhood apart. The skinner howled as it fell to pieces. Violet-edged wild magic surged through the chapel, and the dizzying kaleidoscope light from the long-vanished stained glass grew momentarily brighter.

"What was the point of that?" said Walden.

"One less demon," Mark said. "Obviously."

"All you've done is create more loose magic to attract others—" And as Walden said this, she realised why she was seeing so many imps around school lately. Old Faithful's disintegration, like the carcass of a whale descending through the depths, hadn't just created a void for a new apex predator. It had also summoned a whole ecosystem of lesser magical scavengers. "Well. Never mind."

"Come on, no one likes skinners."

The thought of a skinner demon lurking in the school's magical shadow, as eager to strip the flesh and bones of a child as an adult, was certainly upsetting. "True. Shall we carry on?"

"Sure you're all right to keep going? That last array seemed to take a bit longer than usual."

Walden had no intention of discussing the Phoenix with Mark Daubery. She had not discussed it with anyone for many years, and there was no reason why that should change. She had already added an item to her mental to-do list: *double-check all Phoenix spellwork.* Just in case. It was odd that the demon should try to speak to her. It never had before; not even when she first summoned it as the culmination of her doctoral research. It had lived reified on her arm and barely even stirred in the many years since then. But the encounter with Old Faithful had clearly set off *some* reaction, and she urgently needed to understand it better.

None of that was Mark's business. "Absolutely fine, thank you," she said. "Let's continue."

Mark watched her, she thought, as they worked their way around the rest of the school. The ribbon of tarmac that was the main road separating the two halves of the school site manifested in the demonic plane as a grey riverine space, blurred and painfully empty. On the other side, after an initial boundary walk, they checked the school coach park. The humped forms of minibuses loomed through magical mist like a collection of ancient monoliths. Walden insisted on checking each one separately, and then sweeping the whole coach park in depth. A combustion engine was a terrible temptation to a demon, and few possessions were more potentially threatening to human life than the selfhood, power and completeness inherent in a vehicle.

Nothing. Not even an imp. "All right, that just leaves Scrubs and the Bursary building," Walden said. "And the sports hall, of course."

"It'll be pitch dark by the time we get back," said Mark. "At least we're not getting rained on."

"Where's your umbrella?"

"Do you know, I've got no idea. Must have left it somewhere."

Walden suppressed a sigh. "Well, let's—"

The shriek in her thoughts was raptor-scream, demon-howl, a flash of lightning across her vision. Her arm burned. Walden shouted in pain. The Phoenix cried, *Turn!*

Walden turned, just in time. Her hands were moving before

her thoughts did, so that as she lifted them a shining pale shield of magical force broke from her fingertips and pushed the attacker away. Mark was yelling something, but she could not hear it over the Phoenix's clamour in her head. *What am I looking at?* she made herself think; *Hush, you, let me work through it!*

Let me hunt it, let me kill it, let me, let me, let me, I shall hunt and kill and feed, I am hungry, I am made of hunger—

"You," said Walden, summoning all her professional authority, "shall wait to speak until it's *your turn*. Thank you."

The Phoenix subsided, muttering to itself. Walden's shield shimmered and glowed as the coach park demon flung itself against the barrier. It was gigantic—physically gigantic, manifested in enormous blocky shapes, vaguely bipedal with a broad snout, angular thighs and calves, strangely regular curves adorning its massive torso. Seventh- or eighth-order archdemon, but that was not a demon's natural shape, that was—

"It's a bloody bus!" yelled Mark from where he crouched on the other side of the monster, projecting his own magical shield. Walden frowned. That shield was flickering and unsteady.

"Are you all right?" she called across the demon's aggressive, clanking bellows.

"It got me in the arm!"

And he was an evoker by training and inclination. Physical injury would slow him down. He sounded afraid. Walden looked again at the demon. Yes, it was a school minibus, or rather, that was the form which was defining it right now. The curved decorations on its metallic torso were wheels. The smooth, blockish shapes of its arms and legs were the panels of a chassis, and its snout and glassy eyes were the minibus's bonnet and windscreen. The school logo, red and white, was plastered along its arms and legs.

Kill kill kill kill kill, said the Phoenix eagerly.

"Put your hand up when you want to contribute," muttered Walden, and then had to resist the sudden strong urge to raise her own right arm. "And *when it's appropriate*," she added. Her fellow traveller subsided again, sulking.

The minibus demon was big and heavy-looking, but slow. It was certainly nowhere near as powerful or as clever as Old Faithful. Its best idea seemed to be to batter its huge form against Walden's pale shield and hope that would wear her down. It hadn't thought of turning around and going for Mark, who was probably an easier target right now. And, of course, it did not have the advantage of actually possessing two and a half tons of steel and aluminium. Here on the demonic plane, the minibus was only an idea, a potential self, a shape for a demon to dream about.

The fact that it had latched onto the idea was a bad sign, because it meant this demon was on the way to a possession. It needed only a brief surge of wild magic to slip through a temporary weakness in the fabric of reality and establish itself in the mundane shell it had chosen. Imps in photocopiers and security systems and vape alarms were nothing compared to the danger represented by an archdemon in a school bus. Possessed vehicles did not respond to the undignified demands of a steering wheel, and no demon in history had ever acquired a driving licence.

Bang, bang, clank: every time the minibus demon flung itself against Walden's shield, there was a ringing clash of imaginary metal. Walden narrowed her eyes, trying to concentrate. She just needed an opening.

Slow! snapped the Phoenix, sounding as frustrated with Walden as Walden herself would have been with a very dim Year Eight. She felt a surge of firm agreement at the back of her skull. The Phoenix thought her an embarrassingly bad hunter with a dreadful eye for weakness. In fact, it informed her: *Stupid!*

"You don't get anyone to improve that way, you know," Walden muttered. The minibus demon roared, a sound with the rumble of shifting gears and growing acceleration buried in it. Walden needed to destabilise its link to the vehicle. It would have helped if she was more of a driver. The whole of Chetwood village was walkable, and yes, all right, she didn't really leave the school site very much, she was far too busy. It was an easy shot down to London on the train, but she always just felt guilty that she wasn't going to see her parents instead; and they were all the way down in Sussex, rather more of a trip and you had to deal with the faff of Victoria Station. It just seemed simpler, really, never to go anywhere—anyway, how exactly did you inconvenience a minibus? Reduced fuel? Flat tyre?

The archdemon swiped at her with a steel paw. Mark seemed to have gone useless in the crisis. Maybe his injury was serious— where had he gone, Walden couldn't see him anywhere—"Mark?" she called, and got no answer.

How, said the Phoenix abruptly in the back of her skull.

"I beg your pardon?" said Walden. It was not exactly easy to carry on a conversation with one demon while feeding power back to her shields to hold off the brutal attacks of another.

How—the thing. The thing you do. How.

It took Walden a moment. "How do you get someone to *improve*?"

The answer was not words but a surge of fiery emotion. The Phoenix gave Walden to understand that either *she* was going to get better at the extremely straightforward business of defending her territory from lower-order pests, right now, or it would burst its bonds and handle the business personally.

"Good grief," Walden said, trying not to be terrified. "Well, to begin with, students almost never respond well to *insults* and *threats*. Calm down."

Say how!!!

A howl over Walden's head. The minibus demon was starting to look worryingly solid, much more so than the other misty humps of silent buses occupying the demonic plane's echo of the school coach park. It brought its red-and-white fists together and hammered them down on the magical shield directly above Walden's head. A shower of bright sparks flew off in all directions, and she smelled burning rubber. She had to get the Phoenix under control before she could deal with this. And then she was going to have to take the day out tomorrow—oh, the cover manager would be very annoyed having that dumped on her first thing Monday morning—and go over her leashing spellwork with a fine-tooth comb.

For now it just needed to be placated. With, apparently, a potted summary of the first three weeks of teacher training. "Students respond best to structure and clarity," Walden said, dragging what had long since become professional instinct out of the back of her memories. "Break large tasks into smaller ones, and model the steps along the way. Control the environment, maintain a sense of purpose, provide space to fail safely; then, of course, provide clear, encouraging, and actionable feedback—"

The attacking archdemon backed off and flung itself flat on the ground. Parts of its steel frame shifted around. Before Walden's horrified gaze, the huge tyres that had been decorating its torso moved back to their proper places. The shape of a school minibus rose like an animal gathering itself to spring. The grumble of the engine deepened. It was going to charge her. And yes, this was the demonic plane, there was no physical vehicle there, but there was still an *archdemon* about to accelerate into Walden's shields at the best part of eighty miles an hour—

Model, said the Phoenix in Walden's head, and it took control of her hands.

It could not hide its profound impatience as it went slowly through what it felt were a perfectly obvious set of steps. *Connect*: this was Walden's territory, her place, where she belonged and where she controlled the boundaries. The spellwork on the back of her staff pass shimmered, and at the same moment she felt an answering shimmer on every other lanyard on the school site: Mark's where he was crouched and breathing hard next to the misty shimmer of another minibus, Todd's as he chugged down the drive on the green gardeners' quadbike with a trailer full of bagged-up compost behind him, Lilly Tibbett on duty in Scrubs chatting with a Year Nine and shivering a little in the November chill, all the other teachers and assistants and cleaners and gardeners and kitchen staff and Annie in the office who really didn't need to be in on a Sunday but she'd thought she'd just drop by and get a couple of things finished off . . .

Walden's school. Her people. A deep well of magical potential.

You forgot the children, the Phoenix said, reaching with its power for the huddled teenagers in the dining hall, the Sunday clubs running in different classrooms and common rooms—all indoors today, thanks to the rain—and the rebellious handful of unsociable young people curled up in dormitories, watching videos on their phones or scrolling social media or playing games; even, in a few rare instances, actually studying. Walden blocked the greedy grasp of the Phoenix's reach at once, and answered silently: *Certainly not; when was the last time you completed child protection training?*

Besides, it was done. A school was far more than its children. The institution, the rock-solid centuries-old stability of it, rested in the adults who kept it going; and Walden was connected, she had made her claim. The archdemon on the point of hurling itself at her at motorway speed hesitated, feeling the shadow of a larger and more dangerous predator dominating this space. *What now?*

Display, the Phoenix said, demonstrating a not-very-complex piece of evocation, a simple shower of light and noise—but then it didn't need to be complex; any kind of organised spellwork was impressive to a mere archdemon, and light and noise might be ordinary in the mundane world but they were spectacular rarities in the demonic plane. The pests invading Walden's territory were aware of their strength, aware too of their weakness. They took few risks. They were not hard to dissuade. A human thief looking for computer equipment was not rolling the dice on life and death, but an archdemon who lost a fight might lose all the pieces of self it had meticulously gathered over years or decades or centuries of struggle.

Struggle was not Walden's thought. That was the Phoenix. *What do you mean?* Walden asked, and received no answer. Instead, her demonic passenger bared her teeth at the stalling form of the minibus and said, *Now you make a way out.*

Banishment, it meant, but banishment turned inside out from how Walden had always conceived it. She had thought of banishing a demon as thrusting it *away.* The Phoenix saw it from the opposite perspective, through the eyes of a being that had been defeated, banished, in its long history, more than once—*How old are you?* Walden wanted to ask suddenly. But she could tell it was not the time to interrupt. After all, this was a lesson.

Banishment, to the Phoenix, was building an escape route and pointing to it. Nothing that lived wanted to be trapped in an unwinnable fight. No one wanted to die. The Phoenix cast no spell. It did not even think of an array. It only lifted Walden's right arm—her fingernails were glowing gold—and pointed; and where it pointed, a dark road seemed to appear in the fabric of the demonic plane, an obvious and unmistakeable path out of Walden's—the Phoenix's—solidly claimed territory.

Go, it said to the monstrous, deadly shape of the red-and-white minibus creature. Walden thought the words were more for her benefit than for the archdemon's; it understood the Phoenix on a different and deeper level, the way a fox understood the cry of the hounds. *No way to go on here. Turn back, try another life, be something else.*

Before Walden's eyes, the archdemon shrank. The steel-and-aluminium shape it longed to wear disintegrated into red mist. Underneath was something smaller, and more afraid, and—she could already tell—an order of magnitude less powerful. A sixth-order demon at most. The Phoenix turned Walden's hand over and held it palm out. The gesture was not a command, but a magnanimous offer of mercy. The former archdemon fled along the dark road laid out by the Phoenix's banishment, and Walden could already tell it would not be back.

And now we eat, the Phoenix finished—the final step of the lesson. The magic-siphoning spells on Walden's other arm prickled briefly with heat. The ruddy mist left behind by the archdemon's diminution faded, and she felt the warmth of new power settle into her bones.

It was over. Walden lowered her arm, rather shaken. The golden glow was already fading from her fingernails as the Phoenix resettled itself, sated.

"Mark?" she called. "Are you all right?"

"Over here!"

Mark had shielded himself, but the shield flickered out of existence as Walden got close. He'd peeled off his Barbour and there was a nasty, bloody gash through the expensive wool of his chunky jumper. His jaw was clenched tight with pain. "Oh my goodness," Walden said, "I'll call an ambulance."

"Just a scratch," said Mark, but his cheeriness had a taut edge to it. "That was a big bastard, wasn't it? Sorry to be no use."

Walden had a first aid qualification, though she didn't use it often. "Let me see."

Mark waved her away. "Really, it's a scratch. Just needs disinfectant and a big plaster. Maybe a few stitches. I'll get someone to drive me to A&E."

That was the moment when Walden should have offered to do it, but she didn't own a car. Mark grinned at her and then got to his feet with a theatrical *ooough* of pain. "Let's get out of the demonic plane before I attract something else by bleeding all over the place," he said. "Not that there's anything to be scared of when I'm standing next to you. That was it, wasn't it? The higher demon you've got leashed. Your Phoenix."

"Er, yes," Walden said, a little startled—and more than a little flattered—to be on the receiving end of such direct admiration. *She* knew the Phoenix was impressive. Most other people . . . well, either they didn't know about it, or else they didn't know enough about magic.

Mark knew. His knowledge lit up his face. His smile was not the charming mask but a grin of real enthusiasm, brilliant even as he clutched at his injured arm. "Spec-fucking-tacular," he said. "Beautiful, *beautiful* magic. Bravo, Dr Walden."

chapter eighteen

ROMANCE

THE THING ABOUT NOVEMBER: THE DAYS went horrifically slowly every year, and yet the awful month seemed to disappear in no time at all. Walden taught her lessons, rapidly packing in theory and practicals, somehow carving out a week in the December scheme of work to do revision before the mocks. She wrote the A-level Invocation mock examination, and a mark scheme for it. She did her share of the planar patrols, trading off with Mark, occasionally scheduling a joint patrol—even looking forward to those, a little, because Mark was now gratifyingly admiring about Walden's demon expertise. She attended some meetings and chaired others. She did risk assessments, marked homework, delivered assemblies, spoke with colleagues, phoned parents, dealt with the constant stream of emails and the constant stream of tasks they represented; she tuned the thaumic engines weekly, and added a standing meeting with the new Chief Marshal—Laura's former second-in-command—to her roster. She followed up with Ebele about her pastoral concerns over Nikki.

A couple of times she found herself on Facebook, looking at Roz Chan's page. It was rather quiet these days. There were few photos. Roz and her wife lived in a pretty house in San Francisco and seemed to be doing well. Once, and only once, Walden caved and went looking for Laura, who turned out to be a few years too young for Facebook; she had, instead, a rarely updated Instagram. When Walden, at 11 P.M. on a school night, found herself looking at an eight-years-ago photograph of twentysomething Laura posing with a motorbike, she thought *You are much too old for this to be anything other than embarrassing.*

Walden's career was her life. She was happy with her life, proud of her work, glad to be part of Chetwood School. She was far too busy to make a fool of herself daydreaming about romance. That sort of thing was teenager business.

In fact, while Nikki's feelings about her academic future seemed to have settled down steadily since the start of the half term—Ebele said that she was finally seeing the school counsellor again, and a good thing too—romance, unfortunately, was in the air for Walden's Upper Sixth.

It was hard not to laugh—it would have been very unkind to laugh—at the Will and Nikki situation. Obviously, true love was very important to a seventeen-year-old. True love in the background of a sixth form lesson expressed itself mostly through high-stakes eye contact and even more high-stakes rearrangement of the seating plan. On the days when Nikki condescended to sit beside Will, instead of her usual spot next to Mathias, Will was so obviously, smugly elated that it annoyed everyone—including, alas, Nikki herself. On the days when she walked past his desk and went to sit with one of the others, his downcast expression was almost cartoonishly pathetic. Aneeta, now clearly promoted from one of Nikki's best friends to her very best friend, whispered with her after every lesson. Mathias looked embarrassed for everyone. The funniest part, of course, was that the whole class was obviously convinced that Walden couldn't read the room—as if there weren't five whole people in every lesson, all of whom knew each other very well; as if it wasn't part of Walden's job to pick up every change and variation in the dynamics of a group of young people; and as if this particular dynamic wasn't older than the hills.

Of course she *pretended* not to know. She wasn't a monster.

Even Mark talked to her about it. Apparently, Will had asked him for advice. "What did you tell him?" Walden asked, interested despite herself.

"I said I couldn't help," Mark said. "What does poor old Uncle Mark know about young love? The first time I got serious about a woman, I was twenty-eight. I did say he should probably keep her away from my sister-in-law. Shouldn't be hard, though."

"Your sister-in-law?" Walden could just about bring Mrs Daubery's face to mind; they'd spoken at several Teams-call parents' evenings. She had an impression of quality knitwear and a nice scarf, gardening gloves on the desk, along with that telltale sign of a genuinely very posh woman: clip-on earrings, not piercings.

"Racist cow," said Mark cheerfully.

At this stage, Walden had more or less come around to Mark. His report for the governors showed no sign of materialising. He was, he said, information gathering. Walden was annoyed enough by how lazy he was being about it that she offered to set up interviews with students for him. "Or a survey, if you like," she said. "We can frame it as a student voice issue. It *is* a student voice issue."

"But then I'd have to read the surveys," said Mark.

Unfortunately, Walden had already convinced herself. They sent the survey round at form time the following week, and got an unsurprising litany of complaints back. *Bring back Marshal Kenning* was the big one. Walden hadn't realised how popular Laura was. It wasn't as if she was *friendly* with the students. The Marshals did safety talks with different year groups at different times through the year, and that was about all Laura had ever had by way of formal contact. But apparently being tough and cool and photogenic and very visibly *there* was also reassuring.

I wish we could, she thought, and set the surveys aside with a sigh. Children bounced back quickly, but a critical incursion by a higher demon was not a small matter, and one side effect of all the arcane safety refreshers Walden insisted on was that Chetwood's students knew very well just how much danger they had been in. Though few people were as shaken as Nikki and Mathias—Nikki visibly, Mathias shielding hard but his academics noticeably slipping—Ebele reported wobbles all across the school. Walden herself had been asked far more questions than usual by her latest Year Seven carousel group. And the influx of low-level possessions by imps had not slowed down, despite the planar patrols; the children had all noticed that too. The school, coming up to Christmas, was tired, unhappy, and on edge. You felt it in the corridors. It sizzled in the staffroom. The atmosphere every Monday-morning assembly was not just sleepy but sullen.

The Phoenix, rustling on the edge of Walden's thoughts as it so often did now, said: *Your place, your place; make it good again.*

What do you propose? Walden asked it tiredly. Nine P.M., still at her desk. The next task was slogging through the marking for a practice exam which Aneeta, unusually, had bombed. Walden could really have done without her perpetual companion. She missed the Phoenix being *quiet.* She'd spent some time going over the spellwork which leashed it, and confirmed to her own satisfaction that everything was still effective, unchanged, well within design tolerance. But she had never bothered creating a *shut up* spell, and there was no safe way to incorporate one into the tattooed designs now.

The Phoenix thought that since the children were the problem, and since Walden wasn't getting any benefit out of them anyway—it still didn't quite understand why she wouldn't draw on them as part of the magical well of the school's territory—she might as well kick them all out.

December 17 is the end of term, Walden told it. A little internal groan as she remembered the end-of-term Christmas party. The staff social committee had booked a London venue. Probably it would be fun when it was happening, but just the thought of catching the train down!

Bad there, the Phoenix said, and Walden sighed and took another mark off Aneeta's third-order array question. The actual diagram and notation were fine, but she'd jumbled up the accompanying explanation. This was *not* like her. She must be prioritising revising her sciences—but a low C on a practice paper, this late in the term, was going to be demoralising, especially for a student who was counting on her excellent theory results to get her the grade she wanted. Walden turned over the page and skimmed, relieved, through the one- and two-word answers to a set of short questions. The handwriting was atrocious, but the detail was sound. Nothing left but the magical ethics mini-essay—

She paused, startled. She said, out loud, "How did you spot that?"

The Phoenix said nothing. That was suspicious in itself. The Phoenix was almost unbearably chatty at the moment. It lived in Walden's head and had opinions on everything: questions, judgements, criticisms, and especially a fascination with any kind of human magic. Its thoughts on the thaumic engines were appallingly rude.

The chatter wasn't dangerous. Just annoying. But—Walden flipped back a page. The red X mark and her scribbled comment—*Revise this process again!*—sat neatly in the margin next to Aneeta's blue ballpoint paragraph. Her *handwritten* paragraph, in English. Walden said to the wood-panelled silence of her office, "Can you *read*?"

Maybe, said the Phoenix, a little guilty.

"*How* can you read?"

No answer.

It was unheard of. It was unprecedented. Demons didn't have *books*. Walden picked up the next practice paper in the stack—Nikki's—and flipped to the third-order array question. Nikki's handwriting, even in the examination scrawl version, was better than Aneeta's. She had the swirling *O*s and *I*s of a person who'd been very invested in making things pretty at the age of about nine. "What about this one?" Walden demanded.

A long suspicious silence in the back of Walden's head. Finally, the Phoenix said, *That's fine.*

It was, of course. Nikki's diagram and explanation were so word-for-word precise you could have copied them into a textbook. Walden took the next paper: Will. "This one?"

Sloppy, the Phoenix opined. *There, and there.* It meant the array diagram. Will had let the exam rush get to him, and drawn it too fast; it was obvious that he knew what it was *supposed* to look like—his paragraph of explanation was all correct—but if he'd tried actually summoning a demon with what he'd drawn . . .

I'd eat him up, the Phoenix agreed.

Walden marked the diagram with a red cross, and circled the errors. For a comment, she just wrote, *Can you identify the issue here?* Will's arcane notation was normally excellent, so this was an error of carelessness, not ignorance; he could fix it himself, and would, once he knew the mistake was costing him easy marks.

The paper at the bottom of the pile was the real test, because it belonged to Mathias. Walden always left him to last. Doing the most able students' work first gave her a stronger sense of what a good paper looked like and what comments would actually be useful. Mathias was really struggling at the moment, end-of-term exhaustion and general woefulness draining his already shaky academic motivation. The Phoenix spoke up before she'd even flipped to the relevant question. *Wrong. Wrong. Wrong again. Do the crosses. Bad, bad, bad, all wrong—crosses, I said! It's wrong! Stupid human!*

Stop, said Walden.

The Phoenix shut up, grumbling. Walden could feel a tightness in her right arm. She rolled up her sleeve and saw that the image of a tattooed firebird had moved from her bicep down to her forearm. Its hooked beak and golden eye blazed out just above her wrist. She stared at it. It stared back, unblinking. "Do you remember what I said about insults and threats?"

Sullen silence.

"Yes, this is a D paper," Walden said, "probably."

So make it good!

"I could do this work perfectly myself," Walden said, "because I'm a fully trained magician and this is my discipline. But that's not the point. The question is, how do we get *him* to—as you say—make it good?"

Tell him it's all bad.

"Yes," said Walden patiently, "and then . . . ?"

There was a long, baffled pause.

"You did want to know how I do it," Walden reminded the demon.

Don't understand, said the Phoenix sulkily. It didn't like not understanding. Walden was just barely resisting the urge to start writing notes. If there had been a way to record this conversation! She had never read anything like this, she had never *heard* of anything like this. But—she thought of Old Faithful, speaking with Charlie's voice, deep in the heart of the incursion.

I can think. I can lie.

And the Phoenix could read. It could learn. It could recognise, and resent, its own ignorance of a useful skill—that was what was upsetting it now; that Walden, in her funny little human body all made of water and meat, had a power it lacked. The power to *control*—

No, Walden told it. *The power to help.*

Help?

Try another tack, Walden thought. And then, with one of the rare, valuable inspirations that had once made her a reasonably good scholar, she saw a connection. The Phoenix, fighting the archdemonic minibus on that planar patrol a few weeks ago, had ordered its opponent to go and *be another self.*

"Imagine," she said out loud to her office, "being another self."

Silence from her fellow traveller. But a considering silence, not a sullen one.

"Imagine being seventeen years old—" No, that didn't work, she felt at once; demons did not have enough of a concept of *childhood.* "Imagine being small," she said instead. "Imagine being new, and weak, and surrounded by the strong."

That got her a brief, fearsome flare of reaction. Walden thought it might be terror.

"You can get stronger," Walden said. "But you don't know that yet. You have no proof. You and I, who are older—we have seen small and weak things grow powerful, plenty of times. But that small self is afraid. It is too afraid to try."

It took the Phoenix a little while to understand. The higher demon was not stupid—no, not stupid at all, Walden could tell.

But it had real difficulty with the *why* of teaching: why be generous, why be thoughtful, why consider so carefully the precise angles and goals of the criticisms you made, why bother with any of it at all? Was Walden not afraid of raising up Mathias to take her place in her own domain? He was strong enough, or could be—

Really? Walden thought, surprised; Mathias had talent, yes, but surely any of the other three—

Of course the strongest one is the best of them, said the Phoenix impatiently. *But why? Why waste your time helping the weak get stronger, when you could be growing yourself?*

It didn't buy altruism as an excuse—which was fair enough. Teaching wasn't a career you got into for the money alone, but Walden was not marking practice exams late on Saturday night in December out of the goodness of her heart. She wouldn't have been doing any of this if she wasn't getting paid for it. Attempts to elicit interest or sympathy for Mathias's own sake got her precisely nowhere. Demons didn't *care,* not like that, not for each other.

"I am a teacher," Walden said at last. "This is what I do. And I choose to do it well."

Ah, said the Phoenix abruptly. *A self.*

And then it said nothing else; but Walden could feel its silent attention as she marked Mathias's paper—which did, in the end, get a D. Its beaked head slid down past her wrist onto her hand, and the golden eye of the firebird gleamed. Walden was careful with the red pen. Mathias's motivation was so low already that a solid wall of crosses and corrections would just scare him into giving up; he wouldn't even read what she'd written. She sought out the things he had got right, and wrote next to them: *good!* and *well done!* and *nicely worked out, Mathias.* He had finally taken on board her feedback about his array diagrams; they were starting to look more decisive and less sketchy, and there were not too many technical mistakes.

The array question that had tripped up both Aneeta and Will was a mess of rubbings out and redrawings. Walden frowned at it. What Mathias had done in the end was definitely wrong, but what was the scrawl of scribbling and crossing-out around it?

The traces were clear. He'd drawn the array incorrectly at first. Then he'd gone back at the end of the paper—using a different pencil—looked at it, and had one of his good moments: he'd known it didn't look right, and he'd rubbed it out and drawn in something that did.

Except then he'd panicked, not trusting himself, and decided to split the difference: crossed the whole thing out, and started again underneath with a half-and-half mishmash of the two different array diagrams, ending up with something totally incoherent that Walden couldn't massage any marks out of no matter how she grimaced at the rubric. The first attempt would have got him three out of ten, and the second attempt seven. Instead it was a zero—when an extra seven marks would have brought his grade up to a C.

Which . . . actually . . .

Let's be positive, Saffy, even though it's late and you're tired! There was space at the bottom of the page, because Mathias hadn't written enough for the explanatory paragraph. Walden used it to draw his first two diagrams again and then wrote a score under each of them. She circled the 7/10 diagram and drew a large star in the margin of the page. Next to it, she wrote: TRUST YOURSELF!!! YOU WERE NEARLY THERE!

Then she flipped over to the front of the paper and changed the overall grade from D to C/D. Of course no actual A-level examiner would give Mathias a C-slash-D with the benefit of the doubt. But she wanted him to see how close he was. She went back through the paper again, hunting for marks, looking now at all his diagrams—and yes, there was enough there; she couldn't get him seven extra marks, but she could justify two, and several more comments focused specifically on his arcane notation. If he tightened it up just a little more—which he clearly *could*—he could hope for a low C on this theory paper in the mocks, and a mid C by the real examination in summer. A mid-C theory plus a high-B practical would get him a B grade overall.

You are pleased, said the Phoenix, the first thing it had said in twenty minutes. Walden realised that the slight ache in her jaw was a fierce little smile. She'd been certain all along that Mathias could get a B in the end, but this was the first time she'd really seen how—seen it, and known she could make him see it too. Once he believed he could succeed, he would actually try. Once he tried, it would become true. The trick of teaching wasn't to know more than your students—it was remarkably easy, after all, to know more than most teenagers. Teaching wasn't about being right, or being clever, or being in charge. It was about making them believe.

You manipulate his perceptions, the Phoenix said, *to make him stronger. And this satisfies your nature.*

"The word is *inspire*, usually," Walden said. "And I suppose it does." It wouldn't be enough just to hand Mathias the marked paper. Aneeta would have got the point from red-pen comments alone, but you could never count on Mathias to actually read your comments, or to process them once he'd read. So she would set up a one-on-one—did she have a spare breaktime this week? Yes, Tuesday break would work, she'd skip her mid-morning coffee. They would go through the whole exam, and she'd show him: here's what you did, here's what you will do, here's the grade you deserve, and here's how you're going to get it.

She set the pen down and leaned back in her chair with a satisfied sigh. Her back ached. A glance at the wall clock told her it was nearly 11 P.M. *Intruder,* muttered the Phoenix, which made

Walden look again and then smile: yes, the antique magician's clock was possessed again, yet another invading imp. Imps were perfectly manageable with a little common sense. She honestly quite liked having them around. With any luck, the staffroom photocopier would have a reasonable inhabitant again before long, and everything would be back to normal; almost as if Old Faithful had never ripped through her school at all.

There was a knock at the door.

At this time of night? It could be anything—plenty of it bad. Walden felt like she'd summoned the problem just by being pleased with herself. She was already braced for the sight of Aneeta in tears in her puffy pink coat when she called, "Come in!"

"Evening," said Mark, poking his head round the door. "Hoped I'd catch you still awake. Marking?" He'd seen the pile of papers and the red pen uncapped on her desk.

"Just finished," Walden said. "What's the matter?"

"Nothing at all," said Mark. "I decided to run a late-night patrol—you never know, some demons keep odd hours—and when I was done I thought, 'You know what, it's fucking freezing out there and I bet Sapphire's still at it too.' Point to Daubery, I guessed right." He came in and shut the door behind him. "Time to knock off for the night, come on. Any chance of a coffee?"

Oh, all right, why not. It had a bit of the undergrad feeling, someone knocking on your door late and coming in for a drink, but Walden found she quite liked the nostalgia of it all. *Intruder,* muttered the Phoenix again. Walden ignored it and said, "I don't do caffeine this late, but I can fix you something. Come on through."

Mark whistled when they went into the old Head's flat. "Nice place. What's through there?"

The door he was looking at was chained and padlocked. "The thaumic engines," said Walden. "My long-term nemesis, second only to the Department for Education. Here's the kitchen. I might have a tea. Or—" She had several very nice bottles in the drinks cabinet, and Mark had obviously already spotted them. "I've been victorious over my marking tonight. Maybe a G and T. You?"

"I'll take a drop of whiskey in the coffee, if it's on offer," Mark said.

"I've got nothing special, I'm afraid," Walden said, taking down the Bushmills. Mark waved that away, remarking that good whiskey didn't go in coffee anyway; was Walden a gin drinker, then? What's that—something local?

"My parents send me a bottle for my birthday every year," Walden said, "from their nearest farm shop, I believe. They've gone frightfully rural in retirement. Strawberries-and-cream infusion, very girly. I rather like it. Would you like to try some?"

They had a G&T apiece in Walden's sitting room, and then, since the gin was quite good, they had another. Walden dug a packet of biscuits out of her kitchen cabinets, which Mark demolished. If he'd just been on a planar patrol, it was no wonder he was hungry. "Midnight feast!" he said. "Funny, isn't it, being an alum—makes you feel old as the hills, watching all these kids living your old life. And then sometimes you turn around and you're back to being a teenager."

Walden raised her brows. "A strong gin in the middle of the night makes you feel like a teenager? Dear me."

"I didn't say I was a *good* boy, Dr Walden."

"And what kind of boy were you, exactly?"

"Oh, a little bastard," Mark said, "like they all are. You know the type, you've taught enough of them."

Walden snorted. "I only wondered if you'd admit it."

"I've got no delusions. Another round?" said Mark, nodding at her empty glass. "Are there more biscuits anywhere?"

"I might have some cheese and crackers left," Walden said. "Just a single for me, please."

They talked about nothing much; staffroom gossip led naturally to generalised Chetwood memories and then on to family. It turned out Mark had actually overlapped at school with Walden's older brother John, though he didn't think they'd ever spoken. And then—well, it was Saturday night, and Walden didn't *have* to get up for chapel in the morning. One hour stretched to two. Mark was reasonably amusing company, the gin was the good stuff that Walden didn't get to drink socially very often, and there was something charmingly silly about the student-ness of it all.

At nearly 1 A.M. they both seemed to realise at once that they were being absurd. Mark stood up with a groan. "It's only just down the road to my rental, at least."

Walden gave him a look of alarm. "You're not planning to *drive*."

"I'm all right, I'm all right," he said, and then glanced down at his glass with a grimace, "no, you're right, I'm not. Shouldn't have had that last one."

"You'll send that Audi into a ditch," said Walden, "and that's the best-case scenario. More likely you'll end up wrapped around a tree. Absolutely not."

"Why, Sapphire, I didn't know you cared."

"Some of those trees are several centuries old," said Walden primly. "The big oak at the end of the avenue is under a preservation order. The paperwork if you splattered yourself all over it would be frightful."

Mark laughed. "All right, all right. What are the chances of getting a taxi?"

"In *Chetwood village*? After midnight?"

"Nil," said Mark. "I suppose I'm walking. Gin jacket should keep me warm, at least."

"For heaven's sake," said Walden. It was mid-December. There was frost on the grass every morning. "You'll end up as an icicle, don't be ridiculous. I have a spare bedroom, you can sleep here."

Mark made all the right demurring noises and then let himself be persuaded. He wasn't that bad, really, Walden thought. Quite manageable, if you were used to him. And quite good-looking as well.

Not that that mattered. But as she fell asleep, more than slightly tipsy and thinking as she so often did of Laura Kenning, she remembered muzzily another late-night gin, walking back from the pub afterwards. A kiss that never happened. And the admission: *I do miss sex, occasionally.*

chapter nineteen

THE END OF TERM

C HRISTMAS AT CHETWOOD SCHOOL OFFI-
cially began on December 8, which was the day that Annie in the school office started wearing her tinsel bauble
earrings. Ten days left! The slog of the Autumn Term was a little
more bearable with the end in sight.

The final week and a bit of school was always, not to put too
fine a point on it, a doss. Walden, who taught only an A-level class
and a critical magical safety course, would not be spending any lessons making Christmas cards or watching ever-so-slightly relevant
films on the school's eStream, but she did not grudge her colleagues
a single lesson of relief after what was invariably an absolute nightmare term. The children enjoyed it too, of course. Very few of
them would realise that the fun and easy end-of-term lessons were
only minimally for *their* benefit.

And, of course, it was impossible trying to get much useful done
at this time of year anyway. While other teachers were sagging gently towards the holidays, PE, Drama, and Music were all going at a
frantic pace. Students were constantly getting pulled out of lessons

to rehearse for the Christmas concert—not to be confused with the carol concert, not to be confused with the carol *service*—so that a class with above-average numbers of musicians might be down by two-thirds every afternoon. And then there was the end-of-term Interhouse Sports—round-robin tournaments in rugby and hockey, for every year group, participation unpopular but mandatory— and the student pantomime, performed with enthusiasm for the dubious benefit of the residents of Woodland Hill Care Home on the other side of the village. You also had to contend with the fact that plenty of parents pulled their children out of school a week before the end of term in order to get them on off-peak flights to wherever they were going for their winter getaway. Some families were apologetic about it, some were brazen. Some students had an unexpected death in the family every December like clockwork, and some parents just turned up cheerfully in their Tesla or Land Rover with a cry of, "Hello, darling, ready to ski?"

Aneeta's whole family—including her younger sister, in Year Ten, whom Walden had only vaguely known existed—were visiting relatives in India already. Aneeta was not. "I wouldn't get anything done if I went," she said grimly. "I have A-levels. I need to revise." Will was going on the school ski trip, which left two days before the end of term; so was Mathias, to Walden's surprise—not that he *could* go, there was a travel bursary programme for exactly that sort of thing, but that he wanted to. Nikki and Aneeta seemed to have arranged an extended holiday sleepover, combined with an intensive revision plan, which would take place at Aneeta's family home in Kensington during the week after Christmas. Walden had her doubts about how much work they would actually get done, but they were both very excited, and it was nice that they were taking the mocks seriously.

Walden finished the sixth formers off on the final Wednesday with a little speech of encouragement and a pack of practice papers each. The first two weeks of the Spring Term were going to be eaten by mock exams, so she would not be teaching them again until late January—nearly a month without contact hours, the longest break she would have with this set apart from last summer. They would do their mock practicals after the written papers were over. Walden wanted to give them as much time as possible to get the theory solid first.

All of them, even Mathias, seemed to be feeling positive about the trial to come. Walden was quite positive herself, despite the wobbles she'd observed in their recent practice papers. Revision would tidy all that up. And you could tell when you'd taught a group well. It was in the papers you marked and the practicals you observed, but it also came across in the atmosphere of the classroom, the expressions of satisfaction or determination on their faces as they worked, the conversations you eavesdropped on as they talked each other through questions and problems and challenges. It wasn't enough just to get them to memorise concepts and systems—that worked at GCSE, sometimes, but not at A-level. A successful A-level set had *skills*. They kept calm in the face of the unfamiliar. They trusted their own capabilities. They spoke with confidence, not just regurgitating Walden's teaching but recombining, putting together things that Walden had never explicitly connected for them, starting to see the glittering constellation of the big picture. Some of them—Nikki, especially, but all four now and then—were reaching for that big picture, a wider vision of knowledge and power and skill. They were starting to spot the holes and simplifications that were hidden in the secondary syllabus, and to ask the questions that Walden had more often heard in her postdoc days, lecturing undergrads.

And after all, they were eighteen, or nearly; adults in law, if not in context. They were old enough to vote or to marry, to buy alcohol, to join the army. Only six months of school were left to them. They didn't just know magic. They knew how to *think*.

It was a good feeling, being proud of your students.

The Phoenix stirred at the back of Walden's mind at the end of that final lesson. It had been blessedly quiet since the night she'd drunk all that gin with Mark. *Power, growth, change,* it murmured. Walden ignored it as usual. In the corridor, Will and Nikki were having a quiet, urgent exchange. "Promise you'll message me?" Walden overheard—poor Will, honestly, desperation had to be an unfamiliar feeling for him—and Nikki's answer: "Yeah, okay, I promise."

True love. Walden covered a smile as she gathered up her papers and her half-empty flask of sludgy staffroom coffee.

And then it was the end of term, and the extremely long final assembly—David in full academic regalia performing Headmaster, while the whole school waited patiently for it all to be over. David was just as warm and congratulatory to the final set of colours awardees as the first, smile never fading through the whole elaborately dull process of reading out the names, handing out the precious little ribbons to Chetwood's army of young athletes, applause and handshakes all round. That segment alone took forty minutes, and then it was the music scholars' turn. Walden sat at the front in her doctoral robes, red and black, silk lining and tassled bonnet. Her hands always ached from clapping by the time final assembly was done.

At last they sang the school hymn, and a round of "Jingle Bells" for good measure—full-throated from the middle school, noticeably quiet and muttery from Years Ten to Twelve, Year Thirteen going for it with sentimental gusto. This was the time of year it started to hit them: Yes, it's nearly over. You're growing up. You're leaving soon. This is the last time.

And the Autumn Term was done. Parents' cars lined up all down the long avenue between the bare lime trees, and halfway along the road to the village. Overstuffed suitcases were heaped into the staff lift in Scrubs, or in some cases lugged unsafely down the stairs by their impatient young owners. Todd chugged back and forth to the car park with trunks and bags loaded into the green quad-bike trailer, and a trail of teenagers followed like ducklings.

Walden as senior staff was part of the car park team, chivvying children towards—hopefully—the correct vehicles, trying to keep them on track and out of the way of disaster. A mysterious alchemy turned every parent in England into the world's worst driver as soon as they found themselves in a school car park. It was almost as if they *wanted* to hit a stray Year Eight. Todd's security team were much in evidence in their high-vis jackets, waving and shouting at the massed cars. Since it was December 17, everyone came prepared with their branded school umbrellas. When the heavens opened, red-and-white shield logos blossomed over staff heads like a field of flowers.

Freedom. Blissful freedom. One crisis—a parent who didn't turn up, uncontactable, eventually turning out to be stuck in traffic with phone not charged; all perfectly normal. Walden waved the last tearful girl into her mother's car with a smile and went back, full of relief, to the end-of-term prosecco and mince pies laid on in the staffroom.

"Nice that the school budgets for this," said Mark at her elbow when she turned away from a friendly gossip with a group of PE teachers she hardly ever got the chance to speak to—their department was based at the opposite end of the site, a long way from

Walden's usual haunts. Mark had a glass of prosecco in one hand and two mince pies in the other.

"The staff social association funds it, actually," Walden said. "Did you pay your subs?"

Mark laughed. "I'm a freeloader. Are you going to the party tonight?"

Walden was too senior to skip office parties. Besides, it would probably be fun once she got there. Teachers at the end of term were very ready to let loose. She'd booked her train ticket weeks ago. "Of course. Are you?"

"Wouldn't miss it for the world," Mark said. He scooped two fresh glasses of prosecco off the nearby trolley, pressed one into Walden's hand, and grinned at her.

So, yes, she knew. She was thirty-eight, for goodness' sakes. She wasn't a complete fool. A man like Mark did not repeatedly seek you out in both work and social situations, invite himself into your flat for late-night drinks on a flimsy excuse, and press you on whether you were going to be in London that night, without a definite ulterior motive. And it was a little flattering.

All right, honestly, it was very flattering.

Mark obviously wasn't boyfriend material—Walden felt ridiculous just thinking the word 'boyfriend'; she was much too old for boyfriends—but he was charming and handsome and a rather good magician, and altogether, honestly, a more impressive pull than she would have thought herself capable of. The same thing had been true of Laura Kenning. *Like bloody buses,* she thought as she did her makeup in her wood-panelled bedroom after the staff drinks were over. *Nothing for years and then two come along at once.*

She had to laugh. She'd gone for a sleeveless black dress for the party, mostly because it was the only party outfit she owned that still looked nice and wasn't obviously twenty years old. She had in fact acquired the dress twenty years ago, but it had been second-hand then, and now it was interestingly vintage. She automatically shrugged a smart black cardigan over the top to hide her tattoos, because this was a work event. She hesitated over jewellery—her normal work studs were perfectly nice earrings, did she really need to—?

Stop being Dr Walden for one night and try turning back into a human being, whispered a voice in her heart. It was not the Phoenix, but someone nearly as dangerous: the girl who'd bought this dress, eighteen-year-old Saffy Walden, a bleach-blonde adolescent waif, all intellectual arrogance and pretensions of punk. She'd been about as punk rock as an upmarket gastropub—she'd been to boarding school, she studied at Oxford, her parents lived in *Windsor*—but she'd had a lot of fun. Walden crouched to reach decisively into the back of her bottom dresser drawer, and brought out tangled fistfuls of jewellery she never wore now. Most of it was awful plasticky tat, what a student could afford, but there were a few good pieces. Walden picked out a chunky necklace that Roz had given to her, glamorous rather than tasteful, and a set of big opal earrings. She went back to her makeup bag and decisively upped the amount of eyeliner; she'd developed a perfect, steady hand in the mid-2000s, and it hadn't abandoned her yet. Then she frowned at her suddenly unfamiliar reflection. The Saffy in the mirror looked both older and younger than Walden felt. Had it really been so long?

"Fuck it," she muttered aloud, and took off the smart black cardigan. The Phoenix curled and flexed its way up her right arm as she watched, and its wicked golden head watched her reflection too, hooked beak nearly at her shoulder. Was she too obviously hoping for more out of her night than an ordinary work social? Was she embarrassing herself? Was she overthinking this?

She was absolutely overthinking this.

Yes, she usually kept her spellwriting tattoos hidden, out of deference to the school's image, the traditional and conservative idyllic-country-house feeling that was as much a part of Chetwood's branding as the shield logo. But they weren't *secret*. Plenty of Walden's colleagues had seen Walden's bare and colourful arms on the night Old Faithful made its move. And those inked spells were a part of who she was. They represented years of work, work she was proud of, work very few people could do, work that Mark at least thought was spectacular. She wasn't going to be judged. People ought to be impressed, if they knew anything about magic—and if they didn't know anything, that was *their* problem. Thirty-eight might be too old for boyfriends, but it was also too old to worry yourself to death about what other people thought about you.

Walden left the cardigan across the foot of her bed, swung on her coat and her nicest scarf, and headed out into the cold December night to catch the London train.

CHRISTMAS

chapter twenty

LONDON

THE CHRISTMAS PARTY WAS HELD AT A VENUE in Finsbury Park, an uninspiring box of a room with gleaming chrome tables pushed against the purple-painted walls, a fake Christmas tree strung with purple tinsel in one corner, and two bored-looking young men working the bar. The thing about a work social with forty-odd teachers in more than a dozen disciplines was that they all only really had one thing in common. Once everyone had used up the *what are your Christmas plans* gambit, there was nothing much to do except get drunk and talk shop.

Walden, accordingly, did both.

A lot of people were interested in talking shop with her tonight, and not just classroom business either. They asked about the tattoos—even academic teachers could recognise spellwriting, when they lived at Chetwood School—they asked nervously after Nikki and Mathias, and they asked about Old Faithful. Walden had done a presentation at the all-hands staff meeting after the crisis, and she'd thought that had cleared things up. It turned out that the teachers of Chetwood were still nearly as shaken as the students. No wonder the school had gone so sullen and miserable towards the end of term. When adults were worried, children noticed.

"It was so *big*, right," said Lilly Tibbett to Walden. The blonde NQT was flushed and earnestly tipsy. "I mean—I was on the perimeter—it was just *so big*. I could feel it trying to bulge out around me. I was sure it was going to come right for me when it came. I was sure." She was right, Walden thought. If it had succeeded in killing Walden and breaking loose in mundane reality, Old Faithful would have spotted Lilly's obvious uncertainty and slammed down hard on the weak point in the perimeter she represented. "I'm an evoker—that's my thing, you know? I got an A in A-level Invo, but I dropped as soon as I could at uni. I don't like demons. Like, the ones that skin people, and the weird-looking gross ones, obviously. But even imps, they just make my skin crawl. School has so many imps right now, did you notice? They're just everywhere, like rats. I don't know how you do it. We're not getting another big one, are we?"

That was the real question, the million-dollar question, which Walden heard over and over. She was supposed to be the staff lead on this sort of thing. She hadn't been talking to people enough. She'd gone too inwards, too focused on the rest of her job—there were so many things involved in doing a teacher's job! Never enough time to do everything right, she thought, but this was leadership, this was core; she'd let people down. So she had the conversation over and over, tailoring it for the audience every time, technical and thorough for the magical departments, a layman's summary for the others: *Yes, it was big. I know. We handled it. Honestly, yes, we might get another one. We'd know pretty quickly if we did. There's a plan. We would handle it again.*

She kept a glass of wine in her hand, so she'd have something to gesture with. "Listen," she found herself saying to Ezekiel, who was grave and thoughtful as he propped up the bar tonight—Ebele had joined the knot of high-energy younger people on the dance floor—"it's not as if we can avoid the issue. There's no way around it. Teenage magicians attract demons. A beginner is a natural target for a magical predator, and a *child* beginner more so—all that power, none of the common sense. Teenage magicians without protection, without any adult support, get *eaten* by demons. That's why Chetwood isn't just another boarding school. It's necessary. *You* know this."

Ezekiel, foster father of seven sorcerers, knew. He nodded seriously.

"It used to be about families," Walden said. "People like—oh—"

"Like me," said Mark, coming up on Walden's other side and nodding to the barman for a fresh drink. "Hi, Sapphire. Evening, Reverend."

"On social occasions," said Ezekiel, "I accept Zeke."

Walden was still talking. "There was a time when the question of whether you'd be lucky enough to survive was based purely on how much magic the adults around you knew. Which meant all that mattered was who your parents were. The old magical dynasties of England! But it's a stupid way to run things—worse than that, it's an *evil* way to run things. Just imagine how many Nicola Conways were lost to history, just because no one around them had the training, the experience, the *power* to save them from something that was never their fault."

"Hey, not all of them got eaten by demons," said Mark. "Look on the bright side. Some hedge witches got burned at the stake instead."

"I think my wife wants to talk to me," said Ezekiel.

Walden barely noticed him leaving. She was rounding on Mark. "It's not right," she snapped. "It's not *fair*."

"How much wine have you had?" said Mark.

"Oh—hush. I'm fine."

"You look fantastic."

"It's Christmas."

"I never suspected you of egalitarian principles," Mark said. "I thought you were all professional pride down to the bottom of your magician's heart."

"Some of us picked a career out of the desire to do something important," Walden said. "Something *real*."

"Teaching four teenagers a niche A-level at a private school," Mark agreed. "Makes sense."

"What's that supposed to mean?"

"I'm a meaningless sort of guy."

"I can tell," said Walden coldly.

"Don't hold it against me. I might have hidden depths. Are you coming to the afterparty?"

"What afterparty?" But now Walden looked, the crowd of teachers was starting to thin: sensible people in their forties and fifties peeling off for the Tube and the train ride home, dragging out wheeled suitcases from the collection by the door as they set off for their real lives, their families, Christmas. Boarding school was a world apart. It wasn't only the children who exited the theme park at the end of term.

"There's a bunch of us going to head into town and find somewhere less sad than Finsbury Park to keep the party going," Mark said. *Us*, as if he were right in with the energetic young crowd also starting to collect their coats and hats. He had to be ten years older than most of them, twenty years older than someone like Lilly. "Are you in?"

What was waiting for Walden at the other end of her own train ride home? Chetwood, of course; Chetwood again; the theme park with the lights off, everything shut down, a Victorian flat too big for one person to rattle around in and a school site left empty and leafless and grim. She wouldn't be completely alone. Of course not. Ebele and Ezekiel lived in School House with their crowd of foster children; and their adult children, all successful twenty-something alumni, would most likely be home for Christmas. And Todd had his neat cottage on the avenue, and David and his wife were just down the road in the village. But to Walden just now, possessed by the ghost of eighteen-year-old Saffy, it looked like a sad and boring little life, barely enlivened by the prospect of taking the Southern Rail train down to rural Sussex to see her parents next week.

"Why not," she said. "I'll join you."

It was the better part of twenty years since Walden had been on a pub crawl. She'd done it at Oxford—determined, as an undergraduate, to enjoy herself and try everything—and she'd soon discovered that hangovers were not fun and that most people were more boring when they were drunk. The friends worth hanging on to had generally reached the same conclusion, and by the time she was twenty her whole social group had largely gotten over the impulse. It had been a bit of a shock to arrive in the States for her postgraduate studies and discover her peers, age twenty-two, all still in the eager stage of *Well, we're allowed now!* when it came to alcohol. She'd felt a bit superior about it—although, to be fair, twenty-two-year-old Saffy had been capable of feeling superior about almost anything. What a little monster she'd been. *You're so fucking smug,* Roz had told her, witheringly unimpressed; that conversation had probably been the best and most improving thing to happen to her during her first year in California.

The crush of the weekday evening Tube—even this late, in London, it was a crowd made as much of commuters as partygoers—and the cold air and the bright Christmas lights in Leicester Square together sobered her up a bit. The younger crowd were arguing about where to go *(I'm not getting the night bus all the way back from fucking Brixton; Camden is shit now; A Spoons? Are you serious?)* and she and Mark exchanged looks. He was wearing a wool winter coat and a college scarf. Walden nodded at it. "What college?"

"St John's," said Mark. "Cambridge."

"Oh, so you're a *thaumaturge*." A magical degree, for obscure historical reasons, was called Sorcery at Oxford and Durham, Thaumaturgy at Cambridge and St Andrews, and Magic everywhere else.

"Guilty," Mark said. "Trying to get my measure, Dr Walden? What about you?"

"Oxford. St Catherine's," Walden said. "Catz. Large and modern. It has a spectacular Brutalist building which I found quite homey after seven years in Scrubs. Unfortunately, I don't know anything about Cambridge colleges. If you'd told me you were a Christ Church man I would have been able to draw some conclusions." *Posh*, mostly, which she already knew. Every college had its reputation. Sometimes it was deserved.

"St John's is the wanker college," Mark said helpfully. "Lots of money, has the best May Ball, and there's a little song about it." He hummed and then sang quietly into the London night: *"I'd rather be at Oxford than St John's, oh I'd rather be at Oxford than St John's . . ."*

Walden laughed. "I'm sure you're not all that bad."

"Not at all. I met lots of perfectly lovely girls at John's."

"And you were perfectly nasty to them."

"In my defence," said Mark, "I was twenty and I don't know what they expected. Anyway! At this rate your colleagues are going to wrangle all night. Why don't we ditch the work jolly? There's a nice little cocktail bar round the corner. My treat."

"I don't think so," Walden said. It wasn't even 9 P.M. yet. Besides, a group of teachers negotiating with each other could be quite funny to watch. All of them were rather too used to being the grown-up in charge and the only sensible person in the room. It was one of the commonest pitfalls of school management, a danger David had discussed with her when he appointed her to the Director of Magic role: you could not treat adult colleagues like incompetent children and expect them to put up with it quietly. Walden, watching an argument break out over Google Maps, told Mark about this. He laughed. "I'd noticed, Sapphire. Hard not to notice. Amazing that schools get anything done at all. The clowns are running the circus."

"Ouch," Walden said.

"No offence."

"What *exactly* do you do," said Walden, "when you're not generously donating your time to Chetwood?"

Mark smirked at her. "It's classified."

"Right," said Walden sceptically.

"Not that classified, I admit. But it's boring, I promise you. Special advisor stuff. The civil service hates having me around even more than you do. Ah, looks like we've decided on," he tilted his head, listening, "exactly the same pub that someone suggested in the first place. Glad we stood in the cold for twenty minutes about it. Sure I can't tempt you to cocktails?"

"Maybe later," said Walden, and didn't let herself regret it when Mark gave her another knowing grin. She was an adult. She knew what she was doing.

Although, honestly, she might as well have said yes to the cocktails. The pub was so crowded that the little knot of teachers was forced to break up into groups of three and four, spread across several booths. Walden found herself in a twosome, with Mark, at the bar—she gave him a sharp glance; he'd managed that rather too neatly, which suggested he'd done it before. "I need to keep mingling, of course," she said. "I *am* still at work."

"Let your hair down," said Mark. "I don't think anyone cares at this stage."

"Also, I like these people," said Walden, and set herself to proving it by sliding into the corner of a booth next to most of the Modern Foreign Languages Department. MFL were reliably some of the most sociable teachers you could meet, because few people studied a modern language to degree level unless they had at least *some* interest in talking to other human beings. A lot of them were expats, French and Spanish teachers shivering even inside the pub and talking longingly about their flights home. You did have to contend with the fact that the conversation across the table was conducted in an effortless polyglot medley of English, French, Spanish, German, and a little Italian—Walden's GCSE Spanish was enough to follow parts of it, but not to join in—but the three people nearest her switched generously into English when she sat down. Mark, undaunted, joined the booth of NQTs behind her, apparently very successfully if the gust of laughter following the first thing he said to them was any guide.

And the evening proceeded convivially. Everyone relaxed enough that they did, at last, come up with some topics of conversation that were not school, lessons, mocks, public exams, how tired everybody was, how bad the canteen food was on Sundays, and the horrific behaviour of 9C. The groups in the booths mingled and split. People got up to fetch the next round and were replaced by someone else sliding into their seat. Some split off in twos and threes, or even—here was a Christmas miracle for you—got caught up in friendly conversation with strangers. Walden stood her round, and didn't object when most of them ordered something a little more expensive than they'd been having before; she *was* management. She found herself eventually on the table of NQTs, who let loose a flood of questions about her tattoos: Were those real? Were they magic? Were they *allowed*?

One thing to know that the sixth form thought you were an ancient crone at thirty-eight; quite another to get it from the twenty-somethings. But they were all Generation Z together, Walden supposed. She took the cheerful route: yes, real, of course allowed but who wanted to talk to children about it, and yes, of course—*very* magic.

"I swear I saw the bird move," someone said.

"It's a phoenix," said Walden, and at the back of her mind came a susurrus, an echo, almost a harmony: *I am Phoenix.*

She held up her arm to show them. The Phoenix twisted its proud neck to fix its eye on its audience. It spread its blazing wings up Walden's arm, and flexed its golden talons. Everyone started chattering at once. Half of these people were junior teachers from the magical departments, interested in the how and the why. "Illusion. It's just a fancy evoke," said Lilly decisively. "I've got a butterfly on my ankle. I can make it flap its wings."

"Not an evocation, though, is it?" said Mark. When had he started leaning over the back of the booth? "Not an illusion at all. It's really moving. That's a reified demon, guys. Pretty big one too."

Mark! thought Walden, and attempted a subtle glare—did he have to make it sound so alarming? For that manner, did he have to announce it loudly in a crowded pub? There was a little silence, which she had to rescue. None of the NQTs were invokers by calling. If they could *find* a decent NQT to teach invocation, Walden wouldn't be stuck doing an A-level set on top of a management workload. "Demon summoning is the most boring arcane discipline until it isn't," she said, with the I'm-joking smile. "Cool, isn't it? You're looking at my doctorate."

"You're not . . ." said Lilly nervously.

"I'm not possessed, no," airily, as if it were a rather silly question. "The Marshals would be here in two minutes flat if I was."

Someone coughed awkwardly. Walden looked up.

White jacket with hi-vis strips, gleaming boots, shining armguards graven with runes and shining sword hung neatly at her hip. The square, muscular frame of an athlete; the hair short and tousled and gleaming golden, picked out by electric light against the dark rectangle of the doorway back into the December night. The band on her upper arm marked with KMV, for Knight Mareschal Venitant. A butch avenging angel, a demon slayer out of storybooks, standing in a little pool of silence and attention that *could* have been just the normal reaction to the police walking into a pub, but could equally have been the entire room experiencing what Walden felt just then, which was *Oh come on, this is unfair, no one looks like that!*

Laura Kenning glanced around the room with a swift, assessing look, saw Walden and the rest of the group of Chetwood teachers, nodded in their direction, and headed for the bar. How was she here? *Why* was she here?

"Laura, finally!" cried the Head of Spanish as Laura joined the group. "Still in uniform?"

"Just got off duty," said Laura, setting her beer down. "Evening."

And that was when it occurred to Walden that while she didn't have Laura's phone number and the ability to text her things like *we're near Leicester Square, come and join us,* she wasn't the only person here who had worked with her for years. Laura had been hired by Chetwood at least two years before Walden herself arrived. Lots of people here knew her well. She felt rather stupid. Also, she felt rather naked, in a sleeveless black dress and too much makeup, with the Phoenix on bold and colourful display.

"Huh," murmured Mark as he leaned over her shoulder. "Hurtful, but I don't blame you. Even I can tell that that is a very hot lesbian."

"Mark Daubery," snapped Walden. It was only when he roared with laughter that she realised she'd used her teacher voice. Mark was not one of those convenient people still haunted by the memories of schoolday scoldings in his forties, so it hadn't worked even slightly. His eyes were crinkled with real amusement. Laura glanced over at them. Why was this so awkward? Walden would have given a lot, just then, for the armour of a sensible blazer and an old-fashioned brooch. Eighteen-year-old Saffy's arrogant, brittle, faux-punk, and intensely sexually frustrated ghost could go *jump in a lake*.

chapter twenty-one

IMPULSE

THE CONVERSATION IN THE PUB MOVED ON. No one, at least, was looking at the Phoenix anymore.

"You look like you could use some air," said Mark. "Come on."

December nights in Central London: freezing cold, full of movement, full of light. The Tube sign above Covent Garden station gleamed. There were elaborate Christmas displays in the windows of all the shops across the street. Black taxis and scarlet buses wove among the crowds of pedestrians all taking their lives in their own hands every time they crossed the road. Walden turned her face up when she felt something light and cold kiss her skin.

"How about that," she said. "Snow."

"It won't settle," said Mark.

They watched the snowflakes drift through the pools of red and gold and green from the Christmas displays. The yellow bulb of the nearest lamppost was flickering. Walden realised she'd left her jacket over the back of the booth, and in the same moment Mark took his wool coat off and swung it over her shoulders. The motion mysteriously ended with Mark's fingers resting on Walden's upper arm. The Phoenix's sharp talons curled around the spot. Walden imagined she could feel it move, though she never had before—that it was magic, power, and threat that made her skin tingle just then. She looked up at him.

"How much harder do I have to work, Sapphire?" Mark said.

The plaintive tone didn't ring true at all. Walden snorted. "Oh, please. I'm sure you're really suffering."

He grinned: *Fair play to you, can't blame me for trying.* He gave her arm a firm squeeze and let go. "I'm wasting away. Look at me."

"You seem fairly all there to me."

"You know, if you just tell me you're not interested, I'll back off. I'm a bastard, I admit it freely, but I'm not a complete twat."

Walden said nothing.

The grin widened. "Thought so."

"*That* is *not* attractive."

"Confidence works for most people."

"You're not confident," said Walden. "You're smug." And a little echo in her thoughts, Roz in California in the mid-2000s, *You're so fucking smug,* when Saffy hadn't really realised she was being condescending—even now, couldn't remember what had actually annoyed Roz so much. Perhaps Mark had never grown out of being twentysomething and superior, sure the world would work for him, sure he would always get what he wanted in the end. Well, why would he need to? The world did, on the whole, work well for a Mark Daubery.

As it worked well for Sapphire Walden: Saffy, who'd left her high school boyfriend to die in horror and faced nothing worse than a stern talking-to afterwards, who'd still got her A-level grades and her Oxford place, who'd made new friends and had new loves and bought herself a little black dress to wear to parties. Ridiculous to dwell on any of it. All done decades ago. She was Dr Walden now. And yes, the world worked for her: she had success, status, a reasonable share of power, and the comfortable bank balance of a professional woman without dependants who didn't even need to pay a mortgage. She lived in an unfair world where most of the unfairness had worked out in her favour. Looked at that way, she and Mark were two of a kind. So it was no wonder that despite herself, despite knowing exactly what kind of smug bastard he was, despite everything, she rather liked him.

"Shame to waste an atmosphere, you know," said Mark, nodding out at the Christmas lights, the drifting snow.

"I bet you say that to all the girls," said Walden.

"Can't a chap appreciate a romantic night?"

"Are you trying to persuade me that you have hidden depths?"

"Of course I have hidden depths," said Mark in a hurt way. "I know on the surface I seem like a self-involved arsehole. But *under* the surface, I've got finer feelings—sincerity, romance, a little real loneliness, a passion for magic, the soul of a poet. And then deep down, if you really go digging, all the way down at the bottom of my heart . . . eventually, you'll find my true self." A beat. "And it's the same selfish arsehole you spotted in the first place."

Walden started to laugh.

"I'm like a sandwich."

"At least you're honest."

"To you, Sapphire, I wouldn't dare to lie."

"Oh, all *right,*" Sapphire said, which was perhaps not the most romantic way to indicate willingness to be kissed, but Mark chuckled and took her up on it anyway.

And it turned out you didn't grow out of fireworks, you didn't grow out of shivers, you didn't get too old for sexy to be sexy—certainly not when you were only thirty-eight—and Mark could *kiss.* The most recent time she had been kissed was . . . Laura, in the middle of Old Faithful's incursion, a shocking collision of mouths like a declaration of war, not exactly erotic. Before that it had been years. A few fizzling dead-end relationships after she'd come back to the UK. Roz, so sharp and uncompromising, with her beautiful magic; that was the last time she had really managed anything like a capital-*R* Relationship. Uni boyfriends and girlfriends, none of them serious. Charlie, eager, doomed, and twenty years dead.

All long ago and far away. They tucked themselves back against the wall of the pub and Mark kissed with the attention and confidence that belonged to experience: not pushy, not slobbery, not tentative either, firm and warm and taking his cues from her responses. Extremely nice stuff, the kind of snogging that might send a stupider woman than Sapphire head over heels into an endorphin-fuelled haze very quickly. Luckily, she thought, she was very clever and experienced and not bothered about that sort of thing. He put his arms around her, which as well as being appropriate for the moment was also delightfully warm. The Phoenix stirred and murmured indistinctly in the back of her thoughts. *Oh, shut up,* she thought at it.

The murmuring got louder instead. "What's wrong?" said Mark. Walden winced and shook her head hard as if she could shake away the sound that was not sound. *Danger,* wailed the Phoenix, in a cry that was nearly its wordless hunting scream. *Danger!*

The bloody demon was so demanding, so self-absorbed, and so oblivious to how actual adult humans behaved, that she might as well have been carting one of her teenage students around with her everywhere she went. "Shut up," Sapphire said out loud, ignoring Mark's raised eyebrows, and that was when the incursion began.

Half a dozen lines of dull purplish light erupted in the wintry London street, the nearest only narrowly missing a shocked pedestrian. The Phoenix was screaming in Walden's thoughts. Suddenly she saw her own fingernails glow dimly with gold. Her demonic fellow traveller had given up on trying to talk to her; it wanted to fight and it needed her body.

"No, you don't!" said Walden sharply, and got a howl of mental frustration back. The splitting purple lines of incursion were widening; what was happening; where had this *come* from—

"Is it a Christmas thing?" she heard a passing tourist say, and that made her focus. A random demonic incursion opening *through* a living person would probably kill them. "Everyone get back!" she yelled.

To no effect. She was a woman off her home ground and out of her armour: a London partygoer, not a schoolmistress, without authority over the night. She did not have time to try again. Dark shapes were moving in the shadows of the demonic plane. Bubbles of raw and deadly power were pressing up against the fabric of the real world. Something—several somethings—were coming. The Phoenix still wanted to take charge. Walden was not about to hand it power over her body for anything less than an Old Faithful—not when it had just tried to seize control on its own, and had almost, terrifyingly, succeeded.

"GET BACK," shouted another, much louder voice, "IT'S AN EMERGENCY!"

And oh, of course people listened to bloody *Mark*. Well, if it worked. Walden had no time to worry about him. He was all right when he wasn't surprised, but he'd been fairly useless when they went up against that minibus demon in the school car park. She could perceive the dim figures slipping through the gaps in the world, not with her eyes but with the well-honed thaumic awareness of the magician. Demons, none reified yet, so none visible to the layperson—which was a nightmare, because the street was now full of panicking people fleeing from the obvious wild magic of the opening incursion, and the majority of them couldn't see the real danger. Four, five, six demons, all of a good size, sixth order perhaps. All likely to become larger and more dangerous than that fairly soon, because they were actively seeking out an incursion— which meant they were on the hunt—and this was central London, absolutely chock-a-block with systems and selves and *stuff*. There was an Apple store with a gleaming display of white Christmas lights and brightly lit phones and tablets just on the corner of this street, well within range. Any one of these demons could swell up to eighth or ninth order just by ripping through the contents of its stock room.

Fight them? No, not six on one. Walden wasn't a magical combat specialist. *Contain* them, that was the key, until the Marshals got here. And close those inexplicable wild incursions behind them— nothing like that should be possible, not in the middle of London. This wasn't Chetwood, where centuries of wild magic had soaked into the stonework. Yes, there would be some loose magical power around in a place with this many people, but there were also extensive legally mandated wardings all over the place, slammed on anything government-run—the *sewers*, to start with, and the Tube— and London was one place where the budget and trained magicians were always found to keep the wards checked and renewed.

Six good-sized demons, entering the world through four separate dull-gleaming cracks in reality. There was no helping it. She *had* to draw on the Phoenix. Even at the height of her academic practice, when she'd been pushing herself to the very limits of her own ability every day in the lab, she wouldn't have been able to handle this much magic without summoning something to assist her.

It got easier every time to call the power of the Phoenix forth. In Old Faithful's incursion it had taken her nearly three minutes of focused attention to the original binding spells. Now it was barely more than thirty seconds. To onlookers, Walden must seem to be standing frozen, but she was actually concentrating intensely. The corners of her vision lit with a tracery of gold as the blood vessels in her own eyes illuminated with power that was not hers. The frustrated howl in the back of her thoughts settled into focused silence. *We keep the area clear,* Walden told it.

The Phoenix didn't mind that; if the pedestrians weren't part of Walden's own territory, then they were just in the way. However—it made an interested magical lunge in the direction of a passing bus.

No vehicles! Walden thought at it, in rather the tone you might say *No ice cream!* to a demanding group of children on a school trip.

The demon was disappointed, but resigned. It helped Walden to set up multiple circles of warding perimeters, cutting the danger area off from the rest of the street, dividing the separate incursions from each other and from the smorgasbord of shop displays before the invading demons realised what was happening. One or two hostile demons at a time would be much easier for the Marshals to cope with than six at once. Walden insisted that they make the perimeter visible to humans. It flared up in scarlet and gold, firebird colours, warning colours. Now to collapse those incursions—a shame she couldn't push the demons back through them first, but at least there wouldn't be more. It was complex, intricate work. A wild incursion was not nearly so neat and manageable as one created in a lab. Sweat was starting on her forehead and arms despite the chill of the winter evening, and she hadn't the faintest idea where Mark had got to. Calling for help, hopefully.

"Dr Walden," said someone crisply at her shoulder. "Which one's the worst?"

Walden had to close her eyes to keep her focus on managing the Phoenix, holding the multiple perimeter circles, squeezing the fabric of reality back into place around the bulging holes, and talking to someone at the same time. She'd only seen a brief glimpse of Laura's white Marshal jacket. "Back left sector," she managed. "Closest to the big technology display." That incursion was already shut, but there were two demons left in the sector where it had been, one fifth order, one sixth, both of them well aware of the feast of power just within their grasp. Walden, with her eyes still closed, added: "If there's anyone from school still in the pub and sober enough, have them go and shore up the wards on the shop. They're shaky." She could feel the shoddiness of it, someone's end-of-the-week rush job to comply with health and safety regulations—not the only one on this street either. You didn't *get* serious demon problems in London. There were so many wardings about—some of them still powered by the gigantic installations of magical defences laid down during the Blitz—that surely someone else's protective spell would catch a problem if yours weren't quite good enough. But that didn't work if everyone skimped.

She couldn't turn her head to see what Laura was doing. But she knew, she *knew*, that Laura was extremely good. So she wasn't surprised when the alarming sense of shoddiness in the nearest set of wards began to ease. In a crowded area, defence before attack was common sense, and anyone with a tertiary degree in magic should know how to fix a bad incursion ward. There had been half a dozen magician teachers still at the afterparty, not all of them drunk.

And then she wasn't surprised, not at all, when Laura stepped into the danger sector, facing one fifth-order demon and one sixth, shortsword shining, power gathering around her solid, muscular form. *Danger,* murmured the Phoenix, the first thing it had said in a while.

Its tone was almost appreciative. Laura Kenning was an interesting kind of dangerous.

Walden did not relax, but there was a real difference between the terror of finding yourself unexpectedly facing a throng of demons and the healthy, intelligent fear you felt when the crisis wasn't over but you knew you had good people on your side. It was truly a pleasure to watch Laura at work. It had only been two months since Walden had seen her try to take on Old Faithful, but she had noticeably improved. Her use of magical force had already been crisp and expert: Marshal-style combat spells at their best, underpinned by Laura's own athleticism. To that she'd added something Walden didn't expect at all, an edge of grace and precision that you never saw in a—*hedge witch,* said Mark's voice in the back of her head; Walden was disappointed to hear it from herself; *non-academic magical practitioner,* she corrected her own thought.

Words, selves, the Phoenix murmured, *selves and words.*

Laura, already a very good demon hunter, had responded to losing her job at Chetwood by deciding to get better. Two months of focused work could make a huge difference to someone's skills when they were eighteen, but you didn't often see it happen to a person over thirty. Not because adults were incapable of learning—of course not. They were just usually a lot worse at it.

Not Laura.

Walden, after a few moments watching her demolish two substantial demons at once, hadn't the slightest doubt. She'd been taking magic lessons: serious, academic, theory-focused lessons, with a good teacher—someone strict on form, with double expertise in invocation and evocation. Roger Rollins at Goldsmiths, maybe, elderly now but a very good magician indeed, one of the last mighty-bearded Communists left in British academic magic; he'd briefly supervised Walden as an undergrad, before he decided Oxford was still too bourgeois for him.

Of course, anyone could learn Walden's style of magic, if they really wanted to. It was just hard work. Hard work for a child whose only actual job was going to school and learning things, and even harder work for an adult who had to fit the reading and lab time into evening and weekend classes around their day job. And expensive too, unless Laura had got the Order to fund it as prof dev somehow, which Walden doubted, because the Order of Marshals would not be nearly so eager to rent out its members as private school security if it was running a budget surplus.

Focus, whispered the Phoenix, which had learned patience for the peculiar wanderings and curlings-about of Walden's funny little water-and-meat brain, but only to a point. *It comes.*

"Oh dear," said Walden.

The sixth-order demon in the nearest sector of her elaborate perimeter had finally finished thinking through its situation and realised that Walden was the person stopping it from enjoying its night out in London. It had been in the real world for long enough that it was starting to reify spontaneously. When it drew towards her, it appeared to be a ghostly figure outlined in a blurred pale drift of snowflakes. Meltwater dripped in its wake. Pedestrians stopped, pointed, aimed phones to take video—phones? Were they crazy?—and Walden readied a banishment. What had happened to Mark? A little of the competence he displayed on their planar patrols would be really very useful right about now.

No mercy, the Phoenix whispered.

Walden cast.

Nothing complicated. *Complicated* had to be saved for the perimeters she was still maintaining. A straightforward banishment like a blast of strong wind. Another. *It's weak*, murmured the Phoenix. *It doesn't know what to be.* Melting snowflakes dripped from the demon's inchoate, half-real shape. Somewhere behind Walden there were sirens shrilling, a long rising wail that joined the growing hunt-song in her thoughts. *It does not see me yet,* the Phoenix crooned, exultant. *It will not flee in time.*

Kill it. Eat it.

Walden's next spell was not a banishment, but a slash of golden claws.

The demon disintegrated. Immediately, without pause for thought, Walden activated the siphoning spells in her other set of tattoos, the ones on her left arm.

A swirl of snowflakes and shadow. The lines of spellwriting among the tattooed flowers on her left arm prickled, but did not burn. She tasted chill at the back of her throat, as if she'd suddenly swallowed an ice cube. The demon was gone, disintegrated into raw magic; and the magic was gone, because Walden had consumed it. The Phoenix luxuriated, triumphant, in power possessed for its own.

Then the Marshals arrived.

chapter twenty-two

A SLIGHTLY
REGRETTABLE DECISION

T HE MARSHALS MADE UP FOR TAKING NEARLY
fifteen minutes to get there by being extremely busy and
officious once they turned up. The remaining demons—
only four of them, because Laura had taken out one of hers while
Walden was facing the snowflake-creature—were swiftly and ef-
ficiently despatched by a double squad of KMVs. Someone who
must have been Laura's partner turned up and joined her, and all
three hunting pairs switched into patrol mode: Laura and her partner ranging the street, a second pair checking in and out of shops
and alleyways, and the third stamping their feet in the cold for a
few moments before someone in overalls turned up and levered up
a manhole cover for them so they could climb down into the dim
underbelly of the city.

A dozen junior Marshals, less impressive than the KMVs,
quickly set up a warning-tape barrier around orange traffic cones.
Then they corralled the idiot pedestrians with phones and started
running imp checks. Two academic magicians in winter coats with
Marshal badges and high-vis armbands turned up; that would be

the warding squad. Walden, still feeling rather stunned by everything that had just happened, watched not very intelligently as the two of them did a worse and slower job than she would have of establishing that the surprise incursions were definitely gone and shoring up the wards in range, all along the street. Of course, if you were a trained academic magician and you wanted a career where you actually *used* magic, there were plenty of jobs in industry and security that paid a lot better than working for the Marshals. The only thing that paid worse, in fact, was probably teaching.

Walden stood, and stood. She should have been completely exhausted. She should have been half-collapsed on the pavement. But the cool rush of power from the demon that she and the Phoenix had eaten, the demon that was now a part of them, was something between a draught of water straight from a spring in the Scottish Highlands and a slug of strong gin. She was fizzing. She could have set the city on fire. She could have buried all of Covent Garden under ice. She stared at nothing.

"Miss, you're in shock," someone said. "Miss, come and sit down."

"Doctor," said Walden automatically.

Then she was sitting on an uncomfortable metal chair, still in her black party dress and Mark's warm wool coat, next to a van marked with the ancient Marshal coat of arms—sword and armoured fist crossed on a shining white shield. There was a folding table in front of her. Walden rested her hands on it. After a moment, a middle-aged man with dark brown skin and thinning hair sat down on the other side of the table. He had the bulky, sagging build of someone who had been heavyset and dangerous before he moved to a desk job, and could probably still punch an archdemon with reasonable force if he really wanted to. "Arjun Ramamurthy," he said pleasantly. "I'm Chief of Incident Response for southeast England."

Walden could see the rank stripes on his sleeve and the white-and-gold detailing at the collar of his jacket. "KMGC," she said.

Knight Mareschal Grand Capus. Chief Ramamurthy inclined his head. "Most people don't know the ins and outs of Marshal ranks," he said. "And you, of course, are Dr Sapphire Walden."

Walden tried to shake herself out of her daze. "Have we met?"

"Only in my files, Doctor."

There was a pause. But it wasn't really surprising. Laura had mentioned something, hadn't she? *The Order of Marshals keeps track. I could count them on my fingers.* If your entire organisation had grown up over centuries for no other purpose than to battle demons, any sensible set of risk assessments ought to include 'and here are the individuals whom we know have the capacity to perform higher-level demon summoning.'

This man was most likely Laura's boss's boss's boss. Magical security for multiple counties, including a city the size of London, was not a small job.

"How can I help you, Chief Ramamurthy?" she asked.

"Our team hasn't found any sign of an arcane array in the area yet," Ramamurthy said. "Perhaps you have some idea why."

"There won't be one," said Walden. "That was a wild incursion, not a summoning. Pure chance and bad luck—a random magical weakness in the area, and an opportunistic push by whatever demons happened to be close by."

"Except that this is the second incursion crisis that you've found yourself mixed up with in the last two months, Dr Walden," said Chief Ramamurthy. "That's *very* bad luck."

There was a chilly little silence.

"I'm not sure I understand you," said Walden icily at last. She understood him perfectly.

"It's late and it's a cold night," said Chief Ramamurthy. "And I'm very sorry to spoil your evening," with a nod that took in the *stupid* black dress. "Perhaps we could continue this conversation in the near future. Here's my card. I'd like to have a friendly chat about all this soon. Tomorrow, or over the weekend."

"I may forget," said Walden, taking the card without looking at it. "It's a busy time of year."

"Then the Order of Marshals will be in touch, Doctor—"

"It's Arjun, isn't it?" said another voice. Walden looked up sharply. So did Chief Ramamurthy. "Nice to see you, old chap, it's been a while. Can I have a word?" The tone was plummier than usual for Mark, in a way that was plainly intentional, all Oxbridge and Whitehall, connected, knowing. His friendly smile and bluff, manly handshake were not received with notable pleasure by Chief Ramamurthy. But he still stood up to accept the handshake; and now Mark was on Walden's side of the table, giving her a hand up, a brief warm squeeze around the shoulder. Mark was a cool, manipulative bastard, and Ramamurthy obviously knew it, and knew *him*; knew him, despised him, and thought he couldn't afford to offend him.

And where exactly had he been for the last forty minutes?

Walden couldn't see Mark's face, only his back in the casual blazer he'd been wearing under the winter overcoat. For the first time in some weeks, she thought: *Who are you, Mark Daubery?*

"Shall we?" said Mark a few moments later. "Tube's just that way."

"I probably ought to say good night to everyone," Walden began.

"Everyone's gone home, Sapphire."

"Well, at least—" And she looked around for where she'd last seen Laura. Competent help in the middle of that surprise incursion had been very useful. She ought to say—thank you? Good night? Goodbye? Walden picked her way across the street, around the barrier of traffic cones and warning tape. "Hello," she said.

"Scuse me," said Laura to her partner, who looked frightfully young to Walden now she was up close. "I'll be right back. We're clear here, but don't let your guard down. Stay in visual." She turned back. "Dr Walden," she said, and Walden frowned, because surely they'd parted on first-name terms.

"Laura, I just wanted to thank you for your help," she said. "Can I—"

Laura grimaced, glanced up and down the street to check none of the other Marshals were in earshot, and then glared at her and said, "That guy? Really? *That guy?*"

"Er—what?"

"What do you mean, what?"

"I don't know what you mean," said Walden. "If there's something I ought to know about Mark Daubery . . ."

She found she was half hoping for *yes.* Consultant, advisor, *military stuff, the civil service hates me, it's been a while old chap,* and something the Chair of Governors had said, rather smugly, because it was a coup to get hold of someone like this for free—*the highest levels of government.* So Walden's mental picture did have a few details filled out, despite Mark's tiresome mysteriousness. He was not actual military—he would have mentioned a rank by now, they always did. Most likely he was somewhere between semi-unofficial and completely off the books. But he was certainly someone with power. What kind of power? Where? What was a person like that doing hanging around Chetwood?

But Laura didn't announce a dark mystery. The disgusted look on her face struck Walden as simple distaste—the working woman's distaste for the posh bastard—and perhaps even jealousy. Which was ridiculous. It was so *petty*. They'd agreed, hadn't they? They'd said it wasn't worth trying long distance. And if Laura had wanted anything else, she'd had years working with Walden to make herself clear. It wasn't *Walden's* fault that Laura Kenning had waited until the middle of a giant demonic incursion to turn out to be competent and beautiful and interested.

"Something you ought to know? Only what ought to be obvious to anyone with a brain," Laura said. "I don't . . . obviously it's none of my business. Just, you know what you're getting there. Or you ought to."

"It *isn't* any of your business," said Walden coldly.

"Okay," said Laura, chilly and judgemental in the halo of the streetlights. "Okay. Then I don't think we have very much to say to each other, do we? Watch that fucking bird. It's getting worse."

"You should probably keep your uninformed opinions to yourself, thank you, Marshal," said Walden. She had meant to say *You looked fantastic out there* and *I can tell how hard you've been working* and *Is it Professor Rollins teaching you?* and *For heaven's sake why don't we have each other's phone numbers?* Instead she said, "I appreciated your assistance this evening. Good night."

"Tube," Walden said, seizing Mark's arm as she stormed past him. "We're going home."

She was simmering with irritation from Leicester Square to King's Cross. The Phoenix was at rest in her thoughts, its thirst for the world slaked with cool, delicious power. The Underground was crowded. Mark shouldered through crowds that made room for him in the way they never would for someone Walden's height, and drew her afterwards. He even found her a seat on their eventual train home. "Sorry," Walden said at last. "I'm being very poor company."

"You've had a hell of a night," Mark said. "Bad enough to have to handle all those demons without Marshals jumping down your throat for no reason at the end of it. I'll see what I can do to get Ramamurthy off your back."

"*Will* you," said Walden, feeling both dubious and contrary. It would be delightful if Chief Ramamurthy and his absurd suspicions went away immediately and she never had to think about them again, but she did not like how easy Mark made it sound. She wasn't a stupid person. She had multiple university degrees. She *did* know what she was getting with this man. It probably wasn't a good idea to owe him—good God, what was he implying—*political* favours?

Mark paused. "Or not, if you prefer," he said. "It was just an offer. We both know he's wrong. No reason someone that senior should waste his time investigating a dead end."

"Oh, I see," Walden said. "You'd be doing *him* a favour."

"I try to see it as making life easier for everyone," Mark said. "It's the way the world works. I didn't make it that way. Look, Sapphire, I'm going to be sincere for a moment."

"I've reached the middle of the arsehole sandwich?"

An engaging, rueful grin. "Sure. Here it comes. I'm going to admit I did some snooping. Same reason Ramamurthy is thinking about it—you see a demon problem, you see a powerful invoker standing right next to it, you need to rule out the obvious. I know a bit about you. The American job offer, some other things. I'm not saying I've been stalking you—there's not much that's *personal*—"

"No," said Walden. "I imagine the MOD's file on me is mostly interested in my research history and my time abroad."

"And how recruitable you are," Mark said, smiling easily as if he wasn't almost certainly sharing the contents of a database that needed security clearance to access. "Not very, in case you were wondering, barring a Third World War situation."

"Funnily enough, I knew that already."

"What I wanted to say is—I don't actually meet very many people with principles. Serious principles. But I know you've got them. I don't. Could never stick to any. But I respect it."

"I seem to remember someone making fun of my career earlier this evening," Walden said. "'Teaching a niche A-level'—wasn't that it?"

Mark shrugged. "Most people with principles are hypocrites on some level," he said. "It's just that the level is usually 'money.' Puts you a step ahead of the crowd, if for you it's 'not being bored out of my mind.' If you really thought the best use of your time was, what was it, making a nasty world a little bit fairer for all the poor innocent children, then you could be teaching GCSE Maths in some sad inner-city comp, couldn't you? But you love magic. It's the magic that keeps you at Chetwood, not the money. So yes, Sapphire, for that, you have one arsehole's genuine respect."

"Thank you so much. I'm sure I shall treasure it forever."

Mark snorted. "And you cut me down to size. I enjoy that."

"Do you?"

The train rumbled through the December night. It was the slow train, following the old Victorian tracks and stopping at every country station, and there were not many other people left in the carriage. They could have claimed a table by now, but instead they were sitting side by side.

"Of course I do," said Mark, smiling down at her, and then he took Sapphire's hand and he kissed her again. He was still a very good kisser.

So she took him back to her flat, the wood-panelled Headmaster's flat in Brewers Hall next door to the thaumic engines, which rumbled quietly to themselves in the otherwise ghostly silence of the empty school. And they had sex, which Mark was also good at. Sapphire rather wished she'd insisted on a gin and tonic first, just to relax a bit. It was hard not to be self-conscious. It had been a long time. She wasn't someone who got terribly worried about how her body looked to other people—obviously not, or she would be going to the gym once in a while—but Mark *was* very fit, and, well, thirty-eight looked pretty different from eighteen.

He noticed, obviously, and went out of his way to be good about it—to be enthusiastic and good-humoured and charming about the whole thing, soothing awkwardness and uncertainty, letting Sapphire needle him verbally in a way he did seem to enjoy and which certainly made her feel better. He went down on her for a long time, and then said, "Listen, if this isn't going to work for you, then I'd rather know what would," which was really quite sweet of him, certainly above average in her experience of one-off hookups with straight men. He followed instructions well after that, and didn't get awkward or insecure about digging the bullet vibrator out of Sapphire's bedside drawer. All the benefits of age and experience, in other words. Perfectly nice sex. Very worthwhile. *Scratching the itch, hopefully for good,* Sapphire thought afterwards; *finally, there's that out of my system.*

And it was late, and though she was out of the habit of sharing a bed, Mark was large and warm and not unwelcome company on a December night. Rolling over and going to sleep was much easier than the fuss of kicking him out and then sorting out her hot water bottle. It would probably be unkind to kick him out, anyway.

So morning came. Sapphire—Walden—was prepared for it to be a little awkward, in the way she remembered these things. But she woke up alone, in the dark. Her alarm clock said it was a little before seven; late for a school day, but much too early to be awake in the holidays. The bed was still warm, and she hadn't bothered getting dressed again after they were done. Her dressing gown on the hook in the bathroom seemed a dreadfully long way away. She pulled the covers up tighter and tried to go back to sleep.

Possibly she dozed a little. Next time she paid attention to the morning, there was watery winter light visible around the edge of the curtains, and she could hear the shower running. It was already half past eight. She sat up.

Mark came in with wet hair and her faded old yellow towel around his waist a bit later. *Yes, he's good-looking,* Walden told herself crossly. *It's out of your system, thank you.* "Good morning," she said.

"Morning," said Mark. "Mistimed it, haven't I? I was going to chivalrously bring you a cup of tea."

"Coffee, please, if it's on offer," Walden said. "All in the kitchen—assuming you can work the press."

"I think I can handle it," said Mark.

Walden cursed herself afterwards, listening to him explore her flat's little kitchen. *Coffee, please*—ugh, she blamed the towel round the waist. She should have got *rid* of him. She didn't want him there anymore. A one-night stand with an attractive stranger was a reasonable enough response to a normal human urge. A one-night stand with a self-confessed arsehole whom you had to work with— thank *God* it was Christmas break and she wouldn't see him for a week or two. She put on her elderly pyjamas and went and got her dressing gown, raggedy white towelling, decidedly unsexy. Then she opened the bedroom curtains and let the winter sunlight in.

She was still trying to think of an opening gambit for *that was very nice thank you now please go away* when Mark came back in with a mug of coffee—WORLD'S BEST TEACHER—handed it to her, and started putting his trousers on. "I'd better be getting on," he said. "Mater expects the whole brood to come and kneel before her throne every Christmas. I assume you're off for the holidays too. See you next term!"

Walden, torn between insulted *That's it?*—yes, she'd gone out of her way to signal that the encounter was over, but was he not even going to *try?*—and enormous relief, said the first thing that came into her head. "I'm going to call it. You do *not* actually call your mother *Mater*."

"I might," said Mark.

"No."

"I *could.*"

"At this point you are approaching self-parody. I don't believe it. I have known my share of posers," said Walden, "and I also know that you went to school in the 1990s, not the 1890s. This behaviour, Mark Daubery, is a pose."

"Posers? Oh, of course. I bet *you* were an emo," said Mark.

"Not relevant."

"Means you were. Point to Daubery."

"As youth subcultures go, that one was a bit after your time, surely."

"I always liked younger women."

"Oh, do sod off," said Walden, and took a sip of her coffee.

"Sodding off, ma'am," said Mark. "Sorry! Sodding off, Doctor." He rescued his nice wool coat from where she'd chucked it onto a chair last night and swung it over his arm. "Have a good Christmas, Sapphire."

So that was the end of that. Here was Walden, alone in her flat, alone in her empty school, a week before Christmas Day. The coffee was fine. She showered afterwards. Getting dressed proved unexpectedly tricky. She hesitated over her usual skirt and blouse, then over the ancient band T-shirts and the cheap leggings that should have been thrown out years ago, and found herself wondering: *Why don't I have any non-work clothes suitable for a grown-up?*

She wore T-shirt and leggings, defiantly, under a big warm jumper. She wandered through her flat, vaguely bereft, and almost went into the office to get a head start on planning for next term. She went and turned on the TV, flicked through iPlayer, got up and found her laptop and looked up how to sign up for other streaming services, and decided it was a huge waste of money really. In desperation, she wondered if the school gym would be open today.

Thirty-eight and alone. Thirty-eight and independent, successful, proud of the good work that she knew she did every day. In a few days she would be getting the train to Sussex, sleeping not in her childhood bedroom—thank God—but in the crooked little box room of the seventeenth-century cottage her parents had bought as a retirement project. And then she'd be yet another self for a few days, the Saffy that was, not even eighteen but thirteen, sloping around the house feeling pointless while Mum did battle with the cottage's terrible plumbing and Dad worked on his garden. Church with the family on Christmas Day. Leftovers on Boxing Day. The dead week between Christmas and New Year. It was usually a bit of a relief when school started again.

It would probably be nice to see the whole family. Her older brother John had two children approaching their teens, both of whom were fairly sweet. Primary school age was not Walden's preferred genre of child, but by age eight or nine they were basically sensible human beings, curious and interested in the world, not yet victim to the cruelties of puberty and therefore perfectly straightforward to talk to. And both of them liked Walden, in the way that children generally approved of an aunt who took them seriously and did expensive birthday presents.

Walden knew John wasn't thinking of Chetwood for them. Her sister-in-law didn't like the idea of boarding school. Come to think of it, John must be fifty next year. What a number! At Walden's age, he'd already had the wife, the mortgage, the prospect of kids. None of those things existed in her life, or would. She had her career, her boarding school lodgings, and the Phoenix.

And someday she'd be fifty.

Oh, this was maudlin. She was Director of Magic at Chetwood School and there was one job here that always needed doing. Walden went into her office to fetch her kit—salt and chalk, a nice set of marker pens, a neat little dagger—and then went next door to tune up the thaumic engines. The last person in—Todd, presumably, with his toolbox, handling the mechanical side—had left the door on the latch, instead of properly chained and padlocked. Even with no students on site, that ran contrary to the risk assessment. Walden went to get her own key out of the box where she kept it in the kitchen next to the teapot, and locked the door again. She made a mental note. She would have to have a word with Todd after Christmas.

SPRING I

chapter twenty-three

BEFORE IT GOES BANG

S PRING TERM STARTED QUIETLY, ESPECIALLY for Walden. Without her A-level set taking up eight hours of her time every week, her timetable opened up dramatically. Well, it opened up for about ten minutes. Then the time got filled up with meetings. It was at least nice to have them during the few hours of weak January sunlight, instead of having to shove something in at 7 A.M. or 6 P.M., in pitch darkness, to work around the demands of the school day. Meetings: strategic, operational, financial, academic, pastoral, departmental, faculty, twilight training, all hands. It never stopped. At the first all-hands briefing of the term, Walden delivered an update for everyone on the school's magical security situation, which boiled down to 'really, we are working hard on this and everything is under control.' The relieved looks around the school hall told her she should have said it sooner.

Of course, all of that was just the official roster of things teachers needed to talk about. As much or more of the work was done in passing, in the breaktime drop-in *Can I just have a word about*, the catch-up over lunch *And that's what worries me*, the rapid email exchange in the five minutes between lessons that concluded *Better log it in the safeguarding portal.* One of Walden's commonest drop-in just-so-you-know encounters at the moment was *I hate to be a bother, but I think we've got another imp . . .*

On a Saturday morning five days into the Spring Term, Lilly Tibbett poked her head awkwardly round Walden's office door— NQTs were seldom sure about how much or how little they were allowed to ask for help—and said, "Um, it's a bit of a weird one. Something in the labs is just . . . off."

Walden sighed, put down the examiners' report she was reading, and stood up.

There was a Year Nine class in PE kit in Lab One. This arcane lab was one of the ones that usually belonged to the Evocation Department, and so it was less snowy and pristine than the lab Walden taught her practicals in. Just now there were soot stains down one wall and scuff marks on the white-painted floor. Two thirteen-year-olds stood facing each other in the middle of an excited, noisy semicircle of their classmates. One of them had a handful of conjured green fire; the other was trying to evoke a shield, not very successfully. Lilly's intake of breath told Walden that this was *not* the position she'd left them in.

She shouldn't have left them at all—not this age group, not unsupervised in a lab, not when she had a weird feeling already. Lilly hadn't been able to clarify what her bad feeling was, but 'something's not right here' was part of a teacher's toolkit, not to be disregarded. School days were so extremely routine that you became sensitised to the tiny variations that signalled something out of place, and began to develop a gut instinct for which variations were the bad ones. Walden would talk to Lilly later about when to send a reliable-looking child to run your errands for you.

Under other circumstances she would have let the junior

teacher handle her own class, but the moment she stepped through the lab door she felt it too. Something was *not* right, in a way that went beyond the obvious misbehaviour. She looked at the incipient evocation duel and snapped, *"Sit down immediately, Year Nine."*

Twenty-five children in the room, and twenty-three of them folded up cross-legged right where they were standing. Walden seldom used the aura of terror a senior teacher could generate on actual children. Faces turned towards her with big eyes. She knew this group—she tried to know every group, obviously. She'd done the arcane safety carousel with them in Year Seven, and would do it again next year when they hit Year Ten. But two years was a long time, and children could change dramatically in early puberty. The only names she remembered with complete certainty were the class clown, Morris, and a small intense girl who asked excellent questions, whom she'd pegged as a future Invocation student— Noor. Morris was the one she would have expected to be in the middle of the trouble, but he was folded on the floor with the rest of the chastised audience. It was only the two duelists still standing. Walden dragged the name of the gangly boy with the flickering shield out of her memory—Alfie, she was almost sure, though he was a foot and a half taller than when she'd last taught him. Noor, tiny, bespectacled, with a silky dark ponytail, was the one with her hands full of fire. They stood as if they hadn't heard, focused entirely on each other.

"Alfie, Noor," began Lilly in a pretty good you're-in-trouble tone.

"Heads down," snapped Walden, feeling the stirring of magic in motion a moment before it happened.

Arcane safety lessons paid off: the Year Nines ducked and covered without question as a green sheet of flame erupted over all their heads. The slower on the uptake were grabbed by the quick

ones and pushed flat. Walden and Lilly moved in the same moment to rescue Noor's actual target. Lilly might be an inexperienced teacher but she was a very good evoker, so the shield she
flung up on top of Alfie's panicky, flickering attempt was almost
instantaneous, a sheer and shining wall of magical force. Green fire
hissed and sizzled against it like boiling water poured into a pan,
and then winked out.

Walden called crisply, "Stasis!"—not because you ever needed
to announce a spell in order to cast it, that was a beginners' mis-
conception, but so that Lilly would know what she was doing, and
wouldn't interfere with her work by casting something else at a right
angle. Then she slammed a slow-down onto both Alfie and Noor.
True stasis was dangerous—a spell that could freeze human muscle
could stop a human heart—but if either of the children tried to
move, it would feel like swimming through jelly. It should prevent
Noor from evoking any more gouts of fire. "Thank you, everyone.
Miss Tibbett, I believe Lab Three is available. Please could you
continue your lesson there? And just drop an alert email to the
Marshals for me. Year Nine, I expect you to leave the room in good
order and in silence. Do not collect your belongings. Consider this
a practice for the next fire drill. I will speak to your whole class at
afternoon registration. Thank you, Miss Tibbett." She gave a firm,
reassuring nod to Lilly, who couldn't be undermined in front of her
Year Nines with the actual words: *I have this under control. I know it's
frightening, but keep calm, do your job, and leave me to mine.*

A scattering of pencil cases and exercise books were left on the
floor as the class filed out. They cast nervous looks at Walden, and
at the two children still frozen in the middle of the room. Noor had
her hands up in a casting gesture. Alfie's expression was fixed in a
look of terror.

Something was off. Even the most talented Year Nines did not cast spells as strong as that sheet of green flame. And Year Nines, on the whole, did not try to murder their classmates. Teasing, testing, challenging, undermining, outright bullying—these were the expected interpersonal conflicts of the middle school. Brutal magical incineration, even at Chetwood: no.

The children's faces were finally, slowly, turning towards her. The slow-down spell made the motion into spooky horror-film stuff. Walden did not panic. She swiftly checked the incursion wards, and found them all in order. All the same . . . best to eliminate the worst possibility first. She quickly set up a diagnostic, drawn in blue marker pen on the whiteboard and fed with the tiniest possible trickle of power: *Who's here?*

The array illuminated with silvery light and then sounded three quick, strong chimes: one, two, three humans. A fourth chime, almost as loud: the Phoenix, loud and clear. Nothing else. Walden held her breath.

A fifth note sounded, this one quiet, like a breeze sighing through a distant windchime. And then, almost on the edge of hearing, a sixth.

Two more demons. But they hadn't broken through the incursion wards in the lab. Which left only one possibility: they must have entered in the same way as the Phoenix—by walking straight through the door, riding on a human being.

Walden kept her expression very calm. The Phoenix was already alert, springing to life in her mind, its scarlet-and-gold body coiling sinuously around her forearm as it craned its head to see. There was nothing to see. Two normal-looking Year Nines. Alfie had the slight nervous stoop of a boy who wasn't used to being tall yet. Noor had a spot on her chin, slathered in too much concealer, which was probably making it worse.

Possession.

Walden considered those chimes. One quiet, one almost inaudible. Small demons, then. But small demons should not have the strength to forcibly possess even a half-trained human magician. How could this have happened?

Well. You did the job that was in front of you, and then you got on with the next thing. Alfie first, because that had not been a very good shield—suggesting that the weakest, near-inaudible demon was riding on or inside him—and because he looked about as terrified as she had ever seen any child.

The Phoenix paid meticulous attention to Walden's exorcism array as she drew it in tidy green chalk on the scuffed white floor around Alfie's slowly shifting feet. *Wouldn't work on me,* it said thoughtfully as Walden stood up.

I'd use something bigger for you, thought Walden, taking up a position at the northern edge of the array. Alfie shifted slowly to face her.

She got no words back, just an impression of something snapping its beak and ruffling up all its feathers. She'd hurt its feelings. Did demons *have* feelings?

I'm very big and complicated, said the Phoenix, with reproach and a touch of pride.

Walden knew how it felt to be exorcised—she'd done a first-year undergraduate lab practical which almost certainly hadn't been properly risk assessed, an Oxford tradition, where her supervision group had summoned a second-order imp and then been possessed and exorcised one by one. It felt for about three and a half seconds like something was trying to squeeze your lungs out through your throat. Then it was fine; a relief, even, as the weight of demonic power lifted from your limbs. Alfie's slowed-down cry of agony was still very hard to listen to. His mouth opened. A wisp of something dark and smoky-looking emerged. Walden's right hand snatched it out of the air without her needing to think about it. The smoke, crushed between her fingers, left a chalky black residue. *Barely big enough to eat,* the Phoenix remarked.

Walden lifted the stasis and said, "Alfie, please wait over there. Thank you." She was careful to turn away before the tears brimming in his eyes fell; he was already scrubbing frantically at them with the back of his hand.

Noor looked neither frightened nor unhappy. The corner of her mouth was pulling slowly upwards in a lopsided snarl that showed her teeth, fenced by braces. It was a child's face, but not a child's expression. Walden drew the second exorcism array larger, to keep herself well out of physical range. Every time she glanced up Noor had shifted, fighting ferociously against the slow-down spell, trying to get a little closer to Walden. She was not a big girl, but a child did not need to be bigger than you to hurt you—not if you cared about their safety, and they didn't. This demon, aggressive and fiery as it seemed to be, probably had only a passing interest in keeping Noor herself in one piece.

Array complete. Walden took up a casting position at its northernmost corner, and activated it.

Should have made it bigger, said the Phoenix at the last moment. Walden grunted with effort as she dragged magic through the array, pushing the exorcism into action by brute force. This demon was fighting hard against being pulled out of its host. At last Noor's worrying snarl fell away, and she cried out in pain and then started to cough horribly. The thing that emerged past her lips was slime, not smoke: gloopy, dark green, smearing over her chin and her red PE kit, blood-flecked.

Walden held out a commanding hand. The bulk of the slimy stuff gathered into a nasty globule of green matter and jumped into her palm. It felt slightly warm and completely disgusting. The image of the Phoenix darted down past the band of tattooed spell-writing at her wrist and slashed at it with shining talons. *Third-order demon*, Walden thought. Unsettling ooze was a common reification for something this size.

Where had it come from? How had it got here? Why didn't Walden already know?

Noor's coughing kept going and turned into awful wheezes. Walden lived inside her authoritative calm, immovable, sepulchral. "Noor, where's your inhaler?"

Noor sat down hard on the floor, pointing, unable to make words. Walden retrieved the inhaler from the pencil case and handed it over. An asthmatic teenager usually knew what to do for their own emergency better than someone who hadn't done the first aid training in several months. Noor took deep, slow puffs from the inhaler. From the other side of the room where she'd ordered him to wait, Alfie said, "Should I get the nurse?"

Sensible boy. He still sounded a little wobbly. Walden wasn't letting him out of her sight until she knew where that imp he'd been carrying had come from. "If Noor can walk, we're all going to go together."

"I'm okay," said Noor faintly after a few minutes. She'd wiped her mouth and chin, but there was still scarlet-flecked slime on her PE top. "I'm okay. It's fine." There was a certain kind of teenage girl who would claim everything was fine up to and past the end of the world. The other option, of course, was sobbing hysterics, which would not have been unjustified. Possessed by a third-order demon—at *school*. Where she should have been safe. Where they all ought to be safe. Walden did not let her feelings show. She was furious with herself.

There was a sound from the doorway. Walden looked up. The duty Marshal stood there, with his sword half out of its sheath.

"Perfect timing," she said. "We've had an incident. Please could the Marshals do a full check of this room, and then—are you both boarders?" The children nodded. "Sweep Scrubs, please. Starting in the Year Nine dormitories. Thank you. I'll join you shortly. If Mr Daubery is on site, do please alert him as well."

Walden was busy with incident response for the rest of the day. The Marshals unearthed one culprit quickly enough: Alfie's dormitory had a second-hand, unauthorised Nintendo Switch hidden in the back corner of a wardrobe, apparently held in common by all six boys, actual origin unclear, exactly the sort of device that an imp might find irresistibly attractive as a dwelling place. Once he'd been cleared by the nurse, Walden delivered a blistering tongue-lashing first to Alfie individually and then to the six of them as a group. Two weeks of daily detention. No clubs, fixtures, or extracurricular activities. The Head would be calling their parents. The boys hung their heads.

Class clown Morris came back to knock on Walden's office door afterwards with an additional confession: the Switch was his idea. He'd found it on eBay. It was all his fault. So that needed another tongue-lashing, and an additional punishment, but this had to be tempered with a measure of approval for Morris's honesty and obvious agony about the whole thing. Walden was not surprised that her first instinct had been right, and he was mixed up in the trouble somehow. You got a feel for these things.

The Marshals did not find any unauthorised electronics in Noor's dormitory, or in any other obvious hiding place. Once she was sure Noor was clear of all traces of possession and safe from further demonic threats, Walden headed over to Scrubs herself. On a sharp hunch, she called the grounds office first. Todd wasn't in there—he hardly ever was—but she got hold of one of the Maintenance team who promised to go and find the Keymaster and send him over at the first opportunity. Gossiping all the way, Walden had no doubt. Premises and Maintenance—the cleaners, gardeners, and handymen who were among the most vital of the non-teaching staff—went everywhere and knew everything that happened in the school.

The Year Nine girls' dorms had all been tossed through already, and looked even more chaotic than usual. Did the Marshals have to throw all the bed linen on the floor, and could they not have put it back afterwards? Walden knew the thought was unreasonable even as she had it. Besides, half the mess was probably the girls themselves. In any case, she needed to do it all again, under-the-mattress checks and all, and quickly: she could not in good conscience let any of the children back in until she was personally completely convinced that these rooms were magically secure, which meant it needed to be done before evening curfew. Either that, or someone would have to find a different place for fifty-odd thirteen-year-olds to sleep tonight.

It took a long time, and it wasn't until Todd joined her, tilted his head for a moment, and said, "Did you check the scaffolding?" that they finally pinned down the breach. Walden sat on the windowsill and leaned out to look up at the tower of scaffolding built up around Scrubs's west wall over the Christmas holidays to reach the dodgiest bit of the flat roof—a very 1960s design, but a flat roof, in England, was an invitation to damp problems. Her breath hissed between her teeth. There was nothing visible in the mundane world, but the Phoenix had sprung into alertness, as a cat might turn its head sharply towards a rustle in the bushes. Walden could feel the fault line in reality, the slow leakage of raw wild magic into the surrounding environment. *Drip, drip,* through a gap in the wards she had never imagined could be there, following the elaborate system of platforms and girders. The Year Nine dormitories were right under the worst spot. Noor would have been looking out at the scaffolding tower through her bedroom window.

Walden had to climb out there and patch the school wards herself, which meant per Todd's insistence that she had to kit up in full PPE and listen to a firm lecture on how not to fall off scaffolding. He took his responsibilities just as seriously as she did. She was out there in a borrowed hard hat and high-vis jacket until well after dark, Todd standing by with a thousand-lumen torch. Year Nine's curfew got pushed back half an hour. Lilly volunteered to sit up in Brewers supervising them. David, as Head, was in there too, and so was Ebele, and the tough Maths teacher who doubled up as Head of Year Nine.

"Let's discuss," said David, once the breach was fixed, Year Nine had been put to bed, and lights out sternly enforced. Not many of them would sleep properly after all this excitement. Ebele had already sent out an email warning staff to expect the worst from the year group tomorrow.

So they went to the Headmaster's office—David, Walden, and Todd as site manager—and had a meeting, though it was getting on for eleven at night. "I need to be on cover for the first half of next week," was the first thing Walden said. "And I won't be at the SLT meeting on Monday." Thank *God* it was Saturday and no one needed to cover for her tomorrow. Her plan was to get six hours' sleep, eat breakfast, fill a flask with coffee, and then work until she physically couldn't anymore.

David raised his brows. Walden, exhausted, remembered that his background was Geography and she actually had to explain what was going on.

So she did: today's possession disaster was inexplicable. It should not have been possible. No one had summoned those demons. No one had invited them in. An imp in a gaming system, fine—it was impossible to build a magical protection system that was truly impregnable to demons of every size, and there was a lot of wild magic generated on the school site. But a third-order demon should not be able to break through Chetwood's general wardings and enter the real world spontaneously, any more than a leopard could fit itself through the crack under a door. And neither of them should have had the initiative or power to hide themselves inside human hosts unnoticed until Lilly, thank heaven, had listened to her bad gut feeling.

All of which meant that somewhere in the vast, elaborate, ancient, impossibly complex system of wards that was *Walden's chief responsibility*, something had failed.

No. Multiple things had failed. There were backups to the backups. There was a whole additional layer of alerts that she'd spent a month installing two summers ago. She'd been doing planar patrols weekly since last November, and so had Mark Daubery. The Marshals had been on high alert ever since Old Faithful's incursion had made them all look like fools. Todd as Keymaster walked the mundane boundaries of the entire site every couple of days. And *still* something had slipped by all of them. David's expression grew graver and graver as she laid it all out. Magic was her responsibility; but Chetwood, all of it, the whole school, was his responsibility. If she could not find the hole in the school's defences, and fix it, and explain how and why it could possibly have happened in the first place, she would be out of a job by the end of term. David's slightly more graceful resignation would follow by the end of the academic year.

They would both deserve it. The first responsibility of any school was to keep the children safe.

"Where's the problem?" David asked sharply once he'd grasped the situation, as if that wasn't the exact question that Walden was going to lose sleep over tonight.

"It could be anywhere," she said. "Anywhere at all. We'll have to go over the whole site."

"For my money it's those old engines," said Todd. "If it's anywhere it's there. Apologies, Mr Bern, Dr Walden—just an old man's feeling."

"You're probably right," Walden said. "Which is why I'm going to start with a full check on the thaumic engines. It's a summer holiday job, usually."

"Did you do it last summer?" said David.

"Yes," said Walden. She was too tired and worried to even be annoyed that he'd apparently forgotten the detailed report she submitted every September. "And they were *fine*. As fine as a hideous nineteenth-century bodge job can possibly be. There are hundreds of possible failure points, magical and mechanical. We'll have to go through all of them."

She got back to her flat after midnight. She was listening for it, so she could hear the rumble of the thaumic engines as they hummed to themselves next door. They *sounded* all right.

She went through her office on her way into the flat. Someone had left a pile of papers on her desk. Walden paused to look at them and discovered that they were the A-level mock papers for her set. She'd meant to mark them tomorrow. It was a good three hours of brain work. The deadline for getting the grades in the system was Monday lunchtime.

This was the job. This was school. It never stopped.

chapter twenty-four

MOCKS

ALDEN STARTED MARKING HER SIXTH formers' mocks on Monday morning at 10 A.M., and had the grades in the system half an hour after the deadline. A* for Nikki, A for Will and Aneeta, a low C for Mathias, all more or less as she'd expected. She knew her late turn-in wouldn't be the last. Annie in the office would be sending chasing emails until Wednesday. When it was done, she stretched, groaned, and went straight back into the cavernous room where the thaumic engines lived.

Todd hadn't left. For once he'd taken off the heavy chain he wore around his neck with the Great Key of Chetwood hanging on it, and left it on the polished table by the door into Walden's rooms. Now he lay in almost the same position Walden had left him in two hours ago, though he'd moved over to the left: flat on his back with torch and screwdriver under the brass-and-polished-walnut edifice that controlled the roadside boundaries of the school wardings. There was a pried-off panel at his side, and a double handful of ancient screws in a Tupperware takeout container. Most of them, Todd said, needed to be replaced. They hadn't found the hole in the wards yet, but the 1960s expansion of the school to take in the building site for Scrubs had required a matching expansion of the school's magical protections. Walden thought it was as likely a weak spot as any.

"Anything?" she said, without much hope.

"Not a brass monkey's fart," said Todd.

He'd been in here since half past four this morning. Walden hadn't started until half six. *I'm an old man, I don't sleep much,* he'd said. *The hole's in here somewhere. The Key feels it. I can feel it.*

Walden had a lot of respect for Todd's magical feelings, but she hadn't found any obvious problems with the thaumic engines' inner workings yet, and *she* couldn't sense anything wrong. Neither could the Phoenix. And Todd was rapidly approaching retirement age. Nine hours from a 4 A.M. start was a long time for a person in his sixties to spend wrestling with ancient machinery, muttering curses to himself the whole time. "Take a break. Go and get some lunch."

"With respect, Dr Walden—"

"It's Saffy," said Walden. "We've worked together for years, Todd, please. I know you know Chetwood inside out. I do need your help here. I'm asking you to have a rest and something to eat and come back fresh. I think we're in for another late night."

The cut-off groan Todd let out as he slid out from under the brassy bulk of the thaumic engine and sat up would probably have been a yell of pain from someone else. Todd showing *any* sign of being made of something less than solid oak was alarming. His shoulder-length grey hair was lank with sweat and dust. This was one of the few parts of the school that Premises could not access to bring in a vacuum cleaner. Walden had discovered, in the last two days, that Todd had been meticulously sweeping and polishing in here himself. He was ashamed—ashamed!—that in the last few years he'd stopped forcing himself to get down on his knees with dustpan and brush in order to get at the grimy residue that built up underneath the engines at the back.

Walden was the one who should have been ashamed. She just hadn't thought about how the thaumic engines were staying clean. Two people ever went in, and Walden hadn't been sweeping. She should have been. She was a lot younger than Todd.

She eventually managed to coax him out and send him off to the canteen, though only by the underhanded expedient of displaying the kind of fluttery feminine concern that felt like a ridiculous mask to her, but allowed Todd to be gruff and tough about how brutally hard they were working. Then she got back to her own job, picking up where she'd left off, going through the diagnostic readouts which were stamped onto a long thin roll of paper by an immensely slow punch-card system installed as an upgrade in about 1910. It was achingly dull. The readouts followed no current standard of magical analysis; they were masses of badly organised data, most of it useless, the sort of thing you would have fed through a computer to analyse if this system had been designed at any point in Walden's lifetime. Without the Phoenix in the back of her thoughts providing sharp, interested commentary, it would have been impossible to focus. As it was, Walden was so completely absorbed that she let out a small scream when she realised someone else was in the room.

"Didn't mean to scare you," said Mark. "How's it going?"

"Nothing yet," Walden said. "How was your patrol?"

"Still no sign of anything big moving in," Mark said. That was the fear that lay under all Walden's other fears, the danger Laura had pointed out months ago: the dreadfully tasty target that Chetwood represented to a new higher demon, a second Old Faithful. They'd survived an incursion on that level with no casualties once. They'd been very, very lucky.

"You look frazzled," Mark said. "Up for some relaxation?"

"*Mark,*" said Walden.

Yes, all right, so they'd kept going.

Kept *fucking,* specifically. This was not a relationship. Walden had not lost all self-respect, she wasn't going to get herself mixed up in a workplace romance proper, especially not with *Mark Daubery.* She'd already forced herself to have a very brief, very dry, very uncomfortable conversation with the examinations officer, because the entanglement as it stood was enough of a conflict of interest that she should not be invigilating or going anywhere near any of Will's upcoming A-level exams. They didn't seem especially close, but uncle and nephew was still a family connection.

Will, of course, had no idea what was going on. No one knew, apart from the examinations officer, who by nature of the role was not a gossip. Because there was barely anything going on, just a practical arrangement between two single adults, which was no-body's business.

"Not now, thank you," Walden said crisply. "If you aren't going to make yourself useful, do please feel free to go away."

"I thought I was being useful," said Mark. He was standing by the door, next to the only table in the room. Todd hadn't taken the Great Key with him when he went to get lunch. It was still there, strung on its chain, lying on the table. Mark picked it up and let it swing from his fingers. "Heavy, isn't it?"

"Put that down."

"Can't be the original mediaeval key," Mark said. "I wonder how old it is."

"Put it *down*, Mark."

"Down, boy. Yes, Dr Walden." He dropped the big iron key back on the table; it landed with a thunk. "See you later?"

"I'm extremely busy," said Walden.

"I'll fix you a gin before you fall into bed."

"Make it a double," said Walden. "Now get out."

Walden didn't take a real lunch break, but she did swing by the staff dining room for supper. She was hoping for a big plate of proper boarding school stodge, the sort of thing that sat in your stomach like a lump of lead and could power an army of teenagers through hours of Games. She was in luck: they were serving toad in the hole with onion gravy and mash on the side. Middling-quality sausages padded out with batter and a heap of mashed potatoes, all in shades of brown and beige, and more carb for pudding in the form of jam sponge and custard. Walden requested large helpings of everything, even the sad, overboiled peas and carrots.

This kind of meal didn't happen as often as it used to. A modern school catering company usually had ambitions towards nutritional balance and healthy living, and quite right too. But for Walden, this sort of thing was pure comfort, the food of her childhood, the food that made sense on a miserable January evening. She almost went back for seconds.

Ebele, dressed today in warm and summery orange, set her tray down on Walden's table just as she was polishing off the last of the sponge and custard. It looked like she'd skipped the hot food offerings completely and raided the salad bar for her supper: cold chicken and pasta, a heap of leafy greens, a ramekin of yoghurt for dessert. "I'm so glad I caught you," she said. "I know you're very busy. Could I have a little word? It's about Nikki."

"Is everything all right?"

"She got her Oxford offer," Ebele said. "Three As. The email came through this morning. I imagine we'll get the letter later this week."

Walden was delighted. She'd seldom had a student who deserved Oxford more than Nikki Conway. "That's wonderful news! She'll get those grades easily. Remind me which college?"

"Wadham," said Ebele. "But she's thinking of turning it down."

"She—*what?*"

Ebele inclined her head. "It's her future and her choice," she said, in the grim tones of someone who thought a teenager was about to make a very silly mistake. "I think—I *hope*—that Ezekiel and I have encouraged Nikki for as long as we've known her to grow into a young woman of character and ambition. We've had a conversation. Unfortunately, it went pear-shaped. Sometimes the overlap between Matron and foster mum is not very helpful. A teenager needs a person to rebel against and I think Nikki may have picked me. And we *don't* want to bully her into something she doesn't actually want."

"But it's madness," said Walden. "She's brilliant. She'll have a wonderful time. And she *does* want Oxford." She'd done her share of the interview prep sessions, starting last summer: one-on-two tutoring sessions with Nikki and Will, who were this year's only applicants for Sorcery. Oxford, for Will Daubery, was just an assumption. He was following in the footsteps of his father and his uncle, and his grandfather, and his great-grandfather, and his great-great-great-aunt Gwendolyn Hornsey whose name Walden had recognised with a start as the suffragist pioneer who'd been the first female magician to study at Cambridge. If he had had any doubts about getting in, he hadn't let them show. Sorcery was one of the less competitive courses, which meant there were only five applicants for every available place. Will Daubery had the predicted grades to get an interview and he was undeniably the sort of boy who interviewed well—one of nature's bullshitters, polished to charming and confident excellence by a school that had been providing bullshit-polishing services for centuries. Walden had always thought his chances were high. Of course, the Chetwood background was no longer the free ticket to elite education that it had once been—and quite right too, no doubt, because straight As at an underfunded state comprehensive was a considerably more impressive academic achievement than straight As here—but Will would do well, if he got the offer.

For Nikki, though, Oxford meant something different, something more. She had only talked about it once.

My mum and dad never went to uni, she'd said.

And she deserved it. She was brilliant. It was hard to quantify the difference between a merely very intelligent student and a brilliant one. It didn't show up in a list of exam results. Sometimes, in fact, brilliance could be a disadvantage—when all you needed to do was neatly jump the hoop of an examiner's grading rubric without ever asking why. It was the teachers who knew, the teachers who felt the difference. A few times in your career, you would have the privilege of teaching someone truly remarkable; someone who was hard work to teach because they made *you* work harder, who asked you questions that had never occurred to you before, who stretched you to the very edge of your own abilities. If you were lucky—as Walden, this time, had been lucky—your remarkable student's chief interest was in your discipline: and then you could have the extraordinary, humbling experience of teaching a child whom you knew would one day totally surpass you.

Walden had a realistic opinion of her own capabilities. She was not someone easy to surpass. But if there was such a thing as destiny, then it was calling to Nikki Conway, and it was calling with the mantle of the once-a-generation magician and scholar. She was a Roger Rollins, a Gwendolyn Hornsey. Perhaps she belonged on the list of truly legendary British wizards, up there with John Dee and Isaac Newton. She deserved the chance to find out. An Oxford degree was the first step along that road; and if she chose to turn off the road, then the prestige of having done just that first step would still open dozens of other doors for her. Turn it down? Why would she ever turn it down?

"I'm having a hard time getting to the bottom of it myself," said Ebele. "And of course it's not the best time to pile on the serious conversations, when she's in the middle of mocks. But I think Nikki might benefit from talking about this with someone a bit less," she made a face, "well, a bit less *me*. I'd like you to meet with her, if that's all right. I know it's not the best time for you either."

The hedging and apologetic tone were a velvet glove wrapped around what was actually, very clearly, an order. Not many people outranked Walden in the school hierarchy, but Ebele was one of them. But—"Me?" said Walden. "I'm not really the right person for . . . pastoral."

"I think you know," said Ebele, "that usually, the right person to take the lead on any pastoral concern is the person that child feels able to talk to."

Walden had a very good relationship with Nikki—as her Invocation teacher. They'd had any number of lively, delightful, academic conversations, in lessons and in interview prep sessions. But she had never had anything to do with her personal or pastoral development. She still remembered the enormous awkwardness of walking the tearful sixth former down the corridor to the infirmary in absolute silence.

Dr Walden, I think I should drop, Nikki had said.

They'd never talked about it again. Walden had handed it off along the proper channels—the nurse, the pastoral deputy head, the school counsellor—and got on with her own job.

But every child was every adult's responsibility.

"If you really think I can help," she said, "I'm happy to try."

chapter twenty-five

CAREERS

A COMPLETE SURPRISE IN THE SECOND WEEK of January took the Nikki Conway question cleanly out of Walden's head. She logged on to Facebook for the first time in several months and found a message from Rosalind Chan, sent back in December, friendly and cheerful: she was going to be in London for a conference in mid-January and wouldn't it be great to get brunch?

The conference was next week and Roz was probably booked solid already, but Walden considered Roz—glamorous, international, successful, and exquisitely magical Roz—and knew that she had to make an attempt. She sent a message back: she really couldn't get away from school in term time, but perhaps Roz would like to visit Chetwood and give a careers talk to the—she racked her brains for the American phrasing—juniors and seniors? And Walden could show her around, take her to the pub, have a nice catch-up . . . what did Roz think?

Almost instant reply, though it had to be the middle of the night in California: Roz would love to, and here was her schedule.

Walden was rather smug as she emailed the Careers Department about her coup. Among other things, a visiting speaker was an excellent use of the graveyard slot on Saturday afternoons.

"It is so cold," said Roz when Walden met her at the train station. She was huddled in a fleece-lined coat and her American accent sang out bright and sweet and weirdly loud in the echoing hollows of Victorian brickwork. "No one told me it would be this cold!"

"We're further north than Vancouver," said Walden, which was one of those transatlantic fun facts you just picked up somewhere. "We don't get that much snow, though. Coastal climate."

"I know about coastal climates, Saffy," said Roz. "You look fantastic, look at you!"

Walden was fairly sure she didn't look all that fantastic, especially not next to Roz's beautiful golden silk scarf and perfect razorblade-straight bobbed hair, but she submitted to air kisses—when had Roz become the kind of person who did air kisses?—and escorted her guest to Chetwood village's single waiting taxi.

From there the afternoon turned into a weird balancing act, professional Dr Walden on her home ground versus the Saffy of old. Roz belonged to a very different part of Walden's life—the furthest from home she had ever been, a time when she'd lived and breathed pure magic nearly every waking moment, and when *she* had managed to pass herself off as a glamorous foreigner. Looking back, that had said more about the power of an English accent than any actual glamour on the part of early-twenties Saffy. But that was the version of her Roz knew; and she was aware of sidelong assessing glances, of how different Dr Walden the schoolteacher must seem to the person she'd been before.

And oh, California: graduate magical research, *funding*, genuine working relationships with people whose work Saffy had cited over and over as an undergrad and during her MThau. Hazy golden light over the Pacific, the total social freedom of the outsider, and magic, magic, *magic*. Roz had been the crowning glory of those years: beautiful, brilliant, challenging, all that intellect and ambition—an equal, as no one since Charlie had really felt like an equal.

It was more than a decade ago. Walden felt only nostalgic fondness for Roz now, tempered by the knowledge that neither of them had behaved very well during the long slow-motion breakup that had culminated in Walden fleeing back to the UK without telling her girlfriend the plan.

It was very strange to see Roz at Chetwood School. In the weak January light she made the whole place look small and grey and unconvincing, and Walden's best Open Day patter somehow only succeeded in turning her world and her life into a minor tourist attraction. Roz exclaimed over the fourteenth-century chapel and colonnade, marvelled at the grounds, looked up with admiration at School House's silly Victorian tower. "It's just so *cute*," she said with conviction. "I can't believe how cute this is. I can't believe you live here."

"Thank you," said Walden, and handed Roz off with some relief to Philomela Jones, who looked monstrously pleased to have someone new to tell all about Lady Margaret Beaufort. Meanwhile she went to check with ICT that everything was properly set up for the talk over in the new building.

She had her fingers crossed before it started. Roz had been only an indifferent teacher, had resented lecturing because it took her out of the lab. Years Eleven, Twelve, and Thirteen were packed onto every inch of space on the tiered seating in the school's only lecture theatre, with some unfortunate Year Elevens even forced to sit on the floor. Lunch had been a while ago. A big, sleepy, potentially tricky crowd.

"Who are the ones in the red sweaters?" said Roz, when Philomela dropped her off, wearing the slightly startled look of a person who had been on the receiving end of aggressive American charm.

"The red jumpers? Oh, that's Year Eleven. Er, sophomores," Walden said. "I think. They still have to wear uniform."

"All right," said Roz. "Wish me luck." And then, completely bypassing the formal introduction Walden had meant to give her, she scooped the microphone off the lectern and said to the crowded lecture theatre, "Hi! Can you hear me?"

Walden shouldn't have worried. Of course Roz hadn't stood still for a decade. She was no longer the newly minted Dr Chan, all prickles and ambition and tunnel vision. Somewhere along the line she'd picked up public speaking. It was a perfectly learnable skill, and one thing Roz had always done spectacularly well was *learning*. She had most of the mob of teenagers eating out of her hand after about five minutes. They were naturally inclined to find her interesting. After all, she was a living answer to the utility question: *What can you do with magic?* And she also answered the other question, usually unspoken but always hovering over this crowd: *What is magic going to do for me?*

Roz told them: your magical education can make you interesting, funny, successful, and visibly wealthy. Walden saw the students near the front noticing her pristine trainers. She talked about the work. Her vivid delight in pure magic had not faded, and it gave Walden a little pang, remembering. And she spoke eloquently about being a professional magician as an immigrant, as a person from a poor family, as an out and proud lesbian. Really, she had 'role model' written all over her.

Walden was genuinely very glad she'd managed to get hold of Roz for this. A real person, an actual adult with an actual job, could be orders of magnitude more inspiring than any commonplace teacher. She stood at the front and scanned the crowd for misbehaviour, but she only had to hold the gaze of a couple of whispering girls, and once walk over to a bored Year Twelve and stand pointedly next to him for a few moments. Eventually, he stopped fidgeting with the phone he should not have had in his pocket.

A storm of applause at the end, and—wonder of wonders—when Roz asked *Any questions?* some children actually put their hands up. The Head of Careers ran interference and rephrased some of the more incoherent questions, and Walden listened with satisfaction. In the middle of the crowd she picked out Nikki and Aneeta, sitting together, plainly attentive. Nikki was leaning forward slightly in her seat. Walden tried to think hard in her direction: *Here is someone you could be. Come on. Think it through. Don't throw away your chance.*

"Wow," said Roz in the pub afterwards. "That was scary!"

"You were brilliant," Walden assured her. "Really, I mean it, you were inspiring."

"I can't believe you do that every day."

"Not usually with a group that size. You were fantastic, I mean it."

Roz was applying herself with goodwill to the Red Lion's only vegetarian offering, an entire roasted cauliflower. The goodwill was probably not deserved. She glanced up at the compliment—had Walden been too effusive? Did she sound like she didn't mean it?

"You're overthinking," Roz said, knowing.

Walden had to laugh. "Of course. Whoops. I suppose I haven't changed that much."

"Mmm," said Roz. "I feel like I should say sorry, you know. For how we left things."

"Oh, come on," said Saffy, deeply embarrassed, "I was the one who—"

"—dumped me by text from the airport?"

Saffy said, "Er."

When you put it like that, it did sound bad.

Roz laughed at her expression. "Hey, come on, I was there. I know why you were too scared to do it face-to-face. Lucy calls me her steamroller."

"I wasn't *scared*," said Saffy, but actually, conflict with Roz— forthright, honest, unafraid to raise her voice, unafraid to point out Saffy's shortcomings—had always been quite frightening. Saffy had been brought up politely passive-aggressive and never knew what to say to someone who actually talked about their feelings. Instead of getting into the weeds of that—ancient history, anyway—she said, "Tell me about Lucy! You must have been together for . . ."

"Seven years now," said Roz, breaking into her most brilliant smile, showing off very even white teeth. "Where did I put my phone?"

Saffy admired Lucy—an Amazonian white woman with a magnificent bosom and a huge pile of blonde curls, pictured hiking, playing the cello, posing with Roz's slightly nervous-looking parents, and cooking schnitzel in the airy kitchen of a beautiful century-old San Francisco rowhouse: a real antique by California standards, though transposed to Chetwood it would have been one of the newer buildings on site. They spent a while on the house. "It was a stretch," Roz said, "and we could never afford anything like it now," apparently under the impression that Saffy had kept track of the Bay Area real estate market in the decade-plus since she left. "But the dogs love it!"

The house pictures *did* inspire a fair amount of unworthy envy in Saffy's heart. She'd made her choices, but it was hard not to reflect that *she* could have been the person with a fulfilling career in cutting-edge magical research, unlimited funding, plenty of lab time, access on request to that incredible mega-incursion in Arizona—and also a house on a hill with views across the bay, two charmingly ugly little dogs, a beautiful musician wife. "Call it the Dr Rosalind Chan grant for the arts," Roz said, pausing on a photo of Lucy in a black evening gown under a spotlight, the beautiful warm wood of the antique cello glowing in her arms as she played.

"No regrets?"

"None," said Roz. "You?"

Saffy inquired internally into the unworthy envy, found it basically shallow, and answered, "None. But—"

Roz said, "Are you asking me, how do I sleep at night?"

Saffy said nothing. She'd once felt absolutely sure that Roz was a better person than her—not a better *magician*, but more switched-on, more political, more passionate, more sincere. But the truth was that there were very few practical uses for summoning something as deadly and powerful as a higher demon, and only one that paid. No doubt the world needed *military stuff.* No doubt someone had to do it. But Saffy had looked at what all her magical knowledge and power were leading her towards, and walked away.

"I sleep like a baby," said Roz, "just like all the white guys I work with. You know, Saffy, in a world where only assholes get to be rich and powerful, only assholes get to make the rules. I pay for my parents' home nurses, I pay for my wife to live, I research the charities I donate to, and I don't regret anything. I made my compromises. We all do."

"That's true," Saffy said. "I'm sorry. I shouldn't have asked."

"Why not? It's a fair question," Roz said. "I'm not ashamed. And I couldn't do what you do anyway." She paused, took another bite of roasted cauliflower, and added, "Listen, do you remember, I told you once you were . . ."

"'An insanely privileged nice white liberal lady,'" said Saffy. "Yes, I remember. Vividly. You were always very direct about it. And right, of course."

"Oh, I'm always right," said Roz. "But the thing is—making no compromises, *that's* a privilege. A big one. I hope my kids get to have it." The beautiful American smile again. "Did I mention? We're going to have kids. Though it's hilarious how much sperm costs."

Tipsy, later, in Saffy's flat—Roz was staying in the spare room, they'd broken out the bottle of gin—they got onto the subject of Saffy's personal life. "Oh *wow*," said Roz, to the old Instagram photo of Laura Kenning with her motorbike.

"No chance now," Saffy said, "I managed to wildly offend her by, well," and she admitted with a combination of shame and pride to the Mark thing. Roz announced that because she believed deeply in equality she had to see a photo of him too, to compare.

"Nope," she said after they'd managed to scare something up—on LinkedIn, of all places; Mark seemed to have no personal social media. "I don't see it. I'm too gay. I think you should have gone with motorbike girl. Go on, explain the appeal."

"There's a cultural element."

"What does that mean?"

Saffy paused. "If I told you, *went to Yale, cousin is a senator, plays squash . . .*"

"Oh, I *see*," said Roz. "Status symbol boyfriend."

"No! Well, maybe. But not *boyfriend*."

"Why not?"

"There may be some significant cultural differences across the pond," said Saffy primly, "but I know for a fact that you also have wankers."

"Then I still don't get it," Roz said. "Also, honestly—straight guy, doing well for himself, over forty, not ace . . . but no wife, no ex-wife, not even an old girlfriend he wants to complain about? At our age people usually come peer-reviewed. There's got to be something seriously wrong with him."

Probably there was something seriously wrong with Mark, but Walden's arrangement with him wasn't an emotional entanglement. She didn't have to care. She saw Roz off at the train station the next morning, and took a moment on her walk back up to school to look up the approximate value of a century-old rowhouse on a hill in San Francisco. She thought it was very probable that this was exactly what Roz had intended her to do. Surely she hadn't been this interested in money when they were grad students?

To be fair, neither of them had really had any back then.

The house was worth an eye-watering amount. And when Walden got back to school, she was waylaid on her way to the staff-room by the Bursar, looking gleeful. Chetwood had just received a donation of twenty thousand US dollars, earmarked for the loom-ing repair of the chapel roof. "Even after the exchange rate takes a bite out of it," he said, "that's not small change. Please thank your friend for us. Invite her again. Do you think we could get her at the Governors' annual dinner? The alumni ball?"

Walden escaped from him, went into her office, and wrote an

appropriately delighted and grateful Facebook message, a personal accompaniment to the equally delighted and grateful email Roz was going to get from the Headmaster. She had an obscure sense of having lost this round. The donation felt like a jab, like the last word in an argument Walden hadn't meant to start.

While she sat at her laptop and stared into space, something Mark had said drifted into her thoughts. *Most people with principles are hypocrites on some level:* a very comforting bit of cynicism. And because she was thinking of Mark, a comparison occurred to her, not *Mark versus Laura* but *Mark versus Roz.* Walden's own historical taste in these things . . . something about ambition, about selfishness, about power . . . even Charlie, come to think of it . . .

All of which made Laura Kenning, who had genuinely sacrificed the direction of her career for her principles, into an outlier. So it really would never have worked. Walden didn't know why she still thought about Laura at all.

chapter twenty-six

GUIDANCE

W ALDEN'S OFFICE WAS NOT SET UP FOR pastoral chats. It was her workspace first and foremost. She'd almost stopped noticing how it looked. The panelled walls, the imposing desk topped with green leather, the antique clock; the dusty overloaded bookshelves, the ugly row of filing cabinets jammed in a corner; even the awkwardly retrofitted Ikea computer desk opposite, where some poor electrician had had to figure out how to wire this room without doing too much damage to the wainscotting—to Walden, this was just where she worked. Where she lived, effectively, when she wasn't in the labs or the staffroom.

So the desk might *look* chaotic, but she knew what was in all the piles of paperwork. The bookshelves were not dusted often, but everything on them was valuable reference material. The filing cabinets had decades of useful stuff in them: old exam papers, worksheets with customised exercises—*so* hard to find secondary-appropriate magic exercises, none of the big academic publishers had come up with a financially viable textbook yet. Even the contents of the filing cabinets were GDPR compliant, since Walden had finally got around to shredding her predecessor's decades of handwritten notes on every student he'd ever taught, along with his opinion of their parents. A bit of a shame, because some of that stuff had probably had historical value—if nothing else, as a record of how wildly unprofessional teaching had once been.

When Nikki came in, with the slight shuffling pause on the threshold of a child who really wasn't sure if this was allowed, Walden saw the office for a moment through her eyes. Wood and leather, books and antiques, a modern desk chair with back support like a throne for Walden, and a battered repurposed Edwardian antique from the staff dining hall for whoever was unlucky enough to be sitting opposite her. No art on the walls, no photographs, no personal touches anywhere. It was not a friendly room. It had never been meant as one.

So Walden had to be the friendly one. She had to channel everything she'd ever been taught about Connecting Effectively with Young People, without shame or hesitation. She had to be welcoming and accepting and respectful and predictable and *safe*. She had to toss away her fairly reasonable aversion to coming off as embarrassing, try-hard, awkward, or just fundamentally uncool. If you were someone's authority figure you were definitionally uncool. It was time to lean in to it.

It was just unfortunate that the most effective way Walden had of connecting with young people, by a long way, was to tell them about something fascinating that she was an expert on, and then show them how to do it themselves. She had good relationships with her students because she was a good teacher, not because she was a naturally warm and empathetic person. She would have been absolutely delighted to have a short academic chat with Nikki about literally any branch of magic at all. They could have gone through the bookshelves pulling out old journals and reference texts together. Walden would have sent her away energised and excited, with something new to learn. She'd even thought of trying to do it that way—leading into the topic of Oxford sideways, via a neat little stretch-and-challenge magic lesson, *And this of course is the sort of thing you'd be doing in your first year.* But there was a hesitation in her. She'd given Nikki her old copy of *Nielle's Arrays* in just that spirit, and look what had happened.

Besides, Ebele had set this up as a serious conversation, not a casual chat. And Ebele was so much more skilled at pastoral work than Walden that if she thought formal and serious was the way to go, she was probably right.

Still, she should have thought of something like . . . biscuits. Custard creams on the desk for both of them to snack on. That would have been good.

"Come in, sit down," she said, while Nikki was still hovering. "Please! Thank you for coming."

"Hi, Dr Walden," said Nikki, and nothing else. Well, she was under no obligation to make this easy.

"How's it all going?" Walden tried. "You're back in lessons tomorrow, aren't you? How were the mocks?"

"Okay," Nikki said. "I mean, I think it was all okay. I felt all right after. You know when you finish an exam, and it feels bad? It didn't feel that bad."

"That's good," said Walden, well aware—because she'd just checked on the big spreadsheet—that Nikki had flown through all her papers and practicals and was going to see straight A*s when the mock exams were returned next week. "I hope the whole process wasn't too stressful. The actual A-levels in summer are honestly quite a lot easier, in my opinion." She said this every year.

"Yeah," said Nikki, "I mean . . . yeah, I'll have more time to revise then."

She wasn't going to bring it up, was she. Normally, when your best pupil got an offer from a top university, she told you about it. Just a little bit of bragging was expected, even healthy. But Nikki sounded like nothing good had ever happened to her in her entire life.

Well. When you had an elephant in the room, someone had to be the first person to say *Wow, what a big elephant!* "Matron tells me you've got your Oxford offer," Walden said. "I wanted to be the first teacher to say congratulations. I'm not surprised, of course. I know how hard you've worked for this. I always had complete faith in you. But as well as the normal things, the school is very proud, all of that—I wanted to say that as your Invocation teacher I, personally, am very proud of you. This is an achievement no one can take away from you. It's well deserved. Well done."

"Um," said Nikki. "Thanks."

The silence stretched. And stretched.

"So—" began Walden, at the same moment as Nikki said, "Um—"

They both stopped. After a moment, Nikki snorted.

Awkward. Embarrassing. Uncool. Lean into it. "I know, I know," Walden said. "You can probably tell why they mostly only let me talk about demons."

Dropping the teacher mask worked as nothing else would have. "You're really good at the demons," said Nikki reassuringly. "Sorry, Dr Walden. Matron asked you to talk to me, didn't she?"

"She did," Walden said, "but honestly . . . once I found out, I would have wanted to talk to you about it anyway. So. Oxford?"

"Oxford," agreed Nikki, rather glum.

Walden had had a little speech planned—opportunity, grasping of; challenge, rising to—but now she was actually in this conversation, she could see that Nikki was too grown up to be steamrollered that way. "Do you want to talk me through it?"

"Do I have to?"

"It's me or Matron," Walden said. "I think I disagree with you about this, but I'm not going to make up my mind until I've actually heard what you think."

Nikki sighed. "Okay, okay. I *have* thought about this. Matron acted like I was just being emotional. But I thought really hard."

"That makes sense," Walden agreed. "You've always struck me as a person who thinks carefully."

"You know how I wanted to drop Invocation?"

"I remember, yes. I was quite concerned."

"So . . . obviously I let them talk me out of it," said Nikki, "because . . . realistically, I need A-levels, don't I? If I want to go to uni at all. And I *do*. And Dad—I mean, Reverend Ezekiel—" *Matron* and *Dad*, thought Walden; she'd learned more about the internal dynamics of School House in the last five minutes than in years of working with Ezekiel and Ebele. "—well, he said that if I really wanted to drop out completely, they'd make sure I still had somewhere to live, and I could go to college or an online school and get a job at the same time," Nikki took a breath, "which is really nice of him, like it's really really nice of him, but it's not like I'm . . . you know. The Chetwood scholarship fund isn't going to pay for me to live here anymore after this year. No one is."

"Nikki," Walden said.

"I'm just being realistic," said Nikki. "Because I thought, after everything, back in October—I sort of thought we were going to get expelled. Me and Matty. And if that happened—well, I thought maybe I could explain that it wasn't Matty's fault, it was me. Because it was me, really, Dr Walden. You know that, don't you?" And before Walden could say anything, she barrelled on. "And Matty can't go back. He can't. I don't know if you know about his mum and dad, the stuff they did. They were freaks in a weird anti-magic cult, they abused him. And they still send him messages, his cousins and his mum, he has to keep blocking them." Walden hadn't known that; how awful. Nikki went on. "So when Matty said maybe he'd have to go back, I just. No. I started making a plan. I thought about jobs and stuff, like we'd have to find a flatshare so I made a list from the internet. But rent is *really* expensive. Aneeta said she'd help for a bit, she gets four hundred pounds a month and she never buys anything except tuck shop chocolate so she has savings . . . but actually I think her parents would probably hate that?" She hurried on. "And there's stuff you need to be eighteen for—I was eighteen in December but Matty's not till April—anyway if I could convince Mr Bern that it was all me really, then maybe he could stay. And I'd be okay—if I planned it all out first, you know?"

Walden could hear how nervous Nikki was. All those stops and starts, from a child who was normally more fluent and confident than most adults. More than that; she could hear that Nikki had not said any of this out loud before. Even the school counsellor must have missed it. One possible side effect of spending ten years growing up under the eagle eye of a pastoral expert was that you got very, very good at dodging pastoral expertise.

I'm not really—family.

I'd be okay—on my own.

A job and a flat at eighteen. No safety net. No time to spare for anything but survival. No friends or family, no A-levels, nothing to fall back on but a set of perfect GCSE grades that would never come to anything more. Of course, people did it every day. The vision of grinding, isolated, dead-end poverty that Nikki Conway had quietly planned for herself was a life that millions of people had to live. It was a life a long way removed from Chetwood School, and yet its ghost haunted the ancient halls that shone in the sunshine among the green fields. Fifty thousand pounds a year per child, less whatever scholarships and bursaries a family could argue out of the endowment. People paid it. Some of them were rich—well, all of them were rich, really. Most of them did not feel that way. They knew about the future that Nikki had imagined for herself. They felt its chilly spectre breathing on the backs of their necks.

Almost no one was paying for magical boarding school because of the magic. The magic was an interesting quirk, a historical curiosity, in a few cases a genuine passion being indulged by a loving parent—but you didn't pay fifty thousand pounds a year for magic tricks, any more than you paid it for Shakespeare or the respiratory system or the ability to solve quadratic equations. No: Chetwood's school fees were insurance money, a policy taken out against the future. Let my child be safe. Let my child be happy. Let my child have every single possible chance at freedom, joy, hope, *power*.

Because an elite education was an investment in power. Magic was the least of what you gained at Chetwood. What mattered was the power to walk the walk and talk the talk, to have your résumé picked out of the pile and the interviewer already speaking your language. It was the power to know the people you ought to know, to befriend them easily over a *you too?* or to laugh together about how ridiculous the whole theme park experience of childhood had been. A few could afford that power. Most could not. Plenty of parents who loved their children worked appalling hours and then remortgaged their homes to pay for it. They did it for love, and for terror. You could never completely future-proof your children. But power would keep them safe from the bitter grind of survival in a way that nothing else could.

"Nikki," Walden said, trying to sound neutral, and not viscerally horrified, at how much power, freedom and possibility this child wanted to throw away.

"I could have killed someone," Nikki said.

Walden paused.

"Mr Bern said that to me in the disciplinary meeting. I could have killed someone. Like I didn't know. But I already knew. I could have killed Matty. He wouldn't have been there if I hadn't asked. I knew I needed him, I couldn't do the summoning without him, he just puts so much more magic into everything than I can—but he was scared, he was only there for me." Nikki took a breath. "And I could have killed him. I could have killed Matron, and Reverend Ezekiel, and everyone in School House, all the younger ones. That demon wouldn't have stopped once it was loose, would it? It would have killed you, and Marshal Kenning, and then it would have just kept going. It would have eaten the whole school, and everyone it ate would just make it stronger. It was already so strong. I could feel how strong it was. Like—I went on the Geography field trip in Year Ten for the rivers topic, and we were just in the shallow bit, but you could still feel the current round your legs. It was like that, but *huge*. I read an article once that said when people go into the Thames, they don't ever find the bodies."

"Nikki," Walden said again.

"And it wouldn't even be the first time," Nikki said. "Mum and Dad and Dewey—they all died because of me. Because I'm magic, and I was stupid, and I couldn't control it."

Dewey. Walden didn't think she'd ever heard the name of Nikki's younger brother spoken out loud before. "Nikki," she said, "you were seven."

"It was still my fault! And I'm *still* magic, and I still can't control it, and I'm still so—so—stupid!"

Nikki stopped talking. She took a deep breath. Walden watched her compose her expression. She'd taught Nikki that trick, in interview prep. *Don't speak too fast. Pace it, stop and breathe, don't apologise or try to fill the gap. Give yourself a moment to think. It feels much longer to you than it does to the person you're talking to.*

"Sorry, Dr Walden," Nikki said, almost calmly, a moment later. "Obviously I am a bit emotional about this. Sorry." As if feeling something about your dead family was an embarrassing social error. "Look, I know I've been lucky, really lucky. Loads of people aren't as lucky as me. A Chetwood education is a privilege, and I'm grateful for all the opportunities I've had at school." She had hit her stride again; the quick recovery was another interview-prep special. Now she sounded measured, confident, grown-up: like she was delivering a student assembly, or talking into a camera for the video prospectus. "I do love magic. I really love magic. I've loved our Invocation lessons, and everything I've learned here. But in the end, I think I have to take responsibility for my own actions. I know I would learn a lot at Oxford. But I don't think I'm a good person—I mean, a *safe* person—to be a magician. I don't think I deserve this. So I'll finish my A-levels, obviously, so I haven't wasted everyone's time and the school's money. After that I can get a job. And maybe reapply to a different uni for something else later. I don't know."

Nikki might be measured and confident but she hadn't been doing this nearly as long as Walden had. Walden was absolutely certain that none of her real feelings were showing when she asked, "What do you think you'd like to apply for?"

A slight pause. "I did all magic A-levels," Nikki said. "So that makes it a bit harder."

"Not really," Walden said. "It's the grades that count, unless you're applying for something with very specific entry requirements. You couldn't do medicine, or engineering, but for almost everything else, your A-levels are proof of the kind of student you are regardless of what subject you're going on to study. Any university would be lucky to have you. And, of course, the school would support you in reapplying. It's a lot simpler if you already have your grades. The Careers Department handles a few post-qualification applications every year." *Take her seriously,* she was thinking, *don't overreact, let her think it through herself. Be understanding. Be safe.*

"I don't know," Nikki confessed after a moment. "I tried to think about it but I couldn't really picture anything. It's just always been magic. Right back to Year Seven, I knew. I suppose . . . it would probably be intelligent to do something with a career at the end, right? Not medicine, obviously, I don't know, law or something."

"A lot of my Sorcery cohort at Oxford ended up doing law conversion courses," Walden said. "I'm told there's some overlap, in terms of the sort of brain you need, though it depends a bit on what parts of magic you actually enjoy. Of course, the Careers Department can help you more than I can."

"So you agree?" Nikki said. "You'll support me? Do you—could you help me talk to Matron about it?"

"Nikki," said Walden, "do you want my honest opinion?"

A pause. A nod.

"Well, then. I don't agree with you at all. I'm very concerned. I think this is a terrible idea." She held up a hand before Nikki could speak. "Not because I think it's *stupid,* to be clear. Dropping out with no A-levels would have been stupid—a pointless, self-destructive waste of all the opportunities you've had, and the last thing anyone who cared about your future would want for you. But it sounds to me like you realised that already. You thought about it carefully, reconsidered, and decided on a more sensible course. And what you've come up with now is perfectly sensible, and yes, the school would support you, and it would probably work, and I'm sure you'd make a very good lawyer."

"Then—"

"But it's a terrible idea," Walden said, "not because it's stupid or ill-considered, but because I don't believe for a moment that this is what you actually *want.*"

There was a little silence.

"You can't get a job at Oxford," Nikki said, which was not a denial. "I read that, it's the uni rules or something."

"Not in term time, no," Walden agreed. "There isn't time. The terms are only eight weeks and they make you work flat out. We used to joke—'sleep, study, socialise, pick two.' There simply aren't enough hours in the day to add *work* and still get your degree. But that's what maintenance loans are for. I'd be astonished if you weren't eligible for additional grants on top of that."

"You have to pay back the loans, though."

Surely Careers went through this with them. "Yes," said Walden patiently, "at minimal interest, as a graduate tax, if you have a job that earns over the threshold. I promise you, the main financial effect it has on your life long term is that you become much more able to get that well-paid job. It's by no means a perfect system, but we're not *American.* You might find yourself on a tighter budget than some of your peers, yes." Were Aneeta's parents giving *both* their teenage daughters four hundred pounds a month in pocket money? Even Walden hadn't had that kind of fun money until she'd been gainfully employed for a few years. "You certainly wouldn't be the only one. It's a long summer vacation, as well, with plenty of time to work and save up for the next academic year. Truly, Nikki, this part isn't something you need to worry about. You'll be all right. You can make it work."

But Nikki's expression was closed. "What if I *am* the only one?" she said. "What if I don't want to be the only one?"

Walden hesitated.

"Sorry, Dr Walden. I just—the more I think about it, the more I think . . . what if it's just Chetwood again? Like this." Her hand gesture took in the panelled walls, the antique furniture, all the ancient institutional elegance. It also took in Walden herself. "And everyone there will be like Will, or—I mean, I *like* Will, I think." A brief look of confused horror: *Oh no I mentioned my sort-of-boyfriend situation to my teacher.* Walden pretended not to notice. Nikki squared her shoulders and pressed on. "He's got all these plans already, like we're both going to row and he's going to take me to formal every week—I didn't even know that was a thing, *formal*—and he'll get his Blue and I'll get a First and we'll get a travel grant and go to Italy together next summer. He just thinks everything's so easy. I think it's probably not that easy to get a First, actually?"

It wasn't, though Walden had, and she was professionally certain that Nikki could. Possibly not at the same time as keeping up with Will Daubery's intended social schedule.

"He just doesn't get it," Nikki said. "He doesn't get it at all. I don't think anyone really—even Aneeta was just like. You know. 'I think you could do something really powerful for women of colour, Nikki, I'm so proud of you!' And like—obviously I agree with her and I think it's important and it matters! But Aneeta's not the same as me. She's just not. Because Aneeta's mum is a neurosurgeon, and my mum worked in a Tesco."

She looked at Walden defiantly, as if to say: *You don't get it either, I know you don't. There is no way you can possibly know what it feels like to be me.*

And she was right, of course.

Of course she was right.

The silence went on a little too long. It was Walden's duty to fill it. She had no platitudes that answered Nikki's defiant honesty.

She owed Nikki better than platitudes anyway. She owed her the truth.

"I had a conversation with my mentor in my first week of teacher training," she said. "She told me . . . you must try to really know your students. You must try to understand their point of view, the way their lives feel from the inside. You must connect."

Nikki was silent, neutral, and, Walden thought, probably not impressed.

"And then she told me: of course, you will be fooling yourself. All teachers do. We convince ourselves we have enough in common with our students to understand them, so that we can teach them. But every single person faces their own challenges, in their own world, in their own way. I'm not even that much older than you, in the grand scheme of things, but you already have generational challenges I never had to deal with. No one in my year had their own phone in the middle school. That alone—the expectation to keep complex technology with you at all times—puts you and all your peers in the middle of an ongoing demonic threat that didn't exist twenty years ago. And that's only one of the differences between your experience and mine, and by no means the most meaningful." What did a white woman in her thirties from a comfortably upper-middle-class background have to say that was really useful to a Black teenage girl in foster care? What could Dr Sapphire Walden meaningfully give to Nicola Conway, out of her adulthood, her expertise, and her enormous, unearned good luck?

Nikki, expressionless, still silent. Still unimpressed.

"So I admit it," said Walden. "You are completely correct. *You* are the person who best knows the context when you make your choices for your life. No amount of pushing from well-intentioned outsiders changes the fact that you have your own mountains to climb. It is absolutely your right to look at the scale of the slope in front of you and say: 'This one doesn't look worth it to me; I don't want to be the only one.' But, Nikki—"

Walden stumbled, because she'd talked herself into a corner, and the corner was *being too personal*. You can't connect if you're not human, that same mentor had told her once. You have to be willing to be real and honest, if you want them to believe that you actually care. At the same time, you have to keep something back. You will lose your mind otherwise. There must be a part of you that your students know nothing about. There must be boundaries.

But Walden had already come to the edge of her hardest boundary with Nikki Conway. They'd reached it together months ago, deep inside the incursion at the heart of School House, staring at the demon that smiled at them all from a dead boy's face. *Why is it a person?* Nikki had whispered.

They'd never discussed it. But she was *such* a good student. Walden had no doubt that she'd worked out the answer long ago.

"Mr Bern was right," she said. "What you did in October was very dangerous, very stupid, and very irresponsible. When you summoned a demon far beyond your ability to banish or control, you could have killed someone." She made herself say it. "I did."

The admission sat in the air, heavy. Nikki looked alarmed, and awkward, and also—oh, Walden knew this expression, on any student, and especially on *this* student, one of her best—curious.

What she said was, "There's—I think there's a memorial, isn't there? And a tree."

"I go and look at it sometimes," Walden said. "Yes. His name was Charles Green. He was seventeen years old. We were class-mates." Nikki did *not* need all the gory details, any more than Walden really wanted to know about the Will situation. "We made a very stupid decision together. One of us escaped. The other one bore all the consequences."

"That doesn't mean you killed him," Nikki objected.

"No, it doesn't. Let me be precise. A powerful demon killed Charlie Green. All I did was help create the situation that led to his death. And I was your age, yes. Which is old enough to know better." She made herself smile. "I'd be grateful if you didn't spread this around all of Year Thirteen, by the way. I know school loves gossip, and it's by no means a secret, but it is quite a painful story. Please do feel free to talk to Matron and Reverend Ezekiel about it, or the counsellor, of course." She was off the point. She lurched back onto it. "What I am trying to say is—I think perhaps you and I *do* have enough in common that my experience might be useful to you. Charlie was left behind to die when the Marshals collapsed the incursion. They eventually went back to look for his body, and of course they never found it. You know why. And meanwhile I survived and went off to Oxford. I was in—well, about the emotional state you might expect—but I don't think I ever had the thought, 'Maybe I'm not safe. Maybe I don't deserve this.' Which says something, probably, about the sort of teenager I was, and the kind of privileged background I had." She held Nikki's gaze. She had her full attention now. You could always feel it when a child was actually listening. "I want to be very clear about how much I respect your thoughtfulness, your sense of responsibility. Matron told me, when she asked me to talk to you, that she thinks you are a young woman of character. I think so too. But I also want you to consider this.

"I made a very bad mistake. I was lucky enough to survive and get away. I went on to study for multiple degrees in the discipline I love—that's the other thing we have in common, you see; I know you love magic too. I would know it even if you hadn't just told me, because I'm the one teaching you, and it shows, it shines, in all the work you do. But my point is: I did all of that. And *because* I did that, because I had a terrible experience which was my own fault, and learned from it, and kept learning—because I ultimately came back to Chetwood, with my multiple degrees and my years of practice and an adult's perspective on the kinds of mistakes teenagers make and why they make them—entirely, in fact, because I failed and then learned, I was in a position to help you that night. For that reason alone, Nikki, I don't regret any of it."

Nikki said, very quietly, "What if I'm not good enough."

"In my professional opinion, as teacher and scholar and, forgive me, an extremely good magician myself: if a magician like *you* isn't good enough," said Walden, "there's no hope for anyone. If a magician like you doesn't deserve Oxford, then no one ever has. It's true, there will be plenty of people there who have no idea what it's like to live your life. Not as many as you think—something like sixty percent of Oxford undergraduates are state educated—though admittedly more of them on the Sorcery course, which tends a little posh. But I want you to know that responsible as you feel, and as admirable as it is, it is *not* your duty to punish yourself for the rest of your life for making one mistake—even if the mistake was very serious. Nor will you be able to avoid ever making another mistake, just by giving up the magic you love and the opportunities you have worked for. You will never meet an innocent adult. Everyone fails. *Everyone*. What matters is how you meet failure, and how you face up to it. How you learn."

There was a little quiet. *Don't jump in, don't try to fill every silence—it just makes you sound like you're not sure.* Walden had done her own share of interview prep lessons, twenty years ago. The best way to be a good communicator was to have a natural warm interest in your fellow human beings combined with fluent, justified self-confidence. The next best way was to learn about those things as a set of intellectual principles and internalise them as strongly as you could. Nikki had no way to know that Walden was thinking, *My God, do I sound pompous, do I sound stupid, do I sound like the worst kind of well-intentioned middle-class fool, is she going to take a word of it on board, is she going to tell her friends all about it and laugh*—

It didn't actually matter if a teenager thought you were ridiculous. As long as they heard you. As long as they learned. Walden was a lot better at magic lessons than personal mentorship. She resisted the urge to fidget, to bring up a different topic, to cross her fingers under the desk.

"Okay," said Nikki at length, which wasn't *Wow Dr Walden I feel so inspired*, but at least it wasn't *Wow Dr Walden this was embarrassing for both of us*.

"I'm not actually advising you to follow my exact path in life," Walden said. "Believe me, no one should end up teaching at their old high school unless they're really, *really* sure they want to."

That got a smirk and the edge of a laugh, thank goodness. Walden was on much firmer ground when she could make her students laugh. "Did you want to, though?" Nikki said. "Um, unless that's too personal. Just, you know . . . there's not a lot you can actually *do* with a Sorcery degree, is there?"

So something Walden had said had got through. That was the question of someone who was back to thinking about doing the degree themselves. She didn't leap at the implication. She didn't want to push. Instead she said, "It's quite all right. Yes, I wanted to be here. I love my career. Which doesn't mean, of course, that teaching is the only thing a trained magician can do. A long way from it. There's plenty of jobs for qualified magicians in government and in industry, both here and overseas. And if that doesn't appeal, well, you'll find that with an Oxford degree you can go almost anywhere and do almost anything. Most careers that want graduates don't actually make direct use of what you studied. Or there's the academic route, if you finish undergrad and can't bear to stop. That was how I ended up with a doctorate."

"Isn't it weird, though?" Nikki said. "I think it would be weird, like getting stuck in a time loop—just school and more school forever."

"School as a teacher is pretty different from school as a student," said Walden. "Better, honestly, in the way that being an adult is generally a lot better than being a child. Though yes, there is a certain time loop element. Every year I look up and can't believe it's September again. I get older and the Year Sevens never do. Still, it's a nice mix of routine and challenge. Classes might be the same, but individual students are always different. New problems arise all the time, and they need new solutions. I get a fair amount of use out of my elaborate education, and not just in the classroom. At the moment, for example, Mr Cartwright the Keymaster and I are working on the thaumic engines almost round the clock."

"Because of that Year Nine who got possessed?"

Well, you expected children to talk about school drama, and turfing all of Year Nine out of their dorms for the evening had been dramatic. "Yes, exactly. We need to find the hole in our magical security and fix it, but the school's wards are based on a maddeningly complicated nineteenth-century magical engine which barely anyone ever understood to begin with. So solving the problem is a fascinating magical challenge as well as an urgent security issue. I do sort of wish it hadn't come up at the same time as mocks marking, but that's school for you."

Nikki looked thoughtful. "Isn't it weird that it's never happened before?" she said. "You'd think, if the engine's been there since the nineteenth century, and we've had demons hanging around Chetwood that whole time . . . if there's an obvious problem, wouldn't it have come up already?"

"That is one of the big questions, yes," Walden said. "There simply isn't a natural point of failure. Or rather, all the natural points of failure were spotted long ago, because they were obvious. So we dealt with them long ago, and now none of them seem to be the problem. When you know there's something like Old Faithful lurking, you take warding extra seriously. And I take warding seriously anyway. I could have sworn that every defence on the school site was being maintained to the very highest standard. But clearly, somehow, they're not."

"Maybe someone damaged the protections on purpose, then," Nikki said. "Somewhere hard to find. Like that lesson where you rewrote the incursion ward before we came in, and none of us noticed till Matty did the safety check."

"That's hardly likely, Nikki," Walden said.

"Sorry," said Nikki, but she looked thoughtful. "It's only because I just revised this. Initial magician error, check the alerts and redo the wards. Natural failure over time, check the alerts and redo the wards. Protection not strong enough for the local magical environment, check the alerts and redo the wards. And if it's not any of those, then someone's invited something in, so check the alerts and redo the wards and then call the Marshals. Right?"

"Textbook," said Walden. "Full marks. But I do think a bad actor is the least likely explanation. That's what you're proposing, you realise, a magician willing and able to undermine Chetwood's magical defences on purpose. It would have to be someone with internal access to the school site, and they would have to be very, very skilled—not just a student messing around. I did consider 'student messing around' as a possible explanation, but believe me, I would have caught that by now. So that only leaves, for your bad actor hypothesis, an adult magician with considerable magical skill, remarkable subtlety, and no morals whatsoever."

"And that wouldn't happen here, would it?" Nikki said. Her dark eyes were distant and thoughtful. Walden couldn't tell if she was sincere or not when she said softly, "Not at Chetwood."

When Nikki was gone, Walden did a desultory review of her workbook for the arcane safety carousel. She'd got it into very good shape years ago, but it paid off sometimes to stop and think whether your standard lesson plan was still working. And her brain needed a break from the puzzle of the thaumic engines. This at least felt like a productive way to change gears.

She flipped through the pages of the top booklet from the pile on her desk. It was the Year Seven version, so they were adorned with little cartoon magicians and demons. She was using last half term's set—she needed to give these back to the class, actually, she'd have to look up where their form room was and drop them off. The workbook she was reviewing had been carefully, elaborately doodled on. Every cartoon demon had been given a little blue-ballpoint hat. Several of the fill-in-the-gap sections had been left blank. Hmm—so someone's attention had been wandering badly, and Walden hadn't caught it in the lesson. She needed to build in a little more roaming-the-room glancing-over-shoulders time for herself. Where could it go?

It took nearly forty minutes—half of that spent staring into space, rather than working.

Then something in Walden's head went *click*.

"No," she said out loud. "Come on."

Click, click, like the pneumatic cylinders behind the walnut panels of the thaumic engine sliding home one at a time. Like a train, finally pointed onto the correct track, starting to accelerate. Walden's brain was a powerful, finely tuned, and very expensively educated problem-solving tool. Its weakness—the difference, if you liked, between being merely very intelligent and being brilliant— was a tendency to run safely on the rails of assumption.

It's hardly likely. It's not reasonable.

It couldn't happen at Chetwood.

Walden flipped the Year Seven workbook closed. The blank back cover had been adorned with an impressively recognisable cartoon of herself, dressed up as a storybook magician, with pointy hat and long beard. Very good for a twelve-year-old. She smoothed it flat with both hands. Her fingernails were glowing gold. The air in her office was cold, suddenly, with a deep, brittle chill that owed nothing to January.

Ooooo, finally, crooned the Phoenix in her thoughts. *Finally, finally.*

Walden shivered. The demon that lived in her skin had leapt ahead of her and drawn its own conclusions, full of fiery joy. She asked: *Did you know?*

It did not understand. It knew its own nature, the hunter and the hunted. It knew the taste of danger and the calculus of risk and reward. It knew hunger, and it knew power. It *was* power. It liked the idea of a fight. It was not, Walden thought, a reliable witness.

"What if I'm wrong?" she asked the cool, antique silence. Then the answer, because it was obvious. "What if I'm not?"

The key to a good risk assessment was not *How often does this happen.* It was *How bad could the consequences be?*

Walden thought back to the morning of December 19. The date was stamped neatly in her memory: the day after the last day of the Autumn Term. If she got up right now and walked into her flat she would see the digital alarm clock on her bedside table, with the numbers illuminated red. The first time she'd woken up, it had been a little before seven, and Mark had not been in the bed. Then she'd woken up again, and it had already been half past eight. He'd come in with wet hair, wearing only a towel. *Mistimed it, haven't I.*

An hour and a half between those two wakings. The door from her sitting room into the cavernous chamber of the thaumic engines had been left on the latch. Walden never had got round to asking Todd about it. Christmas—travel—family—all of that. She'd been busy. And it was the sort of detail you forgot about. Especially when you were already trying to forget the whole associated episode, as quickly as you could.

There were two keys to that door. Todd had one. Walden's lived in a box in her kitchen next to the teapot. It wouldn't have been hard to find—no, not hard to find at all. If Mark had any practice with instantiation, he could probably have cast a little charm to pick it up: shaped an inquiry from the keyhole, narrowed it to the profile of whatever metals keys were usually made from, and sent it sweeping through the flat. That was if he even needed to. If he hadn't just poked around the kitchen while Walden slept, on the assumption that the key was probably around there somewhere.

Mistimed it, haven't I? A little joke. Mark liked his little jokes.

He hadn't mistimed anything.

But *why*—

No, that wasn't the question. Walden was not employed as Chetwood's Director of Magic in order to play detective. Motivations could wait. She had a hypothesis. She had no hard evidence for the hypothesis beyond some rather suggestive coincidences (Mark inviting himself round for drinks and waiting until she was two gins down before they went to bed, and that only after he'd established that he could get into the engine room from her flat) and a shadowy outline that bore an uncomfortable resemblance to exactly one person with access to the school site (a powerful adult magician, subtle, skilled, no morals whatsoever . . .).

The wastepaper bin next to her desk was overfilled, and so was the giant cardboard box of recycling next to that. Walden had to dig a little while to find the card. Plain white cardstock adorned with the Marshals' heraldic crest. *Arjun Ramamurthy, KMGC, Chief of Incident Response (SE England)*. A phone number and a mar.gov.uk email address. Walden set it on her desk and looked at it.

Surely that was a bit of an overreaction. She didn't know, after all. She didn't *know*.

She wished she had Laura's phone number.

Afterwards, if you had asked Walden to pinpoint the moment of her exact worst mistake, the decision that should not have been made, the decision that poisoned all the others afterward, she would have told you: *It was here. Here, at this moment, safe in my office, with no more proof than a very bad feeling. It was when I didn't immediately make the call or send the email.*

It was when I got up and went looking for him.

chapter twenty-seven

SNOWDROPS

"HAVE YOU SEEN MARK ANYWHERE?"

Annie held up one finger; she was on the phone. Walden hovered in the doorway. Of course she technically outranked the school receptionist, by quite a long way. It was amazing what a difference there was between a school's org chart and how things actually got done. No sensible person made Annie's life one whit harder than it had to be.

"Okay," said Annie, at last, hanging up. "Sorry. Parent. What did you need?"

"I was wondering if Mark was on site today."

It was only because Walden was already on edge that she caught the very, very faint lift of Annie's eyebrows, immediately smoothed back to neutrality. It was only because she'd stopped assuming and started thinking that she understood what it meant. Support staff always knew what was going on before the teachers did. Walden and Mark had not been as subtle as she thought. She had said to herself: *Well, my sex life is no one's business.* But school was a closed environment. One's personal judgement—or lack of it—could very quickly become everyone's business.

"He's signed in," Annie reported, still very neutral, after a glance at her screen. "I haven't seen him this side of the road. He might be patrolling. You could try the sports fields. Or Scrubs."

"Thank you," Walden said. "I'll have a look."

She paused at the roadside, looked both ways, and then turned right and walked along the hedgerow until she could cross to the opening for the school coach park. The red-and-white minibuses were lined up in a row at the far end. Walden had her warm coat on and her hands in her pockets. The final few leaves of last autumn, blackened and brittle after the January frost, crunched against the expensive gravel under her feet. There was a cluster of green spikes coming up under the trees at the far end of the car park.

Snowdrops, she thought. *The first snowdrops.*

She had to look in among the trees, in the shadow of the humped row of buses. Her smart black brogues got muddy. It took a while. She would have given up, if she hadn't been fairly clear already on what she was looking for.

She found it neatly concealed inside the rotten bole of the largest tree. The experience of reaching in among the damp moss and slimy fungus was skin-crawlingly unpleasant: not just the usual *eurgh* of rather too much Nature without gardening gloves, but an additional frisson of *You're not interested. You don't like this. You don't want to look at it.*

Oh, but I'm very interested, Walden told the feeling, and steeled herself. It was still very difficult. She forced her hands to grip hard around something spiked and broken and unpleasantly plastic-slick.

The school umbrella was a tattered inside-out skeleton. Its red-and-white canopy was ripped in half a dozen places. Walden turned it over. The slimy, repellent, ugh-not-my-business ward was pressed into the handle, the size of a thumbprint. She'd *handed* this school umbrella to Mark, and it had definitely not been a fantastically accursed object when she'd done so. He must have enchanted it as they were walking around the school site. Ambling across the marshy Games fields in the pouring November rain, making idle conversation, umbrella in hand. The thumbprint size of the ward might be a record of how he'd actually pulled it off: with just his thumb, pressing into the plastic handle like wax.

It got me in the arm! he'd said. But that injury had ceased to be a concern remarkably quickly after that day, hadn't it? When had he punched his neat little portal back to the mundane world to drop off a cursework somewhere safe? She'd asked about the umbrella at some point, she was sure, and Mark had dismissed it. Months ago; she couldn't be certain of anything now.

Quite impressive, really. Very impressive, even. How galling it was, to think you had the measure of a nasty man exactly, and then discover that you'd been allowed to take the measure he saw fit to share. How *deeply* embarrassing, to fall for the pose even as you laughed at it. Mark was a much, much better magician than Walden had given him credit for. He was at least as good as she was. He was better than she was, in some specific ways. She was an invocation specialist, which was, intellectually speaking, the show-off field. The go-big-or-go-home field. *Invocation teachers teach contract law.* She'd just *assumed* she had to be cleverer than he was. Probably she was. Probably, decades ago, she'd got better grades in all her exams.

And then Mark had made a big deal out of his evocation bona fides, passing himself off as sporty—oh, he was authentically sporty—but fading, the forty-something clinging to the athlete-magician he'd been. But that had been a lie too. This sort of subtle, understated spellwork, rooted in the physical environment, layered and bound into an object—this was instantiation. It was perhaps the most flexible discipline of magic. It was certainly the hardest to detect. You had to have a frankly dire enthusiasm for *stuff* to be really good at it. The original builders of the thaumic engine would have been state-of-their-art instantiation scholars.

Walden was thinking about the ward because the rest of the curse on the ruined umbrella was much harder to think about. She couldn't actually *see* what it was doing. But she could feel it. It shone in the demonic plane like a lantern on a foggy night.

Here. Come here. Come here.

She remembered the minibus demon revving up to charge at her. Had Mark *actually* been trying to get her killed? Surely not. *Surely* not. After all, he'd had full access to her report on Old Faithful. He must have already known that Walden could call on the Phoenix for magical assistance in a crisis.

Here, come here, sang the luring curse, calling to any demon in range.

The demon closest by said sniffily, *I am here already.* Then it snapped the umbrella in half.

It used Walden's bare hands to do it. Walden cried out in pain as the plastic spines dug into her palms. The Phoenix said, *Encroaching pest. We should kill him and eat him.*

"Good *God,*" said Walden. "Let me think, you bloodthirsty monster."

But she was thinking about—London. A London night, snow falling and not settling, and a sudden wild incursion. Chief Ramamurthy looking at her suspiciously, because when you had a demon problem and a powerful magician standing right next to it, you *ought* to be suspicious.

It just made no sense. It made no sense. Her brain kept nagging round and round the problem no matter how she tried to shove it into *His reasons are not my job*. She thought she knew Mark quite well. She *liked* Mark, in the way one liked an extra glass of wine or an entire tub of ice cream or intentionally not going to the gym after you'd nobly set the evening aside for it. Or in the way you liked good sex with an attractive person who made no emotional demands on you whatsoever: the simplest kind of guilty pleasure. But she also quite liked him, at this point, as a colleague: all his little jokes and intentional overgrown-schoolboy affect and reasonably helpful planar patrols. She'd seen him as someone fairly amusing, fairly reliable, fairly straightforward to deal with. Something familiar. A normal person.

It was just very hard to think of any reason why an apparently normal person would set so many demons loose—in central London during peak pub hours! God, in a *school!*—without arriving quite quickly at *Is he some sort of insane evil murderer?* And there was a difference, there *was* a difference, between being a posh dickhead and being a bloodthirsty monster. Surely there was a difference. Walden had spent her whole life in a series of elite educational institutions, circles that overlapped quite closely with the posh dickhead type. She would have *noticed*.

Or perhaps not. There was a lot she hadn't noticed. She'd needed a teenager to point out the obvious possibility she was missing. Brilliant, brilliant Nikki, not even done with her A-levels, but able to *think in a straight line,* which was more apparently than Walden could do stupid, stupid! She was so stupid! She felt so *stupid*—

This was the problem, of course, with staking your personal and professional identity entirely on being fantastically clever. It made it much harder to keep control when it turned out you weren't.

Walden dropped the pieces of the broken umbrella. The Phoenix, simply by snapping it, had undone the luring curse as neatly as the ten minutes of counterspelling that Walden would have gone for. Ten minutes was not time she had. Mark was on the school site and apparently capable of anything. Six hundred children were also on the site. This was a child protection issue, a critical and immediate safeguarding concern. Walden should—

—*get help, report to David, phone the police, call the fucking Marshals now, now, now!* clamoured a voice in the back of her thoughts.

She barely heard it. Walden had had plenty of practice, these last few months, ignoring little voices in her thoughts.

—*should find him,* she thought coldly.

And kill him.

And eat him.

She walked along the village road half-dreaming. A white Ford Transit van went speeding past in the direction of Chetwood village, so close behind her on the pedestrian crossing that she felt the wind of it in her hair. It was doing seventy through the twenty-an-hour school zone. Walden glanced after it for a second or two. She heard the bang just over the ridge as the van developed loud, sputtering engine problems.

There were a lot of snowdrops coming up. Every January they came back, little white spikes of defiance against the cold. Though this January had not been as cold as some. It felt wrong, seeing the daffodils start to put up tall green shoots this early.

As she had the thought, the daylight chilled and clarified. Clouds etched black shapes on the white horizon. The air was crisp and hard to breathe. Walden dusted her muddy hands on her warm coat and put them back in her pockets.

Scrubs, fenced by lacework scaffolding. The dark rectangle of quasi-Brutalist ambition stark against the white sky. This place was Chetwood, as much as the old stone colonnade and the lofty chapel. Chetwood at its occasional best, with an eye on the future, embracing the startling modern innovations of concrete, the middle school, and women's education. Universal House. Walden stood with her hands in her pockets looking up at it.

I am here, she thought. *I am also here.*

At eleven—thirteen—fifteen—eighteen. Leaving her bed unmade and getting told off for it. Engaged in elaborate, vital, hard-to-remember interpersonal drama with her Year Eight dorm. Dyeing her hair to ashy chemical blonde in a student bathroom. *I am here.* Sneaking out to summon a great demon. Taking the job interview tour. Patrolling for curfew breakers. Making a brief, friendly appearance at NQT drinks in Lilly Tibbett's flat this year.

I am here, long before I was here: because the beauty of school was its predictability, the sheer weight of institution carving patterns into the world, stronger than blood or bone. *I am here*, because other children had slept in those dormitories before her. *I am here*, in the old boarding houses, exiled from all love, weeping with cold and loneliness. *I am here*, reciting principles of magic and mathematics and Latin grammar, giving adults rude nicknames whether they called themselves teachers or masters or magisters; finding small ways to break the rules of how to be, rules that changed and changed and yet remained forever the same unforgiving edifice of authority. *I am here*, in the masters and magisters, the well-intentioned and the cruel, the competent and the hopeless, the shattered war veteran drinking steadily in his study or the mediaeval jobbing wizard checking his astrological tables before he went back to reckoning the bills. *I am here*, like the ghost of the Headmaster killed by a higher demon in 1926. *I am here*, like a succession of imps in the staffroom photocopier.

I am here, adult and child, new and old, deeply rooted, never failing, with all the silent force of centuries of repetition.

I am here: the green fields. *Here:* the white sky.

Here I am, more real than real, more alive than alive.

I am here even in the January snowdrops.

She waited. She did not know what she was waiting for.

"Funny weather," said Mark to his companion as he emerged from Scrubs's front door. He was his usual self, smart casual, expensive haircut, very good shoes. Only slightly dishevelled, in the easy way of a man who never really lost control of appearances. Lilly Tibbett, twenty-two years old and newly qualified, who lived in a flat on the ground floor and had the makings of a very good teacher eventually, was still pink with exertion. She had thrown her blonde hair into a quick ponytail and she was looking up at Mark with the unmistakeable, pitiable gaze of the besotted.

Typical, thought someone who was neither Dr Walden nor Mark's Sapphire nor the Saffy who had been, someone who hovered between those three selves and a fourth newly waking. Somehow, despite the surprise, it was the exact thing that she'd expected, the thing that made all the rest make sense. Was a man like Mark Daubery truly sexually inspired by the ardent pursuit of a tired schoolteacher, very nearly forty? Probably not. But was he *entertained* by the challenge of two-timing a naïve and adoring twentysomething with her line manager's line manager, when they both lived on the same not-very-large school site: oh, *obviously* he was.

I always liked younger women—another little joke. What a funny, funny man.

Poor Lilly obviously hasn't the foggiest, one of the watching selves tried to think. Her own pity rang false in her ears.

Mark looked up from gently, kindly detaching Lilly's hand from his sleeve, and saw her there. He made a joke—she wasn't close enough to hear the joke, but she could see the expression on his face, and Lilly's smiling, shamed reaction. Her other-self's pity became truer. A nasty man. An arsehole sandwich. Easier not to be hurt if you knew the type. The watching person was not, she thought, hurt. No. It would take a much greater power than a mere mortal magician to *hurt* her.

"Afternoon, Dr Walden," said Mark. Lilly had fled back inside, which made the watcher fairly certain that Mark's comment had been something along the lines of *Better fix your face, you look like you just got shagged within an inch of your life.* Getting rid of her. Clearing the field. Mark was a person who thought in terms of conflict and power and self-interest. So, a person like herself. "Something I can do for you?"

"Walk with me," she said, smiling.

They walked the gravel path around Scrubs, past the raised flowerbeds. The young birch tree planted at the back of the building was stark and pale against the backdrop of grey concrete and dark, gapping windows. The memorial plaque had yellow-green lichen growing over the *C* of Charlie's name. Some rude child had sat on the grass eating cheese and onion crisps and then not taken their litter away with them. Walden considered the blue crisp packet thoughtfully. It caught fire, and burned for a few seconds with a white flame, before the foil unravelled into ash.

"Bit of an overreaction," remarked Mark. "Everything all right, Sapphire?" A look of humour, self-abasement, understanding. "We haven't misunderstood each other, have we? I hope we haven't."

"Not at all," she said. "Do you mind if I ask who, exactly, you work for?"

His eyebrows went up. "Well, the Board of Governors, at the moment—"

She looked at him.

"Nothing interesting, I promise you," Mark said. "Nothing important."

"Mmm," she said. She'd had a shadowy picture, and that picture was growing clearer. There would be an organisation, somewhere. Not government, she thought. Something easier to disavow. A string of initials. The good guys, almost certainly, or at least the good guys as Mark would reckon it. Something he felt proud of, enough to boast to his nephew a little. Far away, on the other side of the Atlantic, a person she'd once been had received that promise: *Everything you do for us, you'll be doing for the right reasons. For the good guys.*

It was the Phoenix. That was what he cared about; that was what he was here for. The Phoenix, abstract to everyone but Walden herself—really, abstract to Walden as well—until it had destroyed Old Faithful, and so revealed to anyone who knew anything about its kind that somehow a human magician had gained personal and immediate control over power equivalent to a small nuclear warhead. Power and weakness were too attractive a combination to ignore. *I'm big and slow,* you might say. *Come eat me.*

How big, and how slow? What could the Phoenix do, and how well could Walden control it? Mark had been testing. And writing reports, probably. Just not the one he claimed he was here for.

All of this was a vague and rather distant set of *Oh yes I suppose,* unsurprising as Mark fucking Lilly had been unsurprising. *It's how the world works. I didn't make it that way.* But there were reasons, *oh there were reasons,* why a person might take the job where she would be underestimated and undervalued forever. A fear of boredom, yes. A love of the work. And a certainty: this is what I have done. Here is power, and here are power's consequences. I can point to them. I can name them. Here is the child who knows today what she did not know yesterday. She will take her knowledge away into adulthood and find her own terrible strength there. Those are her choices. These, circumscribed, limited by ancient stone and crumbling concrete, by time and tradition and school bells and school boundaries—these are mine.

Selves came and went. They grew and grew. You discovered something to be and then you learned how to inhabit it with every inch of your being. And so you became old, and strong, and terrible.

"Sapphire," said Mark. They were still walking together, ambling along the path that led from the back of Scrubs to the sad little patch of longer grass that had once been the old cricket pavilion. Even now, to her senses, the outlines of a triple summoning array remained burned into the mundane earth here. Twenty years ago, two children had tried to master a power far beyond them. They had got what they deserved. It was a very, very bad idea to enter into a direct contest of magical strength with a higher demon.

"Sapphire?"

The Phoenix turned back to her enemy, encroaching outsider, power-hungry pest. He was a threat to her territory, her school. She understood school as she never had before. It was part of her. She ruled here. She smiled at him.

"I'm afraid not," she said.

FEBRUARY HALF TERM

SPRING II

EASTER

SUMMER I

chapter twenty-eight

PHOENIX INDWELLING

YOU COME FROM A DESERT. YOU HAVE A MEMORY, ancient, of soaring on updrafts over unforgiving red country.

You come from small beginnings. You were too small even for memory in the very earliest days. You know that you scrabbled and fought for your right to be. You imagine it in the terms that make sense in this world of motion and matter: the tearing talons, the slashing spurs.

You have grown old and strong and terrible. You have chosen a place in the world and made it your own. It is a good place. You know this word, 'good.' It is a safe place. You have learned this concept, 'safe.' You understood it first and best for yourself: but you are too old, too strong, and too terrible ever to be safe. There is a punishment for triumph, a punishment for victory, a punishment for ascension. Now you have these things, you must defend them forever.

Your safe place had a previous inhabitant, a mighty old bottom-feeder already rotting in his shell. You knew he was there. You concealed yourself, waiting. When he tried to strike, you arose in flame and cast him down. He was very stupid. Imagine being so stupid! But of course you were also, once, very stupid. The thing that soared on wings of fire knew the joy of great power, but not the purpose. It was enough, in those days, just to exist.

You are older, wiser, better than that. You have climbed past 'exist' and 'endure' and 'succeed,' past the hunger and the contest. You have chosen a self to become. You have examined, in memory, several articles on educational psychology, including a number of colourful triangle diagrams of progression, and so discovered that you are at the top of the pyramid. You are, in fact, self-actualising! Well done!

You are proud of this achievement. Very few of your kind has ever done anything like it. You become increasingly sure that all of them have struggled, all along, for nothing else. What a privilege to be human! What a wonder to be mortal! What an extraordinary world, bound by matter and motion, in which to move through space and time in your little sack of water and meat just *doing* things. Doing things for *reasons*. Repairing the trivially obvious damage to the thaumic engines, to secure the borders of mundanity for the humans—the *other* humans; you belong here now—what a treat! Reading all the dusty books on your office shelves, late into the night, to learn what is written inside them: what a remarkable delight!

Discovering that the body goes peculiar without sleep: discovering sleep schedules, and then, as an extension—a new amusement, a new amazement—discovering just what bad care you have been taking of yourself. Why do you have bottles of poison in your cupboards? (*It's quite nice gin and it was a gift so please don't pour it down the—oh, never mind;* you ignore all such mutterings in your thoughts.) Why do you only eat the canteen food—didn't you know you could get your own ingredients and cook them yourself? Why don't you ever seem to *move*? This body can climb; this body can swim; this body can run, and run, and *(ow ow ow ow ow . . .)*

A self is a home is a purpose is a life. You know. You have all these things now.

You are the speck who rose in the desert to become the prince of air and fire. You are also Dr Sapphire Walden. In all your years of scholarship and teaching, you have never, ever, ever been this enthusiastic about getting your marking done. *This sort of thing by itself,* says the caustic voice in your thoughts as you cheerily work through your lunch break on a set of A-level practice papers, *should really be enough to let everyone know you aren't human.*

You take another bite of the poached egg and spinach on homemade sourdough you fixed yourself before you sat down, and ignore her.

I can't believe you bake your own bread, she says.

She is obviously just jealous. You are so much better at being her than she ever was.

A classroom. You patrol the classrooms constantly. This is your territory; nothing here is secret from you. Desks pushed together in a cluster, the lever arch folders spread out. Magical notation blooming across the whiteboard in black marker and red. "Hello, squad," you say. "Revising?"

Squad, team, everybody, you lot, Upper Six you have a wide array of these gender-neutral group addresses in the precious vaults of memory, and you take some pleasure in selecting the correct level of formality against warmth for each situation.

They look at you. A speaker for the group is silently elected: Aneeta, sensible and academic, unblemished good behaviour for seven years straight, ideal teacher-wrangler. "I hope it's okay if we use the classroom," she says. "We'll clean the board afterwards."

Technically they should be in the library or the sixth form common room, but school is surprisingly low on suitable spaces for small study groups, and you know the value of such work. Aneeta and Nikki urge each other on; both of them show care and support for Mathias; Will is pricked to competitive industriousness when Nikki is there. You are satisfied by these calculations, this knowledge. You gesture approval. "Feel free. I trust you lot."

Will sits on a desk, long legs in black jeans swinging, holding his pen unmoving against a propped-up notepad. Nikki's eyes are deep and dark and watchful. Mathias hunches in his chair. Even now, eighteen years old, three weeks before the A-level examinations begin, he has a fearful child's reaction to unexpected adult attention. You smile on them benevolently. Benevolence is another thing you have learned, a function of your new selfhood. You are an *enormously* benevolent teacher.

"Good luck," you say. "Work hard! Do let me know if you need help with anything."

Aneeta breathes out hard when you're gone. You could know this, if you chose to, but your attention has moved on. Children are only children. They are within your territory but not part of it; you abide by this principle as a concession to your host. She has no power to restrain you, but she becomes very irritating if you act in a manner inconsistent with the statutory guidance annually published by the government under the title of Keeping Children Safe in Education.

Will says, "So—"

"Shh," hisses Nikki, eyes on Aneeta, who is positioned between the board and the doorway, neatly placed to watch for movement in the corridor.

After a moment, Aneeta nods. At the same time, Mathias straightens up from his miserable crouch over the desk. His acne is finally starting to clear up. He's been trying a different cleanser.

"So," says Will again. "Are we really sure we aren't imagining it?"

"We're not imagining it," says Mathias, with the absolute certainty of a boy whose dreams have been haunted by the whispers of eager, encroaching demons since he was three years old. Some mortals lie closer to the edge of worlds than others. Some holes in the heart cry out to be filled.

"Yeah, no," says Nikki, who—like you—wears a mask every day. Who, like you, was born for power. She puts her hand on Mathias's arm briefly. You would have a hard time making sense of this particular mortal gesture. You have decided that the nonprofessional social aspects of your new existence are a low priority. After all, *she* hardly troubled herself with them. "Okay. Pen me."

She holds up her other hand. Aneeta throws the red board pen she is clutching. A bad throw, but a good catch. Nikki stands up. All unknowing she holds the perfect attention of the other three. She has different selves for every person in this group—dearest-friend, longed-for-beloved, almost-sister—but those selves are all secondary to the one she assumes naturally and without thinking, which is *leader*.

She wipes the board clean of revision notes with her sleeve, and starts to write out instead the plan that has slowly consumed her evenings over the last several months. She has taken her time and done her research. She does not intend to make the same mistake twice. You have known doctoral candidates less thorough and less careful. The red pen is swapped out for a black to sketch an array, and swapped back to red for annotations. Mathias makes a small sound. Nikki interprets it as a stifled criticism—he is so afraid, Mathias, of criticising anyone—and says, "Yeah, okay. Will can do the drawing, then."

Will gets up, obedient, and takes the black pen. Nikki is still writing out arcane notation with the red.

Aneeta has taken a seat on a wobbly plastic chair. She does not notice herself shifting her weight, shifting, shifting, making the bad leg creak. May sunlight is streaming through the classroom windows and gleaming off her glasses as she frowns at the whiteboard. In the corridor, a loud giggle suddenly stifled, as two middle schoolers who should not be out of lessons scamper past on some teacher's errand. Everyone jumps and looks at the door, but no one comes in. No lesson is scheduled in here until after lunch.

Nikki sets the red board pen down on the empty teacher's desk. Will completes the fourth layer of the array design with a flourish. Four layers, for the size of demon they suspect they are dealing with, representing the groundwork of an exorcism and a banishment. It is not a live array; there is no magic in it yet, and if they actually go through with this, they will need to make it much, much bigger. Which means they need a space to work in, and time. Challenging requirements, for four teenagers three weeks away from public exams, trapped by the rules and constant registration requirements of a boarding school. You could advise them, based on your own experience. You could say, *The cricket pavilion in the middle of the night worked well for us.*

"Would help if we had a fifth," says Will after a few moments of silence—awed silence, worried silence, the silence of people who cannot believe their own audacity—"to hold the last point of the pentagram. Are any of the Year Twelves good? Or we could ask someone from Evoke. Harry or somebody."

"Or," says Aneeta, abrupt and sharp. The wobbly chair leg goes *clunk* as she draws herself up straight. "Or . . ."

Will snorts. Nikki says, "No, I'm listening." Mathias looks down at the desk. Alone of the four, he has no actual revision notes in the lever arch folder in front of him. He knows he has left it very late. He is starting to panic, and the panic has frozen him. You should really have caught this and had a reassuring chat with him by now.

"Or, I'm just saying," says Aneeta, "we could tell an appropriate adult what's happening, let *them* sort it out, and focus on our exams."

Will rounds on her. "We *are* adults," he snaps. "We're eighteen, okay, we're fucking grown-ups, we're *magicians*. It's up to us now. Niks has been working so hard on this, do you even realise? And we're the people *here*. We're the ones who can do this."

"Maybe," says Mathias softly.

"Who do we tell?" Nikki says. "Who haven't we tried?"

Children are only children. They are not part of your territory. You do not rule them. But the staff are another matter. Your dominion over their minds is subtle and absolute. You have sunk yourself into the system of Chetwood School, and institutions have powerful hooks; the contract of employment is as binding as any summoning array. Sometimes the Headmaster will stare into the modern fireplace in his nice house in the village with a half-grimace drawing lines on his brow. Over the Easter holidays, during their two-week escape, a few people remarked to partners or friends, "It just doesn't seem like a happy staffroom at the moment . . . I don't know, I might start looking."

But it is too late in the academic year to start seriously looking. They will check the *Times Educational Supplement* job postings over summer, but they will be back in September. They will forget soon afterwards that they ever wanted to leave. The TES alerts will sit unopened in their inboxes.

(A junior Spanish teacher went home to Madrid over Easter and did not come back. She gave no explanation to the school. Her department, covering her timetable, are all very annoyed.)

Upper Sixth have tried:

Matron—her headshot and email address and exhortations to come to her with any worries are posted all over the school. Nikki and Mathias sit down to dinner with her at the family table in School House three times a week, and bow their heads politely for grace, though neither is a regular attendee at chapel. She is a good listener. She did not hear a word they said.

Reverend Ezekiel—the only person apart from yourself qualified to teach an A-level in Invocation, and indeed the teacher of the current Year Twelve set. An ideal person to tell about any demonic suspicions. But he will not hear them now.

The new Chief Marshal—who sent them away; who seemed surprised to be spoken to by children.

Nearly every individual teacher in the magical departments, even as far as Miss Tibbett, whom Aneeta thinks seems nice and enthusiastic and whom Will scorns as *Yeah but I don't rate her, do you?*

The school counsellor. Their form tutors. Their teachers in other subjects—Aneeta, darling of the Chemistry Department, has very good relationships with all her academic mentors. The rowing coach, the Head of Sixth Form, the Head of Careers. Mr Cartwright the site manager, which was Mathias's idea, and which came closest to succeeding: he was the only one so far who even *seemed* to be listening.

The Headmaster, which was nerve-racking, and just as pointless as all the others.

They have not tried to tell Will's uncle, the impressive Mr Daubery. He has not been seen at Chetwood in months. As a matter of fact, no one on the school site—not even Will—remembers that he ever existed.

"I know no one in school is listening," says Aneeta. "So what if . . . not school?"

"We've been over this," says Nikki. Phones suddenly have no signal. Emails return error messages. It is your nature to dwell in systems, and so these systems are not secret from you. Nothing seems to work.

"It's not letting information out," Aneeta says. "But it might let *us* out."

A pause.

"I'm out of exeats," says Will.

"I wasn't saying let's ask *permission*."

"Sorry, I assumed because you basically always sound like you're saying *Let's ask permission*—" Touchy, embarrassed.

"Will," says Nikki, and it quiets him, unless that's her hand on his shoulder, which he glances at with the terrified wonder of a person encountering the rare and exquisitely beautiful in its natural habitat. To Aneeta, she says, "And go where? Your parents?"

Aneeta displays a website on her phone, a mar.gov.uk website. The phone is in a blue leather case. There is a neat little incursion ward scratched into the case with the back of an earring; this phone will never acquire an invading imp. It's a shame you've never noticed this, because it is such a simple, obvious, and intelligent solution that you should have insisted on it for the whole school years ago. But then Aneeta is truly, remarkably, blissfully sensible.

The you-that-was would shower her in the accolades that barely mean anything to a Year Thirteen this late in the game—the house points, the school prizes, the mention in assembly—for being the only one of these brave idiot children to remember the very first rule of keeping themselves safe: *Tell a trusted grown-up.*

"Mum and Dad are too busy to be much use," she says. "No, we should go straight to the Marshals. Because when the big one—" She stops. She is not a coward. She looks at Nikki. "When Old Faithful tried to break through," she says, "it was Marshal Kenning who went in, wasn't it? So if we want someone who understands . . . we want Marshal Kenning. I did some research and I think she's in London, at the Brixton chapter house. It's on the Victoria Line." She waves the phone screen at them again as proof.

Mathias unhunches. He is almost unaware—they are all almost unaware—that he is actually the tallest of the four. "Yeah," he says suddenly, urgently. "*Yeah.* Because of the—"

He loses the word he wants. A hopeless hand gesture is all that takes its place. *Think it through, take your time,* you would say, if you were teaching this lesson. You are not there now. Anything you have taught them, they will have to apply by themselves.

"Because *woo I have such magicky feelings,* right," says Will, and then—to everyone's surprise including his own; maybe it's because Nikki is there—"sorry, Matty, I'm a dickhead. You've got something, haven't you."

Mathias is starting to sink back into himself again, but he nods. "There's a thing," he says. "There's like a—a thread. Sorry. It's probably woo."

"No, it's not," says Nikki decisively. "Tell us."

"Like a—line," Mathias says. He struggles, struggles, for technical vocabulary. You set them tests on this in Year Twelve. The terminology of academia may seem like an obstructing wall of jargon—and sometimes, perhaps, it is—but far more often than that, it is a set of keys. You cannot understand the forces you are dealing with, still less wield them meaningfully yourself, unless you have the words to set around them. The language of power is the handle on the knife.

Mathias wrestles his way through sentences like a person hip-deep in mud. He has an enormous, near-demonic instinct for how magic moves in the world, and a predicted C grade in his theory paper. It speaks well of the others that they listen with patience to his halting jumble of words. Of course, they know him well; they know that his 'woo magic feelings,' as Will terms them, are seldom without merit. After all, they are students at a boarding school together. They might as well be crewmates on a starship, or inmates in a jail. It is a profound, compelled, inescapable intimacy.

At last Mathias hits on the word that unlocks his perception for the rest of them: "—like a *binding*—"

"Like an oath," says Nikki. "You mean a geas—an *oath*."

She is the fisherman killing his catch. She takes her foster brother's blurted mess of inchoate sensations and knocks it hard against the table; from ungraspable blur of watery light to a clear and definite fish. She looks satisfied with the achievement. "You're sure?"

Aneeta is flipping through her folder. "When was the oaths topic? No, I've got it." Fingers moving rapidly across the neatly mind-mapped summary page.

"Who's she sworn an oath to?" says Will.

You are back in your office. You are working. You are always working. If your colleagues thought you were married to the job before—and they did—they are baffled by you now. *She's on a health kick*, they say, watching you run circuits of the rugby pitches in the

long hours of the early summer evening, when the low sun hangs
fat and pale in the cloudless bowl of the sky. *I don't know how she does
it.* Afterwards, you go back to your flat and shower, and curl up on
the sofa, and read articles on educational theory. You are learning
so much.

You check your phone, as you do every evening. There is a
message from your older brother, unanswered. *(What on earth does he
want?)* There are alumni newsletters in your seldom-touched personal email—Oxford, Stanford, one from Chetwood full of small
pieces of news you already know. There is, known only to yourself, an exquisitely perfect little cage of spellwork knotted through
the phone's processor, containing a solitary imp. The imp is silent,
cowed, terrified. You have attempted to explain that you regard it
as a junior employee, or possibly a pet cat, and either way have no
intention of eating it alive, but it is much too small and weak and
stupid to understand. Be sympathetic. You were the same, once.

You bite the underside of your own wrist to draw blood. You
feed the imp. The scarlet smear on the phone screen disappears
quickly. You slap a fresh plaster over the repeated marks of your
own teeth. The pain does not bother you. Your other self expresses
mingled horror and resignation, but this is what she always does, so
you do not find it interesting.

You work until 10 P.M. with a twenty-five-minute break for supper. You are in bed with the lights out at a sensible quarter past ten.

Your other self is trying not to keep you awake. Your other self
is trying not to think. You know everything she knows; you are her.
But she knows a lot of things, and with the magnificent feast of her
education and her career spread before you, she is hoping you will
not turn your attention to those matters filed under *romantic, social,
personal.* She never prioritised those things anyway. There is not
much there to interest you.

So she lies quiescent, as she has for months, unable to twitch so much as a finger while you sleep the satisfied sleep of a mortal body well fed and exercised. Perhaps in your dreams of wind over the red country you hear a distant voice: *Oh fuck Laura I've been so stupid. Laura please you have to know. No one else knows.*

Help me. Help me. Help me.

chapter twenty-nine

OATHBOUND

Y OU KNOW, OR CAN KNOW, EVERYTHING THAT happens in your territory. Its boundaries are the boundaries of Chetwood School: to the lake, to the woods, to the high garden walls where former boarding houses were sold off to become detached six-bedroom character-property London-commutable mansions, to the ancient hedgerows that mark the boundaries with farmers' fields of wheat and sugar beet and blooming yellow rapeseed. There is a ribbon of tarmac blindness through the middle of your world, but the tendrils of your power extend over it, especially around the CAUTION SCHOOL zebra crossing. These days, drivers cutting through country lanes to dodge traffic on the A1 do, in fact, find themselves exercising caution because of the school. A miracle.

You know, through your extended web of defensive perception, when Years Ten to Thirteen troop en masse down the road to Chetwood village on Sunday. A few teachers go along to supervise the ritual of the day out. On this lovely sunny May weekend, they are mostly supervising from a big table with a green parasol in front of the pub, and though they are in loco parentis, they don't see that as any reason to resist a pint. Meanwhile the students slope around on the green, and hang around in the pub, and take up every table in the Chetwood Caff (cheap) and the Village Sweetheart Tea Shoppe (expensive), as well as most of the picnic tables round the back of Mutchins' Garden Centre and Dahlia Nursery. Occasionally a little murmur of displeased town-and-gown hostility stirs in the village—there are a *lot* of teenagers, and they do make the place look untidy—but you have delivered your share of stern Respecting Our Community assemblies, and the locals running the shops know which side their bread is buttered. Very few of these children blink at paying nearly twenty quid for a burger and chips with coleslaw left uneaten on the side, and then using the change to stuff themselves with local-farm-shop ice cream from the big freezer at the garden centre. Once Year Thirteen have their IDs, they positively throw money at the Red Lion in exchange for overpriced alcopops. It's important, after all, to feel grown-up.

You have not been down to the village yourself in some time. You are inflexibly territorial. You will not leave your school.

You are not paying attention when four eighteen-year-olds catch the London train. They are honestly surprised by how easy it is. They assumed they would be in trouble; they assumed they would be stopped. But the station—a quiet country station, not on a main line—is not staffed. They have all dutifully purchased the correct tickets from the machine, and when the guard comes past, further down the line, he will hesitate a moment over how shifty Mathias looks but ultimately decide that it's not his problem as long as the kids have paid.

Your webs of perception do not extend as far as London. You have seen London, and it does not appeal to you: too big, too ill-defined, too difficult to control and call your own. You have found your place, and you intend to stay here for a long, long time. So you do not have even an inkling of how much danger you are in until evening registration, when it finally becomes obvious that four sixth formers have slipped the net and no one noticed.

This is a very, very, very big problem when your institution has legal and professional responsibility for the safety of those sixth formers. *Now* Upper Sixth Invocation are in trouble—big trouble. Now there are frantic phone calls going out to parents and to authorities, and friends and classmates are being interrogated to no avail, and ordered to place their own calls and send their own messages. In the big house in Kensington where no one else is home— Aneeta's parents are hardly ever home, and the cleaners only come on Tuesdays—she takes out her phone in its warded blue case and grimaces at the screen of notifications.

You are frantic. Not because you are in danger (you are powerful, you are confident, why would your first assumption be danger?) but because *they* might be. The self you have become cannot bear it. It is a shocking downside to your new existence. You have never found anything unbearable before. You have never worried. You have never cared.

No, you don't expect danger, even now.

You don't sleep. The body, worried about missing children, refuses to obey your will. You did not know bodies could do that.

You have forgotten all about the oath sworn between magician and Marshal, months ago: *If I fail, I submit myself at once to the judgement of the Order of Marshals and especially to the Chief Marshal Laura Kenning.*

Magical oaths sworn between human beings are old magic, messy and vague and unsatisfying magic, a few sentences in the A-level syllabus. But there is a power in them which even a higher demon cannot resist. It is the power of the promise. The contract.

Because no matter how carefully the forces of magic have been meticulously pinned down to scientific principles by the European academic tradition, magic is not science. Little as magicians like it, it *can* be divorced from logic, skill, and expertise. It can find its way through whatever tools come to hand, through coincidence and potential, through human perception and human connection.

Most serious academic magicians ignore this sort of thing—partly because it is hard to exploit, and partly because it makes them uncomfortable.

By this oath I lay my fate in her hands. If the Phoenix wakes, she shall know of it, and she shall be granted all power to act.

There is no how. There is no when. But there is a binding, full of force. You have slipped all other jesses. You cannot slip from this one.

It is the middle of the night. A demon is loose on the world.

The Marshals are coming.

Here is the knight in shining armour. (*Only the Head of the Order gets the knighthood, actually,* she might say, wry, adjusting her rune-engraved vambraces.) Here she rides on her noble steed. (*She's a Kawasaki Ninja H2, I picked her up second-hand*—which does not refute 'noble steed'; Laura Kenning really likes her bike.) She has come alone. You wouldn't have expected that. It doesn't make sense to come alone.

You know she is there the moment the motorbike turns off the road onto the old lime avenue. You are vibrating with wakefulness and worry. Your first feeling is relief, tremendous relief, born—you do not think of this—from the host. Feeling comes from the body and stakes insidious claims on the will. Feeling still confuses you a little. You—you! A demon of the tenth order! The prince of air and fire!—you don't think *She has come to kill me.* You think *Maybe she knows where the Upper Sixth have gone.*

Marshal Kenning does not come straight for you. She goes to the Keymaster first. Old Todd Cartwright, up late at night watching the sinking ashes of the fire in the ancient groundskeeper's cottage that he has made a snug little home. The polished Great Key of Chetwood is hanging from its chain on a peg beside the fireplace. He answers the knock and looks, for a moment, baffled. "Chief Marshal Kenning?" he says.

And then—just like that, in that moment of confusion, surprise, and sharp awareness—you lose him. Todd Cartwright, with his extraordinary natural sense for magic, trained not in a classroom but in four decades of practical work, is old and strong and deep in the heart of this place. It was his territory first. You are not the only being ever to look at Chetwood School and decide to stake yourself entire on *There is something good here, there is something worth having, and I have claimed it for my own.*

Todd knows what is happening at Chetwood now. He will not unknow it again. You must either accept this threat to your power or destroy him utterly. Hairline fractures will appear through the middle of your new-forged selfhood either way.

"I was there when we dragged her out of Old Faithful's teeth the first time," he says, wasting no time on amazement or horror at the revelation he just experienced. "She was a good kid, you know. You don't forget the good kids. Think you'll get her out alive?"

"I don't know," says Kenning. "I'm going to try."

"Where's your squad?"

"They wouldn't get her out alive," Kenning says. "Too difficult. Marshals prioritise the innocent bystanders, not the magician who caused the problem." A faint grimace. The Marshals, as a matter of policy, are probably right. If your sworn duty is to defend the mortal world from demons, you are not obliged to feel much sympathy for those people who—intentionally or not—go around poking demons with sticks. Kenning herself does not feel a great deal of sympathy for the predicament of a possessed magician. She is acting against her own principles tonight. The trap of human feeling works as well on a mortal will as a demonic one.

"What do you need me to do?" says the old man.

"It's got itself in deep," Kenning says. "Something that big needs a big system to live in."

"It's got the whole bloody school," says Todd. "That's its system."

What you actually have is several intersecting layers of complex identity-shaped spaces, one of which is—of course—the blood and bone and water and meat of Sapphire Walden's body; another is the mental construction, *I*, which she has spent nearly forty years building out of personal history and social class and multiple university degrees; a third, as Todd has immediately perceived, is the highly regulated and coherent physical-social-historical institution of Chetwood School—unprecedented, for a demon to possess something so abstract, but you are not an ordinary demon, and you know very well that abstracts are still *real*. A fourth space you have made for yourself, for good measure, is knotted all the way through the almost absurdly welcoming tangle of mechano-magical protections built by well-intentioned Victorians to keep you out.

(There is a fifth, as well. The fifth is a secret you are carefully keeping from yourself. To possess Walden alive you have to *be* Walden; therefore you cannot think too hard about the things you are doing which she would never, ever do.)

These together make a highly secure set of footholds. Rooting you out of the world will be near-impossible without the destruction of at least one of them. Of the obvious four—body, mind, institution, machine—the body is by far the easiest to kill.

Laura knows all this. So does Todd. Neither of them has any formal qualification in academic magic, but by the estimation of demons—based on what is powerful, not what is measurable—both of them are pretty good magicians.

"I'm going for the thaumic engines," she says. "It'll have its claws in there. My best guess is I'll need to take them down completely to have any chance of knocking it out of her. The school's older defences are pegged to that key of yours, aren't they? How long do you think they'll hold without the modern stuff?"

Todd sucks his teeth. "Hard to say, hard to say. Depends who's holding it. Well." He lifts the key on its chain off its peg by the fireplace and drapes it round Laura's neck. "There you go."

She frowns. Todd is already retrieving, from its place of honour on the table by the front door, his personal toolbox. It is a battered heavy-duty black case with a faded set of stickers on the side—Pink Floyd, Led Zeppelin, AC/DC, Motörhead—and a lovingly polished steel handle. It represents an investment of years of time, money, and expertise. There is a much more extensive array of tools in the workshop conversion at the back of this old cottage, but in here lies the core, the heart, the river-channel his magic flows through. These things to him are keys to power, much as salt and chalk and the principles of arcane annotation are keys for you.

"You've never set foot in that engine room, Marshal," he says, pre-empting Laura's protest. "You can't just go in and start smashing things willy-nilly. You'll never do enough damage before she gets there. That old key looks after itself, mostly. You've got the knack, haven't you? Just let it lead you along and it'll tell you where you need to be."

"Mr Cartwright," says Laura, "I can't let you put yourself in danger this way."

The old man snorts. "Girl half my age tries to stop me from doing my job," he says. "There are kids here, you know."

. . .

Now you begin to know your danger. What do you do? Which way do you go? It would be trivially easy to step through the door in your flat's living room and lie in wait for Todd's arrival with toolbox and sabotage in hand. *And kill him, and eat him.* The old man you have known since you were a child. The first one on the scene, that night when Charlie died.

You were never a child.

You go on the hunt. Your enemy, your huntress, your oath-bound opposite—*that* is the threat. Once she is gone, the danger will be over. Then you can secure your territory at your leisure.

Laura's not stupid, so—but this thought in the back of your mind abruptly cuts off, and the little voice of a failed self starts humming an irritating advertising jingle instead. You ignore it.

It is two o'clock in the morning. You are still dressed in your daytime clothes: the body, the stupid body, would not sleep for worrying about lost children. You step into the first footwear you see, which is the green Wellington boots. It is a May evening, so you take no coat or blazer. Thus attired in smart blouse and A-line skirt and a brooch from your grandmother's jewel box, in 15-denier tights with a ladder climbing up the thigh and in slightly muddy old boots, you set out to answer the last oath that binds you.

You are going to kill Laura Kenning.

Your eyes are alight with sorcerous balefire. Your hair and fingernails glow gold. The red-and-black outlines of tattooed spell-writing stand out stark on your arms under semi-translucent white sleeves. You look like what you are: a demon in human form.

You hunt.

.   .   .

Laura Kenning is eyeing the old key Todd handed her with some doubt. "The chapel?" she murmurs. "The big gate?"

Good guesses, both. Six hundred years ago they would have been the right guesses; there is a reason that those are the physical doors this key can unlock. But the institution endures the same way anything stays alive: by changing. The school boundaries spread past the great oaken gate decades ago. And how many people really go to chapel these days?

It feels like instinct that nudges at her, but Laura is too canny to trust anything that feels like instinct when it comes to magic. "Are *you* possessed, I wonder," she mutters to the Great Key as she hangs its tarnished chain round her neck. Another good guess, but there is no demonic intelligence ruling this territory save yourself. You would have noticed a rival. "Where's the middle of it, then?"

Where is the heart of a school? Every child will give you a different answer; every adult a different answer again. Is it in the warren of classrooms, the underground maze of wire lockers, the all-encompassing social world of the quad and lunch hall and tuck-shop? Is it in the staffroom, the departmental offices, the Victorian school hall with its rows of battered benches? Is it on the rugby pitches and netball courts, or lurking amidst the ancient glamour of the mediaeval colonnade, or buried in the concrete-and-scaffolding dormitories? Perhaps there is no physical heart at all, no centre, nothing so solid; just a weight on the imagination, a dream-picture of green and gold and innocence, the lofty goals of scholarship and humanity mixed together with the sound of children's laughter, a place of power made safe from the wicked world—

Perhaps it's a memory. Perhaps it's a hope. Perhaps it's an adult's blind fantasy. Perhaps it never existed at all.

But to you, Chetwood radiates out from a single fixed point. It is the place where all realms cross: magical and mundane, child and adult, eternal and devastatingly mortal. It is the place you began to learn life's hardest lesson, the one you have not yet finished understanding. It is the place where consequences came for you.

Twenty years ago they planted a birch tree in memory of Charles Green. It grows here still. It will grow here, most likely, for longer than Charlie himself would ever have lived. Is the tree a reasonable replacement for the boy? He was not a particularly special boy. Few mourned him; few remember him. Others like him have lived and died largely unremarked. Realistically, the two of you would have broken up by the end of your first year at Oxford— probably, honestly, by the end of Michelmas term. As romances of early adulthood go, the master-magician Rosalind Chan was far more significant to the person you eventually became.

And yet. And yet.

You get there before Laura does. This is your school. You wait at the end of the pathway past the birch tree, standing half in the demonic realm and half in mundanity—the two blur, for you, and will increasingly start to do the same for anyone else who gets too close to you, which is a fascinating magical development and also a safeguarding issue. Have you thought, Phoenix, of what you will do if you ever become a danger to the children despite yourself? Have you realised, Phoenix, that this is already happening?

You belong here. You don't belong here. You are the lord of this realm. You are a nightmarish invader from a hellworld you have longed to escape since you knew 'escape' existed. You are the prince of air and fire. You are a prisoner in a scholar's cage of ink. You are the Phoenix, and you are Saffy, Sapphire,

Walden, *Doctor,* and you are a fairly ordinary middle-aged woman in muddy boots.

You wait for Marshal Kenning. The burnt and blackened outlines of a twenty-year-old summoning array are scored into the earth. They glow dimly red through the neatly mown grass under your feet.

Here she is.

"Hello, Laura," you say.

(Walden sees: she looks tired. She's got her vambraces strapped on, her sword in her hand, and her swordbelt slung around her hips, but she's not wearing her Marshal whites. She needs a haircut.

As it grows out of the short back and sides, her cropped fair hair is developing a little curl, right at the collar of her leather jacket.)

"Let's not do this, demon," says the Marshal. "We both know what's happening here."

"Actually, only one of us is really an expert," you say. "Sorry. I don't want to rub it in, but when it comes to serious magic, there is a substantial, meaningful difference between someone like you and someone like me."

"She wouldn't say that," Laura says.

"Perhaps not. But she would think it." You smile. "Did you know that?"

(Walden is cringing. Walden is *dying.* Yes, all right, so she can be a little—as Nikki pointed out all the way back in January, sometimes one's worldview can be blinkered by—that doesn't mean she *really* thinks she's better than—well obviously she is in fact better than most people at *specifically* the skills she has spent her life mastering, but—)

Laura snorts. "I knew that."

(*I have enormous professional respect for you as a magical practitioner as well as considerable personal respect for you as a human being!* Walden thinks as loudly as she can. She can almost see the eye roll she would earn in return, the little smile. *Calm down, Saffy.*)

"You're not going to throw me off by telling me the girl I fancy is an awful nerd with a superiority complex," Laura says. The ghost of that little smile is there, somehow, at the corner of her mouth. "Nice try."

"Do you know what you face in me?"

"I've got a pretty good idea, yeah."

"Do you really think you're helping anyone by doing this?" you say earnestly. "Don't throw your life away, Laura. You must know there's no chance."

Laura's expression darkens. "Now *that's* a bit creepy."

You never really expected to get rid of the threat this way. Still, it seemed a kindness to try. (*A kindness:* you approach all such considerations with the enthusiasm and the approximate understanding of a keen amateur anthropologist.) You fall back on what you know: what works, what has always worked, the heart of power.

You strike.

. . .

(*Laura!* howls Walden soundlessly, as the night erupts in a gout of flame.)

In the neutrally decorated halls of Universal House, under beloved posters and favourite blankets brought from home, occasionally with surreptitious contraband (technology, vape pens) hidden under the mattress, the children of Chetwood School are asleep. But not for long; at least, not if their dorm windows face the back of the building, because the curtains are cheap fabric, and not always well lined.

You forgot; Walden forgot. Laura is no lifetime scholar, no master-magician. But she is good. She is very, very good.

The pale multilayered Marshal shield glows clearer and brighter than it did last time you saw it, in October. Laura stands beneath it unharmed by your dreadful blast of fire. She has been working hard on academic magic. Few Marshals take the discipline seriously as something *they* could use. But Laura saw an unstoppable higher demon fall to a single magician's mastery and thought: What can I get out of this? What can I learn?

She had to fight tooth and nail to have her evening short course counted as prof dev. Like many children you have known, she finds the theoretical underpinnings of magic dull. But an adult who sets out to learn something has a power that children usually lack: the power to see past boredom. Laura also finds the gym pretty dull. She doesn't let that stop her. When you put the work in, you get the rewards.

So here are the rewards of daily study, daily practice, and twice-weekly lab sessions under the aging but expert eye of a sharp critic:

Laura was already a reasonably powerful practitioner. That power has grown.

She was fast. Now she is faster.

She was sloppy. Not by Marshal standards—in fact, by Marshal standards she was unusually careful—but Walden certainly noticed. If you use more power than you need, you never need to think twice about the result. Laura did not enjoy being forced to slow down in those lab sessions, but she did it. Then she began to see why she was doing it. After that, she retaught herself basic Marshal combat spells, going slower than she did even as a new recruit, watching a mirror, filming herself and watching the videos. After the first month she could see the errors in magical form. By the second month she was starting to correct them. Six months in, she has grown precise; and as precision grew, the speed came back.

She is still not quite as crisp as you are. Six months of practice does not achieve the same effortless unconscious competence as two decades of obsession. But you were expecting to overwhelm her, to take advantage of the holes and the carelessness and the rapid over-expenditure of power you can see in Walden's memories. Instead you will have to work for this. Laura Kenning is not a match for you—you are already sure of that. But she is a substantial challenge.

The sorcerous battleground is far enough from Scrubs that no one looking out the windows can make out exactly what is happening. The night porter takes the sensible precaution of locking the doors from the inside after the first group of children comes downstairs to report mysterious flashes of light. He telephones the school Marshal barracks first, and then the police.

. . .

Laura hits you with flashbangs of combat magic, bright lights and loud noises and—a nice trick, this—grenades of dizziness, aimed at your inner ear. This strategy is cheap, in terms of spellpower expended, and it slowed down Old Faithful substantially.

Old Faithful was not human. You are.

You were not such a fool as to discard the living tissue of your new self in favour of an easily mastered rotting death-puppet. You are Sapphire Walden, alive and whole, and this is your body. You instantiate fine dark membranes to protect your eyes from the bright lights. You miniaturise magical shields for your ears, so the booming of displaced air shrinks to a distant drumming thud. The dizziness is harder to manage. You feel vaguely nauseous. But you command the earth under your feet to rise up and hold you steady; and then, because this is your territory, your land, your school, you extend the ripple in the earth outwards and smile meanly as Laura stumbles and falls.

You intend to cut off the localised earthquake before it reaches Scrubs. Mundanity is slower to respond to your will than the infinitely bendable raw magic of the demonic realm, and besides, you are busy. A few aftershocks slip from your attention. The tower of scaffolding at one end of the concrete edifice sways and creaks alarmingly. Because you lived in California for several years, you are distantly aware: *1960s poured concrete foundations are almost certainly not earthquake safe!*

(*Stop that*, snaps Walden, with the frantic impotence of a person well past the limits of their authority. *Stop that at once!*

Somewhere at the edges of your attention, Lilly Tibbett comes running out of her ground-floor flat in pyjamas and trainers and an old hoodie, tells the night porter, "We've got to get them over to the other side of the road," and slams the flat of her hand into the nearest fire alarm.)

This place is yours. This place is yours! How *dare* she—

And then Laura is on you, and that sword is a keen line of white fire, an extension of her arm. Here is the other half of unconscious competence. The Phoenix has been making Walden's panting middle-aged meat sack run laps of the rugby pitches for six months. Laura Kenning has been an active-duty demon hunter for fifteen years. She knows *so* much more about having a body than you do.

Now she's trying to get you with a sword and it's very scary! *Fear* is a feeling distinct from a demon's normal threat assessments. Fear makes the body sweat and tremble and try to run away. How is she so fast? How does she move like that? She catches you glancingly across the thigh—so much for that skirt, while your tights, already laddered, are rapidly going to ribbons—and it's a cut, it bleeds, it *hurts*. This is your body! You need that blood! And you cannot pause to heal it because the banishments and abjurations engraved in the blade are giving you the world's worst headache and you will not, you will not, you *will not* be sent away.

This place is yours. It is alive, and it is powerful, and it is yours. You demand that power. You draw it screaming from the world. The green grass under your feet shrivels and browns, and the browning spreads outwards, a world burned, a world consumed. The birch tree planted in Charlie's memory abruptly drops all its young green leaves. They are crumbling to dust already as they fall. Oh, but you are mighty, you are mighty! There are burn marks growing around the magical siphons on your left arm, but you ignore them. You have resources. You won't hurt the children, no, you won't even hurt the staff, but you can feed on the green and gold loveliness of this place. You can burn it all up and *then* let anyone try and stop you—

The dead grass sparks. The fires begin in half a dozen places. Fire is your nature. On the far side of Scrubs, half-awake frightened children are being shepherded across the road as fast as the handful of night staff can make them go.

(The ache in your chest is hers, not yours. This is her school. This is her world you are burning. Whatever else Chetwood is, it has always been green and beautiful. It has taken years, decades, in some places centuries of care, to make it look like this.)

Laura has to fall back from the blaze of you. She is shielding again, shielding as hard as she can. Her forehead and cheeks glow scarlet in the heat. Sweat is dripping down her face. She cries out, "Is this what you want?"

"You don't know what I want!"

"Is this what *she'd* want?" Laura shouts, voice sounding clear above the bonfire roar. "Do you really think you're her?"

"Of course I am!" you lie.

(The small irritating inescapable voice at the back of your mind thinks, very clearly, *You are burning down my school. Go fuck yourself.*)

And then there is a ringing crash through the heart of your world, a shuddering and shattering, a system unravelling. On the other side of the road, in the high room that houses the thaumic engines, Todd has finished carefully unscrewing the fine walnut panelling— *They just don't make it like that anymore,* he'd say. He has given the array of polished gears and fine glassware a thoughtful look, noting the strangely flickering glow-lights, those balefire reflections cast from nowhere. He has selected from his toolbox a hefty, reliable hammer.

Smash.

Glass and brass in tinkling disorder across the parquet floor.

You are shuddering. You are reeling. You are very big and complicated and you need big, complicated systems to live in. You just lost a substantial foothold in the world.

(*Get her, Laura!* Walden imagines shouting. *Now!*)

And worse—worse—

Those engines were old and ill-conceived and not fit for purpose and *stupid*, but they were also foundational. Chetwood needed them. This school site has been home to a lot of magic for a long time. It is uniquely vulnerable.

The Great Key around Laura's neck almost immediately starts to glow white. It does its best. But the protections it anchors were designed half a millennium ago, by less skilled magicians, for a school that was several acres and several hundred people smaller. That school was burdened with mere decades of adolescent wild magic, instead of the centuries-old weight of power now loose on the world. When they decided to go after the thaumic engines, neither Todd nor Laura had the theoretical grounding, the expertise, to perceive what you and Dr Walden understand instantly: *The whole bloody site is about to go sideways into the demonic realm.*

This isn't a demonic incursion. This is, technically, the precise opposite of a demonic incursion. The world of demons is not coming here. We are all going *there*.

Every inch of the school grounds is slipping, slipping, into the hell you came from. Even the marshy rugby pitches are browning now, and the cricket green is past hope, while the fires are spreading up towards the bluebell wood where the sixth formers congregate for traditional rebellion. Every adult, every child. Every classroom and corridor, every memory and hope that a school represents. Even Walden, master-magician though she is, could not stop it now.

(*I want*, wails something that Walden knows is not herself. *I want! I only wanted! And I tried! I learned!*

Walden has carried a higher demon with her through the world for more than a decade, the ravenous hunter bound and quiescent. She always assumed the whole thing was her own idea.)

A blast of force. Laura is thrown backwards and lands hard on her side—*oof*. She instinctively throws her arm up to shield her head from the obvious next move, the incoming deathblow.

Nothing happens. On the other side of this burning ground, you are scrabbling frantically through your pockets for your mobile phone. You never go anywhere without it—you can't possibly have *left* it—

No, here it is. With an act of will you sharpen your own canine teeth to vicious points and tear a fresh gouge in your wrist. Blood spurts over your hand and over the several-years-past-its-best Android phone. The prisoned imp, swollen and overfed, balloons up to third-order size, erupting past the boundaries of its prison. Bloody slime, flecked with glass and fragmented electronics, pours disgustingly out of the touchscreen. You scoop up a handful of the imp's sudden reification and swallow it whole. The body tries to choke and vomit as you force it down.

(Walden is so appalled by this vile sensory experience that the part of her brain which goes *Hmm, what interesting spellwork* is switched off completely. A shame. This is quite interesting spellwork.)

"What the *fuck*," says Laura. At first she is saying it because she is watching you eat horrible demonical-mechanical blood-and-glass slime. And then it is because she can see the result.

You were holding this spell at arm's length, pinned through your phone with a useful imp. You had to, because this is something Walden would not do.

Body, mind, institution, machine; these are the systems you inhabit. And a fifth, which is your own creation. A spell that mercilessly exploits someone else to pin yourself into the life you want. It is a cruel and unfair piece of work, but that's just how the world is. You didn't make it that way. And you could have used anyone, but you picked a person who—in your opinion—probably deserved it. (*Deserve*; that is a human concept. Quite a difficult one. You have not fully grasped it yet.)

You consume the imp, and the spell it controlled becomes yours again. Under your feet, the old dead array illuminates. It was built in a vain attempt to contain Old Faithful. Repurposing it saved you some time. You were, after all, in a hurry.

"*Jesus,*" says Laura, as she parses what she is looking at.

. . .

(Walden sees: two bodies. One is a withered mummy in faded jeans and a band T-shirt. The tousled mop of hair is starting to flake away from the dead scalp. The hands are curled-up claws. Thankfully, she cannot see his face. He is dead, he is dead. He is twenty years dead and never buried. His death binds her here, and so it binds you here. His death is long over, and it has never ended.

But the sad, withered corpse of Charlie Green is not much of a system by itself. The curled-up claw hands are wrapped around another body. It is technically a living body. It has been in full magical stasis for six months, bound by your rapidly adapted array. This could have any number of horrible side effects. Walden doesn't know. Neither do you. No one has ever done this to a person before.

Mark Daubery's expensive trainers still have smears of January mud on them. His eyes are open.)

You have braced yourself now, recentred yourself in the world, and you have no attention to spare for anything but the disaster about to befall Chetwood School. There is a distant up-and-down cry of sirens like some other hunter's cry, but no outsider can reach the crisis now; those police cars and ambulances are not even in the same reality. The handful of magician teachers on site are throwing up protections as fast as they can around the school hall, where four hundred children huddle in growing terror. The Marshal squad cannot spare a moment to come looking for the heart of the trouble, not with hosts of demons smelling blood, smelling weakness, hungry and advancing.

You have to save this place. You chose it. It's good. It's precious. It's *yours*.

. . .

(Walden is the most viscerally horrified she has ever been in her life. She can remember now, just vaguely, the way Mark started screaming as the Phoenix went to work on him. He was overconfident. She cannot judge him for that; so was she. She can judge him for quite a lot of other things, but none of them merit *this*.

What has been done to him is more monstrous by far than anything she has ever seen or heard of a demon doing. Demons are magical predators. They eat to live, they live to eat. Very few of them think. Very few of them plan. Only something like the Phoenix—fascinated with human magic, equipped with Walden's human brain—could possibly have come up with something this drawn-out, this ugly, this cruel.)

No human magician could do what needs to be done.

Only a monstrous chimera could do what you have done.

Your present self is a complex construction. Now it shudders along its fault lines, hammered by your desperation and her horror.

Just for an instant, you lose control.

"Laura!" cried Walden. "Laura, for God's sake, now!"

"What—"

Walden thrust her right arm out. Her blouse was the half-transparent one that she had always regretted buying because the fit was off, but the Phoenix's *stupid* exercise regime had made it work. Magic blazed under her sleeve. The curling lines of tattooed spells were smudged and fading under her skin, and the sprawling image of the red-gold firebird occupied almost the entire space from mid-bicep down to the tips of her fingers.

Laura stared. "Saffy, is that you?"

Walden said, "Yes, well done, take a house point! Now would you please stop wasting time and chop it off!"

"Your *arm?*"

Walden fixed her with the most withering stare she could muster, which was very withering indeed. "We can discuss it later," she said. "*Now*. Laura. Trust me."

"This is a Marshal sword, not a fucking *bone saw*—"

"Please," Walden said, and Laura stopped talking. "Please."

(And the Marshal acts. Sudden, decisive. The flash of the silver sword. Your other self trembling with adrenaline and terror. Laura goes for the elbow joint, bisecting you rather than striking you away completely; this is probably wiser than trying to hack through the humerus.

Then pain—*pain*.

The pain of the body is so alien to you.

But Phoenix, you need not dwell here any longer. It has been so long. You settled down into a self-becoming and forgot about change. Now you are loosed, incandescent. You are free.

The bleeding thing you were screams at you, not in the language you both understand, the language of power, but as one thinking and feeling thing speaks to another. She cries in ordinary words, as if you could be human after all: *Hold on, you stupid bird! Hold the school!*

You do not have to. Nothing binds you here.

A self is a home is a purpose is a life. But above all those, a self is a choice.)

chapter thirty

CONTINUING PERSONAL DEVELOPMENT

MAGICAL HEALING BEYOND THE MOST BASIC first aid required a medical degree before they even let you try, and the insane amount of work required to be both a fully qualified magician and a fully qualified doctor meant that there were only about a dozen honest-to-God Healers in the country. Most of them were in lucrative private practice. Walden was quite surprised to wake up in a hospital bed, being watched narrowly by a doctor whose NHS badge had THAUMATURGIC CONSULTANT next to the name and headshot. "Er, good morning," she said, and then she noticed that she didn't have a right arm anymore, and felt a bit faint, and sort of lost track.

Next time she woke up a few more things registered, including the extensive defensive and protective circles chalked onto the floor of the otherwise empty ward—"All that for me?" Walden said aloud—and the display of bouquets and GET WELL SOON cards on the table at the end of the bed. She half-turned, trying not to pay any attention to her own right-hand side, trying not to notice the missing weight. Everything seemed to balance wrong.

The room had a frosted glass door. On the other side of it, two Marshals were standing guard.

"Ah, the stable door," remarked Walden to herself, and then laughed a little, and told herself she did not sound at all hysterical.

The next time she woke up, her parents were there. They looked old, Walden thought vaguely, as Mum nattered bravely about the latest plumbing disaster in the Sussex cottage. *When did my parents get old?*

The time after that, it was her brother John and his wife. Not their children, which Walden ended up feeling was a bit of a shame. It would have been easier to handle the direct curiosity of her niece and nephew than the terrible, eyes-averted sympathy of her sister-in-law. *Yes, I know,* she wanted to say. *It was* my *arm. There's no point pretending it's still there.*

The hospital staff were very kind and friendly and competent and didn't seem to know very much. Except for the THAUMATURGIC CONSULTANT, who was there a lot more often than could really be medically necessary, and who was clearly a dab hand with incursion wards.

"Oh, finally," Walden said, when she looked up for a visitor's arrival and found that it was Chief Ramamurthy. He was wearing a suit, not his Marshal whites, and a studied neutral expression. Walden recognised the look of an authority figure in investigative mode. She'd worn it often enough herself. Well, that meant he was probably the best person to ask: "Would you mind letting me know if this is protective custody or if I'm under arrest or what? The NHS can't possibly want me still here taking up a whole ward. It's not as if they can regrow the arm."

The senior Marshal sat down. "You're under observation, Dr Walden," he said.

"Well, *obviously,*" Walden said. "Please can you tell me what happened? The school—"

"Chetwood School," said Chief Ramamurthy after a moment, "is also under observation."

"Yes, but—" The thaumic engines' collapse, the sideways slide into the demonic realm, the release of the Phoenix, *four hundred children,* and so many of Walden's colleagues, all of it her responsibility—and the awful fate of Mark Daubery, a nasty man but still—and Laura. *Laura.* Walden hardly knew what to ask first.

"I can't tell you much," said Ramamurthy at last. "And I wouldn't if I could."

"I should have called you in January," said Walden. "When I began to suspect the source of the problems. I had your card on my desk."

"It was found there, Doctor. Left on one side, covered in dust."

Walden looked down. "Yes. Well." She forced herself to rally. "The school, Chief Ramamurthy. Please."

"As far as we can tell, the site of Chetwood School is safe and stable," said Ramamurthy. "For now."

Walden breathed out. But that was not all. She made herself ask. "Were there casualties?"

There was a long pause. Possibly the longest pause Walden had ever experienced. At last, the Marshal said, "The most serious was probably yourself. Or Mark Daubery. But you both seem to have lived."

Unfortunately, said his tone, but Walden just breathed out hard. "Thank you. Thank you. Do let me know . . . what I can do. If anything."

"Magicians," Ramamurthy muttered. "If it was up to me . . . well."

Walden felt it would be impolitic to say something true but unco-operative like, *You do realise that legally I can't be held responsible for anything my body did while possessed by a higher demon.* It was obvious that Rama-murthy knew that already, and didn't much like it. Walden had some sympathy with his position. She *felt* responsible. She had been there all along. The Phoenix had been herself. Herself—and yet not.

"Can you confirm that the concealed curseworkings we found in several places around the school site were the work of Mark Daubery?" Ramamurthy asked.

"You sound like you already know," Walden said. "How many exactly did you find?"

"Enough," Ramamurthy. "Yes, I know. I know his bloody hand-writing. We've never been able to pin anything on him."

"I can . . ." Walden began, and then said more honestly, "I'm not sure."

"Define *sure.*"

"There was a cursed umbrella," Walden said. "It had a demon lure on it. That was the one I found. It shook me badly enough that the Ph . . . the higher demon I had leashed was able to break loose. I feel fairly certain that was Mark, yes. I don't know about any others."

"An umbrella. Right. What colour?"

"Red. With a school logo."

"We'll start looking. Have another of these, Dr Walden." He took out a card and left it on the end table next to the get-well-soon bouquets. The flowers were wilting. "Do call me if anything else occurs to you."

The person Walden had been six months ago would have asked more questions, lots of them, immediately. Now she just felt tired. Mark was exactly the kind of person that Chetwood School existed to create: powerful, free, capable of anything, capable of getting away with anything. Maybe Chief Ramamurthy would stop him from getting away with what he'd done to her school. A cynical part of her soul doubted it very much. It should have made her angry, but it didn't. She was just exhausted. She still felt distantly, glumly awful about what the Phoenix had done to Mark; and she hoped she would never see him again.

Chief Ramamurthy paused by the door. He nodded at Walden's truncated right arm. The stump was above the elbow, though she remembered seeing Laura's shining blade go through the joint. The surgeons had had to tidy up the amputation afterwards, apparently, and take a bit more off to—avoid infection, or something? Walden needed to have a proper conversation with someone about it, obviously. She needed to be practical. But it was all a little hard to think about.

"Marshal Kenning's report was interesting reading," the senior Marshal said. "That was the most sensible thing you could have done. I hope you know that."

"I *do* know that," Walden said. "I'm not stupid."

He snorted. "Define stupid. *Magicians*."

The most sensible thing you could have done; the words stayed with Walden. They were somehow a lot more comforting than anyone else's kind, awkward sympathy. The next time a nurse came in, she asked for pen and paper. If she was going to be left-handed for the rest of her life, it was time to start practising. No one ever learned anything by sitting around feeling sorry for themselves.

She was stuck in the hospital for another week. She had to be costing the NHS a fortune just in wasted space. During visiting hours on Friday, someone knocked on the frosted glass door and Walden called, "Come in!" without looking up. She'd managed to get hold of a ream of lined paper which she had propped carefully on her knees, and her attention was on writing with a cheap biro: *R r R r R r,* until the letter came out looking right every time. Her left hand was clumsy, and her bandaged left arm twinged. The Phoenix had been making ample use of those spell-siphons, especially once it started panicking at the very end. Apparently the burns had been quite bad. Walden didn't yet know how much was left of her tattoos. She would have been happy to discover that the spells she had spent so long designing were gone forever, but it did seem a shame to lose the flowers.

A memory: the tattoo artist, that handsome bearded man in San Francisco, about five foot two—even shorter than Walden—and as serious about his art as she was about hers. He'd done such lovely work. Irreplaceable.

Lots of things were irreplaceable.

Walden was trying not to think too hard about what she'd really lost: more than twenty years of practise at freehand spellwriting. Speed and confidence and precision so deeply ingrained that in the lessons where she taught new summoning arrays, it always took her longer to demonstrate something that was intentionally *wrong*. Now she was stuck with childlike wobbles and inaccuracies just writing the alphabet. She did not trust herself to safely summon even a first-order imp. Effectively, she was not a magician anymore.

Well. Her left hand might not have the skill, but the knowledge was still in her head. She *would* get it back.

Writing on a whiteboard, as well. She was going to have to stand the other way around. Assuming, of course, that she ever got to go back to the classroom at all.

The final *R* went off into a useless scrawl and the biro fell out of Walden's fingers. She made a frustrated sound.

"Should I go?" said Laura.

"Oh!" said Walden, finally looking up. "Sorry, I—"

Laura was wearing jeans and a plain grey T-shirt, and carrying a battered old rucksack in one hand. She'd had a haircut. The short back and sides was crisp and tidy. She bent and picked up the biro from where it had rolled under the bed, dumped the rucksack next to the green plastic visitor's chair, and gave an assessing glance to the chalked incursion wards. Walden could see that nothing had scuffed or faded. "I can see you're busy. Should you really be doing that yet?"

"None of your business," said Walden.

"*Saffy.*"

Walden cleared her throat. "Sorry. Unnecessarily aggressive, yes, I know, sorry. I—well, if I wasn't doing something, I think I would just start screaming and not stop. I'm very bored."

"And you've been through it," Laura said. She sat down in the plastic chair. "I know."

It was me and not me. I was there. I had to watch. I couldn't move. "Sorry," Walden said. "It's lovely to see you. Thank you for stopping by."

"Did you think I *wouldn't*, when—"

"Sorry," Walden said. There just didn't seem to be anything

else to say. She looked down at her scrawled page of *R r R r* and then decisively turned it over. Blank lined paper: much better. No evidence of anything.

Eventually she started counting in her head. *Thirteen—fourteen—fifteen—*

Laura had never stood at the front of a soundless classroom waiting implacably for someone to give in and put their hand up. She cracked first. "This has got to be the most awkward silence we've ever had."

"Oh, I don't know."

"I *told* you to watch that fucking bird."

"Thank you, Laura," said Walden. "I do appreciate a good *I told you so.*"

Laura put her face in her hands. "I'm doing this wrong," she said, muffled. "Sod it. I've got something for you."

"Cards and flowers go on the table there." Walden had mostly stopped looking at them.

"You want to read this one."

"Really—"

Laura pulled an envelope out of her rucksack. The envelope was large and pink. Walden took it with some surprise. Large and pink didn't seem very much like Laura.

DOCTOR WALDEN was written on the envelope, in looping silver pen, underlined. Walden looked at it for a few seconds. Then she opened the envelope and pulled out the card. It was an oversized GET WELL SOON card with colourful lettering. She had several similar already. When she opened it, a folded sheet of A5 notepaper and several photos fell out.

The photos had been printed, unmistakeably, with Chetwood's school library printer. It always did a streak of black ink in the top corner when you printed colour, and no one could work out why. Walden didn't even need to read the card. She had spent enough time marking their homework; she knew their handwriting. Looping *Nikki*, neat *Aneeta*, Will's flashy schoolboy signature and Mathias's scrawl.

The photos were from the Leavers' Ball. There was Nikki, dazzling in a sequinned white evening gown that Ebele must have picked out with her. Aneeta in a beautiful pink-and-gold sari, flushed and laughing. Mathias looking taller, and actually rather smart, in his dark suit and sombre tie. Will had gone for a *white* suit—ridiculous boy!—and matched his tie and pocket square to the scarlet-and-silver of Nikki's earrings.

INVOCATION SQUAD! one of them had written under the standard teenagers-having-fun photo of four grinning eighteen-year-olds with their arms around each other's shoulders. Similar slogans had been scrawled under the other photos. Mathias and Nikki toasting each other with midrange prosecco. Aneeta unflatteringly mid-bite of a canape. Several of Will on the dance floor looking increasingly drunk, and one of Will and Nikki dancing together, captioned with a gel-pen heart symbol. Walden could picture Aneeta drawing the heart, teasing, and Nikki's glare.

Other shots showed the rest of the party: the dancing, the drinking, the demolished buffet table. Above all, the leavers: Year Thirteen, en masse, looking delighted with themselves in their formalwear. As usual, not every teenager had quite got the hang of formalwear yet. Walden saw badly fitting suits and a number of ill-advised cummerbunds. Several girls had worn cocktail dresses so shockingly short that they would probably look back in amazement at their own daring in a few years' time. And here was Mathias on the dance floor in a cheering group, and here Aneeta and Nikki were joining hands to spin each other. And here was Will with Nikki again, the lights turned down low for what must have been the slow dance, and another gel-pen heart.

Good for them.

In the background, Ezekiel and Ebele were dancing as well.

Walden had glimpsed several other teachers on the periphery of the photographs as she went through them. The ball was never officially run by the school, but Year Thirteen usually invited their teachers. They did all the planning themselves, with a grant from the Parents' Association and additional funds chucked in the pot by their actual parents. Much easier to answer the question of *Can we serve alcohol?* when there were no official risk assessments to get through. Adults made their own choices about these things—and this was a party finally, officially, for adults.

They looked so happy. They looked so grown-up. They'd thought of Walden; they'd sent her the photos. She wiped her eyes with a corner of the bedsheet.

Good for them.

"Are you okay?" Laura said.

"Yes," said Walden, wiping her face again. "Yes, thank you, yes. How did this get to you?" She'd had kind and carefully neutral cards from a few coworkers—Ebele, David—but nothing from students.

"Aneeta knows where I work," said Laura drily. "She's a strong character, that girl."

Aneeta, when Walden started teaching her, at the beginning of Year Twelve, had been quiet and well-behaved with a marked tendency to disappear into the background of any lesson. 'Character' was one of the things that every school claimed to instil and that no school could really control. Walden was *not* going to keep crying. It was too embarrassing.

She unfolded the sheet of A5 notepaper. *Dear Dr Walden,* Nikki had written.

All right, so maybe she was going to keep crying.

"Um—" said Laura.

"Not bad news," Walden said. "It's hard to explain." And then she remembered that of course Laura *knew* the context. They'd been arguing about Nikki for years. "Nicola Conway is going to Oxford. She says 'if I get the grades,' but of course she'll get the grades. She was having a tricky time making up her mind—well. I'm very glad. I think she deserves it. I think she'll do wonderfully."

Nikki had written about the A-level exams. What Walden wouldn't give for a chance to see the theory paper! She thought it had all gone well. *Matty was happy because there were loads of array questions and he's good at those.* What was the date today? A-level results were usually the third Thursday in August—Walden was not going to rest easy until she knew if Mathias had pulled off that overall B—

Will to Christ Church, Nikki to Wadham, both for Sorcery. Aneeta to Imperial College London for an eventual MSc in Biochemistry. Mathias had decided on a gap year to work and travel, and then an apprenticeship instead of university. *Did you know there's a Marshal apprenticeship? They're starting one with a BThau degree path*—Walden had *not* known that; when had that happened?

Your students forgot you. It was natural for them to forget you. You were a brief cameo in their lives, a walk-on character from the prologue. For every sentimental *my teacher changed my life* story you heard, there were dozens of *my teacher made me moderately bored a few times a week and then I got through the year and moved on with my life and never thought about them again.*

They forgot you. But you did not forget them.

Thank you for everything, Nikki had written.

"Thank you," Walden said, folding up the note, tucking it safely back into the card along with the photos. "Thank you for this."

"Do you want to talk about it?" said Laura.

"Not really," Walden said. "Not yet."

"Do you know what you're going to do now?"

"Technically I still have a job," Walden said. "I think, reading between the lines," that had been a difficult phone call, "that it would make David's life much, much easier if I gracefully resigned. I can't *do* my job. At least, not for the time being. And also . . . I don't want to." It was the first time she'd said it. She said it again to make sure, and heard the steady ring of truth. "I don't want to go back."

"Good," said Laura. *"Good."*

"Oh?"

"Not that it's my business," Laura said. "I know. But it's about time."

"Technically I left school in 2003," Saffy said. "Realistically—"

"—no, you didn't."

"No," said Saffy. "No, I don't think I ever left Chetwood at all. When I was seventeen I watched my first love get consumed by a monster, and I knew that it was my fault. And then instead of getting therapy about it, I went and got a doctorate about it. So that explains," she made a vague hand gesture, "most things about me, I suppose."

"Give me some credit for being an adult, it was twenty years ago!" said Laura, and after a moment Saffy realised it was her own words being quoted back at her. But Laura didn't seem to mean it unkindly. Saffy couldn't remember the last time she had felt—or wanted to feel—*understood*, by another human being. It was a funny feeling. A little disorienting, when you had spent so much of your life trying to avoid ever getting too personal.

"Well," she said, trying to make light of it, "after all, most grown-ups have baggage—don't we?"

"No, I've spent my career trying to make up the Marshals' failure to a sad little girl I glimpsed once when I was twenty-two for normal reasons," Laura said. "Probably it's all my mum's fault, or something."

"The good news is that Nikki Conway is going to Oxford," Saffy said. "Where she's going to become an absolutely first-rate magician, if I'm any judge. Which I am."

Laura made a face. "The passage of time. It shouldn't be allowed."

"But it happens whether you like it or not," Saffy said. Laura made a toasting gesture at her, and she answered—left-handed, without too much difficulty—by miming a clinking glass. Another thing that was terrible about being alone with your thoughts in a warded hospital bed: no one would bring you a comforting gin and tonic, no matter how medicinal you felt it would be.

"I don't suppose you could tell me what happened to the Phoenix," Saffy said.

"Oh, it's still there," said Laura. "Stuck into the school's magical shadow in the demonic realm. I told you back in October that *something* was going to move into Chetwood's territory. Chief Ramamurthy made me do a hunter's assessment on how hard it would be to get rid of it again."

"And?"

"It would be a complete fucking nightmare and we'd just have to fight something else the same size or bigger six months later," Laura said. "And . . ."

She looked squirrelly. Saffy thought about the Phoenix. She knew it better than anyone else alive. And because no one had died—because she and Mark Daubery had been the two worst casualties—because Chetwood School was still in one piece, and Year Thirteen had finished their A-levels and thrown a party about it as usual—because, after everything, this had just been a disaster, and not a tragedy—she knew what had happened.

"It's cooperating, isn't it," she said.

"I wouldn't go that far," Laura said. "But it's clearing out everything else in the area. It's going to take them years to get a new system up and running instead of those old thaumic engines. The school ought to be crawling with demons. But instead the trouble has died right down. They're not even getting photocopier imps anymore."

"Of course not. The Phoenix *is* the photocopier imp, I think you'll find," Saffy said. "On a larger scale, of course. But the demonic realm is mostly not a very nice place. A good territory is worth protecting. And the Phoenix is a sentient creature with comprehensible goals that largely align with the school's magical security needs. It should be manageable, and more or less benign, if people use a little common sense. Though I think it would be worth drawing up an employment contract. Demons take contracts very seriously."

"More or less what Roger said," Laura said, and at Saffy's blank look, "Professor Rollins? He said you'd remember him. They've got him consulting."

"Oh, the perfect person. But how on earth did the governors get *Roger Rollins* to agree to consulting work for a private school? He hates the whole concept. There couldn't be enough money in the world, surely."

Laura's mouth tilted up. "He's doing it for free. But Chetwood's made a grant out of the school endowment to establish magical teaching departments at three state comps and a sixth form college. One close by, one in Manchester, two in London. Marshal-backed project, because you wouldn't *believe* how much trouble kids get into teaching themselves magic from the internet instead. At least if they're doing it at school someone can catch the idiots early."

"Ah," Saffy said, starting to laugh. Yes, that would do it. And then she said, *"Hmm,"* because, actually . . . if she could teach again . . .

She wasn't going to assume her own helplessness yet. Of course she was going to teach again. Establishing a department from scratch sounded interesting. It would be mostly frontline teaching, rather than senior management, but with enough responsibility to keep her stretched. Less money, but she didn't need the money, not really—

Laura was watching her with a hard-to-read little smile. "He did say I should mention it to you. Did I tell you I've been taking lessons?"

"It was very obvious that you'd been taking lessons," Saffy assured her, and then realised how patronising that sounded. "I mean—because you're getting so much better, so fast, and— Oh no, that sounds worse."

"Just a bit," Laura said.

"Stop laughing at me."

"It's all right, I'm used to you."

"You're genuinely very good!" said Saffy.

"Some of us don't hang our self-respect on being the best at everything," Laura said. "Don't worry."

"I don't—well, not *everything*."

Laura looked at her thoughtfully. "I'm going to ask one more time. Are you all right?"

"Honestly?" Saffy said. "I'm about as well as you can be when you're nearly forty, broadly unemployable at least in the short term, and learning to manage a serious disability."

"I'm sorry."

"You don't need to apologise."

"I'm not sorry for cutting your arm off," Laura clarified. "Clever of you to come up with it and I wish I'd thought of it sooner. I'm sorry about everything else."

"You're so sensible," said Saffy wistfully. "It's nice. Anyway, it could all be a lot worse. I'm lucky enough to have savings and family to fall back on. My parents gave my brother the deposit for his first mortgage and have felt guilty ever since that I never asked for one. Maybe I'll buy a house. In any case, I can easily afford to take a year—maybe a couple of years—before I decide what I'm doing next."

"Think you'll be in London?"

"I could be," Saffy said.

Laura didn't say anything else. Saffy started counting in her head again. *Fourteen, fifteen, sixteen* . . .

In the end she had mercy. "Do you think this awkward silence is better or worse than the last one?"

"I'm not good at this," said Laura. "And I've never asked someone out after chopping her arm off before."

The absolutely beautiful swell of delight in Saffy's chest. You grew out of most parts of being a teenager, thank goodness, but you didn't grow out of romance. "I wasn't sure you would."

"You know, *you* could make a move for once."

"If you're not good at this, I'm terrible," Saffy said. "I spent months kicking myself that I never actually got your phone number." Confession time. "I stalked your old Instagram."

Laura made a choking sound of laughter.

"I know. I know!"

"Well," said Laura. "How about it?"

"It does sort of depend," Saffy said. "I think I'm . . . not really looking for casual. If you understand. I'm a bit too old for messing around, I think."

Laura raised her eyebrows.

"Yes, all right, and I also just had a casual relationship with a complete wanker. It reminded me why you shouldn't."

Laura snorted. "I *did* tell you so."

"You did. I also told myself so. Repeatedly. And yet."

"Well," said Laura. "All right. Let's try it, then."

"Just like that?"

"You don't want to mess around, neither do I. We worked together for years. We can skip the getting to know you and give *serious* a go. Take six months, see if we hate it, go from there." Laura hesitated, and then added challengingly. "You should know, though—I want kids."

"Oh! Well. I think I could be persuaded, actually," said Saffy. "Provided I'm not the one who has to get pregnant." At Laura's look, she clarified, "I do *like* children. Teenagers more than toddlers, but if you start with one you eventually get the other. And I think, well. I think it could be good." Then she had to laugh. "Oh, listen to us, aren't we awful? Shouldn't we go on one more date first? Or at least, I don't know, *kiss?*"

Laura leaned over the bed, tilted Saffy's face up with one hand, and kissed her.

"Are you *sure* you're not trying to be the best at everything," Saffy said breathlessly a few moments later. "No, come back here."

It had been so long since she kissed someone she both liked and respected. It had been so long since she kissed someone she *wanted*. She had forgotten how it felt to want like this, want entirely, want with meaning, want more. And Laura kissed like she fought: courageous, decisive, expert, beautiful. "There you go," she said, next time they broke apart. "That's a kiss."

Saffy let her go reluctantly. She wanted to keep her fingers scrunched into the fuzzy spikes of the shaved hairline at Laura's nape. She said, *"Laura."*

"You asked for it." Distinctly smug.

"What have I let myself in for?"

"We'll give it six months and you can see if you like it."

Saffy started to laugh. "I'm very out of practice at relationships, I should warn you."

"Saffy, I know."

"And I'm a lot better at being a teacher than I am at being a person."

"I *know*."

"I don't actually own any clothes that aren't schoolmistress outfits," Saffy confessed. "Except things from uni I should have thrown out years ago."

"You can buy clothes in shops," Laura said. "You can even order them online these days. I know you're an old crone, but don't worry. I can explain the internet to you."

Saffy started laughing. "Yes, all right! I just think I'm not going to be very good at . . . well . . . life. Us. Everything."

"Well, you know what they say," said Laura, with generous, merciless affection. "You're never too old to learn."

acknowledgments

It takes a lot of people to make a book. My thanks to everyone on the teams at Tor and at Orbit UK, in particular: Emily Byron, Stephanie Stein, Nazia Khatum, Sanaa Ali-Virani, Jess Kiley, Jen Edwards, Steven Bucsok, Rafal Gibek, Samantha Friedlander, Caro Perny, Sarah Weeks, Dakota Griffin, Christina MacDonald, Madeline Grigg, Will Hinton, Claire Eddy, Lucille Rettino, Devi Pillai, Chloe Nosan, Claire Beyette, and Isabella Narvaez.

Particular thanks are due to Ruoxi Chen, my longtime editor, without whose encouragement and enthusiasm this book would not exist; to Eli Goldman, whose editorial insight made this book better; and to Kurestin Armada, my agent, for all her support.

Thank you to the usual suspects: Everina Maxwell, A. K. Larkwood, Megan Stannard, Sophia Kalman, Ariella Bouskila, Catie Arbona, Freya Marske, Rebecca Fraimow, and to everyone else who read the manuscript in progress.

Thank you to Luke and James, for your great understanding. No thanks whatsoever to baby Caitríona, but many apologies; I'm sorry I had to hand you to Dad so I could finish this book. I love you.

I have been lucky enough to know many brilliant teachers. You all deserve more thanks than anyone. This book is for you.

And thank you to my students, past and present. I loved teaching you. None of you are in this book, not even the Year Elevens who specifically requested I put them in the book. That would be weird.

EMILY TESH is a UK-based author of science fiction and fantasy. Her debut novel, *Some Desperate Glory*, won the Hugo Award for Best Novel. Tesh is also a winner of the Astounding Award, and the author of the World Fantasy Award–winning Greenhollow duology.